EDGE
OF
STEEL
ELIZABETH DEAR
AF374316

*To the readers who, like me, spent all of 2019 mainlining every
"spicy magic academy" romance they could get their hands on.
Thank you for returning with me to our roots.*

SYNOPSIS

My mates rejected me, and now they've come crawling back. It's too little, too late.

When the men I'd been falling for spurned me and then left me in the woods to die, I vowed to cut them out of my life for good.

But the Moon had other plans for me.

It turns out Heath, Aiden, Elijah, and Wyatt are my Fated. A rare blessing of perfect mates from our celestial deity.

One I absolutely do not want.

But now I'm stuck with them at Guardian training camp, where I'll continue my quest to earn a permanent place among our kind's elite military force. Within their ranks, I'll finally have safety for myself and my beast.

I don't need bonds, and I definitely don't need my Fated, who only want me now because the Moon told them they're supposed to.

But these four powerful shifters aren't giving up so easily. They've come to camp ready to claim what they think is theirs.

They'll find my claws are out and my swords are sharp.

Game on, boys.

This is a paranormal romance set at a supernatural summer camp in present-day USA and should be read after Clash of Claws. *It is a "why choose" romance, which means our heroine will have multiple love interests and will get her Happily Ever After with ALL of them by the end of the series. This is the second book of a trilogy, and it will end in a mild cliffhanger. It is intended for readers aged 18+ and contains foul language and spicy scenes. Detailed content warnings can be found in the Author's Note. Happy reading!*

A NOTE FROM THE AUTHOR

Hey everyone! Welcome back to Avery's story. Just a few short notes before we begin.

You should have read *Clash of Claws before* reading this book. The same content warnings from CoC continue to apply to this book: fantasy violence and (light) gore, discussions of death of parents of main characters, and some bullying/hazing (not from our love interests).

The spice will get spicier, but we are still in a slow burn here, so please strap in as the boys do their best to earn it.

And there are still snakes. But we love them both, yes?

We end on another cliffhanger, but this one won't be quite as painful. This is book two of three, so it will be the last cliff.

I hope you have as much fun reading as I did writing.

- *Elizabeth*

1

AVERY

"We really have to stop meeting like this, Dad."

He was not amused by my attempt at levity. "You almost bled out this time, Avery, even with the shift. If your brother hadn't been on hand to donate blood...." He shook his head and scrubbed a hand down his bearded face. My dad was an Alpha wolf and could remain stoic in the direst of circumstances, but he couldn't fool me. He was struggling to keep it together. "I can't even say it."

I'd been awake for only a few minutes. Somehow, I'd made it to the school's infirmary, and they'd stuck me in a real hospital bed this time, hooked up to all kinds of cables and cords. Some pain lingered, but the doctors must've worked some dazzling healing magic on me, because all my body parts seemed to be in one piece and on the mend. My beast dozed contentedly within me.

When I'd first opened my eyes, some torturous reflex had me checking the chair in the corner for Heath.

For a horrifying moment, I missed him.

And then I remembered that I hated him.

Luckily, it was Dad in the chair instead, and he informed me that it was midmorning, which meant I'd been out for a solid ten hours.

My fox dad, Joseph, had commandeered Dr. Lee's stool, and he rolled over to my side.

"How are you feeling?" he asked softly. He wore his long golden hair down today, a fatherly angel watching over my sickbed.

"Pretty good, all things considered." I scooted to sit up against my pillows. "Where's Ian? And Kai? Did the wraiths kill anyone on campus? What the hell happened to the wards?"

Joseph patted my hand. "Calm. No one died. The Guardians sent a team to protect the wall while the Council's on-call specialists repaired the wards. You and the rather impressive quad who brought you here were able to kill all the wraiths that made it onto campus."

"And your brother and Kai are guarding the door. Ian is insisting that these *boys*—" Dad slanted me a very pointed look. "—should not be allowed in here to see you. He has already stabbed the bear once."

I blinked at him.

"And Kai is understandably concerned for Ian's safety, so he's keeping an eye on things."

I nodded absently. It had been too much to hope that the Blackwell Quad would just go away and leave me alone.

"Honey." Dad peered at me, a smile pulling at his mouth. "They said you're Fated."

"Declared it, actually," Joseph added. "And demanded to be let in here once you'd been stabilized."

"But Ian announced that it would be over his desecrated corpse that they be allowed anywhere near you, then words were exchanged, and after that all the stabbing happened."

Joseph squeezed my hand again. "Is it true? Did you meet your Fated?"

Don't think this means anything, Avery.

She's no one, Eleanor.

You know you aren't an option.

I shut my eyes and sucked in a deep breath. I would not cry. Not now. Not after all I'd just survived.

"It is true," I whispered. "But I don't want them."

My dads exchanged concerned looks. "Why not, honey?" Dad asked slowly.

"Because they didn't want me," I snapped.

Joseph looked taken aback, while Dad's eyes widened a fraction of a millimeter.

"They were just like every other Prime quad—on the hunt for their latent princess," I added wearily. "Which they told me, and they did not mince words. They only care now because it turns out we're Fated."

"Ah." Dad sat back in his chair and gave that some thought. "Well, I wouldn't expect them to give up easily, honey. While we weren't Fated to your mother, I've heard the pull to one's Moon-blessed mate is as strong as the pull that solidifies for the rest of us after a true bonding. It can be all-consuming when there are beasts on both sides. These power quads who've been taught that the strongest bonds are created via a latent partner may be... unprepared for that."

My reply was stone-cold. "My beast and I are on the same page about this."

Mostly. She was sleeping, so she might have a stronger opinion when she woke up and we were no longer bleeding to death, but out in those woods she'd been... conflicted, to say the least.

That was fine. I was in charge, and I'd be *un*conflicted enough for the both of us.

Dad studied me. "All that said, you're in control of your own life, Avery. We'd never push you to accept a bonding with men who don't deserve you, Fated or not. You have two sharp swords and one hell of a beast. Set your boundaries and ruthlessly enforce them."

"If there's anything left of those boys after Ian's finished with them," Joseph added with a grim smile. "His attitude makes more sense now. It sounds like they hurt you, honey. I'm so sorry."

"They did," I said softly. "I'm sorry, too, J."

The door slammed open, and Ian marched in. He wore flannel pajama pants stuffed into his boots and a plain white T-shirt, and his ash-blond hair was askew. His katana was in his hand, the blade resting on his shoulder, and he had bags under his eyes. Did he sleep at all last night?

"Oh, you're awake," he said, stopping in his tracks to look me over with a critical eye. "Good."

"Hello to you too," I said drolly. "Are they really just letting you stab people in the hallways of the school infirmary?"

He snorted, lifting a haughty chin. "The school is going to let me do whatever the fuck I want after their supposedly world-class wards failed and my sister almost died saving their asses. The dean has already been by to let Dad know that our scholarships have been increased from partial to full next year."

I sat up straighter. "Do they know what happened to the wards?"

"They are being very tight-lipped," Dad replied. "But a complete failure at only a segment of the perimeter stinks of tampering to me."

"Kai agrees," Ian said. Kai was the ward specialist in our family. "The fact that even swarmers made it over the wall means a complete erasure, not a gradual wearing down or a part that wasn't charged up enough last Full Moon."

Great. It appeared we were under attack by more than just a bunch of decrepit, festering monsters. A strong Giant could occasionally break through even a solid ward, but my family was right—someone had created a wide-open doorway at the front gates of the campus.

Good thing that was not my particular problem because I had enough of those.

"Who, uh...." I fidgeted with the IV line connected to my hand. "Who all knows about my beast now?"

Ian slid his sword into the sheath on his back, and then he sat down on the end of my bed. He gave my leg a reassuring pat over the covers. "Rest easy, Aves. Brody's been added to the circle of trust. It couldn't be helped—he was with me when I got the call that you'd been—" His voice cracked, and I reached for his hand. He accepted my squeeze, and then he speared me with a terrible glare. "For fuck's sake, can you please stop doing this to me? You almost bled to death! What if I hadn't been here to donate blood?"

"I'm sorry, Ian."

"You're damn right, you're sorry. Do you know how much it pains me to be even a little bit thankful to that quad of dickheads because they got you here in time to save your life?"

I snorted a humorless laugh. "Let me unburden you, then. I only nearly ended up wraith food because they abandoned me alone in those woods."

He was on his feet, his blade back in his hand as he stormed toward the door. "I'll kill them. They left *that* little nugget out of the story, those motherfuckers—"

Dad moved in a blink, sliding in front of the door to block Ian's way. "Nope. I'm not going to allow you to wave your sword at that group of Primes again, especially that basilisk. Sit and calm down."

Ian stomped to the corner and flopped into the chair like a sulky toddler.

"To finish answering your question, honey," Joseph said, "only Ian's boyfriend and those four boys know about your tiger. We did impress upon the boys the extreme need for secrecy, but they'd already reached that conclusion themselves."

"I know you're upset with them—" Dad began.

"Understatement," I said.

"—but regardless, the drive to protect you will be overwhelming. Your secret is safe with your Fated."

Ian peered at me, his face sullen. "So it's true, then?"

"Unfortunately," I replied, just as sullen. "Why else would they be here, acting like they care *now*?"

Just go, *Avery. For fuck's sake.*

Honestly, how *dare* they?

He cracked a wry laugh. "Right. Fuckers."

A knock sounded at the door, and Dr. Lee stuck his face inside. He seemed amused about something. "Hello, Avery. I came by to check on you, but also, I believe you have a visitor."

My hackles shot straight up. "If it's one of the Blackwell Quad—"

He shook his head. "No, although I think he's affiliated with them? He appears to be a purple python."

Joseph's golden brows hit his hairline. "A what?"

I relaxed—slightly. "He can come in."

The door opened, and Dr. Lee slipped inside. Tall, fit, cheekbones that could cut glass, shiny black hair that one could have no doubt would be silky-soft to the touch. Dark, kind eyes and endless patience for bullshit. He looked fresh, which meant I was catching him early in his shift.

At Dr. Lee's entrance, Ian sat up straighter and wiped the scowl from his face. I coughed and rolled my eyes at him.

George slithered in behind Dr. Lee and made straight for my bed.

"Hey, buddy," I cooed at him. "Where have you been?"

Dad stood rigid against the wall, and Joseph went deathly still on his stool. While George made his leisurely way up into my bed, they stared at me like they were concerned I'd lost some faculties out there in those woods.

"Relax, Dads," Ian drawled. "That's George. He belongs to the basilisk, but he's super fond of Aves. I'm pretty sure he'll choose to live with her after the divorce."

George curled himself into a pile next to me and draped his head across my thighs. I stroked the smooth scales on his head.

"Fascinating," Joseph said, relaxing. "Maybe George somehow sensed the Moon-given connection between your beast and the basilisk. Wouldn't that be something?"

I scowled. That was probably true and would explain a lot, but the idea that George's affection for me was only due to Elijah's beast being Fated to mine soured the whole thing a bit.

Dr. Lee reviewed my chart on his tablet, and then he approached the bed. "Do you mind, George? I need to check Avery's injuries. She had quite an ordeal last night."

George hissed at him.

"Sorry about that," I said sheepishly. "I haven't seen him in weeks, so he's being clingy."

Dr. Lee chuckled. Such a saint, this man. "I see. Well, I'll do what I can."

He worked quickly through his exam, humming approvingly at some points, frowning and tutting at others. The frowns were usually accompanied by the soft, buzzing warmth of magic as Dr. Lee used his healing affinity to move things along.

Dull pain lingered in the leg the Giant had broken, and the wounds and lacerations I had all over my body stung a bit as they continued to heal. I had internal injuries that I suspected had taken up the bulk of the magical healing work, both for my tiger and for whoever was on call last night when I was brought in.

I was sore and weak, but with Ian's blood pumping through my veins and my beast in her peaceful healing sleep, I'd be good as new in a few days.

"All right, I'm satisfied," Dr. Lee announced, stepping away to make more notes on his tablet. "Everything is healing as it should. I'd like to keep you here for observation for another twenty-four hours, and then I'll release you. After that, I suggest you head home with your family, since the semester's pretty much over." He smiled at me, a twinkle in those dark eyes. "I'd prefer as many capable hands keeping you out of trouble as possible for the next few weeks."

Ian saluted him. "On it, Doc."

"Good man." He made his way to the door, then paused with his hand on the knob to toss a conspiratorial look over his shoulder. "I'll be seeing both of you this summer at Guardian training. It's my turn to be camp doc this year."

I blinked in surprise, and Ian just grinned like it was his birthday.

Dr. Lee didn't wait for a response. He left, clicking the door shut softly behind him.

Ian sighed dreamily, and then he looked at Dad where

he lingered near the door. "You should go reinforce Kai. He thinks the situation in the waiting room is mostly amusing, but I don't trust those assholes not to try something to try to get back here. Again."

My stomach curdled at the mention of the proximity of my not-mates.

Dad sighed. "Fine. I'll go growl at that Alpha. He's impressive, but now I know why his tail was between his legs earlier." He gave me one last look full of concern. "Now that you're awake, I can give them a definitive yes or no. Do you want to see them?"

We told you the cold, hard truth. You aren't it for us.

I didn't need to think about it. "Fuck no."

2

WYATT

"You're bleeding again," Heath said.

I shrugged and cast a disinterested look down at the dark stain spreading through my hospital-issued Proteus College T-shirt. "Good."

I deserved it. My mate had almost bled out in the middle of the moondamned forest because of us. A little dribble of my blood on the infirmary's sterile floor was fucking *nothing*.

It'd taken almost an hour for Avery's beast to heal her wounds enough to shift back to her human form. Aiden had done his best to channel the New Moon's trickle of magic into one of the basic healing spells he knew, but he didn't have a healing affinity, and we didn't dare risk our wildcat's secret to call anyone else. Once the tiger had given us back our girl—pale, passed out, wounds still gaping—I'd snatched her out from under the basilisk, cradled her in my arms like the treasure she was and sprinted damn near a mile in the fucking nude to the infirmary.

The guys had led the way in their beast forms, and even Elijah had managed to shift back without issues so that he could pass through the infirmary doors behind me.

It was excruciating, letting the doctors take her from me and not following.

Then Ian had arrived to once again act as the world's most infuriating cockblock. After they moved Avery to recovery, we had an altercation in the hallway, and he ran his blade through my side. I let him because his blood had saved my mate's life.

Heath sighed the put-upon sigh of a quad leader. "You're no good to us or her injured, Wyatt."

"I'll fucking heal when I feel like it." I'd refused Dr. Lee's offer of magical intervention, and then I'd scared off the student medic who'd come out here with a suture kit. It'd only taken one glare and an inhuman snarl from my beast.

My bear wanted his mate. He was furious that she was being kept from us, but he was disinclined to maim her brother or fathers for standing in our way. I wasn't sure how long that would last.

Better to bleed so he had something else to focus on.

Heath and I were sitting next to each other in two of the small waiting room's uncomfortable chairs. Elijah had abandoned his chair hours ago to sit on the floor across from us, his back against the wall and his long legs splayed in front of him. The black scrub pants the infirmary had given him were too short, barely reaching his ankles.

He'd spoken maybe two words since he'd transformed from beast to man, and his yellow stare hadn't moved from the doors to the recovery wing where Avery was being kept since he'd taken up that post.

At least George had managed to get back there. Elijah's weird psychic connection to that snake had summoned him here a few minutes ago, and so far, he hadn't been tossed back out. If we were lucky, Elijah could glean a report on our mate from him.

Aiden had abandoned his chair and stood near the doors, attempting to reason with Avery's dad, Kaito, cat-to-cat.

It wasn't working. Kaito was a cougar of ordinary power, but he also might be an actual ninja. It didn't take a genius to figure out he was the one that taught my wildcat and her brother everything they knew, so I wasn't going anywhere near his blade.

Kaito was not at all intimidated by Aiden, who was radiating extreme feline agitation. No, Avery's dad seemed mildly amused by our existence in general and was the picture of tranquility, but the creases in his face and the hard look in his eyes betrayed his worry for his daughter.

"We won't disturb her," Aiden was saying, faking patience. "If even just one of us could lay eyes on her to see that she's okay, it would go a long way toward calming our beasts."

"I understand," Kai replied. "Truly I do, but we'd prefer to ask her what she wants when she wakes up." His face softened with the tiniest hint of sympathy. "And she will wake up. I promise."

"I know Dr. Lee said she was stable, but—"

Aiden was interrupted when the doors banged open, and Avery's Alpha father strode out.

Heath was on his feet instantly. His read on Rand Baxter was that he was an impressive fucking wolf, damn near Heath's own power level. It made Heath's wolf wary and deferential, which was fortunate for the situation we'd found ourselves in.

My bear didn't desire to fuck with him, either, but he was growing impatient.

"She's awake," Rand announced.

I shot out of my chair. "Fuck," I mumbled as my stab

wound tore further open. Blood seeped into my already-soaked shirt and dripped down my side.

Heath squared up to Rand, projecting every ounce of strength and authority he possessed. But the night had been long, and the exhaustion was heavy on his face. "We'd like to see her," he said.

"I understand that," Rand replied. "But Avery has stated in very clear terms that she does not wish to see you." He cast an almost-sympathetic look around at the rest of us glum bastards. "Any of you. It sounds like you boys have screwed things up pretty badly."

I'd expected that punch in the gut, but it didn't make it hurt any less.

Heath's shoulders sagged. "We did. I can't deny that, but if we just had a chance to explain everything to her—"

Rand held up a hand. "Not today. I suggest you give her some space."

"How long will they keep her here?" Aiden asked.

"Twenty-four hours for observation. Then we will be taking her home with us." He eyed Heath, sizing him up once again. "We—all of us, including Ian—appreciate that you boys did everything you could to both save Avery's life and keep her secret. We're indebted to you. I also understand, more than you know, the power of the beast's pull to his mate, especially when that mate is herself a powerful animal. But it doesn't entitle you to Avery's time or attention. She's hurt, and she needs to heal. You will respect her boundaries."

A growl ripped from my chest.

Rand arched a brow at me over Heath's shoulder.

"Sorry," I said, blinking away the red headlights. "The bear is on edge."

Kaito frowned at me. "You're bleeding all over the floor, son."

"I know."

Rand sighed. Bet he knew a lost cause when he saw one. "We'll take good care of her. Your beasts will chafe at the separation, but they should tolerate their mate being cared for by her family members. You have a month to get your shit together, and then I expect you to watch my daughter's back at camp, no matter how hard she makes it for you. Am I clear?"

That was a tiny and unexpected kernel of approval, and it perked me right up. "Crystal, sir," I said.

"There was never a question," Aiden agreed.

"We'll kill anything that touches her," Heath added.

Elijah said nothing. He'd watched this entire exchange from his spot on the floor, his expression calculating.

"Good." Rand waved a hand at us. "Go home and get some rest. You all look dead on your feet. We've got her."

My bear snarled, but this time I managed to keep it inside.

Gold sparked in Heath's eyes, but he shut them and took a deep breath. "Okay. Thank you for taking care of her." He jerked his head toward the exit, gesturing for the rest of us to follow.

Aiden's face was as hard as I'd ever seen it. He managed to shake Kaito's hand before falling in behind his brother.

Elijah peeled himself off the floor in a single graceful movement. He nodded to Rand, gave Kaito a quick smile, then strode off after the others.

I sank the full force of my bear into healing my wound because it was starting to hurt like a bitch. "Until next time," I said with one last pointed look at Avery's fathers. It was a promise—she was my mate, and this would be the last moondamned time I left her.

"Looking forward to it," Rand replied with a chuckle.

"Good luck," Kaito added, and then he muttered under his breath, "You boys are going to need it."

That was the fucking truth. I'd said and done things to my girl that made me sick to my fucking stomach, and I'd let her stab me fifty times for it if it meant I'd have the force of those electric blue eyes on me once more.

You can't fight divine will, Wildcat. I'm coming for you.

3

AIDEN

"This is just more of the same bullshit," I said, slamming the book closed. "Even the driest, most apolitical academic discussions of bond theory and power exchange seem to just *assume* a latent shifter as a central bond is the strongest and most stable. There isn't shit in here about Fated bonds or the potential power of an off-the-charts female Prime as a central." I glared at the books I'd strewn across Dad's reading table, the room's stately centerpiece. After I spent all day yesterday at the college's library and didn't find what I wanted, I'd stooped to raiding my fathers' private collection.

Elijah shrugged lazily. He looked like a man without a care in the world, lounging in my dad's reading chair, tucked into the corner of the library next to the fireplace. "Why would there be? Power females are as rare as mythics, and I'd be willing to bet a lot of them are, like my dove, hiding what they are. There just haven't been any cases for your academic brethren to study."

"And the Fated pairings that've been examined in the journals I found in the college's database are almost exclusively lower-powered pairs like Avery's friend and her wolf mate," I continued. "They all report increased happiness and tranquility. Any beasts with rage or control issues do show some evidence of settling, but pairs like that don't share power like a Prime quad, so they don't report an increase in the strength or dominance of the beast."

"And yet," Elijah mused, "the First Guardians were bonded to a powerful female tiger, and they are heralded as one of the strongest quads to ever live." His eyes glowed eerie yellow. "Somehow that fact has been... lost over the centuries."

He was right, of course. Elijah had long cultivated this lackadaisical air of a guy who could hardly be bothered to put on a whole shirt, skipped class constantly, and found just about everything in life mildly amusing. And while that *was* him to a point, he was also focused, driven, and ruthlessly intelligent.

"You know I don't believe the Moon *actually* disfavored females with a beast or any of that curse bullshit," I said. "A miracle, given the environment I was raised in. I believe in solid, evidence-based magical theory. It is highly likely that our ancestors reacted in a certain way to the massacre at the lunar eclipse and the tiger's role in it—whether it truly was a betrayal or just a terrible tragedy—and it caused them to develop mistrust of shifting females, which led to selection bias favoring latents when choosing mates and bonds." I slumped in my chair. My head hurt, and my beast had been pacing anxiously within me for the entire three days since we'd left our mate in the infirmary. "Which then caused the disappearance of whatever genetic factors predispose a female to merging with a beast soul. Not divine will."

He grinned. "Indeed. The ancestors were so dramatic."

I rolled my eyes. "So, yes, I get it—quads and other

strong groups formed bonds with latent females because within a few generations, that's all there were. And the magical theory is solid—it makes sense that a latent bond would be more stable and magically potent. But we have nothing—*nothing*—on the Moon herself blessing a mating like ours. Arguably the bond will be even stronger because it truly *is* the divine will." I pounded my fist on the table because *fuck* all of this. It may have cost me my *mate*. "Our entire body of research and theory is bullshit!"

"Yes," Elijah replied, still infuriatingly calm, "and it's breaking your professorly brain that we *do* have a few millennia of meticulously recorded history of powerful Primes and their latent bonds—both male and female— that provides evidence of the supposed perfect fit between the two. The significant increases in power, the way the beasts are settled, the bountiful fertility of the females—"

I held up a hand. "Stop right there. The fact that Avery might think we didn't want her because we assumed we couldn't fucking *breed* her—"

Elijah hissed through his teeth, his pupils slitting as his yellow eyes glowed. "Let's not use the words 'Avery' and 'breed' in the same sentence. My beast is... interested."

I arched a brow. "I'm relieved that you might actually be struggling as much as the rest of us. Your composure has been extremely off-putting."

He blinked, and his eyes returned to normal. "One of two mysteries plaguing me has been solved," he said, grinning lazily. "The basilisk was such a problematic asshole around my dove because he wanted to be with his mate. He doesn't want to kill the woman I'm obsessed with. Amazing. Now all I have to do is figure out who killed my mother and why. Things are looking up."

I stood up and began to pace the exorbitantly expensive

Persian rug my mother's designer had installed in here six months ago when she'd gone on one of her redecorating sprees. "To your original point," I said, "our history and theology were recorded by the men who survived the massacre and became our first Council. If they'd wanted to erase shifting females—especially Primes—from it, they certainly had the power and opportunity to do so."

"Our mate sure seems to think that's the case." Elijah replied, alluding to Avery's words as she tore into us at the Blue Moon Ball.

"And why do you believe a shifting female isn't the right choice for the bond of a powerful Prime quad? Is it because you believe in the lie made up by our ancestors to malign a hero just because she was female?"

Those words had rattled around in my skull like hell's echo chamber since that night.

"But why?" Elijah went on. "To what end?"

"Why murder a war widow in the middle of a farmers' market in Lion Valley?" I asked, referring to Elijah's mom's tragic story. "And why murder the bonded mate of an unassuming trio of mixed-power shifters and the mother of two toddlers, whose beast may or may not have been a tiger?"

Elijah frowned. The tension that crept into his shoulders would've been invisible to anyone but me, Heath, or Wyatt.

Or Avery, my mind supplied helpfully.

The fact that Avery and Elijah had murdered mothers in common was not lost on any of us, but we hadn't speculated they could be connected. Why would they be? But nothing was impossible.

"These people have always existed among us," I went on. "My fathers certainly have ideas about the place of females in our society, and they sit on the fucking regional Council."

And it would be over my dead body that we told them

anything about Avery before we had to. It was bad enough they'd been in the crowd for her performance during our final training run against the Simulated Wraith Invasion Magic, or SWIM, as it was known to trainees. My fathers didn't need to know anything else until after we'd bonded with her and Heath put my most powerful father, Holden, in his place.

My jaguar purred at the thought. *We'll just keep dreaming, won't we, buddy?*

I strode to the bookshelf tucked behind Holden's desk and began to rifle through the titles. I'd ignored this shelf because it was dedicated to his most archaic and backwards beliefs—unlikely to be hiding anything resembling progressive thought on bond theory.

The Original Sin of the Prime Female

The Superior Male: Glorifying the Moon Through Masculine Dominance

"Take a break, Aiden," Elijah drawled. "We're not going to find something we've overlooked that proves all modern bond theory wrong. You didn't miss anything, and it isn't your fault we believed what we believed. It doesn't change the fact that we have to fix what we broke with my dove."

King of the Jungle: Traditional Shifter Values in a Modern World

"Stop talking reason," I snapped. "Maybe there's a clue buried in the bullshit written by these reactionary thinkers my dad loves—" I paused to stare dumbly at an electronic keypad that I'd never seen before, which was hidden behind the two-volume set of *Morals and the Moon*, written by one of Dad's favorite podcasters. "What the fuck is this?"

"What?"

"A keypad. I didn't know my dad had a safe installed in here—"

The door swung open, and I had two seconds to replace the books, sit down in the desk chair, and become engrossed in *Shifter Monthly* magazine before Holden strode in.

Shit. He must've left the office early and come straight to his library. He was still in his dress shirt and slacks, his mane of dark hair tossed over one shoulder.

He glanced up from whatever he was reading on his phone as he walked, pausing in the middle of the carpet. "Aiden? What are you doing in here?"

As always, his presence filled the room. He wasn't any taller or broader than Wyatt, but he wore his beast's dominance like a dark sorcerer would wear his cape billowing around him, heavy and threatening.

I pointed at the magazine. "I was hoping to steal a copy of this. There's a feature on one of my colleagues for his work integrating techno-runes into home security hardware."

Dad waved a hand. "Fine. I'm finished with that."

I stood up and slid the magazine under my arm. "Elijah and I were just leaving."

His cool gray gaze slid to where Elijah sprawled in his chair. Elijah watched him with lazy amusement on his face even as his yellow eyes flashed for the briefest moment.

My dad was wary of Elijah, though he'd never admit it. As the head of the Southeastern Council and self-proclaimed strongest Prime in the region, he could show no fear or weakness, not even in the face of a mythic. If Elijah's basilisk challenged Dad's lion head-on, Elijah would probably win, but Dad would give him a hell of a time. An equally likely scenario was that neither of them would survive the fight.

But until a few days ago, I'd have said Dad had something Elijah did not—supreme control over his beast.

Now? I'd never seen Elijah and his beast in more perfect harmony, and he wasn't even bonded yet. It was as if just the *knowledge* that Avery was his Fated had flipped some mysterious switch.

"Ah," Dad said, wrinkling his nose. "Good to see you, Mr. Harrow. I didn't realize you were here, since I haven't seen your detestable python slithering around this house in a few weeks."

Elijah stood up, his posture loose and languid. He grinned and shrugged helplessly. "George's newfound attachment to Clara was a surprise to me, as well, sir. He's his own snake—I can only politely make requests of him."

A half-truth. George was usually inclined to listen to Elijah's polite requests, and he'd dutifully stayed behind at the manor to watch over Clara while the rest of us went back to school and fucked things up beyond comprehension with our mate.

"Speaking of your sister," Dad said, returning his shrewd gaze to me, "where is she?"

It was my turn to shrug helplessly. "She and Willow conspired to convince Mom and Mrs. Gale to let them stay together this summer. Heath drove her over to the Gale estate a few hours ago."

Also a half-truth. Wyatt's mom was complicit in this scheme because she wanted Clara out of this house as much as we did. Dad didn't need to know that part.

Dad strode past me to take the seat I'd abandoned behind his desk. He sat down and steepled his fingers, gray eyes studying me as if cataloging all possible weaknesses. "Fine," he said finally, his lips pursed. "I suppose that since the Nelson boys are summering in Europe, she doesn't have any obligations here. I want her back in this house before school starts in September."

"I'll mention it to Mom."

"You do that."

Elijah and I exchanged a look, and I jerked my head at the door. He followed me out.

"Oh, and boys?"

I paused in the doorway. "Yes?" I said over my shoulder.

"I haven't had a chance to commend you on your recent heroism." He smirked, and the look reeked of both pride and derision—his usual expression when it came to Heath and me. "A full breach in the campus wards, and not a single casualty, thanks solely to the younger Blackwell Quad."

"It's what we've been training for," I replied simply. It was Heath's diplomacy, the dean's embarrassment, and Dr. Lee's iron-clad rules on medical privacy that'd kept Avery's presence in those woods from becoming public knowledge. "Had any wraiths gotten past us, there were other skilled quads and Support Squadron trainees guarding the evacuation location. But we got lucky."

Dad hummed. "Indeed. Well, you'll be pleased to know that the parents of your peers are falling all over themselves to thank our family for saving their precious children's lives. Your mother can hardly keep up with the deluge of brunch and tea invitations."

"How wonderful," I said dryly. "As long as spilling our blood was good for something."

Elijah chuckled.

Dad's grin turned contemplative. "It's too bad the four of you will be occupied this summer. I suspect there will be a parade of society mothers and their daughters coming through this house."

I'd never been more thrilled to be spending two months in a cabin in the woods.

"As much as I hate to disappoint the ladies," Elijah said, "there's no getting out of camp, try as I did."

He'd tried no such thing, but the more Dad found Elijah unserious and nonthreatening, the better. His commitment to the bit was legendary.

"On that note, Dad," I said, "have there been any updates from the Council's investigation regarding what happened to the campus wards?"

He'd lost interest in our conversation, apparently, and was back to looking at something on his phone. He waved a dismissive hand at me. "Likely a miscast by whoever was assigned that segment on the last re-up. We're interviewing our contractors and will fire the person responsible. Nothing for you all to worry about."

I narrowed my eyes at him. That would've been *quite* the mistake made by a supposed ward security expert while dealing with a rune sequence permanently etched into pure fucking silver.

"Sure," I said. "Have a good summer, Dad."

I would be joining Heath at Wyatt's until we moved out to camp in mid-June. I could've gone back to my house on campus, but I wasn't interested in marinating in my fuckups and pining for my mate by myself. Misery did love company.

Dad grunted an acknowledgment, and Elijah and I finally made our exit.

4

ELIJAH

My dove lived with her family in an older Craftsman home on a quiet but eclectic street on the northwest side of Fulton City. The Baxter house was well-kept—a modest two-story with dark red paint, large windows, and a wraparound porch that offset the red house in a fresh, bright white. The small front yard was a neat hodgepodge of flowerbeds, with shrubs and other various plants bloomed in shades of red and pink. The uneven sidewalk was made of brown pavers, and mature trees lined the yards along the street.

The house next door was twice as large and was probably worth upwards of a million dollars, while the house two doors down had fallen into disrepair, its peeling paint and sagging porch a small blight on the charm of the neighborhood. An aging multifamily triplex took up the large corner lot at the end of the street. A few kids played in yards. An elderly human woman watered her plants across the street.

In the distance, the faint rumble of the transit system's trains rolling over tracks was a reminder of our urban environs. I licked my lips and got hints of hot asphalt, smoke from the barbecue joint down the road, and gasoline.

So different from the cookie-cutter suburban neighborhoods and gated communities our shifter brethren had carved out of the hundred miles of forest and mountains that stretched from north of the city to the Tennessee border.

I'd left my Bronco parked a few streets away. The setting sun and the lovely trees had provided me ample shadows to slip through undetected, and the neighbors' large magnolia had many branches equipped to hold my weight.

Avery stood at the kitchen sink, washing dishes from dinner. Her fox dad, Joseph, dried dishes next to her, his golden hair tied in a bun at the nape of his neck. They chatted amiably, and I doubted I'd ever seen a father more full of love and pride for his daughter.

My beast stirred, the sense of calm that'd come over me since I'd climbed into this tree buzzing pleasantly. *Yes, our mate's fathers are worthy of her,* I told him. *We will not have to kill them.*

Pretty mate. Perfect mate.

The words weren't spoken aloud in my head, but I could interpret them all the same. This was a new and not unwelcome development, but it was also frustratingly late. Had I been able to commune so easily with the basilisk three months ago, I might've known he recognized his Fated hiding within our gorgeous new student.

I could've saved us all from making the worst mistake of our lives.

It was the only reason I hadn't just climbed into her bedroom window upstairs and made myself comfortable in her bed while I waited for her to finish up. Even my beast knew our dove needed space. She needed time to heal from what we'd done, and we would give that to her.

For now.

Avery stepped away from the sink and began putting glasses away in a cabinet. I drank in her lovely profile. I was an addict, and it'd been far too long since my last hit.

My dove appeared healthy and in generally good spirits, but I knew better. She'd been my obsession for an entire semester, after all.

Her movements, normally graceful and quick, were slower, like she was nursing some lingering pain. She had dark little puffs under her beautiful blue eyes—eyes that still carried the weight of everything that'd happened to her. Despite the cheerful demeanor she put on for her family, she couldn't fool me.

She was resolute, but she was also sad.

My beast coiled tightly, hissing his displeasure. *She needs us.*

She does, I agreed. *We'll have to show her how much.*

Avery paused, her arm raised, still gripping a glass she'd just set on a high shelf. She turned slowly, her eyes narrowed as she peered over her shoulder and out the kitchen window that faced my tree.

That was our cue.

"Your time will be up soon, Dove," I murmured. "Until then."

I slipped from the tree and made my way back to my car. I had another appointment tonight.

HEATH SLAMMED THE DOOR AS HE CLIMBED INTO MY CAR. "You're late."

Someone was in a fine mood this evening.

"Apologies," I replied smoothly, grinning as I thought of Avery. "I had to make a quick stop in the Upper City."

He snapped his head in my direction like an angry Doberman. "You *what?*"

"Relax. She didn't see me."

He ran a hand through his thick blond hair and groaned. "You cannot creep around in her fucking bushes, man. This situation is precarious enough as it is. Don't piss her off more."

My smile widened. "You're just jealous."

He huffed and slumped in his seat.

I waited.

After a moment, he sighed, relenting. "How did she look?"

"Like a goddess sent by the Moon to break hearts and slay wraiths."

Gold flashed in his eyes, and he shut them like he was in pain. "I already knew *that*, you asshole." He opened his eyes and glared at me. "Is she okay? Does she look like she's hurting? Do we need to send Dr. Lee or preferably one of his less-attractive-but-just-as-skilled colleagues to her house?"

I chuckled, pulling the car out onto the road and leaving our meeting spot—a Walmart on the south side of Fulton City—behind. Heath had parked his Cadillac SUV in the brightest spot he could find and within mere feet of two security cameras like a paranoid rich boy.

"I suggest you focus on the task at hand, Captain," I replied. "The reason you joined me on this little errand was to take your mind off things, correct? So you'd stop stomping around the halls of Gale Manor like an angry ogre?"

"I have not been *stomping*."

"Sure you haven't," I said, waving a hand at his general state of being. Tense muscles, aggression pulsing around him like an electrified fence. His beast was always on the surface these days, just waiting to break free and run all the way from Wyatt's estate to Avery's house. I sighed, taking pity on him. "She looks good," I said quietly, "but some of her vibrance is gone. I have to imagine that's our fault."

He swallowed roughly, and his fists clenched so hard that it was a wonder he didn't break his own fingers. "I know."

We didn't speak the rest of the twenty-minute drive into the industrial wasteland south of the city, where the Low Country Kings MC made their lair.

It was a joke of a motorcycle club, full of minor shifters and run by men with only slightly more powerful animals than would rank as ordinary.

Petty criminals with small dicks and big ambitions.

And, in all likelihood, the hired help who'd murdered my mother twenty years ago.

We weren't headed for their decrepit clubhouse, as much as I'd have loved to sniff around in there. I'd spent not an insignificant amount of time last semester surveilling the place, and there were always at least two club members present and awake in there at any given time. Not ideal for breaking and entering.

Instead, Heath and I were headed to a nearby neighborhood where the widow of the club's ex-President still lived in the house she'd once shared with her deceased husband. The investigator hired by my uncle, Horatio, had located her a few months ago, and I'd already let myself into her empty house once to snoop.

That was how I came to be in possession of an old cell phone that I'd recovered from a dusty drawer in an even dustier little home office. The call log from the days around my mother's murder showed both incoming and outgoing calls to a now-disconnected number simply labeled "Arch-prime" in the contact list.

Add this to the other item I had in my possession—an odd knife, its hilt carved into a flowering plant with trumpet-shaped purple blooms and onyx berries that perfectly matched the description of the murder weapon—and you had the extent of the trove of evidence I was working with.

Tonight, the widow and I were going to have a little chat, and with any luck, I'd have something to add.

"Brenda, stop fucking talking to that asshole!"

Heath buried his fist in the mouthy gentleman's stomach as he lunged at me for the second time this evening. His leather cut said his name was Razor, but Brenda had called him Carl a few times.

"Shut up," Heath growled. He knocked Carl's hand from where he'd been reaching inside his cut. Heath slid his hand in there instead and deftly extracted a hidden dagger. He shoved Carl to the ground, and the unfortunate man crashed through the rickety coffee table with an embarrassing yelp. Heath pressed a boot into his neck and held up the small knife, a droll look on his face. "Really? What were you planning to do with this? Poke Elijah enough to annoy him into leaving?"

Carl gurgled something unintelligible.

I returned my gaze to Brenda, who was sitting across from me at the small kitchen table. She looked a decade younger than her fifty years and wore a tight tank top over frayed denim shorts. Her massive tits were barely contained by her shirt, and her platinum-blonde hair was freshly dyed, if the ammonium taste lingering on my lips was anything to go by.

Brenda had surely been a looker in her day and still was, which accounted for her younger male companion, who couldn't have been a day over twenty-five.

She frowned at Carl's predicament, like she wasn't sure what he was doing on the floor in a pile of cheap wood shards, before she was back to smiling serenely at me. "I'm sorry about him. We only just started dating, and shifter men can get possessive, can't y'all?"

"Of course," I replied smoothly. "Heath and I have a mate of our own, so we certainly aren't here with untoward intentions. Once Carl gets his wits about him, he'll realize you're just helping a boy find out what happened to his mother."

I let the basilisk peek out again, ensnaring her. I was using the lightest possible touch—I didn't want to lose Brenda to the near-blackout daze my beast could unleash on all but the most powerful shifters. Our project today just needed a teensy bit of hypnosis and a whole lot of my natural charm.

She sighed dreamily. "Yes. I just wish I could be more helpful to you, Elijah."

Carl thrashed behind me. The thud of Heath's kick sounded, followed by a pained groan.

We hadn't anticipated Brenda's new beau, and while he was a lively one, he was no match for Heath. His pheromones tasted of inferior canine, and he yelped like a chihuahua. Heath could've held him immobile with just the force of his wolf's dominance, but he needed the exercise.

"So your late husband never mentioned who he was

working for back in those days when you guys had a little extra spending money to throw around?" I asked her.

She shook her head. "He was so secretive about it. Club business, ya know?" She pursed her lips, a look of real disappointment on her face. "I'm sorry. If I'd have known I might need to help such an adorable young man, I'd have paid more attention."

Heath snorted.

"And the name 'Archprime' doesn't mean anything to you?"

"No...." Her frown deepened, and I allowed her to tear her gaze from mine as a thoughtful look crossed her face. "Well, I did look at a bank statement once," she said after a moment, grinning sheepishly. "I was just curious. Usually the money he made from the club was cash, but suddenly we were getting funds in our bank account like a proper job. Doug had left the statement on his desk to go outside to take a call. He shredded it when he came back."

I beamed at her like she was the smartest lady in the world. "But you took that chance to take a little peek before he could destroy it, didn't you?"

She batted her long lashes. "Yeah. Most of it was debits for our bills and stuff, but there was a big deposit from something called 'Lunar Heritage.' I don't remember any Archprime, though," she added, back to frowning.

Bingo. I typed the name into the notes I kept on my phone. Hopefully Horatio's investigator could handle this one too. "That's okay, Brenda," I cooed. "I'll just see what I can find on Lunar Heritage. I bet it will get me going in the right direction. Thank you so much."

The yellow light of the single bulb hanging over the kitchen table cast a dingy glow on her flushed cheeks. "You're welcome. Are you sure you don't want to stay for a drink? You boys are old enough, right? Not that I'd tell if you weren't," she added with a sultry wink.

"Brenda, what the *fuck*?" Carl protested weakly.

I stood up and dusted off my jeans. "We appreciate the invite, but we'd better get going. I apologize for interrupting your date with Carl."

She waved a dismissive hand and waggled her blonde brows. "There's still plenty of time left for our *date*."

"You hear that, Carl?" Heath asked the man on the floor. "Don't move a muscle as we walk out that door, or I'll break your dick in half. That would be unfortunate because it sounds like you'll be needing it later."

I chuckled. "He's not joking. Heath and I have been going through a bit of a dry spell, and we'd both take some enjoyment in preventing someone else from getting laid."

"Fine," Carl gurgled. "Just get the fuck out."

I released Brenda from my hold. She shook her head slowly, her eyelids fluttering.

By the time she realized a couple of college kids had just bamboozled her into spilling secrets and put her boyfriend through a coffee table, Heath and I were already in the car and speeding swiftly out of the neighborhood.

Hopefully this little sliver of information I'd manipulated out of Brenda would bear some fruit. The basilisk and I both needed a target, or the draw to my dove's side could prove too powerful to resist.

5

HEATH

Cars flew by us on the highway in both directions. Billboards lit the horizon against the gloomy Moonless sky, a thick layer of clouds shrouding the stars from view.

"Our exit's coming up," Aiden said from the passenger seat, indicating my car's GPS. He glanced over his shoulder into the backseat. "You're sure this twenty-four-hour diner is walking distance from Avery's house?"

"Yes," Elijah replied. "I parked there last time I... visited."

Electricity buzzed through my entire body. It'd been nearly a month since I'd set eyes on my mate. I hadn't seen her since the moment the doctors had taken her battered body from Wyatt's arms and whisked her away to surgery. It'd taken everything I had to keep from tearing the infirmary apart after that.

"She's going to be so pissed if she sees us out there," Wyatt murmured. In my rearview mirror, his shining green eyes took in the cityscape sliding past the window. He fiddled with one of the small black plugs he wore in his ear lobes and smirked. "I hope she punches me in the face."

"Keep your shit together," I growled at him. "We're doing this to protect our mate, whether she likes it or not. We need you at your best, not bleeding all over the place or with one eye swollen shut because you begged Avery to give you a shiner."

Red rolled across his irises. "You're the one she's going to run through with her blade, you dick. You think you're going to just walk up to her and tell her how it is and she'll get over everything we did. You're fucking dreaming."

My grip tightened on the steering wheel. I wanted to break it in half, launch it out the window, and scream until I passed out. "She's had an entire month. And camp starts in two days. She has to talk to us sometime."

"Does she?" Aiden asked sullenly.

I flipped my blinker on and coasted off the highway. "Everyone in this car needs to get their game face on. Not one of you protested when I suggested we make this trip."

No, the urge to protect our Fated, who would no doubt be traipsing through the streets while wraiths roamed free, had been too much for any one of us or our beasts to handle. The thought of her not being at her best because of her injuries and her inability to shift freely without risking her secret had plagued my nightmares.

The fact that it'd been weeks since I'd had any idea how she was doing or where she was at any given moment had damn near driven me to insanity.

I didn't give a fuck whether she wanted our help or not. She was getting it.

It was nearing midnight as I parked at the back of the diner. At least a dozen cars sat in the lot, the restaurant full of humans going about their night, oblivious to the fact that soul-devouring monsters might wander into the busy streets around them.

We exited the car and collected our weapons from the trunk. Aiden and I wielded identical sabers, the blade we'd trained with since well before we'd ever entered the Guardian program. Wyatt hefted his battle-ax—a new purchase over the break, since he'd previously only ever cared to use the weapons issued by the program. Elijah strapped a long dagger to his belt, just in case. He usually faced wraiths in his basilisk form and only did so when shit got real.

Aiden had performed the Moon blessing on each of our blades under the last Full Moon—something he, the *runes professor*, had learned from Avery when he stumbled across her blessing her own blades last semester, the lucky fucking asshole.

"I still can't believe wraiths wander all the way down here," Aiden said, eyeing the deserted strip mall down the street. Next door was a trendy brewery, definitely not deserted. He slid his saber into the leather sheath strapped to his back. "According to Council records, the only declared Prime living in this zip code is Rand Baxter. Even with the addition of Avery's undeclared beast, it shouldn't be enough to consistently attract wraiths away from the shifter communities, especially L3s or 4s."

"And yet," Elijah said, his yellow eyes alight, "hasn't the recurring theme lately been that everything we've been taught is perhaps not entirely accurate?"

I grunted in agreement, sliding my saber into the sheath at my waist. Like the rest of my quad, I wore broken-in jeans that allowed me to move freely, a dark T-shirt, and sturdy boots. Ideally, we would handle whatever we found out here in our human forms because while those without shifter blood would be unable to see wraiths, the same couldn't be said of our beast forms.

A giant red bear rampaging down the city streets would probably not go unnoticed. I had no idea how Avery's family handled the balance between keeping the secrecy of our kind and the need to shift in wraith combat.

And I had no way to ask her. My own *mate* was unreachable to me.

Wyatt settled his ax on his shoulder and held his phone in front of his face, squinting as he studied the screen. "Dad's patrol maps show the closest Guardian post is twenty miles north of here, and their zone ends at the border of the Redtail Forest, just outside Deerfield."

Deerfield was one of the southernmost shifter settlements—a small town with a predominantly working-class population and, more than likely, the barest minimum of wards.

"How active was that zone last night?" Aiden asked.

Wyatt scrolled. "They marked the zone orange for this cycle. I think that means higher than average."

Wyatt's father, Ward, was a senior Guardian officer and in charge of our region's training program. He had—against official policy—given Wyatt access to the Guardian network when it became clear that we would not be talked out of this excursion.

"Okay, sounds like we need to be ready for anything." I waved a hand at Elijah. "Lead the way."

We followed him as he cut a path across the busy commercial area and into a residential neighborhood. Mature trees lined the streets, and every house on the block had to be at least fifty years old. It was pitch-black, save the occasional porch light. The soft yellow glow of the streetlamps on each corner did little to pierce the still darkness.

My heart beat harder in my chest. My wolf pushed against my skin, ravenous for blood, anxious for our mate.

Her voice ghosted through my mind, as it so often did.

Admit you think I'm somehow defective.

Those haunting blue eyes had been so fierce, so furious, so righteous as she'd torn strips from my skin at the ball. I'd never seen a more beautiful girl in my fucking life.

And I'd never been so *angry* in my fucking life as I stood there, spiraling, trying to do right by my quad and my sister, and there *she* was, invading our space, challenging me, looking so *fucking* hot in that dress.

Taunting me with something I thought I could never have.

My wolf whined in my chest.

I'll fix it. She's ours.

Elijah put up a hand, bringing us to a stop. "Listen."

Up ahead, the echoes of a screech sounded. A masculine voice barked orders.

I tensed and wrapped a hand around the grip of my sword, taking comfort in the feel of its worn leather. "Let's go—"

Another screech, this one louder and coming from somewhere behind us.

Shit.

"Elijah and Aiden, support the group straight ahead," I said, thinking fast. "Wyatt and I will assess the situation to the west."

No one argued. Elijah and Aiden broke into a run, speeding off down the street until they disappeared around the corner. Wyatt took off in the opposite direction, running with his huge ax strapped to his back like it weighed nothing. I followed him, and we wound our way west, farther into the neighborhood and away from the busier streets.

We rounded a corner, and the houses fell away, green space flanking us on both sides. A park lay on our left, complete with a deserted playground and a man-made pond, its fountain feature creating the only noise besides the night insects. To the right, a low stone fence separated a cemetery from the rest of the street.

More shrieks rent the air, and three L2 swarmers careened around the corner and into the street in front of us, their bodies pudgy and piglike but their four legs long, hairy, and bent at an angle like a spider's. Behind them, an L3 Ripper leapt from the bushes, oozing colorless gray blood from where a blade had been impaled in its chest. It had the vague shape of a bear nearly as large as Wyatt's beast, but its head was twice the normal size, and in place of paws, it had three-toed reptilian talons. It was also missing a chunk of flesh from its skull and its entire left side, the patchy, dark gray hide rotted away to reveal decaying ribs. The faint violet glow of the magic that gave this *thing* life leaked through the cracks.

It staggered into the street, screeching at decibel levels the SWIM had never managed to replicate. We sprinted right into the fray. Wyatt intercepted the swarmers, yanking his ax from his back and lopping off heads as he ran.

Before I could take a swing at the Ripper with my own blade, Avery's dad, Kaito, jumped out of the bushes. He took a running leap and shifted seamlessly in midair into a cougar with shiny dark fur. His beast smashed into the much larger wraith with a vicious snarl, and they tumbled over the stone wall and into the cemetery.

Avery sprinted out of the park and shot across the street in hot pursuit, her short swords raised, a light sheen of sweat glistening on her exposed skin.

Time slowed to a crawl.

She wore a black tank top, fitted tactical pants in the same color, and combat boots. Her blonde hair was in a tight ponytail, save the few strands that'd come loose and now stuck to her damp face.

So fucking beautiful. The sight knocked the breath from my chest.

She was laser-focused on where her dad had gone over the cemetery wall with the wraith. Those long legs ate up the distance on the pavement, her beast's strength pushing her to inhuman speeds.

"Avery!" I bellowed, jogging straight for her, Wyatt on my heels.

Her head jerked in our direction, and she stumbled a few steps as she slowed to a stop.

She stared at us, her chest rising and falling as she caught her breath. Surprise morphed quickly into a deep frown.

She may as well have slid a knife between my ribs.

"What...," she said, panting. "What the *fuck* are you doing here?"

We stopped a few feet in front of her, taking care to be outside her sword range.

Wyatt propped his ax on his shoulder and hit her with the most panty-melting smile in his arsenal. "Helping, Wild-cat. What's it look like?"

"We don't need your help," she spat.

"Avery," I growled. "You're our Moon-blessed mate, and you're recovering from serious injuries. Let us help you."

Her knuckles went white around her swords, her jaw tensing as her nostrils flared. "I am not your fucking *mate*. You rejected me, and you left me to die in the fucking woods. Go away, Heath."

"That's not—" I shook my head and took a step toward her. "Avery—"

She raised her blade and pointed it right at my neck. "I said. Fuck. Off."

Wyatt slipped into the space between us. "Come on, Wildcat—"

Another violent screech echoed from the cemetery. Kaito was still battling a wraith in there.

"Shit," Avery swore. She turned and ran for the wall, hurdling it with ease. She disappeared into the trees, leaving Wyatt and me standing there like chumps.

Until a second Ripper stalked around the corner. Another mutant bear, which we should've been expecting. Wraiths usually spawned in multiples.

It was almost a relief to see it. Now we could actually be useful.

The wraith turned the empty voids of its eye sockets on us. We were two juicy Prime souls, ripe and ready to be consumed. It opened its bear jaws to reveal four rows of dagger teeth and two horrifying tentacle protrusions that darted from the corners of its mouth. It roared, the sound like car tires screeching across pavement.

It charged us, and our cylinders sparked back to life.

This was what we'd been training for, and we were the best in the fucking class at it.

Wyatt's bear tore from his body and charged the wraith, his ax clattering to the ground next to his destroyed clothes. I ripped my saber from its sheath and followed. Wyatt took the same tactic Avery's dad had, circling around the wraith before launching his huge bear body at it, tackling it out of the street and over the wall into the cemetery.

I followed them over the wall. Wyatt snarled and snapped at the wraith as they tumbled through the trees and out into an open area filled with grave plots.

The wraith slashed at Wyatt with dagger talons. Wyatt

tore into its patchy gray hide with his jaws. The granite headstones bore the brunt of the force of their huge bodies as they bounced off them like pinballs. Packed soil churned under claws and fur, disturbing the dead beneath it.

Taking a page from Avery's playbook, I vaulted onto the wraith's back and drove my sword straight into its spine. It shrieked and flailed, tossing me off. I landed nimbly on my feet, and then Wyatt smashed into the wraith once more to knock it to the ground. I lunged and tore my saber from the wraith's body. Gripping it in both hands, I swung the blade in a brutal downward strike, severing its neck.

Aiden's Moon-blessing held true. Its disgusting gray flesh hissed, and the wraith began to melt away into thick gray sludge, its foul stench lingering as it went.

Wyatt shifted back into a man, and I threw him a pair of shorts I had in the small pack I wore on my back. We were in human territory, so we'd prepared to be more careful with the public nudity.

I wiped my blade on my jeans and put it away, and then I shucked my shirt, now drenched in wraith guts.

I'd just shoved my shirt into my pack when Avery and Kaito sauntered through the trees.

I spared a passing glance for Avery's dad, now no longer a cougar and who, like Wyatt, wore only a pair of tight black shorts. About Avery's height, he had the lean, muscular build of most cat shifters. Wraith gore decorated his chest and coated his katana blade.

For several long moments, I scanned my mate from her gorgeous head to what I was certain were perfect toes inside those thick-soled boots. She must've caught some wraith claws, because she had three identical slashes through her shirt, her toned stomach taunting me through the rips. No blood that I could see or smell. Streaks of wraith goo marred her pale neck, and the single blade in her hand dripped the same gray guts, which meant she'd probably beheaded the other bear wraith after Kaito had worn it down.

A possessive growl reverberated through my chest.

Avery stopped in her tracks, frowning at the scene. What I wouldn't fucking give for my presence to elicit something other than a frown from my mate.

Kaito's dark brows bounced up his forehead before he schooled his expression into something like mild interest. "Got the twin, I see," he said, surveying the remnants of the wraith. "Thanks for the assist."

Avery shook the sludge from her sword and sheathed it on her back with an exasperated huff. "We could've taken care of it, Kai."

I dared a step in her direction. "Killer, are you hurt?"

She winced, and my stomach dropped into an even lower circle of hell. "That's not your concern anymore, Heath."

"Avery—"

A shrill whistle sounded from somewhere outside the cemetery. Kai returned the call with two short whistles of his own.

A few seconds later, Avery's Alpha father jogged into view. He also wore only a pair of shorts, indicating he'd shifted at some point this evening. Following close behind him were Ian, Aiden, Elijah, and Avery's fox dad, Joseph— all of them still fully clothed and splattered with gray guts.

"Oh look," Ian said, chuckling as they joined us around the grave plots, "the gang's all here. Aves, you owe me fifty bucks. I knew there was no way they were going to wait until camp to butt back into your life."

Aiden and Elijah drank in the sight of Avery like dying men in the desert who'd crawled their way to an oasis. She lifted her chin, her eyes sparking electric blue as she glowered under their attention.

Elijah blinked away his beast, his lips quirking into an almost smile, while my brother's face looked the way my insides felt, which was totally fucking destroyed.

Rand cleared his throat awkwardly. "Well, we do appreciate the assistance. We had to take down a full dozen swarmers and three Rippers in the east quadrant, and the extra blades were handy. It was the most active night we've had so far this year." He met my stare and put the full authority of his wolf behind it. "But it's probably best if you boys head back home now."

Wyatt blew out a harsh breath and cracked his neck. His bear did not want to leave his mate.

"We'll be on our way shortly," I replied. "If we could just have five minutes to talk to Avery—"

Ian snorted. "Fat fucking chance."

"That would be up to Avery," Kaito said, twirling his katana lazily, "and no one else."

Aiden's gaze had yet to leave our girl, the turquoise glow around his irises faint but present. "Avery, can we just—"

Avery held up a hand and looked at Rand. "Give me thirty seconds, please."

He nodded. "Let's go, everyone," he said, motioning for the rest of the group to follow him down the path that led back to the road. "That means you, too, Ian."

"But—"

Joseph snagged him by the back of his shirt and dragged him off.

Once they'd disappeared, Avery crossed her arms over her chest and surveyed the group of us with yet another frown.

And then she let her beast off her chain.

The tiger's presence crashed into the space between us, a tsunami of pure power. I smothered a gasp at the push of such a dominant Prime against my wolf.

How the fuck had she hidden *this* from us last semester?

My wolf floated to the surface, growling his approval as he held out against her onslaught.

Elijah chuckled happily. In any other situation, his beast would've taken over and gone straight for the kill. Not even my father would've dared.

"Fuck yes, Wildcat," Wyatt said with a deep growl. His bear was riding him hard. "Give me those claws."

"Shut up," she snapped, and we all stood up a little straighter. "Whatever this is—" She gestured between the four of us. "—it stops now. We are not mates. We are, at best, classmates and Guardian teammates. That is how we're all going to act at camp."

Wyatt snorted a laugh.

"Not happening," I declared. "You can't deny it, Avery. Your beast felt it, just as ours did. We are *Fated*. It's the Moon's divine will that you belong to us."

"I belong to no one," she growled. "Least of all you four. You made it very clear how you felt about me as a candidate for your central bond."

Aiden blew out a frustrated breath. "Avery, you know what bond theory says, why we thought—"

"Save it, *Professor*. I don't want to fucking hear it."

My wolf pushed hard against her, and she sucked in a breath.

"Killer," I said, my voice low and threaded with dominance, "camp starts in two days. You can't avoid us forever. We fucked up, but we can't fix it if you won't talk to us. We have things to say to you, and you will *listen*."

Her electric eyes went nearly white, and silver fur sprouted along her arms for a flash before it faded away.

My wolf's power swelled against hers. We fought it out for two blissful seconds until she snapped my hold like a fucking twig. A sharp sting of pain reverberated through my bones.

"Just like you listened when I begged you not to leave me alone in a wraith-infested forest?" she snarled.

I blew out a frustrated breath, my heart pounding in my chest. Excruciating silence stretched between us.

"Dove," Elijah whispered. "Please."

"No." She pulled her beast back, and the pressure relented. She shot us one last clear-eyed look full of hatred —or was that *pain*? "Fuck off, all of you."

She turned, giving us her back.

We could only stand there and stare, our beasts mingling into a mess of longing and anger and self-loathing as the object of our deepest desires walked away from us once again.

6

———

AVERY

"Swanky," Ian said as he marched through my cabin's screen door without knocking. He surveyed the sparse but cozy space. "Being the only female in this sausage festival rarely has its perks, but this is definitely one of those times."

I tucked in the final corner of the sheet on my twin bed. "Clearly I need to complain to management about getting a lock."

"You do." He threw himself onto the empty bed situated against the opposite wall.

Since I would not have a roommate for the eight-week duration of Guardian Training Camp, the extra bed would serve as Ian's couch and a depository for my dirty clothes.

"Or," he went on, "maybe I should just sneak in after lights out and sleep here. Help keep out the riffraff."

"And leave your boyfriend alone in a cabin full of hot shifter males?"

He scoffed. "We're rooming with Joon and Nico. Those are the straightest boys alive."

True. Both were bobcats and part of Brody's feline crew

of besties. I'd never seen either of them in a social situation without a girl hanging off their arm, and it was rarely the same girl twice.

I waggled my eyebrows at my brother. "You and Brody sharing a bunk? Who's top and who's bottom?"

He winked. "We'll switch. It's going to be a long summer."

"Why did I even ask?" I said with a roll of my eyes. "And also, ew. I can't imagine anything less sexy than four guys crammed into one small cabin. The *stench*."

"I beg you to remember that when the call of the wild with respect to a certain quad becomes especially persistent."

With a few aggressive strokes of my hand, I smoothed my purple quilt, and then I sat down on my neat little bed and glared at my brother. "Sounds like you don't have any confidence in my resolve."

He held up his hands in surrender. "I have all the confidence in you, Aves. But... I don't know. This is a *Fated* bond. It's rare and powerful. I hate that you'll have to deal with that on top of all the regular bullshit of just surviving whatever camp has in store for us."

He and I both. I needed to be on my game. An ice-cold bitch who cared about nothing except becoming the best wraith-killer in my class and ascending to the level of a Guardian, a valued member of the elite force, a protector of our community.

All so I could just have a modicum of safety and stability for myself and my tiger.

Because my mother's beast was also a not-quite-white tiger, and she was murdered for it. I could not, under any circumstances, allow my family to experience that kind of pain again.

What I was not here to do was get distracted by Elijah's haunting yellow eyes, always so hungry and desperate when he looked at me.

I also wasn't here to entertain Wyatt's shameless flirting and needling me into giving him attention.

Or to allow Aiden to flex his forearms while condescending to me about the academic theory that he claimed justified their dickish behavior.

Or to get into libido-revving dominance games with Heath.

My beast licked a claw and flicked her tail. Aloof but not disinterested.

You're a real problem, I told her.

It'd only been two days since the guys blindsided me by appearing in the streets of my neighborhood. For weeks, I'd been steeling myself, building my walls, and preparing to be stuck with my not-mates nearly 24/7 for two months.

But then, there they were.

Ripping the Band-Aid off early.

The sight of them, first Heath and Wyatt, then Aiden and Elijah, was as easy on the eyes as ever. They seemed a little more haggard, a little more worn down, but it did nothing to detract from how stunning they'd always been.

And that little flicker of desire, the tiny fluttering of butterfly wings in my belly, the perk of my beast's ears, that moment of *longing* for the way things had been before they came back from spring break and turned on me, had sent me straight into a boiling rage.

This is what you wanted, Wildcat. We told you the cold, hard truth. You aren't it for us.

The fucking *nerve* of them riding to my rescue like I was a damsel in need of protecting. Like I hadn't spent an entire semester proving just how well I could protect myself.

And how dare they decide to care *now*, after what they did?

I still couldn't close my eyes at night without seeing Callista wrapped around Wyatt on the dance floor, her lips on his neck, while he looked me straight in the eyes and smiled like he was enjoying it all.

I couldn't even perform my monthly ritual of Moon-blessing my blades without Aiden invading my brain, the memory of his genuine praise at my skill drowned out by the sound of his silky tenor announcing to his date that I was *no one*.

Then there was Elijah's abandonment.

And Heath's cold dismissal.

And, of course, the haunting nightmares that still plagued me of my flesh being torn from my beastly body.

Fuck them. They'd ruined everything.

Ian cleared his throat and raised a brow.

I climbed out of the hole I'd been descending into. "Are you finished unpacking?" I asked. "Is that why you're in here bothering me?"

"Yes and yes." He slid languidly from the bed, getting to his feet and smoothing his white Guardian T-shirt and shorts—one of a dozen pairs we'd all been issued. "And I came to escort you to dinner. I heard it's chicken-fried steak night."

I shucked my forest-green Proteus College tank top and pulled on a black Guardian T-shirt over my sports bra. After strapping the harness that affixed my two wakizashi blades in their X-shaped scabbard to my back, I shoved my phone into the little compartment on the thigh of my compression leggings. Unlike a real summer camp, we were allowed access to our phones because our weekly schedules and other pertinent communications would be pushed to our email throughout the duration of the program.

According to the blast leadership sent out an hour ago, we would start bright and early tomorrow with a four-mile run through the wilderness. My beast and I needed that chicken-fried steak.

I heaved a sigh and faced the cabin's screen door. There was no putting this off. "I'm ready."

Ian and I ambled out into the waning evening daylight. The clean mountain air caressed my nostrils. The grass was soft and lush under my sneakers. Ahead, the waters of the camp's lake reflected the setting sun, deep-blue waves lapping softly against the rocky sands of the small beach on its north shore. Surrounding us on all sides was a thick forest of maples, oaks, and hickory trees that completely covered the terrain save for the narrow path that'd been cleared for the camp's entry road.

We passed a cluster of a dozen cabins situated in two opposing semicircles around a larger building that contained the bathrooms and showers. Shifter males streamed from the area, all in the same white T-shirt Ian wore, indicating they were Support Squadron trainees. The herd moved at a leisurely pace toward the front of the grounds, where the chow hall was located.

A door slammed, and Brody trotted out with Joon and Nico in tow. Brody's dark curls bounced as he ran, his brown eyes bright and pinned to my brother like it hadn't been less than twenty minutes since he'd seen Ian.

Joon had slicked his black hair into a short little mohawk, and he carried his blade, a *Sain-geom*, in a simple sheath strapped to his back.

Nico was the shortest of the crew, coming in a few inches shy of Ian's and my five-foot-ten. He was built like a rugby player and looked like he'd waltzed straight off a yacht in the Mediterranean.

"Greetings, Baxters," Nico said, twirling his tactical Tomahawk ax. "Please allow us to escort you to chow."

"Is that why you're all armed?" I asked. "Are we expecting a wraith to jump out of the bushes?"

Brody fixed me with the world's most patient look. "Of course not. But this place is crawling with Prime quads, and some of them may decide to... bother you. Safety in numbers, Avery."

He didn't just mean my not-mates. Cash and his quad of losers were lurking somewhere, and I had no idea whether any of the recently graduated seniors had a problem with me. This would be my first time training with the Guardian candidates in the class above mine.

"Also, *you're* armed," Joon pointed out.

"Yeah, but I'm always armed."

I'd learned last semester that I couldn't walk around a campus crawling with shifters and expect to be left alone. If I wanted to retain any sort of discretion as far as the tiger soul I was harboring, I had to have other means to defend myself.

Ian nudged me as we walked. "There are the Guardian cabins."

Perched on a rolling hill overlooking the baseball field and sand volleyball courts were several more clusters of cabins. These were larger and a bit boxier than the Support Squadron cabins, so I suspected leadership wasn't forcing their power quads to squeeze into twin-sized bunk beds like they were the ordinary shifters.

In another reality, I'd have put up at least some resistance to being sequestered away from the Guardian trainees, stuck over in the cabins reserved for the scant few female staff. I was here to become a Guardian, not be treated as something other just because I was female.

But in actuality, the distance between me and the Blackwell Quad suited me just fine. It was going to be hard enough to ignore them as it was. I didn't need to sleep two doors down or risk running into any one of them on my way to the bathroom.

I also didn't exactly desire to share a bathroom with half the males in the program, so I'd accepted my cabin assignment with a grateful nod and zipped lips.

The chow hall was located next to the large faux-log cabin that housed leadership's offices and the more utilitarian structure that was the camp infirmary. The lake beckoned from across a hundred yards of freshly mowed lawn.

Ian tossed an arm around my shoulders as we approached the chow hall's front steps. He took a big whiff through his nose. "Ah, the smells of nature and fried beef. Doesn't get much better than this."

I shoved him off. "You don't fool me, Ian Baxter. I feel your beast all coiled up and ready to jump at the slightest provocation." I pointed a finger in his face. "Behave."

He rolled his eyes. "I'm *sure* I don't know what you're talking about."

"*Brody*," I whined.

Brody slipped an arm through the crook of Ian's elbow, and my brother melted into his boyfriend's side. "Everything's fine. See? Look how relaxed and nonviolent he is."

Joon chuckled and punched Nico in his large bicep. "You should try that move on Cynthia next time you see her. Maybe she won't claw your eyes out."

"She'd have to catch me first."

The chow hall was bustling, the air filled with nervous excitement on the eve of the first day of camp.

Maple paneling stretched from floor to high ceilings where exposed beams spanned the width of the room. Long tables with benches were arranged in neat rows, an aisle separating them into two distinct sides. A buffet line hugged the left wall, and a nearby swinging door probably led to the kitchen.

All the white T-shirts congregated on the right side of the room. On the left, the black shirts of my Guardian class were interspersed with yellow-gold shirts—the uniform of the graduated seniors doing their second rotation through camp before being assigned to a real Guardian post.

Flanked by Ian's crew, I attacked the buffet. The few dining staff on hand appeared confused by my presence. Out of the corner of my eye, I clocked some of the gold-shirted quads sizing me up—some with curiosity, others with thinly-veiled disdain.

Our group made our way over to an empty spot at one of the long tables on the white-shirt side of the hall, which was slow going because Ian had to fist-bump or chirp at about a dozen guys on the way.

Before I could sit down next to Joon, I was accosted by one of the males I'd been hoping to avoid.

"Baxter." Cash sneered at me as he hovered in the aisle, arms folded over his chest. He, like all the trainers in attendance, wore the official uniform—black tactical pants, combat boots, and a fitted black shirt with the golden Guardian logo embroidered over the left chest. His dark-blond hair was shorn close to his head in a high and tight military cut, which I'd learned was odd for a lion shifter. He probably valued projecting "military badass" over "stately lion," though he was successful at neither, since all I ever got from him was "raging dickhead."

I sighed. "What can I do for you, Cash?"

"Did you suddenly decide to join the Support Squadron?" he snapped. "If so, you're wearing the wrong fucking color. If not, get your ass over to the Guardian side of the hall."

I gave him a blank stare. "Meals are segregated? Really?"

"They are if I say they are. Move your ass."

Ian glared pure venom at Cash while Brody stroked his arm. My tiger prowled her enclosure, eager to test herself against this asshole lion. I could let her. I could look Cash in his smarmy face and say, "Make me," and then we'd see who was the king of the jungle.

But rocking the boat like that before camp had even officially begun was unwise. Also, I was hungry, my food smelled amazing, and I did not feel like dealing with Cash one second longer than I had to.

I scanned the rows of black and yellow shirts. Everyone appeared focused on inhaling their food, either oblivious to my dilemma or fastidiously ignoring it.

"She can sit with us."

A huge male, as tall and broad as Wyatt, smiled at me from across the aisle. He wore a gold shirt and Guardian-branded track pants. His blond hair was long, the locks flowing in beachy waves around his chiseled face.

I blinked dumbly at him.

"Oh, give me a moondamned break," Cash said, rolling his eyes. "First Blackwell, and now you're fucking Kellan Crimson, Baxter?"

Ah. The fabled Crimson Quad. They of the six-million-dollar lake house. Top quad in the graduate class.

And Kellan Crimson was a griffin—the lone other

mythic at school besides Elijah and one of only a handful in the entire country.

Kellan turned his intense amber eyes on Cash, and they narrowed into slits. Cash immediately lost his bravado. He grumbled irritably and stalked off to the front of the room where the staff table was set away from the rest of us.

With another beaming smile, Kellan motioned to me. "Come on, Baxter. Don't be shy."

Eager to be out of the spotlight, I went to grab my tray from where I'd set it next to Joon.

A familiar presence crowded my back, dominance and hostility rolling from it in harsh waves.

"I don't think so, Crimson," Heath growled mere inches from the back of my neck. "Back off."

I whirled. There he was, dressed in his black T-shirt, arms crossed, his carved biceps flexing under golden-tanned skin as he glared menacingly at Kellan.

Aiden, Elijah, and Wyatt lingered in the cramped space behind him. Aiden and Wyatt were dressed like Heath in their tight-fitting black T-shirts. Aiden wore black track pants, while Wyatt and Heath had on black shorts. Elijah had opted not to wear the required uniform and instead had arrived to dinner in a loose black tank top that did little to hide the snake tattoo draped around his neck or the chiseled muscles of his torso.

Aiden and Wyatt were, like Heath, glaring at Kellan as if they were ten seconds away from murder.

Elijah only had eyes for me.

My beast fluffed her fur and paced, ready for action.

I hit Heath hard with a pulse of dominance, like popping a rubber band against his skin. "No, *you* back off, Blackwell."

He snapped out of whatever stupor he was in regarding

Kellan. He turned those hazel eyes on me, the starbursts in them sparking with the golden sheen of his beast. "Killer," he said softly, "come sit with us. Where you belong."

"No," I growled. "Are you staking a public claim on me like a cave beast?"

His jaw flexed. "That is not what this is."

"Then go away and leave me alone. I'll sit with whomever I want to sit with at meals."

Kellan grinned. "You heard the lady, Blackwell. What's this bullshit, anyway? Last time I saw you, Phoebe Atkins was parading you around like the prized spoils of a hunt."

Heath slowly rotated his head to stare Kellan down like a velociraptor sighting its prey. Sandy-blond fur rippled along his arms, and heavy aggression leaked into the air.

But he had no response to Kellan's accusation because it was a true fucking statement.

"Shut the fuck up, Crimson," Wyatt drawled. His lazy tone belied the red sheen of violence in his eyes. "You have no idea what you're talking about."

Anger swirled through my body. Would they say it? Would they announce to this whole camp that I was their Fated? Would they stake a claim over me like a piece of property?

A few tense moments passed, but there was only silence, Heath's dominance saturating the space around us while Kellan kept whatever he had going on tightly under wraps.

"Enough." My tiger pulsed her aggression again, careful to aim only for Heath and his quad. "Are any of you planning to physically prevent me from doing what I want to do?"

Aiden sighed. *Oh, am I exasperating you already, Professor?* "Of course not. We just want to talk to you, Avery. That's all."

"No, thank you."

I turned away, ready to grab my tray and be finished with all of this.

Heath wrapped a calloused hand snugly around my wrist. "Don't do this," he rumbled in my ear. "Don't go to them just because you're mad at us."

My beast mustered up a pleased little purr at the sensation of Heath's hand on me. I flashed her an image of him looking perfect in his suit with his arm around Phoebe's tiny waist. She growled angrily and snapped at him.

He dropped my arm as if I'd burned him.

I gave the others behind him a cursory glance. Wyatt, looking surly and violent, his big shoulders tense and his green eyes tinged with red. Aiden, wavy brown hair askew like he'd been raking his fingers through it, hazel eyes despondent behind his glasses. Elijah, cool as a cucumber, posture relaxed, which was fooling no one, given his eyes glowed yellow and his pupils had slitted dangerously. His focus had shifted from me to Kellan, which was not good. If those two fought, they'd bring the building down around us.

"I'd like to eat my dinner now," I told them patiently. "I'm very hungry, and this is embarrassing. Please leave me alone."

"Fine," Heath gritted. "But this isn't over, Avery. Not even a little bit."

I picked up my tray and stalked away.

7

AVERY

Kellan beamed with smug satisfaction as I marched his way. He was sitting with the rest of his quad—three large muscular guys I vaguely recognized from the elite student tables back in the Proteus dining hall.

I dropped my tray unceremoniously onto the table and sat down next to an attractive guy with wavy black hair and a short, neat beard. He appeared to be of South Asian descent and had the lean, powerful build of a feline shifter.

My beast bristled at his nearness. *Oh, you* love *Aiden's feline, but this one you have a problem with?*

"Ari Syed," he said, holding out a hand for me to shake. "Prime Sumatran tiger."

Well, that was quite the announcement.

And now my tiger's irritation made sense. Competition.

Tiger shifters were rare for the same dumb reasons I had to hide my beast, but there were a few males running around with the normal orange-and-black stripes of tigers in the wild. No one seemed to think they were the second coming of "the betrayer" or the downfall of our kind, so they were revered just like any other male Prime with significant power.

Hard not to resent Ari for his good fortune of just being born male and bonding with a beast soul that had orange fur.

My beast licked a claw, supremely unbothered. Ari was a Sumatran tiger, but my girl most closely resembled a Siberian tiger, which meant we were larger and better.

But a lot more persecuted, so we'd call it a draw.

"Avery," I replied with a quick shake of Ari's hand. "Undisclosed."

He chuckled. "Sure. You're still pretending you don't have a beast? Come on, we all saw you face the SWIM during the junior quad competition."

I shrugged. "I work hard to be strong and agile, and I was taught how to use my blades by the best."

The burly guy sitting across from me reached out a huge hand. "I'm Hank, Prime brown bear and big fan."

"Oh, uh, thanks," I replied with an awkward shake of his hand.

"And that's Teegan," Kellan announced, jerking his chin at the stoic guy with light brown hair and a jawline that you could break a crowbar over. "He's an Alpha wolf. And as I'm sure you've figured out, I'm Kellan Crimson, quad leader and mythic."

"A griffin," I said, nodding. "Impressive."

His smile was blinding white. "I like to think so."

I began to shovel food into my mouth because I was not actually here to make friends with the Crimson Quad. I was going to fuel up for tomorrow, and I was going to pretend I didn't feel the hot stares of my not-mates searing the skin off the back of my neck.

"She's not that impressed with your mythic status, man,"

Ari said, pointing his fork at Kellan. "I heard she's close with Harrow and that crazy snake of his."

"Snake, yes, Elijah, no," I said around a mouth of mashed potatoes.

Kellan's amber eyes took on a speculative gleam. "Uh-huh. What *did* happen between you and the Blackwell Quad, Baxter? Things seem a little tense."

None of your business, Kellan.

"They made a decision about me and are now regretting it," I told him, forcing a careless shrug. "But they're excellent fighters and will make top-tier Guardians. Our combat styles mesh well, as I'm sure you observed in the arena, and that's the extent of it. We'll figure out how to coexist harmoniously because lives depend on it."

They all stared at me for a beat. I'd taken the wind out of their sails by making this about the mission, which was serious as a heart attack.

"Right, well," Kellan said, "I think you'll find our quad a breath of fresh air. Teegan's sister has a wolf soul, on the cusp of an Alpha. My aunt, who lives in Canada, has a lion, smaller but powerful enough to be considered a Prime. We're not backwards assholes who think females with a beast are an abomination."

"Glad to hear it," I replied, and I meant it. A top quad who respected shifting females and didn't outright object to my presence here was extremely welcome.

"And," he went on, "not all of us think the strongest bonds require a latent central." His amber eyes met mine, and a hot orange sheen flashed over them. He leaned forward and lowered his voice, like he was telling me a secret. "I couldn't imagine throwing away a one-of-a-kind diamond just to pick through pearls."

My beast hissed like a cobra in my chest.

I sighed wearily. *Yes, he went there. Do not kill him.*

The sound of glass shattering behind me made me jump in my seat.

Hank let out a deep, rumbling laugh, and Kellan sent a sharklike grin over my shoulder. "Whoops. Those Alphas do have especially sharp hearing."

They clearly knew more than they'd let on about the state of things between the Blackwell Quad and me, and Kellan was rubbing Heath's nose in it.

Heath deserved it, but still.

This was what I got for thinking the Crimson Quad viewed me as an equal, a skilled and adept trainee destined to fight monsters alongside them under the dark skies.

No, Kellan had fuck-zoned me already, and I hadn't even finished my potatoes.

I took one last big swig of blue Gatorade and got to my feet. "Thanks for letting me eat with you guys," I said. "I'll see you bright and early tomorrow."

Ari the tiger nodded, his dark gaze dipping down my body. "The pleasure was ours, Avery."

Kellan shifted on the bench like he was going to get up. "At least let one of us walk you back to your cabin—"

Loud swearing and the sounds of benches scraping the concrete floor cut him off. George appeared from under a nearby table, his thick body winding lazily in my direction, amethyst scales glinting under the bright lights.

I grinned. "No need," I told Kellan. "My escort has arrived."

Hank pulled his feet up off the floor, and Ari slid six feet down the bench. Even Kellan the great and powerful griffin looked unsettled by the arrival of a large purple python. Only Teegan the Alpha wolf appeared unbothered, but he seemed to only have one mode.

"Come on, George," I said primly. "The testosterone in here is suffocating."

He nosed my leg in agreement and followed me out of the hall.

THE WIND WHIPPED THROUGH THE TREES, AND I STUMBLED, blind to my surroundings. The darkness was suffocating. An ear-splitting screech sounded behind me, and I reached for my swords.

I grasped at nothing. The sheaths on my back were empty.

Where are my swords?

Teeth tore into my flesh, ripping skin and muscle from my thigh. I screamed and called my beast forward.

She didn't answer.

I was still screaming as claws impaled me through the back.

My eyes snapped open. I shot up in bed, heaving panicked breaths. I reached for my sword where it hung in its sheath off the side of the headboard and found it exactly where it was supposed to be.

In my cabin. I'm safe and in my cabin.

I sucked in another deep breath and released my grip on the hilt of my blade.

And then I froze as my gaze met a pair of glowing yellow eyes through my window.

They were there, floating amidst the trees, pupils thin slashes, focused entirely on me as I panted and shivered in the chilly night air wafting through the window screens.

There was a monster outside.

But unlike the monsters that plagued my dreams, this

one didn't fill me with bone-melting terror. My beast wasn't clawing her way to the surface, ready to throw herself into a fight we were destined to lose.

No, those eerie yellow eyes brought me comfort, at least momentarily, and my beast was merely alert, flicking her tail in interest.

The monster ducked away, gliding from under the tree outside my window and toward the cabin's front stoop. I watched, fascinated despite everything that was wrong with this situation, as the towering serpent that was Elijah's basilisk appeared in front of the screen door.

I'd only ever seen Elijah's beast in his full glory once, and it was through my tiger's eyes the moment our Fated bond snapped into place. I'd been torn apart, bleeding to death on the forest floor and clinging to consciousness.

Now, it really hit me how terrifying he was.

Or probably was to others. My body and my beast knew with soul-deep certainty that he would never harm us.

I'd be mad about that fact later.

His serpent body was as thick as the trunk of the large tree outside and covered in rough green-gray scales. His head, almost too large for even that powerful body, was triangular, his nostrils two harsh slashes near the point. Spiked scales jutted like a lion's mane around his face and continued in a row down the center of his back.

The monster smiled, giving me a glimpse of dagger teeth as long as my hand and a jaw that I suspected could unhinge at a horrifying angle—one that would allow the beast to swallow an entire human whole.

In a blink, the basilisk melted into the stunning form of Elijah the man. He shoved through my screen door, breaking the flimsy latch that kept it bolted to the frame.

The darkness blurred his nude body, his glowing yellow

eyes and the clock on my phone screen the only illumination in the room.

Suddenly, I was acutely aware that I wore only a flimsy tank top and no bra. I yanked the covers up to my chin and sank back into the mattress.

Elijah fell to his knees at the side of my bed. "Dove, are you okay?" he rasped.

"Why are you here?" I whispered.

His lips quirked. "Just keeping watch. George slipped out a few hours ago to explore the woods."

I'd registered the absence of the large python at the foot of my bed when my nightmare had woken me up. George did like to come and go as he pleased. He was whimsical like that.

I glowered at Elijah, whose face was inches from mine. "I'm perfectly safe in here and can protect myself. Guard duty is unnecessary."

"Tell that to the basilisk, Dove."

I sighed. Exhaustion washed over me. I hadn't had a nightmare that bad in a few weeks, but the cumulative sleep disruption was taking its toll. "You can't be in here, Elijah," I said softly.

"I know." He caressed my face with cool fingers, his thumb rubbing a gentle path across my cheekbone. "But I am anyway. Have you been having nightmares, love?"

"Don't call me that."

Another grin. His breath somehow still smelled like minty toothpaste, even after the transition to and from his beast. "Okay. I'll wait until you're ready."

"Elijah," I growled. I nudged his hand away from my face. I'd only allowed it there in the first place because his touch had gone a long way to finally calming my erratic heartbeat. "You have to leave. We aren't mates. I don't forgive you for what you did."

His smile slipped away. His eyes sparked, his pupils threatening to change shape again. "I know, Dove. You shouldn't forgive me. I haven't earned it yet." He leaned down, bringing his face even closer to mine. "But I will. Even if it takes me decades of my life. You are more than I could've ever *fathomed* to dream of in a partner and a bond. I'm sorry that I gave you up. I should've fought harder to keep you."

I stared at him. He was so achingly beautiful, and it made me so violently furious. "You hurt me," I whispered, my voice cracking. "I was falling for you, and you hurt me."

His nostrils flared, and he ground his teeth together like he was enduring torture. "I'm so sorry, Dove," he murmured. "We had a purpose when we did what we did, but we were very wrong in thinking you couldn't be part of it."

I didn't want to hear any more, but curiosity killed the tiger. "Were you just going to bond with whichever latent princess the others decided on?"

He swallowed roughly and tore his yellow gaze from my face for the first time since he'd arrived. "Yes."

Disgust curdled in my gut. I shut my eyes and burrowed further into my covers. "Please leave," I croaked.

The air shifted between us, leaving a cold void in front of me.

Without another word, he slipped from the cabin and disappeared into the night.

8

WYATT

Somebody was going to die today.

Would it be Ari, the smarmy fucking tiger from the Crimson Quad, who prowled around my mate in the breakfast line, studying her like she was a sexy puzzle he couldn't quite solve?

Would it be Cash, who tried to force my wildcat to once again eat on the Guardian side of the chow hall and then barked insults at her when she'd simply walked away with her brother and his friends because she'd already finished her breakfast?

Maybe it would be Kellan Crimson, who spent all of breakfast alternating between smirking like an asshole at us and watching Avery with the eager interest and a thinly disguised hard-on I knew all too well.

It might even be Trent, the floofy fucking snow leopard and Cash's second, who would lead our morning run through the woods. He'd just directed us to strap on our weapons for the run, and he hadn't managed to do it without also making a comment about my mate's ass.

No. It was probably going to be Hank, the Crimson

Quad's resident bear, who had just placed his giant hand on Avery's shoulder and wedged himself between her and Trent.

My beast pushed to the surface, and my vision tunneled.

"Later," Heath barked. He tightened the leather strap of the harness that held his saber. "We have to get through this run. And she didn't let him touch her for more than a second."

I cracked my neck and willed my bear to relax. "He knows what he's doing," I grumbled. "He thinks because his bear has a hundred pounds on mine, he's superior. He's provoking me."

"And he'll reap the consequences," Aiden replied. He was stretching, his sword on his back. "But Heath's right. Starting the first day of camp with a brawl isn't going to convince Avery to talk to us."

He was full of shit. We could all feel his jaguar and how close he was to getting into it with that fucking tiger. Ari couldn't know what Avery was, but his animal was clearly sensing something that interested him, and that was on top of the fact that Avery the human was a total fucking smokeshow.

Elijah appeared from the depths of the forest and made his leisurely way over to us. Instead of our black Guardian-issued T-shirt, he wore a faded blue tank top with armholes that dipped below his ribs. At least he managed to put on the little black track shorts we'd been issued and some running shoes. He was also munching on the remains of a bagel.

"Nice of you to join us, Harrow," Trent snapped. "Timeliness isn't optional in the Guardians, even for super-special mythic shifters."

Elijah just grinned at him, his fangy canines on display.

"My apologies. I had to sweet talk the cafeteria ladies into hunting down some dairy-free cream cheese for me."

Trent tried to hit Elijah with a disdainful look, but he blanched and turned away when Elijah's pupils narrowed, his beast telling Trent to go fuck himself.

"Get moving, all of you!" Trent bellowed. There were at least fifty of us standing around the trailhead, a mix of the black shirts of our class and the gold of the class above us. The Support Squadron must've been running a different trail this morning. "I want seven-minute miles at a minimum, or your quad will be running extra this week!"

Heath didn't have to tell us what the plan was. We slipped into the crowd as a unit and forced our way toward Avery. She fell in near a quad we knew to be happily bonded, which meant they were safe from death by bear.

For now.

We began our run a few lengths behind them.

If I had my way, my wildcat would always be in my line of sight. Not just on this morning's run, but all damn day. According to the schedule we'd been sent, we had weapons drills after the run, then it would be lunch, a classroom session, and more combat training. We'd get a few hours of recreation time before dinner, and then we'd decide which one of us would loiter pathetically outside her cabin tonight while she slept.

Speaking of that.

"I can't believe you went inside her cabin last night, man," I said to Elijah, who loped along next to me.

"There was no stopping it," he replied easily. "At least she didn't try to kill me."

"Yeah," I muttered. "I guess."

And I wanted my turn. I didn't care if Avery *did* try to kill me.

In fact, I welcomed it.

The thought had my bear licking his chops in excitement and my dick stirring in my pants.

The four-mile run was long and arduous. My ax weighed nothing on my back, but the terrain was uneven and littered with rocks and roots. The tree cover shielded us from the rising sun, but the slight chill in the mountain air was no match for a bunch of overheated shifter bodies. My shirt clung to my chest, and my hair was plastered to my forehead.

We passed slower quads, including the Crimson assholes, who couldn't leave Hank behind. He was a typical bear, built like an offensive lineman, and he lumbered along like one too.

I made sure he saw me flip him off as we jogged by.

My wildcat was fast and nimble, and she had no trouble keeping up with the front of the pack. Her blonde head bobbed up ahead of us, her ponytail swinging, hypnotizing me into doing anything she fucking wanted.

"Does that girl own any shorts that don't cling to every inch of her ass?" Aiden griped behind me.

"Quit your bitching," I shot back. "That ass is the reason I get out of bed in the morning."

"That ass is going to get a bunch of our fellow trainees murdered if they don't stop staring at it," Heath muttered.

This was what we got for deciding not to kick down the doors of this camp on the first night and announce that Avery Baxter was our Fated. No shifter in their right mind would make a play for another's Moon-given mate, and only one with a death wish would come for *our* Fated.

But Heath, in all his quad leader wisdom, had decided that staking our claim in such a public way would backfire spectacularly. It would also have revealed to everyone, without a doubt, that Avery could shift, because Fated bonds could only form between beast souls.

At the time, I'd agreed with Heath. My wildcat's secrets were safe with us, and she'd made it crystal clear that she didn't want to be claimed. She had to come willingly.

She had to claim *me*.

But now that we were here, it was getting harder and harder to stick with the plan.

My bear grunted his annoyance. *Noted, asshole.*

We finally emerged from the woods, and our run ended back at the front of the campgrounds near the chow hall. Water and Gatorade stations had been set up on the picnic tables there. We rehydrated while we watched the rest of the Guardian trainees drag their asses to the finish line. The Support Squadron trainees trickled in from the other direction, looking as tired and sweaty as we were.

Cash arrived and was in a dick mood, as usual. "All right, shut up, everyone. Support Squadron, head to the obstacle course. Guardians are with me for weapons drills. My group meets at the field house in ten minutes. Do not be late."

I downed the rest of my paper cup of Gatorade and tossed it in the trash. With an annoyed sigh, I lifted the hem of my T-shirt and used it to wipe the sweat from my face.

When I lowered it, I was just in time to catch my wildcat's gorgeous blue eyes darting away from my abs.

I grinned at her.

She huffed, her nostrils flaring, her jaw rigid enough to break concrete. She turned away, her attention firmly on her brother and his cat friends.

My bear fluffed his fur and preened anyway.

I'll take it, baby girl.

The field house was located on the south side of the lake. A simple vinyl-sided building about the size of an outdoor basketball court, it was nestled under some trees and adjacent to a wide clearing, the grass there trampled nearly to dust.

Inside were piles of practice weapons and other drill equipment. Several quads began hauling huge practice dummies shaped like monsters from the building. Three different training frames had been erected in the front yard, with stacks of tires and other hardy items hanging from chains attached to the beams. Staked in the nearby dirt were rows of pells—wooden striking posts for use by those who wielded blades daintier than mine.

Cash barked some nonsense at all of us about warming up, so I found the heaviest unoccupied pile of tires and began swinging my ax at it. Heath and Aiden claimed one of the larger and more complex pells, unsheathed their swords, and began unloading their frustrations onto it.

Elijah climbed onto a smaller pile of tires that hung next to mine and sank into it like he was floating in a swimming pool. He sipped the remnants of his Gatorade, his yellow eyes glued to the furthest station away from us, where Avery attacked her own pell with perfect, whip-fast strikes of her blades.

"I wonder if Kellan Crimson does indeed have a death wish," Elijah mused lightly, as if he was wondering what the chow hall would be serving for lunch. "He and the bear are dragging that practice dummy far too close to my dove."

I swung the flat of my ax into the tires with every ounce of my strength, and the hit reverberated up my arms and into my brain. I shook my head irritably. "You think you could kill the griffin?"

His grin was serene. "There is little the basilisk won't do to someone who's dumb enough to get between him and his mate."

"Good." I swung the ax again, this time imagining the tires were Holden Blackwell's head.

He was the *real* reason we were in this mess, after all.

After we'd been at it for fifteen minutes, Cash bellowed, "All right, that's enough! Pair up and spar. No beasts. Real blades, real stakes. If you get injured, shift to heal, or you can have the dubious honor of being the first camper to the infirmary this summer."

Elijah was off his tire and stalking across the training grounds toward our girl before Cash had even finished barking his instructions. I tossed my ax onto my shoulder and followed him.

Avery didn't want anything to do with us, but that was too fucking bad. The wraith realm would freeze over before we'd let one of these assholes swing a blade at her.

The clangs and grunts of our classmates attacking each other started up around us as we reached the other side of the training grounds.

"Hey, Baxter," Hank said, sidling up next to Avery. "Wanna be my partner? I hear you're vicious with those little swords."

"Oh, uh," she said, startling out of her squinty glare at Elijah and me as we arrived at her side. "Sure, why not?"

"Nope, not happening," I declared, baring my teeth at Hank before I turned to Avery. "Work with Elijah, baby. He's good with a smaller weapon, and your styles mesh well."

She crossed her arms over her perfect tits, lifted her chin, and speared me with that look that made my dick hard. "No. I'm fine sparring with Hank."

Hank decided at that moment that he did indeed want to die. He tossed a huge burly arm around Avery's shoulders and stared me down, a red sheen rolling over his brown eyes. "You heard her, Gale. Back off and quit pissing a circle around her that she clearly doesn't want."

"Wildcat, go stand next to Elijah."

"What? No—"

Elijah lunged with his snake speed. He snatched Avery's hand and jerked her away from Hank just in time for me to swing the flat of my ax at Hank's big fucking head.

He ducked, yanked his ridiculous two-handed longsword from his back, then sprang up and swung it at me with an obnoxious bellow.

I blocked his strike easily and kicked him in the groin.

"Wyatt," Heath growled from somewhere behind me.

I used Hank's momentary incapacitation to jerk an irritated glance over my shoulder, prepared to tell Heath to fuck off with his careful quad leader bullshit. Instead, I found him leaning against a wooden pole of the nearby training frame with half a smile on his face. Aiden was next to him, looking bored and unbothered.

"Try not to kill him" was all Heath said.

I grinned and whirled around, swinging my ax down in an arc, aiming right at Hank's thick middle. He brought his blade up again and managed to knock my strike off target, but not before I sliced a deep gash into his arm.

He roared, brown fur rippling along his arms.

"Hold!" Kellan barked, his oppressive dominance saturating the air around us. He and the rest of his quad lingered at the edge of the trees behind Hank. "No beasts."

Hank shook his head, and the fur disappeared. "Lucky for you, isn't it, Gale?" he said. "My bear would crush yours one-on-one."

"Your bear is fat and slow and only good for crushing wraiths that your quad has already managed to mortally wound. I would run circles around you before I tore out your fucking throat. Keep your hands off Avery, and we won't have a problem."

He swung his sword at me again.

I knocked it completely out of his hands with the head of my ax. "Still too slow," I snapped.

He growled in frustration and lunged at me, fists raised. I tossed my ax to the ground and met him hand-to-hand. He managed a glancing blow off my cheekbone. I sent an uppercut into his gut. We grappled, trading shots. He had at least twenty-five pounds on me and hit fucking hard, but I was faster, in better shape, and was superior in pound-for-pound strength.

"You need to get over yourself, Gale," he said, breathing hard. "You and your quad don't own every hot girl you set your sights on. Or did things not work out for you with Callista Jackson?"

My bear snarled in my chest, and a red haze clouded my vision. I ducked Hank's next wild swing at my head, crouching low as his fist sailed over me. I used his momentum and the last of my reserves to catch him around the torso and launch him over my shoulder.

Heath and Aiden scattered just as Hank's giant body crashed into the training frame. Posts buckled and splintered. Chains and tires clattered to the ground, and then the entire structure collapsed in a heap. Hank rolled to a stop and groaned.

"Hey, what the fuck?" Cash shouted from somewhere across the grounds.

Heath swore. "Maybe we should disperse—"

My wildcat stormed up to me, her eyes electric blue, the strands of her hair that'd escaped her ponytail framing her gorgeous, furious face. She punched me in the chest. "What is your fucking problem, asshole?"

I scooped her off the ground and tossed her over my shoulder.

"Wyatt!" She thrashed, pounding little fists on my back. "Put me down, you insane bear!"

Ignoring her protests, I stalked away from the training grounds. Heath, Aiden, and Elijah watched me go without a word.

I didn't stop until we were behind the field house and out of sight.

When I dropped Avery to the ground, I found myself shoved against the wall, her sword pressed to my throat.

"Finally, baby," I groaned. "Bleed me. I deserve it."

"Yes, you do," she said, seething. "It is the first fucking day of camp, and *we are not mates.* Get control of yourself and your beast, or I will run you through with both of my blades."

The edge of her blade broke through the thinnest layer of skin, and my blood beaded, warm and wet on the steel. "That's where you're wrong, Wildcat," I said with my most seductive grin. "You can deny it until you can't even fucking speak anymore, but we *are* mates. You. Are. My. *Fated.* I won't give you up, and my bear certainly isn't going to let any other bastards put their hands on you. It's instinctual, primal, and all-fucking-consuming. Get used to it."

She leaned in closer, our lips nearly touching. "Oh yeah?" she whispered, and suddenly I knew I was in danger. "But your bear doesn't have any qualms about other girls putting their hands on *you*, does he? How was your date with Callista, Wyatt? Did you fuck her this time, or did you just give her the honor of sucking your cock again? Was she in the running for your quad's bond, or were you just trying to get your dick wet one last time before Heath made you bond with Phoebe?"

Furious despair flooded my entire body.

With a quick flick of my wrist, I disarmed her, removing her blade from my neck and dropping it to the ground. She screeched in frustration, but I'd already grabbed her by the hands. I spun us and pressed her back against the field house wall, locking her wrists above her head.

She fumed as I pressed my sweaty forehead to hers.

"Listen up, Wildcat," I growled, "because I'm only going to say this once. What you saw at the ball was the extent of what happened with Callista. I was trying to convince myself that I could *want* to touch someone other than you, and I failed miserably."

She struggled underneath me, but it wasn't lost on me that she was keeping her beast leashed. I'd seen—and felt— what she could do to Heath's wolf. Her eyes glowed, but she hadn't struck me with the force of her tiger's dominance.

I took that as permission to press my entire body against hers. She was soft and strong underneath me. My bear rumbled his approval.

"I hated every fucking second of it," I whispered in her ear.

"Liar," she snarled. "You looked like you were enjoying yourself plenty. Almost as much as you were enjoying rubbing my face in it."

I kissed her behind her ear, and she shivered against me. I pulled away just enough to look her in her beautiful, livid eyes. "I was *obsessed* with you, Wildcat. But I thought I couldn't have you, so I needed you to hate me."

She blew out a harsh breath, and then the tiger came out to play.

Pressure crushed my skull, demanding that I yield. The sharp bite of her dominance struck me like a live wire, and my bear had no desire to fight his mate. I released her from my hold.

She shoved me away and then buried her fist in my stomach. I grunted and bent over because it fucking hurt.

"Job well done, then, Wyatt," she said softly, "because it worked."

She wiped a tear from the corner of her eye, and I wanted to curl up on the ground and die.

"Baby—"

She turned, giving me her back. Without another word or a backwards glance, she swiped her sword from the ground and stalked off.

9

AIDEN

We hadn't even been at camp for a full twenty-four hours yet, and already Elijah and Wyatt had both managed to take one step forward and then two giant fucking steps backward with Avery.

I looked on glumly as she finished up her lunch, surrounded by her brother, his lynx boyfriend, and their other feline friends. If I could just get her to *talk* to us....

"At least we're split by year for the classroom sessions," Heath said as he tried to burn a hole in Kellan Crimson's head with his stare. "A solid ninety minutes when those assholes can't salivate over her."

The Crimson Quad was sitting four tables down from us, Hank looking no worse for wear. We'd found out that two shifters from rival quads had gotten into it during our sparring time, and one of them had nearly fatally stabbed the other. This had occupied Cash and meant someone else had the dubious honor of being the first to report to Dr. Lee in the infirmary.

The property destruction was another issue. Not only had Wyatt demolished one of the weapons training frames by throwing Hank through it, but he'd also apparently punched a hole in the back wall of the field house.

We had just enough time to shower and change into fresh training clothes after lunch before we had to report to our classroom session. The main administration building housed several small lecture halls in addition to the offices of Guardian leadership, including Ward.

When we arrived, we grabbed seats in the back row, Elijah on the end so that he could stick his long legs into the aisle.

Avery strode into the room, instantly snagging our collective focus. She'd changed into leggings and a fresh black Guardian T-shirt, and her long hair was a little damp and braided over her shoulder. A faint hint of her lavender-and-jasmine scent wafted through the air. Heath's sensitive canine nose would get that full bore.

My brother smothered a groan.

Avery slipped into an open seat near the front, next to Josh Anderson and his happily bonded quad. He jerked a friendly but uninterested nod at her and went back to his phone.

My jaguar luxuriated in the sight of our mate's profile, her slender neck, and her ash-blonde hair—not the silver of her tiger's beautiful fur, but close enough to conjure memories of that night.

The night I was handed everything I could've ever wanted even as I'd known with gut-churning certainty that I'd already lost it.

It was my turn to smother a groan when our instructor strolled into the room.

"Oh shit," Wyatt said, chuckling. "Looks like I might not be the only one getting into a fight today."

Kit Wells.

Kit *fucking* Wells.

We'd been in the same graduating class at Proteus. He was an ordinary shifter—a fox, of all the things—and had been a perfectly adequate Support Squadron trainee. He'd made the cut and gone onto serve in the field, but the Guardians must have determined his real value was his intelligence.

Whenever he and I had shared a class, we battled for who would take the top grade and who would come in number two. And we'd unfortunately shared a *lot* of classes, as we'd both been history majors with a secondary affinity for rune and spell work.

He'd beaten me one more time than I'd beaten him. Not that I was counting.

He was of average height, maybe an inch shy of six feet tall, and he had the lean build of an ordinary shifter who kept in top shape. His wheat-colored hair was thick and wavy, and he still wore glasses with thin wire frames, like he was so above it all that he didn't care to be stylish with his eyewear.

Unlike Cash and the field instructors in their fatigues, Kit wore a simple black polo shirt with the golden Guardian logo embroidered over the chest and light gray slacks.

"Good afternoon, everyone," he said cheerfully. He took up his post at the lectern and opened the laptop waiting there. His friendly smile morphed into a smirk when he caught me glowering at him from the back of his class of students who still hadn't graduated from college. "Welcome to your first classroom session of Guardian Training Camp. My name is Kit—fox shifter and two-year veteran of the Support Squadron. Last year I transitioned to a position at Guardian regional headquarters, where I've been working as a top counterinsurgency and deterrence analyst."

I could not roll my eyes any harder.

Avery had perked right up, clearly excited to learn from someone with real Guardian experience who wasn't a meat-headed blowhard like Cash.

And she probably felt some affinity for Kit because he was a fox shifter like her brother and father.

I hadn't thought it was possible for me to dislike Kit Wells more than I already did, but I'd been wrong about a whole hell of lot lately. It was starting to piss me off.

Kit tapped a key on the laptop, and a map of northern Georgia flashed onto the screen at the front of the room. Outlined in red were the borders of our shifter communities, stretching from the outskirts of Fulton City to the south and ending at the college and the base of the Blue Cliff Mountains. I-77 bisected the map, and miles of rural land and forest surrounded the warded walls of each town.

"You'll of course recognize our community map," Kit said. "As Guardians, you'll become intimately familiar with the vast areas beyond our walls, where our posts are located, and where we patrol for three nights every lunar cycle."

A guy in the row below me raised a hand. "How come we patrol in the woods rather than just guarding the walls of our towns?"

"Ah, a good question. Generations of experience have taught us that the best tactic is to hit the wraiths out where they spawn rather than risk them coalescing into larger groups and attacking our communities. And the longer they're allowed to roam, the greater the risk they could kill someone. Never forget—a wraith that's consumed a soul will immediately become stronger."

The class murmured its assent. That was something none of us could forget. Stories of shifters who'd strayed beyond the wards and had their soul eaten were fodder for our bedtime stories.

Kit tapped another key, and the forests, fields, and towns on the screen became sectioned into zones, each one shaded green, yellow, orange, or red. "This shows the map of each official zone—the area assigned for Guardian patrol coverage. The colors denote the level of wraith activity reported by our patrols during the most recent lunar cycle. Red will be the most active, with an exceptional number of L3 Rippers and L4 Giants. Orange is higher activity than normal, and yellow is normal to low—usually just a few L2 swarmers or the occasional L3. Green marks no wraith sightings for the previous cycle. We also use this light-blue color to mark an area within a zone where L1 wisps have been sighted, indicating a rift between realms is likely to be established within the next cycle or two."

Our training via the school program hadn't focused much on the mechanics of real patrols, since our only job had been to learn to swing a bladed weapon and kill wraiths in a magical simulation. My quad had some notion of how Guardian patrols worked, but only because of our relationship with Wyatt's fathers.

Another hand went up. "Do the zones change color often, or do you find that most red zones stay red, green zones stay green, and so on?"

Kit gave his patented smile, easygoing enough to be friendly but patronizing enough to remind you he was of superior intelligence. "Another great question. As I'm sure you've learned in your training, the areas adjacent to our communities with higher populations of shifters are usually more active, and the places where we have more Primes per capita are the biggest targets for wraiths, especially the L3s and 4s." He waved at the map on the screen. "You'll note that the most red and orange zones are clustered near the Hills, though we've had orange zones popping up all over the place lately. It is a lunar eclipse year, after all."

Nods and grunts all around. We certainly hadn't been allowed to forget the lunar eclipse coming later this fall. It would be one of the longest totalities we'd had in this area in several decades.

"But," Kit went on, "while the color of a zone isn't static, it is indicative of a trend. We can have months where all zones surrounding the Hills, where our illustrious Primes are most numerous"—that got a snort out of Avery, which I found a bit ridiculous, since I was now aware that she herself had a powerful Prime animal—"are yellow rather than orange or red. That tends to lend itself to more quiet green zones to the south and for the rest of our region's patrol map."

Avery's hand shot into the air. "Kit, I see Zone 11, which is the southernmost zone, closest to the Fulton City limit, was orange last month. Is that normal?"

Kit now had an excuse to stare directly at Avery, and he drank her in with enthusiastic curiosity.

"If you don't kill him, I will," Heath muttered.

"Well, Miss...?"

"Avery Baxter."

"Well, Avery," he said with a grin, "I'd have to check the reports, but we've had a lot of our quieter zones become more active lately. It's been an unpredictable eighteen months or so as we approach this area's big eclipse event."

She smiled back at him, and it was gorgeous and lethal. "I would be interested to know the answer, and I would be *really* interested to know why the bright minds at Guardian HQ don't believe Fulton City itself merits at least a small patrol, especially if there are on occasion orange zones directly to its north. Wraiths don't exactly abide by the Guardian's borders."

He frowned. "You think we need to patrol the city?"

Heath sighed and pinched his brow. Wyatt leaned an elbow onto the desk and propped his chin in his hand, looking wistful as he prepared for our mate's scathing tirade. Elijah's grin was nearly giddy.

Instead of the vitriol we expected, Avery only shrugged, her expression patient. "Wraiths do make it into the streets of the Upper City on a fairly regular basis. My brother and I killed a Giant over the holidays. I almost died doing it."

Heath broke the pencil he'd been fidgeting with. Wyatt's bear activated, his rage a tangible thing that set my beast on high alert. Elijah went rigid next to Heath.

Our mate had almost died a *different* time than when she'd almost died because we were high-handed assholes who sent her away during the campus breach?

Kit's brows bounced to his hairline. For a moment, he studied Avery, a look of profound respect on his face. "Wow. Not even a graduate yet and you have real wraith kills under your belt? And in the city? I'll definitely want to sit down with you later. I need to know the locations, the frequencies, the power levels—we may have to redraw our maps!"

Avery's face flushed with a hint of pink, a pleased smile on her face. "Sure. I'll bring my brother."

I jammed the lead point of my pencil into the surface of my desk and snapped it right off.

When Avery announced that wraiths walked the streets of the city on her first day in *my* class, I'd dismissed it as ludicrous. I'd expected Kit to do the same, but for some moonforsaken reason, he'd chosen *today* to become a guy willing to believe he could learn something from a random student he just met.

Elijah raised his hand, and Kit had to tear his adoring gaze from our mate. He eyed Elijah with equal parts surprise and trepidation. "Uh, yes, Elijah?"

Elijah gestured to the map, his yellow eyes narrowed as he stared at something in the top corner. "Why is that zone marked in gray?"

He was referring to a large swath of territory at the northeastern edge of the map. It was labeled "Zone 3," but instead of one of the traffic-light colors of the other patrol areas, it was shaded gray.

"Huh," Heath mused under his breath. "That's fucking strange."

It dawned on me why that part of the map had caught Elijah's attention.

That was where his fathers had died.

"Oh, yes," Kit said, perking up. "Interesting, isn't it? The Guardians took this zone out of active patrol about five years ago. I believe it was normally green, and occasionally yellow —normal for a location on the furthest outskirts of our community. But there hasn't been a wraith sighting there in something like twenty years, so the zone was retired. The adjacent zones rarely see wraiths, either, and those that we do see there are believed to have wandered over from more active areas."

"Really, twenty years?" Elijah asked, his posture lazy and his tone nonchalant when he had to be feeling anything but. "Interesting"

"It is," Kit said, nodding enthusiastically. "We theorize that the rifts that were in and around that zone have closed. Gone extinct, or at least dormant. It's a rare phenomenon, and we don't really know why it happens."

Elijah didn't ask any more questions. We all knew where his mind had gone, and the brutal slaying of his fathers by several Giants and an Apex wraith that happened to occur in that area during the lunar eclipse twenty years ago was not a topic he would want to raise for a classroom discussion.

I filed it away for later. We'd help him get to the bottom of this too.

Kit continued his lecture on the basics of Guardian patrol, regaling us with how he and the other bright minds at HQ develop forecasts before every lunar cycle to provide recommendations for the manning of each zone. He answered a few more thoughtful questions and several dumb ones, and after ninety excruciating minutes, he finally dismissed the class.

"Oh, hey, Avery," he said as we all stood up and gathered our things. "Could you stay behind for a couple of minutes? I just have a few questions for you."

"Like fuck he does," Wyatt snarled under his breath. He was still in a mood.

"Sure, no problem," Avery replied.

I snagged Wyatt by the waistband of his shorts before he could storm the lectern. "I'll handle it," I announced briskly.

Heath, Wyatt, and Elijah filed out, but not before each of them had given Kit some version of a death glare.

Not that he noticed. He'd come out from behind the lectern and was leaning casually against it, his arms crossed over his chest as he peppered Avery with questions about the wraiths in her neighborhood.

"That's enough, Kit," I said, coming to stand behind Avery's shoulder. "You'll make Avery late for our combat session. I'm sure it isn't news to you that a few of the trainers would love an excuse to make her life harder, and I'd prefer not to give it to them."

Kit arched a brow at me. "Ah, Aiden, you must've

forgotten that here at camp, I'm the instructor and you're the student. I know what time the next session starts."

I let my beast peek through my eyes. "And you must've forgotten I'm not a fucking idiot. Flirt with females on your own time, but never *this* female."

"*Aiden*," Avery hissed.

Kit's cocky smile dipped. The rivalry between us was always academic and never about our animals, and it was beneath a Prime of my level to run around exerting my beast's power against lesser shifters. I hadn't touched him, but I was reminding him that I could.

Avery was *mine*.

He cleared his throat and turned to her, his inquisitive smile returning. "What's going on here, Avery? Blackwell is acting a *tad* possessive. Who is he to you?"

She shrugged her swords onto her back and tucked her notebook under her arm. She spared me a passing glance as she turned to leave.

"He's no one, Kit," she said, raking my guts onto the floor with poisonous claws.

She walked out of the room without another word.

10

AVERY

I hadn't made it ten feet down the hall before a hand wrapped around my arm and yanked me into a closet.

Darkness swallowed me as I was pressed from chest to thighs against a hard, muscular body. A woodsy, masculine scent with hints of thunderstorms invaded my nose. Eyes blinked in the dark, now softly glowing with blue-green rings around the irises.

"Aiden!" I yelped. "What the hell do you think you're doing?"

"Shit." His hands landed on my hips. "I didn't know this supply closet was so small. And I have no idea where the light is."

"What?" I glared up at him, my eyes adjusting as my tiger, who was coyly flicking her tail, lent me her keen night vision. "Why are you dragging me into a supply closet in the first place? Have you lost your moondamned mind?"

"Yes," he growled. "My *mate* refusing to talk to me has made me lose my moondamned mind, Avery."

Each time one of them called me their mate, it sent me into a sanity-shredding spiral of pleased preening from my inner beast and barely contained rage from every other part of me.

"I am not your mate," I whispered. My lips were mere inches from his chin. "You let me know exactly what I was to you when I saw you and your *date* at the ball. What was up with that, Aiden? Were you and Heath just going to flip a coin between Phoebe and the hot professor when it came time to choose your bond? Or was that fuckboy behavior just for my benefit?"

He crowded me further, and my back hit the shelves. The neon headlights in his eyes pulsed brighter, and his jaguar floated into the air between us. Not pushing, but caressing, teasing my tiger. She didn't rise to the bait, but she purred in approval.

"Do you want to talk about what happened, sweetheart?" he asked, his lips next to my ear. He smelled so good, and it made me monumentally furious. "Gladly. I know you're angry. You have every right to be. But we are *Fated*, Avery, and that deserves at least one civil conversation." His grip tightened on my hips, and he pressed his body flush against mine. He was hard as a rock in those track pants, and I couldn't decide if I was pissed he dared or would've been more pissed if being pressed up against me *didn't* make him hard. "So, are you going to talk to me, or are you going to continue to act like a brat?"

I squirmed under him. I ached to reach for my sword, but there was no room to maneuver. "Fuck you, Aiden. You broke my heart, and now you have the *gall* to call me a brat?"

He sucked in a harsh breath and returned his gaze to mine, anguish marring his stupid handsome face. "*Fuck*, baby. I didn't know I even had enough of your heart to break. I am sorry, Avery. I was half in love with you—"

"Bullshit," I spat.

"—but we had reasons, sweetheart. Reasons to seek what we thought was a guarantee of power and stability in our bond, and to do it quickly. You *know* why we thought that couldn't be you—"

"I don't want to hear it—"

"For the love of the fucking Moon, Avery," he snarled, his lips nearly touching mine, his minty breath hot against my skin. "We. Didn't. Know. *I* didn't know! But now we do. Stop this madness and come back to us."

I jammed my knee into the steel rod between his legs. He swore and stumbled enough that I was able to slip around him.

He leaned against the shelves, breathing hard and watching me warily. Turquoise pulsed as his jaguar reached for me again.

My beast shoved back, and he winced.

"I know what we are to each other," I said, struggling to keep my voice even. "It is excruciating every time I see you, and my beast longs for the ones the Moon, in her infinite wisdom, has decided belong to us. But do you know what I also feel when I see you, Aiden?"

He sighed, defeated. "Tell me."

"I feel the bile that rose in my throat when you paraded another woman in front of me and called me *no one*. I feel the terror that consumed me when you left me in wraith-infested woods alone. And I feel the pain of my heart being crushed when the moment that should've been the happiest of my life wasn't—because you'd ruined it."

We stared at each other for a long, agonizing moment, me with my hand on the doorknob and him sagging against the shelves filled with cleaning supplies.

"I'm sorry," he said quietly. "For all of it. Those weeks after spring break are the greatest regret of my life because you are *everything* to me, Avery. You always have been, even when I acted like the exact opposite was true. That was torture, but this? This is far worse."

It sure fucking was. My chest was so tight, it was a miracle I could breathe at all. I straightened my posture and lifted my chin, proud of how I managed to keep it from trembling. "Goodbye, Aiden."

I left the closet and slammed the door behind me.

OUR GROUP COMBAT TACTICS SESSION WAS HELD IN ANOTHER large field, its grass trampled to hell. This one was bordered by the lake on one side and the tree line of the thick forest on the other.

All of us were here this time. Gold shirts, black shirts, and the white shirts of the Support Squadron.

Ian unsheathed his katana and twirled it lazily as he looked me up and down. "What's wrong with your face? How is it that every time I see you, you look more and more pissed off?"

"I don't know, Ian, what could possibly be driving me up the fucking wall on this fine day?"

Nico elbowed Ian. "Dude, I know she's your sister, but you can't say shit like that to a chick."

"Yeah," Joon added, "you gotta tell them they always look perfect and chill or else they'll think you're calling them crazy, and I wouldn't call Avery crazy if you paid me a million dollars to do it. I like my guts where they are."

"Thank you, Joon," I said, tickled to be considered so threatening even by my friends. "That's kind of you to say."

Our array of trainers for this afternoon's activities stood

in the middle of the field, surveying the lot of us with mixed expressions.

There was Cash, of course, his posture rigid and a look on his face that said we all disgusted him.

Trent was here, too, his big shoulders bunched and white hair ruffled as he muttered something to Cash.

The other two members of Cash's quad, Jared and Alex, both generic brunet Alpha wolves, lingered nearby. Even after a semester of training, I wasn't sure I'd ever heard Jared speak a word, and Alex communicated more in grunts than fully formed sentences. Neither of them had ever paid much attention to me, content to let Cash and Trent be the ones to belittle me while they ignored me in favor of their favorite trainee quads.

A few Support Squadron leaders stood near Cash's quad. Two of the trainers were younger, maybe in their late twenties, and with them was an older man who could've been anywhere from forty to sixty. It was hard to tell with shifters, since we aged slower than humans, especially those of us in the physical condition required when one fought wraiths for a living. These three seemed in good spirits and generally happy to be here training the next generation of ordinary shifters destined to plow the lower-level wraiths from the path of their Guardian counterparts.

Finally, there was the man who had to be the one in charge of this exercise.

"Is that Gandalf the White?" Ian whispered.

"I think it's Zeus," Brody whispered back.

"Nah, it's a real buff Santa Claus," Nico said, a little too loudly.

"Shh," I hissed at them.

"Greetings, trainees," the large white-bearded man said, projecting his deep voice across the field. "I am retired

Commander Benjamin Moss. I served in active combat as a Guardian for twenty years, and then I spent twenty more years in command at both the brigade level and the division level throughout our region. I know my shit, and I'm here to help you become well-oiled machines out on that battlefield."

I had the vague notion that a brigade was the group of Guardians and Support Squadron forces stationed at a specific post, while a division made up all posts within one of the zones Kit had shown us during class. The "Twelfth Division" would be all the posts within Zone 12 and so on.

"If you've made it this far," Commander Moss went on, "you've proven yourself adept against the wraith simulations, both as an individual fighter and in team formation. You've drilled the basics of how to employ both blades and claws against these monsters." He paused, his deep-brown eyes hard as he swept his gaze across us all. "And there are those of you who have survived one year of real patrols under the darkest skies. But there is always more to learn. This session will be first and foremost about teamwork—specifically, teamwork as a Guardian Unit."

My skin tingled with excitement. A unit was the team of four Guardians and their six-member Support Squadron. Our training against the SWIM hadn't involved working in that formation, but I was most comfortable working in a mixed shifter group.

"We'll be doing a number of games and drills designed to hone your tactical skills as a unit. And of course, we do not have fancy magical constructs out here in these woods. You will be facing each other, which means you can and will get hurt. Toughen up, because at the end of the summer, we'll be tossing you into one of the most active zones on the map."

"Hell yeah," Ian said.

"'Bout time," Joon agreed.

Mumbles of at least some level of enthusiasm sounded all around.

I shifted my balance from foot to foot, anxious to get started and also pretending that I couldn't feel the four stares of my not-mates boring into the side of my face. They lingered on the edges of the group like surly princes, too talented and important to mix with the rest of us.

"All right, settle down," Commander Moss barked. "Today we're just going to play a simple round of blades versus beasts so I can get a feel for what I'm working with." He nodded at Cash. "Since Rogers knows the lot of you better than I do, he and his quad will divide up the teams and assign roles." He clapped his massive hands. "Spread out and get started!"

Everyone hopped to. The Guardian trainees who'd arrived as established quads broke away into their groups. Every other group was at least a trio, though there were a few spares like me. The Support Squadron trainers herded the white shirts into groups of six.

"Baxter," Cash spat, stalking over to where I'd tried to blend in near a quiet trio of black shirts. There was also a second trio of gold shirts nearby, who radiated hostility in my direction. "You're fucking up my numbers, as usual."

"Just stick her in the Support Squadron," one of the gold shirts suggested helpfully, his lip curling as he gave me a passing glance. He was a tall, lanky asshole with black hair and a giant nose. "It's where she belongs."

Cash scoffed. "She *belongs* outside the gates of this fucking camp with a one-way ticket back to the slums of fucking Fulton City. But until Ward Gale gets his head out of his ass, we have to play along with this farce."

I sighed. "This is getting tiresome, Cash. I earned my place here, same as everyone else."

Big Nose cackled loudly. "Sure you did. I don't know who you had to fuck to get let in here to make whatever bullshit feminist statement this is supposed to be—"

A cold, brutal chill swept over my body. Big Nose hissed in surprise, and the others paled and stumbled back a few steps.

The icy force had alarmed and maybe even pained the gold-shirt trio, but it only caressed my skin lovingly before fading away. I jerked a stern look over my shoulder and met the electric yellow gaze of the basilisk peeking through Elijah's eyes.

His pupils bounced back into a round shape, and then he winked at me.

"Baxter can work with us," Mark Ellison announced, his voice soft but decisive. He was the leader of the quiet trio from my year and a Prime jaguar like Aiden.

My beast snorted derisively.

Yes, I know, Aiden's beast is more impressive. Thank you for the reminder.

"How magnanimous of you, Ellison," Cash drawled. "Fine." He turned his slimy leer on me again, and he smiled. "Your team will be playing the beasts, which means you're going onto the field with only the clothes on your back and whatever animal you have at your disposal. And once I find Davidson over here a fourth"—he jerked his head at Big Nose—"they'll be team blades. Enjoy."

He sauntered off.

Fuck.

Mark cast a sidelong look my way, a hint of sympathy there. "We'll do our best. I don't suppose you might decide to actually shift for this? It's cool if your beast is on the small side—we can make it work. The Support Squadron guys they assign to us will be in beast form too."

I shook my head. "Nope."

"Right. Well... don't be a hero." He patted my shoulder awkwardly, then turned to confer with the rest of his trio.

Davidson and his team procured their blades for this exercise, and they began warming up nearby, making harried, violent slashes through the empty air. Davidson's preferred weapon appeared to be a mace, which made little sense for killing a wraith and was going to make this exercise extra tricky.

All three of them watched me, grins wide like they couldn't wait to teach me a lesson.

I'd just have to teach them one first.

11

HEATH

It took us no time to cut down our assigned opponents. Jared had paired my quad with a six-man Support Squadron group that included Ian, Brody, and their cat friends, presumably because we were the two top groups coming out of training this past semester. We'd been assigned to the blades team because no one wanted Elijah's beast to make an appearance, and we'd bled the opposing team's beasts dry in about three minutes.

All the while, Commander Moss had strode through the field, barking instructions.

"If your opponent has drawn blood, you're out! That means you, Killion! I don't care that you can still fight with that gash in your leg."

"Support Squadron should be clearing a path through the ordinary beasts! Assist your Guardians with a kill only if you've eliminated the smaller opponents first."

"No shifting, Moore! You're on team blades—you should be able to stab that gorilla without use of your beast!"

"That's it, draw the most powerful of the group away. Isolate him from his teammates!"

I lingered on the edges of the field as I caught my breath and cleaned my sword with the hem of my shirt. I was also ignoring the intense loathing radiating in my general direction from Ian. Even with the short duration of our bout, we were lucky Ian's blade hadn't "accidentally" found its way into any one of us.

"Fuck, they've put her on the beast team," Aiden said, glaring across the field to where Cash directed Avery's group to square up against Brayden Davidson's trio plus one and their assigned Support Squadron team, who all carried their various bladed weapons.

"Cash is a sadistic asshole," Wyatt growled. "He knows she won't shift, so he's sending her against a bunch of blades with only her fists."

I was about to grind my teeth to dust. "Ellison's quad is decent, but they aren't us, and there's no reason for them to prioritize Avery's safety during any of this."

"Our mate is resourceful," Elijah pointed out. His body and beast were miraculously relaxed—for now. "But I'm going over there, anyway."

Ian and his crew had already taken off and were marching around the perimeter of the field, heading toward Avery and her team. We followed, the grunts and roars and shouts of our fellow trainees who were still engaged in battle echoing through the clearing. The air was thick with shifter aggression, the beasts around us pumping it into the atmosphere like a fog machine.

We weren't the only ones who'd noticed Avery's predicament. A small crowd had gathered, consisting mostly of trainees from our class who were probably there for one of two reasons: They were hoping to finally get a glimpse of Avery's beast, or they were delighting in the fact that Cash had just hung her out to dry.

"Nope." I snatched Ian's katana from his hand and slid it neatly back into the sheath on his back. "That's not going to help her."

He whirled on me, his eyes lit the same electric blue as his sister's were whenever I agitated her enough to bring her beast out to play.

The ache I worked to suppress damn near every hour of the day bloomed to life in my chest, and my wolf whined.

"Don't touch my sword, Blackwell," Ian snapped. "And I won't be taking advice on how to help my sister from the guy who's hurt her worse than anyone ever has, save the three assholes standing behind you."

Aiden let out a defeated sigh, and the red flames of Wyatt's bear rage seeped into the air, tempered not at all by the flash of cold from Elijah's beast. My wolf shoved to the surface and directed all three of them to keep it together.

"You can't just run out there into the middle of your sister's fight and save the day," I said quietly to Ian. "Nor can you lend her your sword. I know you know that, and I sympathize. My mate is constantly finding herself in situations that leave me feeling helpless, and that's something only my father ever managed to make me feel before now."

Ian studied me with narrowed eyes like he was surprised by but also suspicious of my candor. After a moment, he relented, softening slightly. "I'm so fucking pissed at you, Blackwell," he said wearily, and then he cut a glance over my shoulder. "At all of you. The Moon gave my sister the strongest quad imaginable because she *needs* you, and you fucked it all up."

Aiden cleared his throat. "Was.... Was your mother the same?" he asked softly. "The same as Avery?"

Brody had slipped quietly to Ian's side during this exchange, and he grabbed Ian's hand, giving him a knowing look full of sympathy. *He* knew, I realized. Brody knew, but I didn't, and Avery was *my mate.*

Ian looked me in the eyes and lifted his chin. "Yes, she was."

Wyatt swore, but none of us were surprised. We'd suspected it from the moment we were able to wrap our heads around what Avery was and what she could possibly be doing in the Guardians.

"Listen up, Baxter," I said, allowing him to continue to hold eye contact with me. My beast recognized our now-familial connection and only chuffed at the little fox's bravery. "I don't care if Avery hates us for the rest of our days. We are her Fated, and we will *never* let what happened to your mom happen to her. Do you understand me?"

He sniffed, finally looking away from me and wiping his eye. "Yeah. I believe you, Blackwell. And I'm grateful. But it would be a lot easier to watch her back if she didn't hate you, or even better if—and I can't believe I'm about to say these words—you were actually *bonded.* But the hole you've dug is fucking massive. I have no hope for you."

Elijah chuckled. What the fuck he found funny about that, I had no moondamned clue.

"Thanks, man," Wyatt drawled. "We're aware."

"Why the fuck are you all standing around?" Cash bellowed at the combatants on the field. Mark Ellison, to his immense credit, had pulled Avery aside and appeared to be conferring with her. "We don't have all fucking day. I better see beasts on this field in thirty seconds."

The teams lined up facing one another, each in the basic unit formation. The four Guardians stood in a square, two in front and two in back, and the six support men fanned out in front of them in a V-shape, the point of the spade meant to carve through the swarmers so that the stronger shifters could attack the bigger threats.

After removing their clothes, Avery's team shifted into their animals. A jaguar and a snow leopard took the front, and Avery was positioned on the back right next to a panther.

Aiden huffed a humorless laugh. "They have a full quad of Prime felines and don't even know it," he murmured.

On the front line stood two small bobcats and two ordinary wolves. At the last moment, the final two Support Squadron members burst into feathers and launched into the air, one of them a large hawk and the other an even larger falcon.

"Oh, good," Elijah mused, his yellow gaze tracking the raptors. "Maybe they'll peck Brayden's eyes out. I don't like the way he's looking at my dove."

I concurred. Brayden Davidson would be tempting death if that ridiculous mace he was swinging around his head like a lasso went anywhere near my mate.

Avery bounced on her toes and shook her arms loose, her gorgeous face focused on her opponents and devoid of anything resembling fear or even mild concern.

While I was on the verge of an aneurysm.

Cash blew his whistle, and the two teams attacked.

Davidson's Support Squadron did what they were supposed to—carved straight through the four smaller beasts on the front line and separated them into manageable groups. It was three blades against two land-bound beasts while the avians took turns dive-bombing everyone in the group.

The Prime beasts on Avery's team didn't wait for Davidson and his quad to charge through the opening created by the Support Squadron. The snow leopard and the panther bolted down the path and leapt together onto Steven McConnell, the first man they encountered. Claws raked across his chest, opening deep gouges through his T-shirt, but he managed to get his sword through the snow leopard before he was taken down.

"McConnell and Atkins, you're both out!" Trent shouted.

The panther pounced on Bruce Rosenburg, another of the blade-wielders, from behind. Bruce whirled at the last minute and managed to slice the panther across the belly. The panther staggered, and Bruce jeered at him, taking precious fucking seconds to revel in his victory.

It was enough to allow the hawk to attack him from the air. It dove at him, and he'd hardly been able to cry out before its talons opened deep puncture wounds in his neck.

Cash's lip curled as he watched the guy stumble around with his hands on his neck, frantically trying to staunch the bleeding. "Get the fuck off my battlefield, Rosenburg."

That left two Guardian blades versus Avery and Mark Ellison's jaguar. Mark snarled at their approach while Avery lurked behind him, her hand resting on his flank.

Aiden exhaled an angry breath through his nose and commenced an agitated prowl next to me.

Commander Moss had finally made his way over here, too, and he observed the proceedings without an ounce of emotion.

"Give it up, Ellison," Brayden said with a sneer, swinging his mace lazily. "It's the two of us against you, and all you have is that broken female behind you. Yield now, or I'll bleed you all over this fucking field."

The jaguar snarled again. Powerful muscles bunched under fur, readying to strike, as Brayden and Damien Jones, who was brandishing a falcata sword, advanced slowly toward him.

Suddenly, Avery slapped Mark's flank and shouted, "Now!"

The jaguar lunged at Damien, who slashed at him wildly with his sword. Mark ducked the blade, his belly hitting the dirt, which allowed Avery to vault over his back. She slammed into Damien from the side, knocking his sword from his grip and taking him to the ground.

The jaguar launched immediately to his feet and pounced on Brayden while Avery punched Damien right in the fucking throat.

The crowd hissed.

"Perfect," murmured Elijah. He hadn't even twitched a muscle since the fight began, but the icy shroud of his basilisk hovered at the surface of his skin.

Damien gurgled an enraged sort of noise as Avery rolled off him, snagging his sword from the ground as she went. Black fur rippled down Damien's neck and arms as he leapt to his feet. A neon-green sheen rolled over his eyes, and his fingertips elongated, claws threatening to erupt from them.

My beast growled in my chest, pushing hard against my control.

Damien launched himself at Avery, a vicious growl erupting from him as his wolf pushed the shift. She plunged his sword straight into his gut and jumped clear of his attempted tackle.

"Fuck yes," Wyatt said, bouncing on his toes. "That's my girl."

She wasted no time in running to the aid of her teammate. Mark and Brayden were locked in a standoff, the jaguar dodging the mace while Brayden evaded the swipes of Mark's claws.

Avery jumped right onto Brayden's back and put him in a chokehold.

"For the love of the fucking Moon," Aiden groaned.

Brayden flailed, the mace swinging wildly. The jaguar had the opening he needed to duck under the mace and sink his teeth into Brayden's meaty thigh.

"Fuck!" Brayden shouted. The jaguar unlatched, and deep-red blood seeped into his shorts and ran down his leg.

Avery released Brayden's neck, her sneakers landing lightly on the grass. She grinned and dusted herself off.

"Bout goes to the beasts," Cash yelled. "Fucking pathetic, Davidson."

Brayden staggered on his injured leg, bellowed in rage, and then, to my absolute fucking horror, swung his mace at Avery's back as she walked away from him.

Wyatt's bear burst from his body and shot onto the field.

"Avery, watch out!" I shouted.

She turned at the last second, and genuine fear flashed across her face as she registered the heavy ball of the mace and its sharp studs coming straight for her. She dove out of the way, her insane speed allowing her to dodge a direct hit that would've shattered every bone in her rib cage.

But it wasn't quite enough.

My wolf howled as those sharp studs caught the skin of my mate's hip, slicing up her left side and her arm as she dropped to the ground. Blood—my *mate's* precious blood— ran in rivulets down her arm. It bloomed under the tears in her black shirt, and she hissed as she tried to climb to her knees.

Utter chaos erupted.

Wyatt's bear slammed into Brayden, taking him to the ground. He roared and sank his teeth into Brayden's throat. The crowd began shouting, the aggressive pheromones in the air whipping everyone into a frenzy.

Kellan fucking Crimson and his quadmate, Teegan the

Alpha wolf, inserted themselves between Brayden's remaining trio members and Brayden's prone body as he struggled under Wyatt. Kellan shouted something in their faces while Teegan loomed silently.

Brody and his bobcat friends had managed to tackle Ian to the ground ten feet away from where Brayden had been standing before Wyatt's bear mauled him.

Commander Moss marched into the mix, barking orders.

Aiden stood in front of Elijah, hands braced on Elijah's shoulders and neon eyes locked on Elijah's glowing yellow ones as his jaguar tried to radiate calm he didn't feel.

I sprinted past them and into the fray, needing with every fiber of my soul to get to my mate.

"Avery!" I bellowed. I hurdled Wyatt, who had regrettably been pulled off Brayden by Commander Moss before he'd done more serious damage, and I landed at Avery's side.

Just as she was helped to her feet by Teegan of the *fucking* Crimson Quad.

"I've got her, Blackwell," he said, his voice calm and full of quiet menace.

"Like fuck you do," I snarled. "Give her to me. I'm taking her to the infirmary."

"Heath, quit it," Avery said wearily. She hissed in pain as Teegan looped her arm around his shoulders. "I don't feel like dealing with your bossy Alpha nonsense right now."

"You know that's not what this is," I replied between clenched teeth.

Teegan's face remained placid as ever, but his eyes sparkled with quiet glee. "You heard her. I'll get her to the camp doc, if that's what she wants."

"I will kill you."

"*Heath*," Avery growled.

"That is enough of this bullshit!" Commander Moss announced from somewhere behind me. "Davidson, shift and heal, and then you and your trio are dismissed from this program. Teegan, escort Miss Baxter to the doc. The rest of you, get your asses off my drill field and out of my sight."

The corner of Teegan's mouth lifted a single millimeter, his version of a smug smile. "Come on, Baxter," he said softly, still looking at me, "before you lose too much more blood."

"Yeah, okay," she said. Her eyes met mine. Pain, sadness, anger, and for the briefest second, *longing* all flashed in those blue depths before they iced over once more. She lifted her chin. "I don't need your help, Heath."

She might as well have cracked open my ribs and ripped out my heart. I couldn't watch yet another person take my injured mate away when it should be *me* with her.

"Avery," I whispered, the desperation leaking into my voice and laying me bare in front of her and fucking Teegan, "*please*, baby. Please let me take care of you."

She stared at me for a beat, and then she shook her head sadly. She turned her back to me and limped away, leaning on Teegan as she went.

IT WAS NEARLY HALF AN HOUR BEFORE I MANAGED TO GET myself to the camp infirmary. I'd had to make sure Wyatt wasn't going to be punished for attacking Brayden. (He wasn't because Commander Moss clearly thought Brayden deserved it, and it didn't hurt that Moss had trained Wyatt's fathers back in the day.)

Aiden volunteered to be on Elijah duty until Brayden

and the rest of his trio had packed their shit and left the campgrounds. There was a reason Wyatt hadn't even tried to hold his bear back after Davidson's chickenshit attack on our mate.

It was better him than Elijah's beast. If the basilisk had come out, Brayden would be dead, and we might've been the ones sent packing.

Out of the Guardians, away from Avery. An unfathomable disaster.

Cool, sterile air engulfed me as I marched into the reception area. There was a large desk where two nurses in blue scrubs manned the computers. A hallway to the left of the desk led to what I assumed were offices and other staff areas.

It was the large double doors to the right that I was more interested in.

"Excuse me," said one of the nurses as I breezed past the desk. "Where do you think you're going—"

I shoved at the doors. Locked.

My wolf growled. He could feel his mate behind them.

"Sir—"

I kicked the doors in. The steel caved under my shoe, crunching inward before the doors flew open, and the clang of something metal hitting the floor announced my entry into the treatment wing.

Snarling, I stalked inside. A long white room with high ceilings and harsh fluorescent lighting greeted me. Hospital beds lined both sides. Light-blue curtains hung between them, separating each treatment station.

Dr. Lee looked up from where he was sitting on a rolling stool at the foot of a nearby bed. He wore his white coat over scrubs, and his finger hovered above the screen of a tablet.

Avery was perched on the bed, looking tired and

wearing only shorts and a sports bra, her ruined T-shirt in her hand. Her perfect skin was clean and free of blood, but Dr. Lee had placed bandages along the left side of her body. A girl with deep-brown skin and long braids was wrapping another bandage around Avery's upper arm. She wore the same blue scrubs as Dr. Lee and the nurses out front, and I vaguely recognized her as a fellow Proteus student.

"Can we help you, Mr. Blackwell?" Dr. Lee asked, lifting an eyebrow in my direction.

Avery did not appear surprised by my arrival, and she let out a resigned sigh.

Alpha dominance flared in the air, and Teegan appeared from wherever he'd been lurking. He slid in front of me, blocking my way to my fucking *mate*, his arms crossed over his chest and a flat look on his face. "She doesn't want you here."

"You have no idea what the fuck Avery wants," I growled. "Get out of my way."

"No."

"Move." My beast poured the command into the space between us and *pressed*.

Teegan's brown eyes flared amber, and his already tight jaw clenched harder. The faintest tremble ran through his body.

"That's right," I whispered menacingly. "You're strong, but you're no match for my wolf, who's spent the past decade keeping a basilisk in line. If you ever stand between me and Avery again, I'll tear your fucking head off."

He glared, brown fur ghosting along his extremities. He pushed back, the seconds dragging by, and then blood began to leak from his nose.

Shit. That was dangerous, and he should've yielded, but

apparently Teegan was a stubborn asshole who would rather pass out on the floor than submit to me.

"Damn it," Dr. Lee said, sounding only mildly perturbed. "Aisha, get some gauze. Heath, release him now, or I'll ban you from my infirmary for the rest of the summer. You can figure out how to stitch your own wounds."

I did as I was told. Teegan sucked in a harsh breath, but he recovered quickly, his wolf falling away and his posture returning to its usual ramrod straight.

Aisha hurried toward him, gauze in hand, but Teegan grunted and waved her off. He wiped the blood away from his nose with the hem of his T-shirt, conspicuously flashing Avery a glimpse of his abs. "I'm fine," he said. "I need to get back to my quad. Avery, you're coming to the lake for rec time, right?"

She gave him a wan smile. "Yeah, though I'm pretty sure I can't get these bandages wet." She glanced at Dr. Lee, and her smile bloomed brighter. "Right, Doc?"

"Correct," Dr. Lee replied, returning her smile with a fond one of his own. "The healing spell our wonderful student-medic Aisha worked on your wounds should have them closed up by tomorrow morning, but keep the bandages on and dry until then, please."

"I'll save you a spot on the beach," Teegan told her.

"The fuck you will," I bit out.

"Sounds great," Avery replied, pointedly not looking at me.

Teegan turned and marched stoically through the broken doors. Aisha busied herself with a supply cart, and then she wheeled it out of the room behind Teegan.

Dr. Lee rose from his stool. "I'm going to finish up your chart," he told Avery. "I'll be back in a very quick three minutes." He slanted a look at me as he headed for the doors. "Do not break anything else in my infirmary, Mr. Blackwell."

"Sorry, Doc."

He shook his head, though he might've been smothering a grin.

Whatever. Alone at last.

I prowled toward my mate.

She watched me, a challenge burning in her gaze.

"Are you okay, Killer?" I asked softly, coming to a stop a foot from her bed. I ached to touch her but somehow managed not to. "Anything badly damaged, or was it just surface wounds?"

"Surface wounds," she replied, her face hard. "It's not lost on me that you were the one to shout the warning at me, so thank you. It would've been a lot worse if that mace had hit me in center mass."

I swallowed roughly. "I know. I'd say I've never been so scared in my life, but that wouldn't be true, would it? You almost died in the forest at school, and it was my fault."

"I think you share that blame." She shook her arm out and gingerly rolled her injured shoulder. "All four of you told me to get lost. Even Wyatt managed it as a bear."

"It wasn't like that," I growled. "We thought.... Fuck, you know what we thought, Avery."

She sighed, exhaustion weighing on her beautiful face. "It's really pissing me off that you're here, Heath. You only care now because your beast is driving you to. Do you remember when I got a concussion in a bout in the arena and you didn't give a shit?"

"I gave a shit," I snapped. "I punched a hole in the fucking wall of the men's locker room."

That earned me a slight raise of her blonde brow. "But you wanted me to *think* you didn't give a shit, correct?"

Shame churned in my gut. "Yes."

"Then tell me, Heath, truly." She sat up straighter, her eyes blazing like the center of a flame. "You didn't want a central bond with a beast soul because you thought it would be faulty. Weaker. You wanted the assurance of power. Of stability. Of *fertility*. Now you know for certain that a bond with me means a bond with a beast soul. What's changed, really?"

"*Everything* has changed, Avery," I said, my voice a desperate rasp. "You're our Fated. Our perfect match, chosen for us by the Moon. Our deity. The source of every drop of our shifter magic. I don't believe our bond could be anything but the strongest and most perfect union on the planet, but even if it wasn't, I just *do not fucking care anymore*."

I'd shouted those last few words, and she stared wordlessly at me.

"I won't take you from them again," I whispered. "If I'm wrong, I might die for it, but I won't ask my brother and my best friends to sacrifice for me anymore."

She frowned. "You might *die*? What are you talking about?"

Avery was aware of my parents' intentions with respect to Clara's bonding—she'd skewered one of her dates last semester, after all—but she didn't know that everything had escalated. She didn't know about the deal with the little Nelson shits or about my plan to challenge my father by Clara's seventeenth birthday—a deadline that still loomed over all our heads.

If I challenged Holden and won custody of my sister, I could put a stop to the bonding she didn't want to a quad of teenage assholes who were callous fuckboys at best and dangerous abusers at worst.

A month of stewing, of aching for my mate, had given me some perspective. As much as I'd wanted to spill everything to her in the immediate aftermath of the night in the woods, to somehow make her see we had a *reason* for doing we what we did, I knew now that I couldn't.

Avery had only met Clara once, but she'd already performed heroic feats to save her from harm. I wanted Avery to bond with my quad because she forgave us. Because she wanted us. Because she knew in her heart how well we all fit together.

Because she loved us.

I didn't want her to bond with us begrudgingly just to save Clara, nor did I want her to feel like there was anything behind our obsessive need to make her ours other than pure and unadulterated *desire* for a girl we'd all fallen for well before we knew she was our Fated.

So no matter how badly I wanted to stand here, look her in the eyes, and beg her to forgive us for what we did because it was what we thought we had to do to save my sister because maybe, just *maybe*, it would give her a reason to look at me with anything other than distrust, contempt, or *pain*—

I wouldn't.

"Nothing you need to worry about," I replied, inching closer to her. She tensed, but the urge to comfort my mate overwhelmed me. I cupped her cheek, and it was soft and warm in my hand. "I'm glad you're okay, Killer. I would've let Wyatt kill Brayden Davidson if I hadn't thought it would get us kicked out. I know you're angry with us, but we'll never leave you. You're our mate, and we're going to take care of you."

She shoved my hand away. "If the breach in the school's wards hadn't happened, I'd have shown up next semester and had to watch you all fawn over fucking Phoebe or some other latent princess you picked to bond with because you decided you wanted to juice your power. Go away, Heath."

My wolf rumbled a dangerous noise in my chest. I leaned down and got right in her face. "You don't have all the facts, Killer," I snarled in a low voice. "You may be right, but it would've hurt me even more than it hurt you, I can fucking promise you that."

Her tiger lashed at me, but my wolf held strong, reveling in the pain. Our mate was a storm, a force so fucking powerful, it made me want to cry and scream and fuck her until neither of us could walk or speak.

"All right," Dr. Lee announced as he breezed back through the doors. "Heath, step away from my patient and get out of my infirmary. Avery, you're released and on rest until tomorrow morning."

We both relented. I dropped a kiss on her forehead and strode from the room before she could punish me for that too.

12

ELIJAH

I ended yet another frustrating phone call and went in search of my quadmates. George slithered along next to me, doing his best to radiate soothing contentment. He'd rather be with my dove, and I greatly empathized, but I appreciated his willingness to split his time between us nonetheless.

We found Heath, Wyatt, and Aiden, along with dozens of other campers, sunning themselves on the rocky sands of the small beach on the lake's north shore. We were allotted a couple of hours of recreational time before the dinner bell would ring, and it appeared the lake was the popular choice.

"Any news?" Heath asked me. He'd managed to snag a beach chair from the supply hut and had set it up in ankle-deep water. His golden tan put everyone at this lake to shame, but his sunglasses did little to hide his dark mood. Even the wolf head tattooed across his chest looked angry. "It would be awesome if something went right today."

"Sadly, no," I replied. I toed off my shoes, shucked my shirt, and flopped onto an empty beach towel next to Aiden. George curled into a glittering purple pile at Aiden's feet.

"Uncle Horatio's people are hitting dead end after dead end on this 'Lunar Heritage' nonsense."

"Probably because they're used to investigating companies that commit run-of-the-mill financial crimes," Aiden said, ignoring George's friendly sniff of his leg. He lay on his towel, staring up at the sky like it might give him some answers to our problems if he waited long enough. He wore navy swim trunks and had a tan nearly—but not quite—as impressive as his brother's. "Whatever the hell was going on with these mysterious Primes and their targeted attack on your mother wasn't anything like that. We're on the cusp of uncovering something dark and insidious, I can feel it."

He was right. I could feel it too.

My beast salivated for blood.

"Would be nice if we had a name or location for these fucks," Wyatt muttered. He'd gotten a hold of a paddleboard and was straddling it, floating in waist-deep water a few feet away from Heath. Hopefully he'd put on sunscreen—he certainly did not have a tan and was wearing nothing but tiny board shorts. "I haven't beaten the shit out of nearly enough people today."

I arched a brow at him. "You're the only one of us who's gotten to beat the shit out of anyone. Consider yourself lucky."

"Not exactly true," Aiden murmured distractedly. "Heath almost melted Teegan's brain in the infirmary."

I flashed Heath a smile full of teeth. "Good."

He sent me a half-hearted salute, still staring off into the distance behind his sunglasses.

Wyatt let out a pained groan. "Fuck me. Avery in a bikini is going to ruin my fucking life."

Aiden jerked up to sitting on his towel. George shifted irritably at the sudden movement, his nap disturbed.

The basilisk surged forward. My vision sharpened, acquiring our target.

Mine, the beast said.

Down the way, my dove strolled onto the beach, flanked by her brother and their gaggle of felines from the Support Squadron. She wore a sporty purple bikini that showed off every line of her long, lean body. The top teased just enough of her perfect tits to have my fangs threatening to descend, and the bottoms only just covered the round muscle of her ass. Her blonde hair remained in its braid from earlier, and her dainty feet were bare.

I gritted my teeth, fighting against the pulsating wave of lust that her nearly naked body sent thrumming through my veins and the siren's call to battle ignited by the sight of the bandages on her torso and arm.

"Fuck," Aiden said under his breath. "Is she trying to kill us?"

"Probably," Wyatt replied. "We deserve it."

"I'm getting tired of your defeatist attitude," Heath muttered. "If Avery wanted to kill us, we'd be dead. I'm not sure I've ever felt a stronger beast. She'd give my dad a run for his money."

Aiden whipped an alarmed look at his brother. "Truly?"

"Yep."

"Dad can never find out," Aiden growled.

Heath clenched his fists around nothing. "You think I don't know that? Her beast's appearance is dangerous enough, but add the ball-shriveling level of power she's packing, and you've got Dad's worst nightmare."

Avery laid her towel on a large rock and sat gingerly down on it. Brody joined her, and they began chatting happily. The basilisk didn't mind this—the lynx had only brotherly affection for our dove.

"I think you're all missing the bright side here," I said. "Our mate has been blessed with the substantial power she needs to protect herself in this dangerous world. Not to mention she was also blessed with *us*—four brutal monsters who would follow her to the ends of the earth. Trust in the wisdom of our deity."

Heath rumbled a noise of agreement. "And I've told her we're not fucking going anywhere, no matter how hard she fights us."

"Bet that went great," Wyatt muttered.

"Sure did."

I leaned back onto my elbows, the sharpened gaze of my beast never leaving Avery. We'd certainly all had some setbacks since camp began, but it was only the first day.

A small kernel of hope was buried under the despair—Avery had been falling for us before our ill-conceived plan destroyed it all. She'd admitted it to me and to Aiden. I still had dreams about the way she'd softened in my hold when I'd taken what I wanted and kissed her in the school hallway, and you couldn't remove the memories of how lost she'd been in Wyatt during their tryst in the laundry room even if you took a blow torch to my brain.

But her prior feelings for us only amplified the hurt we caused her. My precious dove had her heart broken, and now she was using the pieces to slice the flesh from our hides, cut after devastating cut.

"And there they go," Heath growled. "Circling her like horny fucking sharks."

Kellan Crimson and the rest of his quad strutted down the beach, big torsos and tanned skin on display. Each one of them not-so-casually strolled by Avery's perch on the rock, all smiles and waves for *my* mate.

Hank and Ari set their towels down on a patch of sand

ten feet from Avery and then jogged off to dive into the lake. Teegan, who it appeared had recovered from Heath's assault on his brain, placed a hand on the rock next to Avery's sleek, bare thigh and leaned in close. I couldn't read lips, but he wore the serious, concerned expression of an Alpha checking on the welfare of someone he cared for.

Avery's smile for him was warm, polite, and devoid of the curious interest or low-smoldering heat she used to have for me and each of my brothers.

Still.

A growl ripped from Heath's chest. He surged to his feet in the water.

"Don't do it," Aiden said, sounding exasperated. "Heath, I'm serious. It'll only make things worse."

Heath dropped back into his chair with a defeated groan.

Teegan finally moved on after Ian weaseled his way onto Avery's rock and took up the extra space Teegan had needed to get so close to my dove.

That left Kellan.

He glanced over his shoulder in our direction and smirked at our exile from Avery's general vicinity. His amber eyes lingered a bit longer on me, and an orange glow sparked in them. He'd activated his beast's long-range vision, as I had mine.

I smiled at him, letting my fangs elongate just enough that he wouldn't miss them.

His smirk widened, and he turned back to Avery, engaging her in what I was certain was polite but flirtatious conversation.

Kellan was a unique mythic. We were notoriously violent, erratic, and struggled with control. It was why, even though most of us would lead any quad we decided to join in raw power, we were rarely the quad leader.

My beast versus Heath's wolf one-on-one would result in Heath's death nine times out of ten, but Heath had superior control, and his wolf's dominance was an unwavering and impressive force that gave even my basilisk pause. He was a natural leader, and the basilisk submitted to his command without protest. It was good for us.

Kellan, like the few griffins on record before him, had the temperament and control of an extra-powerful lion. He was more of a super-Prime than an off-the-charts mythic, which meant he had no trouble leading his quad. His grandfather, Jeremiah Crimson, was also a griffin and one of the few mythics to ever sit on a regional council.

The Crimsons were also richer than even the Blackwells.

It was all these things that made Kellan who he was—a shifter who truly believed that there was nothing in the world that could stop him from getting whatever he desired.

But that was where he was wrong.

Because if Avery was what he desired, there was one thing in this world that would stop him from having her.

Me.

George sensed the direction of my thoughts and slowly unfurled from his spot at Aiden's feet. He set off across the beach, winding swiftly through the sand, alarming beachgoers along the way, until he reached the base of the rock where Avery was sitting.

He reared up and hissed violently at Kellan, who startled and danced away, a stream of expletives flying from his mouth. George then slithered his way up the rock while Avery squealed with delight at his arrival. He curled himself loosely around her and then flopped his head into her lap like he was the most exhausted snake in the world.

Kellen slunk away to join Teegan on their towels.

Aiden chuckled, and Heath grunted a satisfied noise.

"Well, thank fuck for that," Wyatt said, still bobbing in the water on his board. "That snake has really been pulling his weight around here lately."

Avery stroked George's scales and chatted with her brother and the felines for the rest of our hour at the lake while the Crimson Quad was relegated to sulking on their towels nearby.

DINNER WAS A QUIET AFFAIR. A FULL DAY OF TRAINING PLUS AN hour or two baking in the sun had subdued all but the most rambunctious shifters, which included Avery's bobcat friends. The basilisk had been unsure about Joon and Nico hovering around our dove, but after a day of observation, we'd learned that while those two may have found Avery attractive in an objective sense—there was no way around it because she was the most beautiful girl in existence—their pheromones tasted of healthy respect and a substantial dose of fear when it came to her.

So, they would live to see another day.

George had done his part keeping the riffraff, including Cash, from bothering Avery during dinner, which left her to enjoy her burger in peace.

Unfortunately, the setting sun and the unexplored bounds of the surrounding forest called to my python, and he disappeared before our last activity of the day.

A gathering around a campfire as some sort of perverse and unnecessary team bonding activity.

"Oh, for the love of the fucking Moon," Wyatt snarled under his breath as we approached the large firepit. Kellan and Ari had managed to snag spots on Avery's log and were sitting just outside the bounds of her personal space. Hank and Teegan sat down on the log next to theirs. "The second her brother and the cats are gone, they descend like fucking vultures."

Support Squadron had its own campfire on the other side of the lake.

"Come on," Heath said tersely. He marched toward the open log on the other side of Avery's.

We followed. Heath, Wyatt, and I managed to smash together on the log.

That left Aiden the odd man out. He surveyed the situation, studying it like he would a complex rune problem, the orange flames of the fire dancing in the lenses of his glasses. He slid a glance at Avery, who was pointedly not looking our way as Ari talked her ear off about something.

Aiden took off his glasses and handed them to Heath.

Then he reached behind his head and yanked off his black T-shirt.

His track pants went next, leaving him standing there in just his tight boxer briefs.

I grinned. This had gotten Dove's attention, her cerulean gaze drawn to Aiden's bare torso like a magnet.

A ghost of a smirk flashed across Aiden's face before his jaguar erupted from his body.

"For fuck's sake," Kellan snarled as the jaguar turned in a circle in front of the fire, his tail nearly whipping Kellan right in the face.

Aiden's large beast stretched languidly, pawed at the ground with his claws for a few seconds, then he curled up between our log and Avery's, his body crowding the space as he basked in the heat of the fire.

Ari snorted in derision, which was certainly sour grapes —Aiden's jaguar was bigger than his sleek little orange tiger.

Aiden ignored him, his turquoise eyes glowing and focused squarely on Avery, and he flicked his tail in interest, deliberately tempting her tiger.

Avery's eyes sparked bright blue, but she blinked it away quickly.

I reached over to stroke the jaguar's back, and he gave a rumbling purr. "Good thinking, my friend."

A bit of commotion broke out as a few of the ladies who worked in the kitchens brought down a crate of ingredients to make s'mores. Campers converged on them, and within minutes, skewers loaded with marshmallows were being held over the flames.

Wyatt returned with our supplies and passed them out, tossing me a consolation bar of dark chocolate. "Sorry, man."

I saluted him with the bar. "I'm used to it."

Ari snorted. "Is the snake too cool for s'mores?"

"Elijah's vegan," Avery replied instantly. "The marshmallows are made with gelatin, so he can't have them."

Our mate knows us. Defended us, the basilisk said.

The jaguar flicked his tail faster.

Realizing what she did, Avery looked away and took a frustrated bite of her s'more.

I let my fangs lengthen just a touch, and I bit into my chocolate bar with a smile aimed directly at Kellan.

He bristled. "A vegan basilisk? That's ridiculous. Only herbivore shifters don't eat meat."

That was not a universal truth, as one's human form didn't necessarily have the same dietary preferences as one's beast, but it was common.

The basilisk had never met flesh he didn't want to consume. My diet was about control.

I *tsk*'d. "That's very judgmental, Crimson. Weren't you touting your quad's lack of judgmental tendencies to Avery just last night?"

Heath and Wyatt chuckled. Kellan scowled, and Avery appeared very fascinated by the flames.

After a tense but quiet few minutes, I gathered my quad's chocolate bar wrappers and took them to the nearest trash can. When I turned to head back down to the firepit, Kellan stepped into my path.

My vision narrowed, and my fangs elongated once more. "Careful, Crimson. You've pissed me off enough already today."

Ghosts of golden-brown feathers rippled along his neck, and the telltale orange sheen rolled over his irises. He crossed thick arms over his chest, doing his best to loom. He and Wyatt had a similar build in their human forms, which meant he was a few inches taller and had several pounds of muscle on me. I found him about as intimidating as a Shih Tzu.

"What the fuck is your deal with Baxter, Harrow?" he growled. "What is the deal with your entire quad? *Everyone* in school knew that you guys came back from spring break and declared an active search for your bond among the latent girls, and it was clear that whatever shit you had going on with Avery was well and truly over. Now she wants nothing to fucking do with you, but you showed up to camp and started acting like psychotic assholes about her, even though everyone and the Moon knows she has a beast."

"I'd say that sounds like none of your business."

He grinned, showing me a mouthful of straight white teeth. "I'd say it *is* my business when my quad happens to also be in the market for a bond. Did you know my grandfather theorizes that a bond with a particularly strong female beast could be superior to that with a latent? He's certainly in the minority, but he has his reasons."

I filed that away for later. If Jeremiah Crimson knew something we didn't about Prime female beasts and bonding, Aiden would do just about anything to find that out, including breaking into his fucking house.

"And isn't it convenient that my quad may have happened upon one of those rare, glorious females?" he went on, and then he dropped his voice. "I can finally test my grandfather's theory."

Scales bloomed along my neck, across my chest, and down my arms. Kellan sucked in a breath, but his eyes only glowed brighter. "I advise you to listen closely, Crimson," I said, this hiss of my beast on the tip of my tongue. "Avery Baxter is off-limits to you, your quad, and every other shifter that walks this earth. Touch her, and very bad things will happen. Understood?"

He chuckled and cracked his neck, extinguishing the orange headlights. "Sure, Harrow. Sure thing."

He strutted away, heading back to his spot next to my dove like I hadn't just issued his death warrant.

Avery watched Kellan return, and then she glanced my way, concern heavy on her gorgeous face.

That's right, Dove. There is nothing I won't do to make you mine.

13

AVERY

My phone buzzed as I stepped out of my cabin, dressed for my second day of camp and eager for breakfast.

MALLORY

How was the first day? Did you kill anyone yet?

I snorted.

No, but it was touch and go.

When are you and Allen back from Palm Beach?

Three weeks! You better make time for me on your night off... or else.

She'd been issuing these sorts of vague threats since the beginning of summer, mostly to encourage me to check in to prove I was still alive.

I'll see what we can do.

I stepped off my cabin's little stoop and almost tripped over eight hundred pounds of rust-red bear.

"Wyatt!"

The bear was sprawled out on the grass in front of my cabin, lying on his side and apparently sound asleep. He stirred at my arrival, stretching languidly and letting out a big bear yawn.

"What the hell?" I tried to march around him, but he rolled swiftly to his feet and blocked my path. "Why are you sleeping outside my cabin?"

The bear nudged me with his giant head. Guileless green eyes stared at me, and my tiger purred at his touch.

Quit it.

"What do you want?" I asked the bear. "I'd like to go to breakfast."

He dipped his big furry head under my hand and then rubbed his nose on my shirt.

"Oh, for the love of the Moon. Fine." I gave him some pets on his wide forehead and a few ear scratches for good measure, and he rumbled happily. "This is under duress, just so we're clear. You did not earn pets for sleeping unin-vited outside my cabin. I'm just hungry and you're in my way."

He snorted and rubbed his head all over my shirt again, and then he nudged me in the direction of the chow hall.

I swatted his nose. "Stop that."

He chuffed, undeterred. I began a brisk stride down the path, and he lumbered along next to me. There wasn't much I could do about the situation, save shifting into my tiger and either sprinting away from him or forcing him to go away with my will alone, and I didn't exactly trust her to behave in the presence of Wyatt's bear or any of the other beasts the Moon had saddled us with.

Ian, Brody, Joon, and Nico waited for me in front of the Support Squadron cabins. At the sight of my companion, Brody's dark brows bounced upward, while Joon and Nico both bit off laughs.

Ian's eyes narrowed into slits. "What the fuck, Gale? Are you harassing my sister?"

The bear ambled over to Ian and butted his head into Ian's side, nudging him toward me like he was rounding up the kids for the carpool.

"What—" Ian staggered, and Wyatt nudged him again. "Avery, call off your bear!"

I sighed. "He's bringing you to me like you're a gift. Trying to butter me up."

Wyatt chuffed again and tried to steal another pet from me. I shoved his big bear head away. "No. No more of that for you."

He huffed a disgruntled noise. The rest of the group—all three of those jerks now holding in laughs—fell in next to us, and we continued down the path.

As we passed the edge of the lake, the path diverged, one way leading up the hill to the larger Guardian trainee cabins and the other toward the front of the campgrounds.

Waiting for us at the fork were Heath, Elijah, and Aiden.

Heath, dressed in our standard-issue black T-shirt and training shorts, his blond hair swept neatly back from his face and glinting in the sun like the sands of a tropical island, the barest hint of amusement on his full lips.

Elijah, miraculously also dressed in our training uniform, his long muscular legs on display beneath shorts that were at least one size too small, his canines sharp as he grinned at my predicament.

Aiden, wavy brown hair rustling in the soft breeze, his T-shirt molded to his shapely chest, hazel eyes alight behind his glasses as he not-so-subtly dragged his gaze slowly up and down my body.

My tiger preened and licked a claw.

Damn it.

I was on my own.

"Did you lose something?" I asked Heath, waving an exasperated arm in Wyatt's direction.

"Good morning, Killer," he said, his amusement blooming into an affectionate smile. "Did you sleep well?"

"Heath," I growled. "The night watch is unnecessary."

"I beg to differ. The beasts don't like sleeping away from their—" He darted a glance over my shoulder at Joon and Nico. "—from you. You're lucky it isn't all four of us there every night."

The bear shivered, and then his big furry body morphed into a very naked Wyatt the man.

He stood there, unrepentant in his nudity, dark-auburn hair tousled like he'd just rolled out of bed. He grinned lasciviously at me, his muscles flexing under his pale, tattooed skin. "Morning, baby girl."

"Damn," Nico said from somewhere behind me. "Are all bears packing like that?"

"Yeah, man," Joon replied. "It's probably the compromise the Moon granted them for being so fat and slow in beast form."

"*That* bear isn't fat and slow, though," Nico protested. "Pretty fucking unfair."

"Will you two shut up?" I hissed over my shoulder.

Wyatt's grin had grown impossibly wider. Aiden threw a black T-shirt and shorts at him, and Wyatt's burning gaze never left my face as he slowly dressed.

I gritted my teeth and willed away the heated flush I felt from my cheeks to my chest. It was anger and frustration that Wyatt dared—that *any* of them still fucking dared after what they did to me—and also anger and frustration at the warmth the sight of Wyatt's naked body elicited in other parts of my body. It had been crafted by the Moon herself to torment me.

Aiden had done the same thing to me last night, and his jaguar had radiated smug satisfaction afterward.

I pointed a finger at Heath. "No more of this, or I will shift and *make* you go away. Got it?"

The starbursts in his eyes lit up the brightest gold. His wolf knew as well as I did that letting my tiger out around him might not go the way I wanted it to. "Looking forward to it, Killer."

I huffed and stomped away. Ian and Brody followed, sticking tight to my back, and the others fell in behind them.

"Dude, could Avery's beast really force that Alpha to leave?" Nico asked in a low voice.

"You know you're not supposed to ask questions about Avery's beast," Brody replied diplomatically.

Joon snorted. "Doesn't matter. Those guys are hella pussy-whipped over her. They'd do whatever she wanted them to do."

"Except leave her alone, clearly," Nico mused. "Quads are weird."

"For sure," Joon replied.

"The bobcats are astute."

I nearly jumped out of my skin. Elijah had appeared out of thin air, like he so often did, and was strolling along next to me as if it was the most natural thing ever.

The cool touch of his beast slid over my skin. My tiger gave a haughty sniff, but her tail flicked in interest.

"What?" was all I managed to say.

"Your bobcats," Elijah replied smoothly. "They're correct. We are pussy-whipped. Every single one of us would stab ourselves in the heart if you asked us to."

That thought made me feel like *I* was being stabbed in the heart, and I waved it away with an internal scream of frustration.

"And quads are indeed weird," Elijah went on, his yellow eyes alight and his fangy smile big and brilliant. "Always in a constant battle between man and beast. The push and pull of primal instincts versus reason. The baser need to protect the ones we love. We don't always make the right decisions, Dove."

I squinted at him. Protecting the ones they love? Was this about what Heath had said yesterday, when he was acting like his life may be in danger?

The tiger's hackles were up.

"Elijah, what—"

He just squeezed my hand and then walked ahead. He jogged up the stairs to the chow hall and disappeared behind the doors, probably to go make himself at home in the kitchen. The ladies who worked here were always letting him back there, probably so he could assemble a meal that met his dietary preferences.

The loss of the ghostly lick of the basilisk on my skin left me feeling flat and empty. I blamed my beast.

Brody linked his arm through mine and led me up the stairs, chatting happily while Ian beamed at him with so much love that it made me want to cry.

Clearly I needed to eat.

And as I made my way through the bustling dining room to the buffet line, I pretended that the quick *knowing* caress of Aiden's hand along my lower back as he swept past didn't also make me want to cry.

After another four-mile run through the woods with my swords strapped to my back, I was all warmed up for our next morning activity.

The obstacle course.

"All right, everyone gather 'round!"

Commander Moss was back and overseeing this exercise this morning, which left Cash and his quad free to stand around nearby and look annoyed and disgusted by all of us.

"Some of you will remember this course from camp last summer," Commander Moss said, "but we've added quite a few new obstacles and increased the difficulty this year." He waved a weathered hand in the vicinity of the large structures staged behind him. Towering obstacles made primarily of wood and ropes cut a twisted path through the trees, thinner here than at the edge of the forest just beyond us. "You'll rack your weapons before you go, but this course is meant to push your *human* bodies to the limits, just as the wraiths will when you need to be a blade wielder. No shifting allowed."

Murmurs sounded among my fellow black shirts. In the distance lay a cargo net that looked at least fifty feet high, and some of us would much prefer to scale that in agile feline form.

"Today you'll be running the course as an individual. No quads, no teamwork. Each obstacle is set up to take three people at a time, so we'll run in heats. The requirement is to finish the course in under twelve minutes. Each fall from an obstacle is a thirty-second penalty."

Commander Moss sent a pointed look around the group, like he was daring us to ask questions, and then he clapped his hands. "Line up!"

Gold shirts and black shirts alike converged into the area at the front of the small clearing where we all waited. A stone-faced Jared and a scowling Trent set about putting them in some kind of order.

I hung back. The longer the rest I had after this morning's run, the better.

"Not excited for this one?"

Ari the tiger sidled up next to me, a confident and relaxed cat without a concern for what lay ahead on this course.

"Plenty excited," I replied. "But not in a hurry. I'm pretty sure the course isn't going anywhere."

He chuckled, and a whisper of his beast's interest floated between us.

My tiger hissed her displeasure.

Yes, thank you, I'm aware of your feelings.

"Well, I think you'll do just fine," Ari said, beaming an encouraging smile at me. "If I had to guess, I'd wager you're hiding some kind of feline within that gorgeous body, and we're excellent climbers." He placed a hand on my arm and gave it an encouraging squeeze.

Feline aggression filled the air, and instead of provoking my beast, she let out a pleased purr.

Ari's hand disappeared from my arm. The snap of bone followed.

"*Shit*," he hissed, shaking out his hand. "What the fuck, man?"

Aiden loomed, turquoise headlights set to high behind his glasses. "Hands off, Syed."

I gaped at him. "Did you just break his finger?"

"I did. He has plenty of time to wander away, shift, heal, and come right back."

Ari growled, and orange fur sprouted along his arms.

Aiden's jaguar pulsed dominance into the space between them, a clear message to fuck off. He wasn't as strong as Heath, but he was close. Heath was heavy and sturdy, like an immovable wall, while Aiden's flavor was sharp and biting.

Ari gritted his teeth.

I stepped between them. "Sorry about him," I said to Ari. "He's lost his mind. We'll be up soon, so you better go take care of that."

Ari shot Aiden a look of pure venom, then stalked off into some nearby trees, ripping his shirt off as he went.

I turned back to give Aiden a piece of my mind. "What the *fuck* is wrong with you?"

He *tsk*'d and gave me a stern look, like *I'd* been the one misbehaving, his hazel gaze hot on my skin.

Then he stalked off to join the rest of his quad where they lingered a few yards ahead.

My tiger flicked her tail, thumping it in time to the pounding of my growing headache.

Whistles sounded at intervals, and the line moved as wave after wave of trainees took off onto the course.

Heath and Wyatt were placed in the same heat, and they easily muscled their way over the first walls, up the ropes, and over the cargo net before they disappeared around the bend in the trees.

Aiden got stuck with Hank and Teegan from the Crimson Quad, and his nimble body and superior climbing skills had him well ahead of those two before they ran out of sight.

When it was finally my turn, somehow the quiet and inoffensive quad I'd been lingering near had shuffled back into the line. Instead, Kellan stepped into place on my left. Elijah materialized on my right.

"Oh, look, Baxter," Trent drawled as he fiddled with the timer app on his tablet. "A couple of your boyfriends have decided to run the course with you. Do you think opening your legs for the mythics will convince one of them to protect you from being torn apart by an L4 when we ship you out at the end of the summer?"

"Dude," Kellan said, sounding taken aback. "What the fuck?"

Elijah said nothing, but Trent paled considerably, his knuckles going white around his tablet. The cool touch of the basilisk glided across my skin like a wink before falling away.

Trent shook it off and blew his whistle angrily.

We were off.

First up: an agility run through rows of tires, straight into the seven-foot-tall "low wall." I easily scaled it by jumping to grab the top and muscling myself over. Kellan hit the ground two seconds ahead of me, but Elijah had somehow gone up and over the wall with a leap and a hop, like he was jumping a fence.

We ran ahead to the high wall, which we were to scale by pulling ourselves up with one of the three ropes hanging from the top. Hands on the rope and feet planted on the wall, I worked methodically, making it to the platform at the top right behind Kellan.

Elijah, meanwhile, was already there because he'd run halfway up the wall and grabbed the rope near the top before swinging himself over the ledge.

He stood there, grinning at me, apparently not in a hurry. "You're doing great, Dove."

I scowled at him. "What the hell is this? You don't give a

shit about training, you hardly ever come to anything, but suddenly you're a parkour champion?"

He licked his lips, yellow eyes alight. "I have a few talents that may yet surprise you."

Kellan huffed and nudged me. "Let's go, Avery. Don't let Harrow distract you."

Our way down was via one of the ropes suspended from a steel apparatus ten feet in front of us. Kellan launched himself onto one, slid down, hit the grass below, and jogged ahead to the cargo net.

Elijah waved a hand. "Ladies first."

I huffed and jumped. The thick rope burned my hands and shins as I slid down. The others would shift to heal, but I would manage with Ian's burn salve, which I had stashed in my cabin.

Kellan was halfway up the towering cargo net by the time we reached its base. Resting Dick Face Jared stood nearby, observing. I jumped onto the net and began my scramble. Elijah—who, it appeared, was not only a basilisk but also Spiderman—crawled up the net at breakneck speed, his feet hardly touching each rope before he propelled himself up to another.

My grip was starting to tire, but I made it back down the other side of the net in good time, cutting Kellan's lead on me in half.

Elijah waited for me there, and then we ran into the maze of trees, hot on Kellan's heels. We dove under a low-lying net and army-crawled through the dirt.

We ran through the trees and vaulted over a series of logs set as high as my chest, passing Cash's quadmate Alex, who did not look up from his tablet, at his station on the way.

We scaled another tall wall, this time with only nooks,

crannies, and rock-climbing holds to aid us. At the top of the wall, we ran across a narrow platform and then entered a rope bridge, walking heel to toe on a shaky tightrope with only even shakier rope railings to hold onto. Slipping would mean a fifty-foot fall to the ground.

Elijah reached the end first and jumped from the landing. He hit the in-ground trampoline below, backflipped, and landed in a crouch on the high platform of the next structure we were to climb. Unlike Elijah, I'd be using one of the ropes hanging below it to do that.

Kellan grunted, shook his head, then jumped down. He bounced off the trampoline and landed in a much more reasonable manner on the grass nearby. I followed suit, allowing myself to fall as gracefully as possible onto the trampoline and then bouncing a few times until I came to a stop. I stepped off onto the grass and faced the last rope climb.

My grip was weak now, but I managed to propel myself upward using the power my beast pumped into my legs. Ten, twenty, thirty, forty feet.

I reached the top and crawled through the circular hole, pulling myself onto the platform next to Elijah. Kellan popped through his hole and muscled himself up with just his giant arms.

We stood at the edge and faced down the final obstacle.

Below us was a downward-sloping hill. Three thick ropes, one for each of us, were strung like zip lines from the base of the platform and down the slope for a hundred yards, the other ends suspended from a simple wooden tower about ten feet off the ground.

Beyond the tower, the clusters of black shirts and gold shirts who'd finished the course were just visible through the trees. Commander Moss was there, too, deep in conversation with a few of the gold-shirted quads.

Cash hovered near the base of the tower below us, arms crossed over his chest, usual glare aimed squarely at me, his hate so visceral, I could feel it from a football field's length away.

The stunt he'd pulled yesterday by forcing me onto the beast team had backfired pretty spectacularly. Not only had I not revealed my beast, nor had I been gravely injured by refusing to shift, but the whole thing had resulted in three vetted graduates with the same female-hating sentiments as Cash getting tossed out of the program.

Cash had never liked me—not from the moment I'd stepped into the arena last semester and announced I was there to become a Guardian. He'd done his best to humiliate me, insult me, and endanger me, but by the end of the semester, it'd seemed like he'd just come to a begrudging acceptance of my presence in the program. He'd mostly ignored me.

But there was a deeper hatred lurking in his glares since my arrival at camp. Maybe he'd been holding out hope I'd decide not to spend a chunk of my summer living in a cabin in the woods with a bunch of male shifters, many of whom deeply resented my presence here.

I met his cold stare with one of my own. *Tough shit, asshole.*

"Ready, Dove?" Elijah asked.

I sighed. "Just go. I'm sure you have some insanely graceful way you're going to get down there. You don't need to keep waiting for me."

He winked, crouched low, and swung himself onto his designated rope. Using that momentum, he spun around it like a corkscrew and shot all the way down to the end. He dropped to the grass on light feet, gave Cash a shitty salute, and then leaned casually against the wall of the tower instead of jogging to the finish line like he was supposed to.

Kellan had already climbed onto the rope to my left and was clinging to it with his hands and feet, hanging like a monkey. He began to scoot down the rope, his movements measured and his pace quick. Pausing, he tilted his head back to look at me upside down. "Come on, Baxter!"

I backed up a few steps, ran, and launched myself out and onto the middle rope. I caught it with my weakened grip only a few feet behind where Kellan had progressed on his, and then I swung my feet up to grab on that way, too, content to use Kellan's method to scoot down to the bottom.

But as I heaved my feet into the air, my rope snapped from where it had been connected to the tower at the bottom, and I dropped.

14

AVERY

I screamed, clinging to my rope as I swung back toward the tower I'd just jumped from. My tiger roared in my ears, helpless to save me. My back slammed into the unforgiving wooden wall.

Bones cracked. My vision whited as searing pain shot through my back and into my chest. I tried to gulp in air, but it hurt too much.

I was still dangling thirty feet in the air.

My grip slipped. I had nothing left.

Male voices were shouting.

"Avery, let go! I've got you!"

I did let go. I had no choice.

With a silent scream, I plummeted to the ground.

Strong arms caught me easily, cradling me like a delicate maiden. "Fuck, are you okay?" Kellan asked, his eyes blazing.

"Yes," I rasped. "Might've broken some ribs."

Elijah must have sprinted up the hill because he arrived seconds later. "*Dove*. Are you hurt?"

I was a little dizzy, but my tiger was working overtime to

squelch the pain and accelerate healing. I was able to suck in a shaky breath. "I'll live," I croaked.

Elijah hissed angrily, his pupils slitting in those yellow eyes. "Give her to me, Crimson."

Kellan turned away from him, putting his back between Elijah and me. "Fuck off, Harrow. I've got her."

I patted Kellan's arm. "You can put me down now."

He began walking down the hill. "No, I think I'll get you down to the finish line and give your beast some time to heal the worst."

Elijah appeared in front of us, blocking the way. His wild, glowing eyes brimmed with an unsettling violence I'd never seen from him, not even the few times I'd met the basilisk. "Remove your hands from my—from Avery, Crimson. Hand her to me, or I swear to the Moon, you will not like what happens next."

As much as I disliked the fact that my not-mates had done nothing but piss a circle around me since camp began, and as much as it would normally give me satisfaction to see them suffer, I was not dumb.

Elijah's beast was about to be in the driver's seat, and that was a dangerous situation.

"Kellan, seriously," I said, my tone more forceful now that I could breathe. "Put me down. I can walk just fine."

Kellan's body heated against me. His features sharpened, and his long golden hair seemed to thicken. "No," he said, no longer looking at me, his glowing stare pinned to Elijah. His voice dipped into a rough growl. "I don't think I will."

Oh, for the love of the fucking Moon.

Elijah hissed again, gray-green scales blooming along his arms and neck.

With all the strength I had left, I drove the heel of my hand into Kellan's throat. He coughed and sputtered in surprise, which allowed me to wrestle free of his hold. I dropped to the ground, the impact like knives through my back, and I rolled down the hill until I was clear of the two of them.

The basilisk erupted from Elijah's body, his training clothes falling to the grass in shreds. He bellowed a monstrous noise and charged Kellan.

Kellan leapt into the air and burst into his griffin form. His head was that of an enormous eagle with amber feathers and a sharp black beak. The feathers faded into the body of a golden-furred lion, larger than any Prime lion I'd ever seen. In place of paws, he had giant bird talons, the scaly brown skin ending in four toes and curved claws longer than my hand.

And then there were the wings. Powerful wings, the span of a small aircraft and covered in the same amber feathers as his head, jutted from the muscles of his lion back.

Those wings beat in forceful strokes, allowing Kellan to hover ten feet off the ground and let out a terrifying noise that was somehow the roar of a lion and the screech of an eagle all at once.

The basilisk slammed into the griffin and knocked him out of the air. Elijah sank his rows of dagger teeth into the feathers of Kellan's neck as he whipped his thick, powerful body around him, constricting, and they tumbled straight through the tower that had just broken my ribs.

The impact knocked the top half straight off, and the rest crumbled into a heap of splintered wood.

"Oh shit." I crawled to my feet and ran after them.

Shouting echoed behind me, followed by the sound of a stampede up the hill. The crowd was on the way to witness the mythics trying to kill each other.

After their crash through the tower, Kellan shook Elijah

loose and dodged the basilisk's next strike with a leap and a beat of his wings. He screeched and dove, talons aimed for Elijah's yellow eyes.

Elijah zipped out of the way, whirling through the dirt like a giant scaled torpedo, and then he spun and launched himself at Kellan again. With another flap of his wings, Kellan avoided teeth around his throat by leaping to the top of the pile of wood that was the ruined tower.

It appeared that even those massive wings didn't allow the griffin to fly like a bird—the rest of his body was too heavy—but Kellan could jump much higher and longer distances than any Prime animal on the planet with their help.

He dove at Elijah again, and they smashed together, a tangle of scales and feathers skidding toward the pylons holding up the rope bridge.

I ran past them, every breath a heroic feat.

"Get down!" I shouted at the trainees who were just about to reach the top of the rock-climbing wall, which was attached to the narrow platform that led to the rope bridge. I waved my arms and jumped up and down, which hurt like hell. "The bridge is coming down!"

"What—" Josh Anderson started to say with a confused look, and then the basilisk plowed through the pylons holding up the rope bridge like a bowling ball. "Oh *fuck*. Shift and bail out!"

A bear and two Alpha wolves fell from the rock wall, landed on their feet, and sprinted into the woods right as Kellan landed on top of Elijah, grabbed his body with his talons, and tossed him through the rock wall.

It didn't splinter into shards, but it did come loose from the top platform. It fell over with a ground-shaking thud like a giant domino.

"Moon *fucking* damn it."

For once, it was a relief to hear that voice.

Heath jogged into view, Aiden and Wyatt hot on his heels. The rest of the trainees fanned out around the edges of the course, trying to get a glimpse of the carnage without getting hit by a projectile.

"What in the name of the ancestors is going on?" Commander Moss shouted from somewhere in the crowd.

"We'll handle it!" Aiden shouted back, although he did not look confident.

Hank, Ari, and Teegan went streaking by, shouting at Kellan.

Elijah had wrapped his thick body around Kellan's beast once again and hurled him at the cargo net. Kellan bounced off it and launched straight at his quadmates, who scattered, swearing up a storm.

"Elijah!" Heath bellowed. He sprinted toward the basilisk and ducked a haphazard swipe of his spiky tail. "Enough! Get it the fuck together!"

Elijah hissed at his quad leader and then struck at Kellan again, who'd just leapt off one of the log vaults, screech-roaring his head off.

Wyatt stood next to me, as serious as I'd ever seen him. "Wildcat, what in the ever-loving fuck happened?"

"My rope broke, I fell, and Kellan caught me." I pinched the bridge of my nose and took a moment to just marvel at how ridiculous my life had become. "And then he wouldn't let Elijah have me."

"Well, that'll fucking do it," Aiden said wryly. "Wait— sweetheart, are you hurt?"

It was as if there were no longer a terrifying serpent monster and a giant screeching bird-lion trying to kill each other in the immediate vicinity. Aiden and Wyatt closed in around me, their beastly eyes burning bright as I became their sole focus.

Aiden cupped my face in his hands and studied me. For a concussion? Wyatt pressed against my back and ran his big hands lightly over my ribs.

I sucked in a pained breath as his fingers hit a tender spot.

"Broken ribs," Wyatt announced. "Shit, baby. Let's go. Dr. Lee needs to fix you."

My tiger stretched languidly, licking a claw. She'd been enjoying all of this—the basilisk's extreme possessiveness, Aiden and Wyatt's concern for our wellbeing, even Heath's fearless march right into the fray to attempt to rein Elijah in like a proper Alpha.

Me? I was just tired.

I shook off my handsy not-mates. "Stop that. I'll be fine. We need to get this situation under control before they break a person instead of property."

Kellan roar-screeched from where he'd flown next—the top of the cargo net. This time he dove at Elijah *and* Heath. Heath jumped onto Elijah's back, clinging to him, and the basilisk rolled them out of Kellan's path, knocking over a line of vault logs as they went. Bellowing his displeasure, Elijah shook Heath off, unhinged his disturbing jaw, and struck at Kellan with all those teeth.

He managed to get a hold of Kellan's back leg. Kellan screeched and pecked at the basilisk with his sharp beak until Elijah was forced to let go.

Hank was now a bear, and he lumbered over to roar some bear nonsense at Kellan. Ari and Teegan appeared to be trying to herd Kellan toward Hank. Maybe he planned to sit on him?

I'd had enough. I marched toward the basilisk.

"Wait, Wildcat—"

"Avery, no! Stay back," Ari yelled, still waving his arms at Kellan. "It's too dangerous."

"Worry about your griffin!" I shouted back.

Elijah reared up, readying to strike again.

I jumped into the space in front of him.

Heath swore. "Avery, get clear! He's lost control."

I ignored him. "Elijah!"

The basilisk hissed, but I'd managed to pull his attention from where Kellan was beating his wings aggressively somewhere behind me. Those glowing yellow eyes and slitted pupils were now focused solely on me.

He hissed again, but it came out more like a purr.

"Come here, please," I said, holding out a hand. The beast dipped his big scaly head, and I stroked his nose like I would George. "Ready to calm down now? You're very impressive, very big and scary. You really showed that griffin who was boss, didn't you?"

The griffin snorted angrily behind me.

"You need to lock it the hell up, man," Teegan said in his monotone. "Or you're going to get us all kicked out of here."

The basilisk flicked his tongue a few times, and then he nuzzled my shirt with his colossal nose. I stroked him a few more times. "That's better. Can I please have Elijah back now? I need him to take me to the infirmary so Dr. Lee can fix my broken ribs."

That did it. The basilisk melted into a very naked Elijah, all olive skin over carved, sinewy muscle, his dark hair flopping onto his forehead, his eyes still those of the snake.

I swallowed my displeasure at the broken skin and streaks of blood that marred that perfect body.

"Dove," he rasped, kneeling in front of me and grabbing my hands. "Your ribs are broken?"

"Fucking finally," Wyatt said, jogging up. He shucked his shorts, which left him in only his tight black boxer briefs, and threw the shorts at Elijah. "Get dressed so we can take Wildcat to the infirmary."

"Why does Avery need to go to the infirmary?" Heath asked, striding over with his big dick Alpha energy. "Killer, what happened?"

"Her rope broke and she fell," Aiden announced. "Kellan caught her and set Elijah off by refusing to hand her over."

Heath forced a harsh breath through his nostrils and cracked his neck. "Well, sounds like I need to kill him."

"Ugh." I wriggled free of Elijah's grip and took several huge steps away from the group of them. "I do not need an escort to the infirmary. I just said that to get the basilisk to cede control." I darted a half-apologetic glance at Elijah. "Sorry."

He grinned, back on his feet, dressed in Wyatt's little shorts, and looking more pleased than was appropriate given this entire mess. "It was good thinking, Dove. The basilisk would do anything you asked."

"All right!" Commander Moss shouted at the crowd, which was dispersing now that both Kellan and Elijah were human again. "Let's just let this be a lesson on the dangers of setting off a mythic. Now everyone get the hell off my obstacle course."

He didn't have to tell me twice. I retrieved my swords and began my march back toward the chow hall. Food would fix me as well as Dr. Lee could.

Heath, Aiden, Wyatt, and Elijah all fell in behind me, hovering as if they thought I was seconds away from falling apart and they were preparing to catch all my pieces.

Exhaustion prevented me from doing much of anything except put one foot in front of the other.

This... sucked. These men—men I'd once known to be savvy, disciplined, and driven—were out of control. Acting like assholes. It was stifling, not to mention embarrassing.

How was I going to survive two whole months of this?

We walked past Kellan, sitting naked on a fallen log next to his quadmates and looking no worse for wear, save for the numerous deep gashes that marred his tanned skin. He watched me go with a speculative look on his face.

Everyone gave us a wide berth as we exited the obstacle course, and I ignored their wide-eyed stares. They'd all watched me stand down the basilisk, sure, but they hadn't seen me shift or anything more concerning. I held out hope that the excitement over all of this would die down soon. Shifters were hotheaded and aggressive and got into it with each other all the time. This was just notable because the combatants were mythics.

Cash had reunited with his quad and was conferring with them over who knew what near the starting line, and he managed to toss one disgusted glare our way as we walked by.

At me. Not at Elijah, who'd just destroyed half the obstacle course. Not at Heath or his other quadmates, who'd failed to get him under control.

Just me.

And it struck me that I finally had the wherewithal to wonder how my rope had broken in the first place.

15

WYATT

My dad glared at us from across his hulking metal desk. He'd trimmed his bushy red beard shorter for the summer, and his bald head gleamed under the harsh overhead lighting.

"To summarize," he said, his tone that of a disappointed parent rather than a pissed-off commanding officer, which I would've preferred, "you all have—" He looked at me and began counting on his fingers. "—collapsed one of my weapons training frames by throwing a fellow trainee through said frame, after which you put a hole in the wall of my field house."

I shrugged. No regrets here.

His glare slid to Aiden. "Threatened one of my classroom instructors and then decided to break the finger of one of my best trainees without provocation—"

"Ward, there was *some* provocation—" Aiden began.

Dad held up a hand, and Aiden shut up. He addressed Heath next. "Ruined the door to my infirmary's treatment room beyond repair and then nearly caused *another* of my best trainees to suffer a brain bleed—"

"It was his fault for not yielding when he should've," Heath muttered petulantly.

"—and if that wasn't bad enough," Dad growled, finally turning his ire on Elijah, "you have also completely destroyed my obstacle course, much of which was *brand-new*, and probably endangered half the Guardian class by letting loose not one but two out-of-control mythics."

Elijah kept the amusement in his expression to the bare minimum, but it was there nonetheless. His beast rarely got to go all out against another shifter like that, so he was mellow as shit right now. "I suggest you send the Crimson family the bill for the repairs," he said lightly. "Kellan was warned, repeatedly, and he chose to ignore those warnings."

Dad narrowed his eyes at Elijah, crossing his giant arms over his chest. He was one of the few shifters alive who would dare to stare down the basilisk, but he was practically a father to Elijah, so he could get away with it. "Uh-huh," he said dubiously.

"Dad—"

"Zip it, Wyatt." He pinched the bridge of nose. "It is the second moondamned day of camp. This behavior is completely unlike you four. You are one of the most talented quads to come out of Guardian training in a generation. You know how to control your beasts—yes, even you, Elijah— and you've always been single minded when it comes to your goals within the program. What in the wraith-infested hell has gotten into you all?"

His question was met with silence. Even Heath couldn't muster the energy to come up with some diplomatic bullshit.

"Um, sir?"

Avery raised a tentative hand from her chair in the corner.

Dad's face softened instantly as he turned to my mate. "You can call me Ward, Avery."

She wrinkled her perfect little nose in confusion. "Oh, um, okay. *Ward*, I was just wondering why exactly I'm here?"

I'd been wondering the same thing, but we weren't going to complain that Avery had been summoned to the principal's office along with the rest of us, which meant we weren't leaving her unsupervised in today's classroom session while Kit Wells batted his lashes at her.

Heath had managed to keep his shit together after the obstacle course mess and hadn't gone overbearing Alpha on our girl about going to the infirmary. He'd counted on Ian to do his dirty work, and it had paid off.

Avery had hardly been able to scarf down a sandwich before news of "the incident" swept through the chow hall, and after giving his sister the third degree, Ian had frog-marched her to the infirmary himself.

An hour later, after we'd all showered and changed for class, the text from my dad hit our phones.

"Well, Avery," Dad said, "I wanted first to apologize to you regarding the rope incident. It's true that all of us assume the risk of grave bodily harm and even death when it comes to our jobs as Guardians, but that isn't supposed to extend to faulty training equipment."

She gave him a perfunctory nod. "Apology accepted."

Elijah shifted in his chair, his beast creeping into his eyes. "I'd suggest, Ward, that you reconsider Cash's and his quad's roles as our primary trainers if Avery's safety is a priority of yours."

Dad's bushy brows lifted the tiniest bit. "What are you suggesting?"

"I'm merely pointing out that Avery's rope had no issues remaining tethered through use by countless other trainees and that Cash, who has made it no secret how he feels about Avery's presence here, happened to be stationed at the base of that obstacle when it broke."

"Do you have any proof that Cash sabotaged Avery's rope beyond his presence nearby when it failed?" Dad asked.

Elijah's pupils slit, and the temperature in the room dropped ten degrees. "Do I need it?" he hissed.

"Elijah," Avery snapped. "Stop it. You know as well as I do that there's no way to prove Cash did anything."

The cold press of the basilisk vanished. Elijah smiled fondly at her. "Whatever you say, Dove."

Dad cleared his throat. "That's the other reason you're here, Avery. I commend you for your bravery in standing down a basilisk lost to bloodlust earlier today. It was reckless, but it worked. It is for that reason and a few others that I've decided to add you to this team permanently."

I could not keep the gleeful smile from my face, and the others were no better.

Avery's eyes widened in alarm. "What—"

"Our first Guardian quintet," Dad went on, an excited gleam in his eyes. "I don't see how it wouldn't work just as well as the usual quad formation, and you're certainly skilled enough to integrate into this quad. And having you on hand to settle Elijah's beast in the event there's a need is an added bonus."

"We're amenable," Heath said eagerly. "Avery is a perfect addition to our group."

"No," Avery snapped at him, and then turned to Dad, softening only slightly. "I'm sorry, Ward, but I have to decline."

Now his eyebrows really did hit his nonexistent hairline. "Oh? And why is that? I've seen you all work together against the SWIM, and you can't tell me there's a better matched group of Guardian trainees for you. No one in your class comes close to your skill outside of these four."

Dad's compliment managed to momentarily crack her wall, and her cheeks flushed a pretty pink. It was fleeting, though. She shook it off, the rigid set of her jaw saying she wasn't about to back down. "I have less fond memories of being paired with them for that last challenge in the arena than you do, Ward."

He stroked his beard. "I do recall some friction, but that seems to have dissipated, yes? I may be an old bear, but I still remember what it was like to be young, hotheaded, and unbonded. It's my theory that all of this bullshit—" He glared at us again. "—will die down if Avery becomes a permanent member of this team. Am I wrong about that?"

"Nope," I said.

"Definitely correct," Heath added.

"The perfect solution," Aiden chimed in.

"No," Avery said again through clenched teeth. "Ward, please do not do this."

He frowned, studying her for a long moment. "What am I missing here?"

Avery looked at me, her face incredulous and confused all at once. "You really didn't tell your own father?"

I lost every ounce of good humor I was feeling. "Of course not, Wildcat. That's our private business, and your secrets are always safe with us."

Her lips parted for the quickest of seconds, like I'd surprised her, but then she snapped her mouth closed, lifted her chin, and gave my dad the coldest of stares.

Fuck.

My bear let out a pained whine in my chest, and I clenched the arms of my chair.

"Ward, last semester these men made the coordinated decision to spurn me publicly and treat me like shit. It is also their fault I almost died in the campus forest during the breach of the wards because they left me there, alone. They've only decided to care about me now because they found out our beasts are Fated."

Heath sucked in a shocked breath. Aiden went rigid in his chair. Even Elijah looked surprised.

My bear slammed against the bars of his enclosure. Our mate had claimed us, openly, in front of my father. It didn't matter to him that she was only doing it to expose us for the assholes we'd been.

Dad stared at Avery in stunned silence. After a moment, a slow smile spread across his face. "You're Fated? To my son and his quad?"

Avery blinked at him, realized she miscalculated, then sighed in defeat. "Yes."

My dad's grin grew, and he turned to me. "Truly?"

"Truly," I replied. "She's our mate, Dad, but she has every right to be pissed at us."

His grin turned speculative. "You've seen her beast?"

"Yes, but don't ask us about her. Ever."

He held up his hands in surrender, then turned his attention back to Avery, wearing the same indulgent smile he reserved for my sisters. "I am so intrigued. And thrilled, Avery, you have no idea. A Moon-blessed match for my son, and to such a talented young lady! I cannot believe how lucky these boys are."

"Did you hear anything I said about how they treated me? Ward, they told me to fuck off out of their lives so they could focus on finding their latent princess."

Aiden sighed wearily. "Avery, you know why we thought —*oof*."

I elbowed the shit out of him.

Dad shot me a reproachful look before turning back to Avery, trying his best to tamp down the excitement. "I'm sorry, Avery. I do perhaps have some idea about why all of that happened—" He darted a furtive glance at Heath. "—but also, this explains *so* much. No wonder these four have been acting up." He slapped the top of the desk, back to smiling. "And this is why Elijah's beast is so docile around you! I should've known. I must be losing my touch. Fated bonds are just so rare—"

"Dad," I growled. "You have to keep this to yourself. You *especially* cannot tell Mom, or half the population of the Hills will know our business within an hour."

My dad pouted. *Pouted.* "Fine. For Avery's privacy, of course."

"Thank you," I said.

Avery had sunk lower and lower into her chair as this went on. She looked more like a sulking kid than the polished professional soldier she'd been when this meeting began.

It was so fucking cute.

"Now, Avery," Dad went on, dispensing with proud dad and back to stern commander. "I understand your concerns, and I don't want you to think I'm not hearing you or that I don't care about your feelings. It appears these boys hurt you deeply and have some things to fix. But this doesn't change my mind. I'm assigning you to the Blackwell Quad's Guardian Unit—"

She sat up straight. "But—"

"—because you all perform at a truly elite level when you're together, and it appears there is a divine reason for that. But I need you to understand that this is for purposes of the *Guardian Unit* only. This assignment does not make you their central or otherwise a member of their quad." He fixed the rest of us with a steely glare. "That part you all will have to work out on your own, preferably with less damage to my campgrounds and my campers. Am I clear?"

Heath nodded, his wolf thrumming with restless, excited energy. "Crystal. You won't regret this, Ward." He looked at Avery, drinking in her sullen face with the look of a victorious predator. "You, either, Killer. We were made to fight alongside each other. You know it as well as we do."

Dad coughed into his fist. "Quit while you're ahead, boy."

Avery stood up and shrugged her swords back onto her back. She moved like she was sore but not in serious pain.

Good.

"I understand," she said to my dad. "I won't waste any more time arguing with you. I just hope that as my commanding officer, you'll be open to reconsidering this assignment at the end of the summer if things don't go as you envision."

"Fair enough," Dad replied diplomatically. "You're dismissed back to class. All of you."

Avery marched out of the office. The rest of us stood up and gathered our various weapons and notebooks. I checked the time on my phone. We still had about thirty minutes left in our classroom session, which would be thirty minutes I got to sit in the back of the class and soak in the curve of my mate's neck and daydream about wrapping her ponytail around my fist.

"Wyatt, hang back," Dad said, snatching that kernel of joy from me. "I'd like a word."

Heath and I exchanged a look. I shrugged, he grunted, and then he followed Elijah and Aiden into the hall.

Dad shoved his giant body out from behind his desk and

came around to the front. He jerked his head toward the door. "Walk with me, son."

I followed him out of the building, and then we began a slow stroll down the path toward the lake. He was contemplative as we walked.

When we reached the lakeshore, he stopped and sat down on a bench. I joined him, taking a moment to stare out across the water. It was a dark, moody blue under the cloudy sky, and I contemplated throwing myself into it and sinking deep enough to hide from the shame of how I'd treated the girl I wanted more than I wanted to breathe air.

"Sounds like you boys fucked up pretty badly," he said eventually. "Your mate is not happy with you."

"Was it that obvious?" I said, my words dripping with sarcasm.

"You shunned her publicly as part of your decision to pursue a bonding?" It was a simple question, with only the slightest bit of censure in his tone. He didn't seem mad or ashamed that I might have done something to hurt my mate. His bear exuded a quiet energy that felt like cautious excitement mixed with sadness at the state of things.

"She was under my skin, Dad. We all thought we were doing what had to be done."

"And does Avery know about Clara?"

I explained that she knew about the plan to force the bonding generally but not the expedited timeline we'd been operating under since spring break.

"And why not tell her?" Dad asked. "She might understand your rush to find what you thought was a suitable bond before you all knew you had a Fated match in Avery."

"Trust me, we wanted to—at first." I raked a hand through my hair, still a little damp from my shower after lunch. I itched to be back in closer proximity to my girl, but it was also... *nice* to have a conversation with my dad about the most important thing in my life. "But she refused to talk to us, and the longer we sat with it, the more we couldn't figure out how to tell her about the ticking clock over Heath's head without it seeming... manipulative."

"Ah." Dad stroked his beard again, lost in thought. "That is a level of maturity that frankly surprises me from unbonded shifter males of your age, especially with respect to being separated from a Fated bondmate. In hindsight, it's a minor miracle you haven't caused more damage to this camp or killed anyone."

"It's been fucking close," I muttered even as my bear puffed up in my chest at my dad's praise. "And I appreciate that, Dad, but the situation is not good. She's the best thing that could've ever happened to us, and we fucked it up worse than you can imagine. We're lucky she hasn't stabbed one of us yet."

That only made him grin. "Yeah. The Moon saw fit to give you a real spitfire of a mate. The best dual-blade wielder this program has probably ever seen."

"I'm glad you're amused by this," I said wryly. "I don't think Avery was expecting you to be so thrilled about it."

"No, I don't think she was," he replied, chuckling, and then he sobered. "She was expecting me to display at least some shade of disappointment that my son's potential future mate has a beast, wasn't she?"

"Would you have been? If I'd have come to you before the whole Fated thing and said, 'This is the girl I want to bond'?"

He sighed, taking a moment to study the lake's glassy surface. "I don't know, son. I'd like to think I would've been just as pleased, especially since I'm lucky enough to know Avery. She's such an impressive female." His expression darkened. "But I might've worried, just as I'm sure you all did, about what it might mean for Heath if he still planned to challenge his father. Holden Blackwell is vicious, powerful, and quite possibly a sociopath. We only know what we've experienced for generations, and that is that the bonds created with latent females from Prime lines are the source of incredible strength for a quad."

"But that doesn't concern you now?" I asked. It didn't concern me, or Heath, or the others in my quad, but we'd *felt* the divine connection snap into place.

It was easy for us to have no doubts.

Dad's smile was in danger of breaking his face in half. "Not even a little bit. You've been given a sacred gift, Wyatt. There is not a chance your bond with Avery will be weak or unstable."

This was nice, actually. My dad was not only on my team but also genuinely excited at the prospect of Avery as my bondmate, despite her beast. I was happy, at least momentarily, and it was a relief to feel something other than my bear's rage or the claws of desperation that had been raking away at my insides since the moment I locked eyes with that beautiful, bleeding tiger in the woods.

My girl would sink her little teeth into me if I tried to pull her into a dark corner to thank her for spilling the beans, and the thought made my mouth water and my dick ache.

Dad clapped a hand on my shoulder. "A word to the wise, son. Avery was handed a loss today, at least in her mind, so you boys should employ some restraint in the wake of this small victory. Give her some space and do not push her. You've got a long summer ahead of you."

I shook my head even though he was absolutely right. "We'll see."

16

AVERY

ONE MONTH LATER

A fizzy pink drink with a sugared rim and an umbrella stuck through the straw landed in front of me. "Drink up, bitch."

I scowled at Mallory. "Why? Not like it'll get me drunk."

"It is for the *vibes*, obviously. We are in a *bar*, and you will act like you're enjoying yourself. You haven't seen me in, like, two months. It's the least you can do."

Allen, her bonded mate and wolf shifter, nodded enthusiastically, his blond curls bouncing. "Let loose, Avery! You gotta take advantage of what little time they let you out of your prison in the woods." He jerked his chin to where the dart boards and pool tables had attracted a small crowd. "Look, Joon and Nico are having fun."

I rolled my eyes. Those two had wasted no time in cozying up to a couple of cute girls I recognized from the rising senior class at Proteus. Joon's shirt was unbuttoned down to the middle of his pecs, his black hair flopping boyishly onto his forehead as he leaned an arm against the wall, bicep flexing. His girl du jour stood on strappy heels underneath that arm, blinking coquettishly at him as she took delicate sips through the straw of a drink that looked suspiciously like mine.

Nico wore a tank top that left little of his chest and nothing of his arms to the imagination. He was standing boldly between the open thighs of a beautiful girl, who was perched on the edge of the pool table and had some truly impressive breasts.

"Those two are going to have to get creative with respect to location if they want to get laid," Ian mused as he slid back onto his stool at our high-top table. He set three pints of beer in front of Brody, which meant he, still six months away from turning twenty-one, had deployed his trusty fake ID again. "A shared bunk in our cabin is not ideal for hooking up." He slid a heated glance at Brody. "Ask me how I know."

Brody chuckled, snagging one of the pints before handing another to Allen and the last to Ash, one of Allen's besties from the wolf contingent.

Ash's dark hair was a bit longer on top than it had been the last time I saw her at school, but she'd freshly shaved the sides of her head. She wore a fitted dress shirt in an eggplant color with the sleeves rolled to her elbows, displaying the myriad colorful tattoos that decorated her forearms. Her many rings clinked against the glass as she raised it to me. "Here's to the first month of camp being behind you. At least you look like you're still in one piece."

My answering grin was wry. "For now."

Mallory, who was parked on the stool next to me, leaned in. "How has it, um, been?" she asked in a low voice so that only I could hear her. "Is your beast... unsettled?"

Mallory knew that I'd been caught in the woods during the breach of the school's wards because she'd been walking the perimeter with me when those first swarmers had crawled over the wall. She was also aware that after I'd sent her running, I was injured and had to shift to save myself.

While I still hadn't told her exactly what I was, I'd come clean to her about the fact that my beast had met her Fated in the entire moondamned Blackwell Quad out in those woods.

I'd needed someone I wasn't related to by blood or boyfriend to discuss it with, and Mallory was conveniently well-versed in this topic. She and Allen were Fated, which had struck their beasts like lightning the instant that Mallory had gathered the courage to shift into her cat form in front of Allen's wolf several months into their relationship.

She was, predictably, both thrilled that I'd also joined this special club of shifter rarities and horrified that my experience had been so completely tarnished.

"My beast doesn't help the situation," I replied. "I just have to remind her of the facts, and usually she settles."

With all the polite acceptance of a hungry cat being told it's not dinnertime yet. She was growing more difficult by the day.

"I am astonished, frankly," Mallory said. "And thoroughly impressed by you. Not that I disagree with how you're feeling about all of this, given those boys' terrible behavior those last weeks of school. But the pull to a Moon-blessed mate is *strong*, Avery, even without a bond, and you've been in such close proximity to them for a *month*. I was preparing myself to come back from Palm Beach and find you fully bonded after the first Full Moon."

That first Full Moon had fallen on a Saturday two weeks into camp, and since Saturday was the day we were allowed to leave camp to do whatever we wanted, I'd spent it at home with my dads and Ian.

Couldn't accidentally trip and fall into a bonding while tucked safely inside my house with my family, watching cult documentaries for hours.

There might've been a basilisk in our tree at one point, but I'd chosen to ignore that.

"They were very pushy the first few days," I admitted. "But then there were some, uh, incidents, and they've been on better behavior since then."

I couldn't help a furtive glance over the rim of my fruity drink to the other side of the bar, where Heath, Elijah, Wyatt, and Aiden were holding court.

It'd been too much to hope that they'd choose to spend our Saturday liberty at one of the dozens of other bars or clubs on this strip, which I'd learned was one of the shifter community's nightlife hotspots, but no. They were never far.

There was Wyatt, dressed in a white V-neck T-shirt that clung to his chest and left nothing at all to the imagination with respect to his chiseled pecs, sculpted arms, and tattoos. He leaned back in his chair and pressed a beer bottle to his lips, smirking when he caught me looking.

Then there was Aiden, drinking amber liquor from a glass while wearing perfectly tailored jeans and a dress shirt. The chocolate waves of his hair had grown longer over the course of the summer, one lock flopping over the side of his glasses as he sipped his drink with a slutty flex of forearm. He was engaged in conversation with a guy I recognized from the faculty in the college's History Department.

At the bar, Elijah was chatting happily with the proprietor of this brewery, an older man in a flannel shirt with a white towel draped over his shoulder as he slung drinks with expert hands. Elijah wore his usual linen shirt, unbuttoned to reveal an unholy amount of chest and his snake tattoo, and tight, ripped jeans that probably did great things for his ass, but I wouldn't know because I hadn't looked.

And, of course, there was Heath, sandy-blond hair styled like a magazine model's, perfect pectorals snug in his T-shirt, jeans molded to his thick thighs. He was pretending to listen to whatever Mark Ellison, the friendly jaguar, was saying to him while he was actually watching my every twitch. I glared at him over my drink, and he didn't flinch. No, his expression remained as stoic and intense as ever, with only the flash of golden starbursts in his eyes betraying the fact that he was affected by my ire at all.

Mallory arched a fiery brow. "Incidents? Those are four Prime animals being denied their Fated. It's a miracle the camp is still standing."

"So I'm told," I muttered.

As incensed as I'd been at Ward for sticking me with the men I so desperately wished to keep my distance from, he hadn't been wrong about it settling everyone down.

I'd kept my mouth shut and my focus only on training harder, and for the most part, the guys had left me to it. They knew as well as I did that Ward had given them a boon they didn't fucking deserve, and they'd decided to accept their good fortune and not push me any more than they already had.

Being around them hadn't exactly gotten easier, but I'd at least grown used to the intense emotions their presence evoked.

It was clear they were still taking turns sleeping outside my cabin in animal form, but they'd been sneakier about it. Sometimes I caught a whiff of wolf or bear on the first breeze I encountered when I stepped outside. Once, I'd spotted Aiden's jaguar slinking through the trees behind my cabin, taking the long way to breakfast. A few days ago,

George had slithered out the door a few minutes after I woke up, and I'd watched in fascination as he and the basilisk disappeared into the forest together.

On our morning runs through the woods, the guys jogged in silence behind me, keeping just enough distance between us that I couldn't hiss at them about being in my space.

During quad-focused activities, Heath made an effort to treat me like a soldier, and I made an effort to give him the obedience and respect I would've given any decent leader of my unit. The bullshit between all of us had to be left off the battlefield, or someone was going to get their soul devoured by a wraith.

I ate my meals with Ian and Brody except when Cash forced me to the Guardian side of the chow hall. Then I'd reluctantly join my assigned quad. Somehow, Kellan and his quad would always end up seated on my other side, so those meals had been rife with uncomfortable silence and unre-strained aggression radiating from all around me.

Being attacked full-on by a basilisk had not put Kellan or the rest of his quad off the flirtatious attention they were determined to give me, but I suspected Ward had dressed them down in a separate meeting because there was no more touching or deliberate attempts to provoke Elijah or the others.

Couldn't say I was mad about it. I had no idea if Kellan had been truly serious that first night about his quad seeking a bond with a beast soul or if it was just bullshit male posturing between the two most powerful quads on the premises, and frankly, I didn't care.

That wasn't why I was at camp.

"So, this is the norm for the weekend that falls after curfew?" Ian asked the table, his blue eyes alight as he looked around the crowded bar. "A little silly if you ask me. It's not like people who live behind the warded walls of the shifter towns don't go out and about even under a New Moon."

A dozen or so more people wandered through the door, and I recognized them from the avian contingent at school. They were bright-eyed, dressed to kill, and laughing loudly amongst themselves.

"It's tradition," Allen said to Ian with a gregarious shrug. "It's taken generations to perfect the anti-wraith wards, so I imagine back in the day, there was reason to celebrate just being alive after a New Moon."

"And *we* are celebrating all of you being alive," Mallory said, pointing at me with her glass. "Since you are trying to make a career out of being outside the wards during curfew."

Ian snorted. "The accolades are unnecessary. They aren't letting us go on patrol until August, at the end of camp. So fucking lame."

It was, but the July patrols had apparently been a bust, so I couldn't be mad that we hadn't been allowed out. The gold shirt trainees, having already had a year of experience in the field, had been shipped off to Zone 12, which Kit informed us had been super active for June. The report was that a few swarmers had strayed into the zone, and Kellan's quad had killed a pair of small Rippers, but that had been it. Zone 12—marked yellow for July.

Kellan had bitched endlessly about how boring it'd been at breakfast yesterday morning.

Kit told us that it'd been that way across the entire region—quiet, hardly any wraith sightings at all. Chalk it up to things being more erratic than normal in a lunar eclipse year, move on, and be ready for the worst next time.

If I was being super honest with myself, our being forced to train another month before going out into the field was a good thing. Our *quintet* formation was a work in progress and hadn't flowed as easily as we'd all expected, used to being the best on the field as we were. The few times we'd gone all out against other quads in training, whether in human or beast form, our attack had been sluggish, hampered somehow by the quintet in a way I'd never felt in a quad.

It would just take some time to adjust, and we had until the August patrol to get our shit together.

"Cash is a bigger annoyance than the wraiths are at this point," I said with a wry smile.

Ian laughed. "The look on his face every time you slice up one of his prized Prime trainees. It never gets old."

"He can't ignore how badass you are forever, Avery," Mallory said, sticking her tiny nose in the air. "Isn't it strange how Prime males, the ones at the very top of our society, are the *most* threatened by powerful females?"

I didn't think it was strange at all, but I was a whole lot more cynical and jaded than Mal.

"It is a bit silly," Allen agreed. "A guy who is supposedly the best Guardian in his year has a problem with a competent female fighter, but I, merely an ordinary wolf, think it's awesome we finally have a maybe-Prime female wandering the campus." He winked at me, and I returned it with a mysterious smile. "Joon thinks you're totally awesome too," Allen went on, flapping a hand in Joon's general direction. At the moment, he had his tongue down his lady's throat. "And so do Brody and Nico, obviously."

I nodded absently, my attention snagging on one of the girls from the avian group. She was gorgeous—willowy figure, long pink hair, a tiny diamond stud in her nose, and dozens of bracelets adorning her slender wrists.

And she was staring at Elijah like she knew what his cock tasted like.

My beast rose and prowled her cage.

"Damn, Aves," Ian said, shivering dramatically. "What's got your fur in a twist?"

"Nothing." I flashed my tiger the image of Elijah walking into our shared class last semester and ignoring the shit out of me.

She returned the memory of a large, violent, terrifying serpent monster attempting to destroy a griffin for touching me and then his naked human body kneeling at my feet afterward.

Quit that, or I'm never letting you out again.

Elijah turned around in his seat at the bar and pinned me with his yellow gaze, a dark brow raised in question. My tiger's agitation must have called to the basilisk.

Inconvenient.

I should've ignored him, but instead I looked pointedly at the beautiful pink-haired girl still staring at Elijah with bedroom eyes. He glanced her way, and then his mischievous smile fell away, replaced with a rigid jaw and the barest hint of guilt.

The tiger let out a menacing growl.

I cracked my neck. *Nope, we are having a nice time with our friends.*

Another boisterous group of Proteus students trickled in through the front doors, interrupting my fight with my beast.

"Oh, gross," Mallory said. "It's Callista and her flock of harpies."

It sure was. A gaggle of latent princesses from the rising

senior class flounced toward the bar, a few burly guys in tow. Callista wore a skin-tight black bandage dress that did amazing things for her ass, and she'd pulled her dark hair into a sleek ponytail. She had on her usual war paint—smoky eyes and deep maroon lipstick.

Her friends crowded the bar, but she homed in on Wyatt immediately, slinking in his direction, a sexy gazelle offering a tantalizing meal to a starving bear.

Wyatt was still lounging in his chair next to Heath, a lazy prince on his throne, when Callista appeared next to him. His smirk slid right off his face, replaced by the same damn guilty look Elijah had worn.

The image of the two of them at the ball assaulted me yet again.

Callista, humping Wyatt's thigh.

Wyatt's hands all over her body.

Her lips on his skin.

His crazed smile during it all.

It took everything I had to keep the fur from blossoming on my skin.

I shoved my chair away from the table and got to my feet. "I'll be right back," I announced. "I'm just going to get some air."

Mallory patted my hand but didn't argue. The whole table could probably feel the beast aggression leaking from my pores.

I shoved through the door and stalked past the bouncer into the large parking lot that separated the building from the street. The warm night air chased away the goose bumps that'd appeared on my skin minutes earlier, which had definitely been a reaction to the bar's air conditioning and not the thought of Wyatt and Elijah fucking other girls.

My destination was my RAV-4, parked near the street,

where I intended to listen to exactly two Celine Dion songs to recenter myself and my beast before going back inside. The tiger needed to be reminded once again that we didn't care who any of the assholes the Moon had tried to force on us had fucked once upon a time.

The fact that I *still* had to fight these feelings, even after a month of functioning behind carefully constructed walls, made me want to stand here in the middle of the parking lot and scream for a minute straight.

I was ten yards from my car when a bright red BMW came roaring down the street and then whipped a high-speed turn into the parking lot. Headlights lit me up, and I darted out of the way, smashing myself up against the back of a Jeep.

The driver laid on the horn as the car screeched to a stop in front of me, and then a piercing squeal erupted from the car's passenger window.

"It's Avery!"

"By the Moon's tits, C," said another female voice, this one a huskier rasp, "that almost shattered my eardrum."

I shoved off the Jeep, strode to the car, and bent down to peer through the open passenger window. *"Clara?"*

17

AVERY

Clara's smile was brilliant as she gave me the most enthusiastic wave I'd ever received. "Hi, Avery! How are you?"

"I'm good," I replied slowly as I took in the car's dark interior. Clara was perched on the cream leather of the passenger seat, dressed in a lacy camisole and trendy dark jeans. Another teenage girl sat behind the wheel, this one wearing a vintage Nirvana T-shirt that had somehow been cut into a flattering crop top. She had auburn hair and familiar bright green eyes. "What in the world are you doing here?" I asked.

Clara held up her phone. A location-sharing app was on the screen. "Stalking my brothers, of course."

"Stalking your brothers," I repeated dumbly. "Um, why?"

The redhead leaned over the center console. "So this is Avery, huh? *The* Avery who sliced Paul Blankenship into ribbons?"

Clara beamed at me with pride. "Yep."

"Badass," the redhead said, nodding her approval. "That

guy is such a prick. Why haven't you sic'd her on the Nelsons, C?"

"Avery is not an assassin for hire, Willow. She's going to be a *Guardian*."

"Hey," I said, attempting a redirect. "Why are you stalking your brothers to a bar you aren't old enough to get into, Clara? Are you in trouble again?"

"Oh, no," she said quickly, waving a dismissive hand. "It's just—"

"Willow!"

A very angry bear was marching toward the car.

"Ah, fuck," Willow huffed, slumping behind the wheel.

Wyatt appeared at the driver's side window, his face livid. "What are you doing here, Willow?"

She raised her chin and tossed a casual arm over the steering wheel. "None of your business."

He gripped the window ledge and leaned in, narrowing his eyes at what he saw in the backseat. "*Winona?* Are you fucking serious right now?"

Now that he mentioned it, there was, in fact, an even younger teenage girl in the backseat. She had strawberry blonde hair that hung in stick-straight sheets around her face, a contrast to her sister's—because yes, these had to be Wyatt's sisters—wild red curls.

"Whatever, Wyatt," Winona drawled. "I'm allowed to be in the car with Willow in a parking lot."

"Don't bullshit me," he snapped. "You three were going to sneak into the bar. How were you planning to manage that?"

Willow held up what looked like her driver's license. "By walking through the front door with ye olde fake ID, obviously," she replied, giving it a flick.

He made a grab for it, but she snatched it away. "Willow,

for the love of the fucking Moon," he growled. "I expect this from you, but Winona is *fifteen*."

"Like you didn't get up to way worse stuff when you were my age," Winona said indignantly. "I remember when Mom caught you sneaking two half-naked girls and a bong into the pool house on Christmas Eve."

Wyatt heaved a long-suffering sigh, and his eyes met mine over the top of Willow's head, frustration and guilt brewing in his gaze. He probably came out here looking for me, since I'd left the bar after the lovely reminder of his transgressions with Callista.

I locked the cage on my beast and returned his look with stone-cold nothingness.

"Our plans have changed anyway," Willow announced. "Go away, Wyatt. We want to hang out with Avery."

Wyatt squinted at her. "Why?"

"It's girl talk!" Clara said brightly. "We're not going into the bar. You can tell my brothers we're just going to hang out with Avery for a minute, since I haven't seen her at all since *that night*, you know?" She gave him a sad little look and wrung her hands. "Please? Then we'll go back to Gale Manor. *Promise*."

Wyatt was no match for the big pleading eyes of the angel among the little devils in the car. "Fine. But if I catch you three anywhere near a bar or club on this street, I will be escorting you home to explain yourselves to Mom." He looked at Clara. "And you will get to explain yourself to Heath. He's not in the mood, I promise you."

"Yes, yes, we get it," Willow said, shooing him away from the car. "Go waste your money on beer that won't get you drunk and let the girls paw at you or whatever it is you like to do in bars."

He clenched his jaw and straightened his posture. He

sent one last dark look my way. "I want to talk to you later, Wildcat."

As if my stare could get any more glacial.

"She doesn't want to talk to you!" Winona hollered from the back.

I pointed at her. "What she said."

"I mean it," he growled.

I opened the car door, slid into the backseat next to Winona, then slammed the door.

Willow cackled. "Bye-bye, big brother."

She cranked the wheel and hit the gas.

I fumbled for my seat belt and then clicked it into place right as Willow peeled out of the parking lot.

I WAS BEGINNING TO REGRET MY SPLIT-SECOND DECISION TO jump into a small sports car driven by a seventeen-year-old just to avoid Wyatt when Willow finally slowed to a normal speed. She paused for an appropriate amount of time at a stop sign, and then we pulled onto a quieter street that was lined by quaint antique stores and coffee shops that'd long since closed for the night.

Clara turned around in her seat to grin at me. "This is nice. We never get to hang out."

"Clara," I said, giving her a pointed look. "Why are you guys stalking your brothers?"

"Because they've been acting weird," Winona said. "All four of them have been staying at our house, you know. They were there for weeks before you guys all went to camp, and they've been back on some of your nights off. We're just *investigating*."

"Weird how?" I asked.

"Well, um...." Clara chewed her lip, considering her next words. "You remember how my dads are making me bond soon?"

"Yes," I replied darkly. "Have you had more bad dates? Do you need to come stay in my cabin? I have an extra bed, and I'm sure Ward would okay it. He owes me."

"That's *so* nice of you to offer," Clara gushed, though she couldn't quite hide the little wrinkle of her nose. Not a camp girl, got it. "But no, thank you. I've been staying at Willow's house, and the quad that I'm, um, *promised* to is in Europe all summer."

"What?" I snapped. "Your parents already found the quad they're going to force on you?"

"Yes, and they suck huge bear testicles," Willow offered helpfully. "Heath and Aiden caught them talking about knocking Clara around if she gets out of line."

My hand jerked like I was going to reach for my swords, but those were stowed safely in my car. "Did Heath or Aiden happen to knock *them* around after that?"

Clara gave me a sad smile. "They would if they could, Avery. But you have to understand, my dad, Holden, is *very* powerful. He's even more powerful than Heath, and Heath's the most dominant Alpha wolf in the South."

"Heath hasn't fought my dad," I muttered as I contemplated climbing through Holden Blackwell's window with my blades.

"They did leave the snake with you, C," Willow pointed out. "He kept those Nelson bastards away for the rest of the school year, and now they're across the ocean, thank the Moon."

"That's where George was last semester?" I asked Clara, frowning. "With you?"

She nodded, and her chest puffed with pride. "He and I

are friends now. After all the, um, suffocating of my enemies and stuff. The Nelson boys stopped trying to take me on dates because George wouldn't leave my side, and he wasn't very nice to them."

A wisp of relief left my body.

Elijah hadn't kept George away from me last semester. Not maliciously.

George had been out on a *job*.

"Anyway," Clara said. "My brothers made a plan to get me out of this whole mess. They're really *trying*, Avery." She bit her lip again. "At least, they *were*."

"Because that *plan*," Willow added, "involved them finding the right girl for their bond, and fast."

Understanding dawned.

We had a purpose when we did what we did, but we were very wrong in assuming you couldn't be part of it, Elijah's silky voice whispered in my mind.

We had reasons, sweetheart. Reasons to seek what we thought was a guarantee of power and stability in our bond, and to do it quickly, Aiden's imperious voice added.

Dread began a slow creep through my veins.

Willow shook her head ruefully. "The literal *second* the word got out that they were truly in the market for their central, everyone in school talked about it non-fucking-stop for months."

"And that's what we're *investigating*," Winona said in a conspiratorial whisper. "It was public knowledge, and they seemed like they were really going to do it, but then they just... quit."

"They didn't go on a single date the entire month they were at the Gales' this summer," Clara went on. "They were always shut up together in Wyatt's suite. Talking."

"Plotting," Winona said.

"Brooding," Willow added. "And they won't tell us shit."

I sucked in a deep breath, my fingernails digging into my denim-covered thighs. "Clara, this plan to save you involved your brothers growing their power," I stated, my throat dry as a fucking desert.

The kind of power they thought they could get through a bond with a latent female from a Prime shifter line.

She nodded sadly. "Heath plans to formally challenge my dad for custody of me before I turn seventeen in October because my parents are planning to make me bond with the Nelson Quad at the first Full Moon after my birthday. He thinks he'll lose without a bond, Avery. Maybe even... *die*."

It was a punch right to the gut. My chest tightened. My tiger let out a guttural snarl and shoved at her cage.

Heath's voice echoed in my head.

If I'm wrong, I might die for it, but I won't ask my brother and my best friends to sacrifice for me anymore.

"When did this happen, Clara?" I asked softly. "When did your dads secure the deal for your bond?"

"Oh, um." She tapped her lip with a polished pink fingernail. "It was when Aiden and Heath were at home for spring break."

The fist lodged in my gut twisted. Dread ignited into something like rage.

Something like *despair*.

Willow pulled the car back onto the brightly lit street with all the bars and clubs, completing our circuit. "But like we said," she went on, "they must've changed their plan, but they aren't telling us anything."

Winona side-eyed me like only a fifteen-year-old could. "It kind of seemed like Wyatt was pretty into Avery. Like *pathetically* into her."

"Oh, they're totally into Avery," Clara announced. "All four of them. It was obvious from the moment I met her."

"What the fuck?" Willow barked, her green eyes flashing as she glanced at me through the rearview mirror. "Those four had this beautiful badass lady right in front of them that they *all* agreed on—which is a fucking miracle—and they haven't locked her down? Idiots."

"Well, the problem is—wait, is it okay to tell them, Avery? About, um, *you know what?*"

"I have a beast," I said distractedly. My attention was entirely on containing my tiger's bad attitude. It was a small car, and I didn't want to scare the girls.

"Ah," Willow said. "Well damn, C. I should be nicer to my brother. He was going to give up his love so Heath was on sure footing when he challenged your dad."

"Maybe they changed their mind?" Clara mused. "Maybe Heath decided he could still gain enough power in a bond with Avery to give him a chance against my dad? Aiden was spending a lot of time in the library before they went to camp. I bet he was researching bonding theory. That's totally something he'd do." She turned around in her seat to grin at me again. "Or maybe they're all just in love."

"It's not that," I said through gritted teeth.

Willow turned back into the parking lot where they'd picked me up. The cars had thinned out considerably. It was getting late.

Just as she was about to pull into a parking spot, Brody burst out of the bar and tore through the lot at top speed, running straight for my car.

Panic was etched into every line of his pretty face.

"Stop!" I cried.

Willow hit the brakes. I rolled down my window and stuck my head out. "Brody!"

"Oh, Avery, thank the Moon," he huffed, skidding to a stop in front of my window. "It's Ian. He's picked a fight with Kace Mahoney."

Clara gasped, and my stomach plummeted through the floor of the car.

Kace Mahoney. The asshole Alpha wolf who'd attacked me in the arena last semester when he was supposed to be my teammate.

The guy who ripped a chunk out of my shoulder and left me to experience a simulated soul death under the ministrations of a Giant wraith conjured by the SWIM.

The guy whose trio Ward had tossed out of the Guardians after that incident.

I could only stare at Brody in horror. "W-What?"

His chest heaved, and words began tumbling from his mouth. "He and I snuck out to the back of the bar and into the employee parking lot to, uh, you know...." He forced a sheepish grin, and I waved an impatient hand. "But then Kace and that panther who's in his trio—Drew, I think?—they came out back with a girl, who I guess works in the bar, like they were going to go home with her, but then Ian walked right up to Kace and punched him in the face—"

"Damn it all to hell," I groaned.

"—and luckily Drew just laughed and told him to have fun and took off with the girl, but I don't think Kace expected Ian to be as good at fighting in human form as he is, and it's getting really bloody back there. He's going to lose it soon, Avery."

Lose it. As in let his wolf out.

While Ian could certainly hang with an asshole like Kace as a man, Kace's wolf would kill Ian, and there would be no justice under shifter law if Ian started it.

"Where the fuck are the rest of our friends?" I growled.

He tossed his hands into the air. "Nico, Joon, and Ash had all left already with girls they picked up in the bar. Allen and Mallory ran back there when I came out here to look for you, but you know Allen's wolf can't do anything against an Alpha."

No, he sure fucking couldn't.

"Get Heath," I said without hesitation. I'd dispensed with my pride—the situation was too fucking dire. "I'll meet you out back."

He didn't need to be told twice. He sprinted back toward the bar.

"Willow, back parking lot, and step on it," I barked.

She was already whipping the car around before I could finish my command. She floored it, and we were around the block and turning into the bar's nearly deserted employee parking lot within thirty seconds.

"Ian is Avery's brother," Clara informed her friends, her tone as panicked as I felt. "He's a fox! What was he thinking, picking a fight with an Alpha?"

It was a good fucking question.

As Willow screeched to a stop in front of the dumpsters, I had five seconds to take in the scene before me:

Ian, illuminated by the dim moonlight and what little security lighting the bar had installed in the lot. He was bleeding from his nose and a cut on his temple, and one of his eyes had swollen shut. The collar of his T-shirt had been ripped, and he was favoring his right side like something was broken.

Kace Mahoney, standing a few feet from Ian. His white hair was matted with blood that gushed down into his eyes, one of his arms hung at an awkward angle, and his jeans were caked with dust and gravel. His gray eyes had gone molten, and his normally pale skin was flushed with rage.

Allen and Mallory stood off to the side, clutching each other, helpless to intervene.

Ian ducked a swing from Kace's good arm, laughing like a maniac. He popped up, quick and spry despite whatever was broken, and he kicked Kace between the legs before launching a punch straight into his face.

Kace buckled, bellowing with rage. "I'll fucking kill you, Baxter, just like I should've killed your bitch sister!"

White fur sprouted on his arms.

Ian staggered. That last move had taken it out of him after all.

I threw open the car door, launched myself out, and hit the pavement at a run.

Kace snarled, and then his large white wolf burst from his body, his maw gaping, those huge wolf teeth bloody and aimed for Ian's neck.

I leapt into the air, hurdling Ian as he disappeared. His silver fox streaked away from the pile of clothes left behind on the ground.

My beast, already so close to the surface, broke through her chains with a murderous roar.

And she met that bastard Mahoney head-on.

18

AIDEN

I chased Heath down the staff hallway leading to the bar's employee parking lot. Wyatt was hot on my heels, Elijah seconds behind him after he stopped to inform Bernard, the bar's proprietor and friend of his uncle's, to lock the door and keep everyone out of the back.

One minute ago, the four of us had been sitting around our table, drinking booze that wouldn't get us drunk and brooding like a bunch of sad assholes because our mate had stormed out of the bar. Wyatt's previous antics with Callista had come back to bite us all once again, as well as, apparently, a brief fling Elijah had with one of the avian girls months before any of us had even *met* Avery.

Wyatt's attempt at damage control had gone as well as expected, and then Avery had left the premises entirely, allegedly out on a joy ride with *our sisters*, who had no business being in this particular part of town at this hour.

So when a panicked Brody ran up to our table, grabbed Heath by the shirt, and told him that Kace Mahoney was probably about to kill Ian behind the bar and that Brody had sent Avery back there to stop him?

We were on our feet and sprinting to the back without another word.

The moment Heath shoved through the heavy exit door, the terrifying roar of a tiger blasted through the parking lot like a detonating bomb.

We breached the first and only line of cars just in time to witness our mate's gorgeous beast leaping into the air, her shredded clothing falling to the ground behind her.

Mahoney—the bastard who'd injured Avery right in front of us in the arena while we could only stand there, helpless, murderously angry, and utterly confused as to why seeing this girl hurt affected us so intensely—had two seconds to comprehend that the girl he'd shamelessly attacked during training had just shifted into a very large and very powerful silver tiger.

And that she was about to tear him apart.

The wolf's gray eyes went comically wide before the tiger slammed into him, knocking him out of the air and rolling him across the asphalt like a furry log.

"Perimeter," Heath barked.

We fanned out, each of us taking up a post around the lot so that we could collectively cover all entrances and exits. Avery's friend Mallory and her wolf mate stood nearby, both watching with wide eyes and slack jaws as our beautiful tiger tore a huge chunk of flesh from Kace's shoulder. Brody jogged over to them, relief evident on his face. He didn't appear surprised—only awed—by Avery's beast, but then he must've known what she was or else he wouldn't have sent her up against an Alpha wolf.

The doors of the red BMW parked haphazardly in front of the lot's entrance opened and ejected Willow, Winona, and Clara, all three of them gaping at the sight in front of them.

Kace recovered from his shock and scrambled to his feet. With a vicious snarl, he lunged, teeth aimed for Avery's throat.

He wasn't going for submission. He was trying to kill her.

My jaguar growled in my chest.

Avery swatted the wolf's head away with her big paw, raking her claws through his flesh as she did. That rang Kace's bell hard, and he staggered away from her.

"Holy fucking shit," Willow hissed.

"What. Is. *Happening?*" Winona stage-whispered, her blue eyes saucers as she blinked at the scene.

"She's *beautiful*," Clara added.

A small silver fox scurried up to Clara. She gasped with delight and picked him up, squeezing him to her chest like a teddy bear.

So there was Ian. The fox was bleeding in a few places, but he appeared to be in one piece.

His boyfriend glowered at him from across the parking lot.

Clara turned her wide eyes on me. "Aiden! Is this what you guys have been hiding? Look at Avery! She's even bigger than your jaguar."

Speaking of my jaguar, he was greatly testing my control. An enemy beast was attacking our mate, and the drive to be in battle beside her was all-consuming.

By the look of the violently glowing eyes of the rest of my quad, they were in the same boat.

But we wouldn't intervene. Both beasts and men knew that our mate could hold her own in this fight, and it was her right to protect her brother and avenge the assault Mahoney had perpetrated against her in the arena.

I cleared my throat. "She's bigger than me by mass. Our beasts' frames are about the same size."

Kace lunged for Avery again, this time getting his teeth into her flank. She snarled and whipped her powerful body around, shaking the wolf loose. Kace flopped to the ground, rolled, and launched himself at her again, snapping and snarling and pumping suffocating pheromones into the air designed to smother a weaker shifter into quivering submission.

My mate hissed her displeasure, rearing up to intercept the wolf's attack.

She batted him with her paws, rending more flesh with every swipe. The wolf's eyes liquified into blazing silver, blood and saliva flying from his jaws as his attack became frenzied, lunging and snapping at the tiger's throat with reckless abandon.

"He's lost it," I barked at Heath.

Lost to the beast. No humanity left at the controls.

"I know," Heath replied. His voice was calm, but his shoulders were practically in his ears and his jaw was rigid enough to break his teeth. "I can feel it."

Across the way, Elijah was still as a statue, his knuckles as white as the wolf's fur. Wyatt loomed near our sisters, his eyes blazing red with the rage of his bear.

Kace managed to get his teeth into Avery's shoulder, *just* below her throat, and she roared in outrage. She reared up again and shoved him to the ground, using her larger mass to pin him down. She tore into the flesh of his chest with her claws, and she used her advantage to sink her teeth into his throat. With those strong deadly jaws and her muscular neck, the tiger shook the wolf violently.

The crack of his spine echoed through the parking lot.

Heath and I exchanged a look. Wyatt met my gaze next, and finally Elijah, the vertical slit pupils of the basilisk staring back at me.

We were all on the same page.

The wolf would not be leaving this parking lot alive. There were scant few people on this planet with whom the knowledge of Avery's beast was safe, and Kace Mahoney was not one of them.

His father, Arthur Mahoney, regularly did business with my dad.

The tiger wrenched her head away from the wolf, taking a huge chunk of his throat with her. She spat it on the pavement and unleashed a growl that sent a shiver down my spine.

Blood dripped from her mouth and stained her beautiful fur. She stared at Kace where he lay on the ground, blood pooling around his upper body, his abdomen heaving with labored breaths.

If we left him long enough, his beast might be able to heal. Avery hadn't taken his whole throat—the killing blow of most big cats.

Intelligent blue eyes took in each of the spectators surrounding her. Finally, she landed on Heath. There was a question there, maybe even a plea.

"Aiden," he said softly. "Finish it."

Before he'd even finished saying my name, I was striding forward, yanking my shirt off as I went, followed by my glasses, which I shoved in my pocket. My shoes were next, and finally my pants.

My body hardly registered the sharp pinch of the shift. My jaguar flowed more effortlessly from my body than ever before, the tiger's presence a shining beacon calling him forward.

With an inhuman growl, the wolf rolled and began to climb to his feet. Blood dripped from his neck and his mouth, his insane silver eyes focused only on Avery.

He'd dug deep, lost in his beast, and he was going to attack her again.

Animal instinct melded with the very human need to protect Avery from harm, and I shot forward, sprinting on powerful feline legs toward the wolf.

With no hesitation, I struck, sinking my teeth into the back of the wolf's skull and crushing it.

Killing him instantly.

"By the Moon," Clara whispered.

Later, I'd probably be horrified to have killed another shifter in front of my little sister, but right now, I only had eyes for my mate. She stood over the wolf's body, those luminous blue eyes blinking at me.

I slinked over to her, purring loudly. She lifted her chin with a haughty little snort, but she didn't move away. I rubbed my head along her soft neck and then against her cheek. She rumbled a noise, not quite a growl, and not threatening enough for my jaguar to even consider stopping what he was doing.

I licked her face.

She snapped her teeth at me.

I nuzzled her neck and purred some more.

"All right," Heath said, striding over to us. He gave my flank a grateful pat, and then he corralled our tiger with a burst of Alpha dominance and a few loving strokes along her furry forehead. "You were fantastic, Killer. You protected your brother and made quick work of an Alpha wolf lost completely to the beast. And you made it look easy."

She huffed, but she couldn't hide the tiger's preen.

Elijah, looking only slightly less vexed, appeared on her other side. "Dove, you are viciously magnificent," he said, running a hand along her back.

Wyatt joined us, giving my head a rub before he stole

some ear scratches from the tiger. "That's our girl, Wildcat. What a fucking show."

She let them pet her for exactly three seconds before she shook them off. She growled, baring sharp teeth, and extricated herself from their huddle. With a shake of her silver fur, the tiger receded, and a gloriously naked Avery rose in her place.

My quadmates stared unabashedly at our mate's strong, nude body, and I was no different, even in beast form. Her long blonde hair hung around her shoulders in gentle waves. We got a glimpse of perky, perfect breasts before she crossed her arms over them. The soft light from the stars and waxing crescent Moon above caressed her curves and the slight grooves in her toned stomach, which led to a trimmed patch of blonde hair between her long, bare legs. She was all silky skin and lean muscles, and the image would be branded onto my brain for the rest of my life.

She sucked in a deep, calming breath. The beast would be riding her hard after a fight like this.

I had to stow that thought before it made me insane.

"Shit," she said.

She looked around the parking lot at the small group of friends and family that were now in on her greatest secret. The girls were still gaping at her. Brody had averted his eyes because she was basically his sister, and Allen had done the same because he didn't have a death wish.

"*Shit,*" she said again.

I padded over to her and nuzzled her again.

She smelled like blood and jasmine and beastly violence and primal *need*.

"Damn it, Aiden," she said. She exhaled another shaky breath and rubbed my neck, and I purred like a buzzsaw at my mate's hands on my fur. She shook her head ruefully, then she pushed me away. "Okay, that's enough out of you."

"Avery." Heath's gaze on her was searing, ignited by the obsession that had consumed us all. "Don't worry about any of this, okay? I'll report to the Council that Mahoney challenged Aiden over some bullshit that happened during Guardian training last semester, and their beasts fought to the death, as is their right. The wolf's wounds are consistent with those from a Prime feline. No one will know the difference between tiger and jaguar, and the killing blow to the skull rather than the neck is consistent with the jaguar. You were never here."

She jerked a nod. "Thank you. He really was trying to kill Ian, so I had no choice."

"I know, Killer. You did the right thing."

Mallory sidled up to her. "Hey there, friend of mine. Quite a *situation* you have going on there. I mean, I'd have put my money on *big cat*, especially after the power your girl used to send *my cat* running through the woods during the whole campus breach thing, but *damn*. We can talk about it all later, after you've, uh, come down from all of this, but at the moment, how about I heal some of these gashes?"

"Do it," Heath said. Avery and Mallory both gave him a flat stare. "Please," he added.

He put his cell phone to his ear and wandered out of earshot, and Mallory began running her fingertips over the flesh wounds in Avery's shoulder and thigh. The soft blue glow of Moon magic, stored like a battery by shifters with a competent healing affinity, bathed my mate's wounds and unclenched the knot in my stomach.

While Mallory worked, Clara trotted up, fox Ian still in her arms. "You were amazing, Avery! I can't even believe this —you could've ended Paul Blankenship's lion with, like, two swipes of your paw and a scary roar! But instead you had to use your swords, and you were amazing then, too, don't get me wrong! I mean, I *get* why you aren't open about your beautiful tiger, I really do, but it's such a shame. People are backwards and stupid about females sometimes."

With one last burst of my will, I forced the jaguar back inside, and he was not happy to go. I shook out my limbs and pinned my sister with a grave look. "Clara, do you understand why no one can know about Avery's beast? *Especially* Dad?"

She paled. "Oh. Yeah, definitely. Not a word from me. I promise."

Avery's ethereal gaze dipped down my naked body for a fraction of a second, setting every nerve I had on fucking fire, before she focused firmly on my face. Her eyes narrowed, studying me for a beat, and then she turned her attention to the fox in Clara's arms.

She pointed at him. "I see you, Ian Baxter. You think you're avoiding being yelled at by me and by your boyfriend, who you scared half to death, by hiding behind your cute little fox face. You are in for a rude awakening."

His whiskers twitched, and then he buried his head in Clara's shirt.

Brody walked over to Clara and held out his arms. "I will take him, please."

"Sorry," she whispered to the fox, and then she handed him over.

Brody clutched Ian to his chest and walked away, presumably so they could have a private chat.

Elijah wandered closer to Avery, bringing the chill of the basilisk with him. He chucked my clothes at me and then produced a T-shirt and offered it to Avery. "Here you go, Dove. Courtesy of Willow."

Willow waved jovially from where she stood next to her car, clad in only a sports bra and jeans. Winona lounged against the door next to her, looking like a fifteen-year-old who'd just seen something extremely impressive but didn't want to let on that she was impressed.

Avery pulled the T-shirt over her head, which only hit her mid-stomach. She cracked her neck and rolled her shoulders, agitation seeping from her every pore, but she managed a smile and a wave for Willow.

Elijah shucked his own shirt, and Avery tried but failed to smother a tiny moan at the sight of his naked torso.

"Fuck," she swore, snatching the shirt from Elijah's hands and tying it around her waist. "I mean, thanks, Elijah."

"You're very welcome, love."

"Don't call me that."

He grinned. "Okay."

Mallory cleared her throat and stepped away from Avery. "Finished. These should be fully healed tomorrow, so take it easy until then." She gave Avery's outfit a quick once over, her nose wrinkling. "I have some clothes in my car out front. How about I go grab you something and meet you in the bathroom so you can look less like you just shifted and brawled in a parking lot?"

Avery chewed her lip and shifted her weight from foot to foot. I bit off a growl at the fact that her feet were bare against the dirty asphalt.

"Go ahead, Dove," Elijah said. "Wyatt ducked inside to update Bernard on the situation. He'll keep everyone out of the back."

She sighed. "Okay. Mal, I'll meet you in there."

Mallory ran off, her still-stunned mate in tow, and Elijah went to help Heath.

Avery glanced at me one more time, her beast still peeking through her eyes. "Thank you, Aiden," she said softly. "I would've done it, but I'm glad I didn't have to."

She was so strong, so fucking beautiful, and it hurt so much.

"You're welcome, sweetheart. I would do it again a thousand times to keep you safe."

She managed a nod before she hurried away and disappeared inside.

And my world was dark again.

19

AVERY

I leaned over the sink in the bar's employee bathroom and splashed water on my face for the fourth time. My tiger paced her cage, testing my control. The aggression, the untamed energy, and the *need* had not abated even a little bit, no matter how many times I'd drenched myself.

The beast was there in my reflection, in my glowing eyes and in my flushed face. Even my hair looked like it was standing on end, cascading in wild waves down the back of my borrowed T-shirt.

Mallory's search through her car had turned up a black cotton skirt that hit me at mid-thigh and a pair of Converse sneakers that were half a size too small. I had no panties or bra on, but that was the least of my problems. I needed to sneak through the bar, which would hopefully be much less crowded than it'd been a few hours ago, and get to my car out front, where Mallory waited with my purse and hopefully my brother, who had better be in human form, fully clothed, and ready with an apology for his reckless behavior.

And then I needed to get the hell out of here. Forty-five

minutes of driving, and I'd be home in my bed for one blissful night before I had to return to camp tomorrow evening. With any luck, my dad Joseph would have a fresh batch of his homemade sleeping tonic on hand because I needed to be knocked the fuck out.

Too many things had happened in the past hour. Too many thoughts, too many confusing feelings. I wanted off this emotional rollercoaster.

First the revelations about Heath's plan to save Clara.

Then I'd let my beast out, in fucking public, and killed another Prime. It hadn't been me who'd struck the killing blow, but I'd issued his death sentence all the same.

And now I was keyed up, debating whether to touch myself right here in this bathroom to take the edge off or ride home with Ian while stinking of violence and carnal lust. My entire body was a live wire. I'd heard it could be like this, but I'd never experienced it.

I'd been in a lot of fights. I'd killed before, many times. But fighting Kace wasn't like fighting wraiths. Those were warped, grotesque monsters that needed to be culled for the sake of public safety. It also wasn't like fighting in controlled combat drills or when I'd had to go up against shifted beasts with my swords.

This had been my tiger, unleashed in her true form, fighting beast to beast against another Prime animal. Kill or be killed. This was primal—a baser instinct engrained in those who carried a beast soul within our bodies.

With one last look at my flushed face in the mirror, I slipped out of the bathroom and into the hallway. It was quiet, a lone exposed bulb hanging from the ceiling, illuminating the bathroom door on one side and what appeared to be an office and a storeroom on the other. At one end of the hall was the exit to the employee parking lot, where Heath and Aiden would be concocting the story of Kace Mahoney's demise and selling it to the Council. The door at the other end led back into the main bar area.

I smoothed my skirt and started for the door to the bar. I didn't care to see the carnage in the back again, nor did I need to be around any of my not-mates in my current condition.

Especially because, despite what they'd done for me here tonight, for which I was truly grateful, I was once again really fucking mad at them.

As I neared the door, it cracked open, sending a sliver of the bar's orange-tinged light into the hallway.

Wyatt slipped through the crack and shut the door behind him. He shoved a few locks of his dark-red hair off his forehead and blew out a breath, and then his emerald gaze landed on me.

He froze, his brows lifting like he was surprised to find me standing here in the dim hallway in borrowed clothes with a raging beast simmering under my skin.

And then in an instant, the mood shifted.

Wyatt's nostrils flared and his eyes hooded. "Wildcat," he purred, taking one small step towards me. "You need something, don't you?"

I raised my chin and clenched my jaw, bracing against the caress of his beast and the scent of him—woodsy pine, fresh rain, cinnamon, *man*.

"Not from you," I said through gritted teeth.

He advanced on me, slowly, carefully, treating me like the wild animal I was. "Baby," he said softly, lifting a hand to gently stroke my cheek. "Your beast just fought another shifter damn near to the death. She's riding you hard right now, I can tell. There's no one left to fight, so you need to *fuck*." He grinned, showing me his perfect white teeth, and then his voice dropped to an inhuman register. "Use me."

I swatted his hand away. "No. You don't deserve that."

"You're right, I don't." He leaned in until we were almost nose to nose, and then he whispered, oh so softly, "But you do."

I sucked in a breath.

"You've been through so much, baby. Not just tonight, but the whole fucking year. All the bullshit at school, whatever happened to you that made you come to school in the first place, the attack in the woods, *us*...." He ran his fingers gently through my hair. "When was the last time someone really took care of you? You deserve to feel good."

He was right.

I *did* deserve that.

With a frustrated cry, I shoved him against the wall and pressed my forearm against his throat like it was my blade. "Fine," I growled in his face. "But you don't get to come. Only me."

"*Fuck*," he rasped, his eyes lighting up like Christmas. "Anything you want, Wildcat. Anything you fucking want."

I leaned in, pressing my arm harder against his throat, which brought the rest of my body flush against his. He was scorching underneath me, his muscles taut, his rock-hard dick settled against the apex of my thighs, a preview of the treat that awaited me. "I mean it, Wyatt. This isn't for you."

His answering grin was hot and wicked. "I know, baby. I'll be good."

Groaning, I released him, and then I grabbed his hand and pulled him into the empty office down the hall. The room was small and dark, the only light streaming in through the lone window from the streetlamps outside.

Wyatt slammed the door and flicked the lock behind us,

and then I deposited him on a worn leather couch nearby. It was the only furniture in the room besides a neat wooden desk.

My beast, no longer in a rage, purred happily within me as I climbed on top of Wyatt and straddled his thick thighs, doing my damnedest to resist cataloging every line of his handsome face that I could make out in the low light.

He ghosted his hands up the backs of my legs and made his way under my skirt. "For the love of the fucking Moon, Avery," he growled, grabbing the globes of my ass roughly. "No panties? Are you kidding me?"

I unbuckled his belt and went to work on his zipper. "Destroyed them in the parking lot with the shift. You were there."

"Mmm, I was. My bear loves watching his mate shred Alphas like tissue paper."

"Not your mate," I grumbled. "What is with this fucking button on your jeans? Is this your new chastity belt? Too little, too late, Gale."

He chuckled, and the sound dripped down my spine like honey. "Let me, baby."

Those strong fingers made quick work of the button and then ripped his fly open. He freed his enormous erection from the confines of his boxers and stroked it slowly, his hot gaze never leaving my face.

I shoved his hand away and lowered my very bare, extremely wet pussy right on top of his dick, pressing it flat against his stomach. I rocked slowly, reveling in the easy slide and the delicious friction. Preparing this monster to fit inside me was priority number one.

"Wildcat," Wyatt groaned, his hands still on my ass as he helped me grind against him. "Holy fuck, that's good. Let me eat your cunt."

I stopped rocking, clamped him with my thighs, and grabbed him by the throat. "No," I hissed in his face. "You'd like that too much."

He barked a laugh, a manic look in his glowing eyes. He grasped the back of my head roughly and jerked my lips to his.

He kissed me like he owned me, taking exactly what he wanted with every press of his lips and every skillful exploration of his tongue. He held my head firmly, moving it to his liking, in control even though I was the one who had him pinned underneath me.

I let him do this for a few glorious seconds because it made my whole body fucking sing, and I was so tired of fighting.

Everything, all the time.

Wraiths, other shifters, our society's expectations, my restless beast, the pull to the men who had hurt me.

In Wyatt's arms, I didn't have to fight—at least for a few minutes.

And a few minutes was all I would allow myself to give to him. This didn't erase what he'd done.

After one last frenzied kiss, I bit down on his lip.

"Fuck," he swore, releasing me. His eyes were so glazed with lust that he looked high as kite. A knowing grin spread across his kiss-swollen lips. "Were you enjoying that too much, baby? Felt right, didn't it? Like I've been kissing you for years."

"Shut up." I grabbed his cock and notched it at my aching, overheated core. The fit was going to be a challenge, but I'd tackled more difficult tasks in the past hour. With a fortifying breath, I began to sink down onto it, and the intensity of the stretch ripped a tortured moan from me. I gasped and dug my fingernails into his shoulders. "*Fuck.*"

His moan was equally as tortured as he gripped my hips and thrust slowly up into me, helping me along. "You can do it, Wildcat. This cock is yours. Take everything you fucking want from it."

I began to slowly roll my hips, letting the motion ease me lower and lower onto him until he was fully seated inside me. He was so big, but my beast had revved every single one of my hormones, and they'd been working over-time to make me wet and pliable and ready.

I leaned back, tossing my hair over my shoulder, and I began to ride him harder. "Yes," I said with a sigh. His dick was hitting every spot I had, winding the knot of pleasure in my center tighter and tighter with every cant of my hips. "I'm already close."

Wyatt groaned like he was dying, and then he took advantage of my new position to jerk the hem of my borrowed shirt up to my collarbone and bury his face in my breasts. "So perfect, Wildcat. I've missed these tits." He wrapped his lips around my nipple and lavished it with the same attention he'd given my mouth, and then he switched to the other. "Let go, baby," he said between licks and sucks. "You've earned it."

I *had* earned it, and I was going to come harder than I ever had in my life.

I shifted again, gripping the back of the couch on either side of his head, and then I increased my pace. "Do. Not. Come," I growled between panting breaths, my nose an inch from his.

He nipped my lip and gave me a strained smile that still managed to be the most sinful thing I'd ever seen. "It'll be the second-hardest thing I've ever done because your pussy is fucking *nirvana*, but you need to get it through your gorgeous, stubborn head that I will do *anything* for you. For-fucking-ever and always."

Suddenly my chest ached and my eyes stung.

No. Not now.

"Ugh," I groaned. "Stop talking."

He chuckled and kissed along my heated skin, down my neck and across my collarbone, his hands wrapped around my hips like a vice. I chased my orgasm, needing to release the pressure that'd been building inside of me for the Moon knew how long at this point—hours, days, *months*—more than I'd needed anything in quite some time. I was coiled so tight, my vision going spotty, but my thighs were burning, exhaustion finally setting in.

"Fuck," I whined. "I need to.... I can't...."

My back hit the couch cushions. Before I could cry out in surprise, my legs were over Wyatt's shoulders and he was pounding into me, fucking me brutally, relentlessly, unlike anything I'd ever experienced in my life.

My body exploded into a million pieces, and I screamed.

"*Yes*," Wyatt snarled. "Fuck yes, baby. That's so fucking good."

I fell over the cliff, the tension rushing from my body until I was a wet noodle. Wyatt gave me two last hard thrusts before he yanked himself away with a frustrated roar. He sank to the floor in front of the couch, his rigid dick encased in the punishing grip of his fist, his knuckles white and his jaw as tense as Heath's on his worst day.

Slowly, I righted myself. I sat up, smoothed my shirt, and adjusted my skirt so that it was no longer twisted to the side and riding halfway up my torso. I finger-combed my hair and retied the laces of one of my shoes that'd come undone.

My beast, to both my relief and everlasting annoyance, lounged peacefully, her bloodlust—and regular lust—sated.

Wyatt was silent, his broad chest rising and falling as he caught his breath. He watched me as I stood up and gave my borrowed outfit one last smoothing. He'd lost the wicked smile and bedroom eyes.

He was all predator now.

"I, um...." I began. My cheeks heated, which was ridiculous given everything that'd just happened. "Thank you, Wyatt. I do feel better."

"Any fucking time, Wildcat," he replied, and it sounded like both a vow and a threat. He squeezed his dick, still hard and full of the promise of another round if I wanted it.

I needed to go.

Resolved, I strode to the door and turned the lock, but then something tugged at me. I cast one last look at Wyatt over my shoulder.

"What was the first-hardest thing?" I asked softly.

He didn't have to ask what I meant. A red sheen rolled over his glinting green eyes as he answered, his voice just as soft. "Giving you up."

I left the room without another word and shut the door firmly behind me.

20

HEATH

"And what were the grounds for the challenge?"

Aiden stared at the Council investigator like he was the dumbest supernatural being he'd ever beheld. "Was I supposed to stand in front of a near-feral Alpha wolf and ask him politely to shift back and state his case? We can only assume things, given our history, as my brother has already explained to your colleague."

His colleague, dressed in the same matching polo shirt and slacks as the man in front of me, was standing over the deceased wolf body, snapping pictures with his phone. As was natural for shifters who died in battle as beasts, Mahoney had not reverted to human form and would be given burial rites as a wolf.

The investigator pursed his lips, irritated at being spoken down to by Aiden but powerless to do anything about it because Aiden was a Blackwell. He looked to be somewhere in his thirties and had the aura of an ordinary wolf, of which there were many in shifter law enforcement. He was clearly tired, unhappy to be dragged from his bed at this late hour to deal with hotheaded young shifters killing each other in bar parking lots. "Just give me the gist for the official record, please."

I cracked my neck, and he winced. The guy was a decade older than I was, but I was still an Alpha. "As I've said, my quad was enjoying a drink in the bar when a classmate informed us that one of our Support Squadron members"—a reminder that not only was I a Blackwell, I was also a Guardian—"and Kace Mahoney had gotten into a fight out back. We came out here just in time to witness Mahoney shift into his wolf and attack a much weaker fox shifter."

The investigator frowned. "Quite the loss of control for an Alpha."

"Quite," I agreed. "The fox managed to shift and escape, but instead of de-escalating at the natural end of the fight, Mahoney chose to attack Aiden."

"I hardly had time to complete the shift," Aiden added, sounding bored. He adjusted his sleeves. "It was fortunate I had extra clothing in the car."

"And the Alpha went straight for the throat?" the investigator asked.

"He did," I replied. "A blatant challenge to the death. We can only assume it was due to a grudge he still carried from back in our Guardian training days. He and his trio were spineless cowards and worthless teammates. We let them know it."

"We also let Ward Gale know it," Aiden added. "Who, as you may remember, is both the head of the Guardian training program and the father of our quadmate, Wyatt. It is entirely possible Mahoney blames us for the fact that his trio was dismissed from training last semester."

The investigator grunted, typing notes on his tablet. "And why, out of all of you, would he challenge the jaguar?" He glanced up from his typing, pinning me with as forceful of a look as he could muster. "Why not challenge the head of the quad, who also happens to be an Alpha wolf?"

Aiden scoffed, and I returned the investigator's look with my most withering stare. "Because he knew without a doubt my wolf would crush him," I said. "So he rolled the dice against Aiden's jaguar, and he lost. Or do you think it would've made more sense for him to try his hand against the basilisk?"

I waved a hand at Elijah, who was leaning against a lamp pole nearby, still shirtless and casually flipping the dagger that'd killed his mother in one hand. He grinned, flashing his sharp canines at the investigator, his yellow eyes bright and unsettling.

The investigator swallowed roughly and then decided he had other places to be.

Aiden and I watched as he went to confer with his partner.

"Masterful work," Aiden murmured. "Plausible story, delivered with authority."

"And it's in his nature to trust me as an Alpha," I replied. "We lucked out there."

Aiden blew out a breath, his shoulders sagging as he let the exhaustion and stress show for the first time tonight.

I could afford no such luxuries. Not yet. I was an immovable rock until this entire scene was cleaned up and the Council investigators left the premises.

Only then would Avery be safe.

The past month had been the longest of my life, and that was saying something considering how unbearable the end of the spring semester had been. Ward's plan to stick Avery with us as a permanent fifth had mellowed our beasts enough to get through the daily camp activities without further property destruction, but each day remained a quiet torture that was slowly driving us all mad.

We'd never been closer to our mate, while also feeling like there were oceans between us.

But my own personal exercise in self-control was about to be at an end. Having to stand by and watch as a piece-of-shit Alpha tore into the flesh of my mate's beautiful beast was going to be the thing that broke the dam.

It didn't matter that Avery's tiger was one of the strongest felines I'd ever seen. It didn't matter that, even though Avery was unable to shift except under rare circumstances, she was an elegant and efficient fighter unmatched by anyone in the Guardians. It didn't matter that I'd had zero doubts about my mate's ability to crush Mahoney's wolf.

I was at my limit.

When we returned to camp, Avery would be lucky if I didn't march straight to her cabin, pin her to the bed, and tell her this bullshit space we were giving her was over. I'd convince her to let me bury myself inside her so she could *feel* how we belonged together.

I surfaced from that agonizing fantasy to find Elijah studying me intently. "Are you going to need me to handcuff you to the bathroom pipes when we get back to camp, Captain?"

Elijah always could read me like a book.

I scoffed. "Like that would contain me."

"You brought your handcuffs to camp?" Aiden asked him dubiously.

Elijah waggled his dark brows. "You never know when they might come in handy."

I pinched my brow, feeling a headache coming on. Elijah had procured silver cuffs through means still unknown to me that he'd used when interrogating players possibly connected to his mother's murder. Prolonged exposure to silver cut off access to the beast for all but the strongest of us.

Unfortunately for Elijah, repairing our relationship with Avery wasn't the only thing that'd stagnated over the past month. We'd had no real breakthroughs on his mother's murder, either, with what little time we'd had to devote to it.

"Hey there, big brothers," Clara chirped, slinking over to us. "Is everything going to be okay?"

My headache intensified. "Yes, Clara. Honestly, you're lucky this situation is taking all of my energy. I have none left to lay into you about whatever you and the Gale girls were up to tonight."

"This is not why we agreed to share our locations with you," Aiden added. "That was for your *safety*."

She tossed her dark hair over her shoulder with a dramatic huff. "Please. You guys have been acting *so* shady. It was only natural that Willow and I wanted to figure out why. The fact that you haven't been dating *does* sort of affect me, you know."

I grasped her hand. "Clara, I swear to you that your safety and well-being has never stopped being our priority. It's just that our plan is... more fluid. Whether I end up challenging Dad or not, we're not letting those little Nelson fucks bond with you."

Aiden nodded and patted her shoulder. "We're going to take care of it. I promise."

She grinned. "You changed plans because of Avery."

Neither of us opened our mouths to deny it.

"I knew it!" She hopped up and down on her toes. "She's so awesome. But I don't think she's on board with becoming your central. She seems kind of mad at you guys, actually."

"Understatement," Aiden muttered.

Elijah licked his lips, and then he narrowed his eyes at my sister. "Clara darling, did you and the girls talk about anything in particular with Avery this evening?"

A flash of guilt crossed her face. "Maybe. What's said in the Beemer stays in the Beemer." She lifted her chin, tossed her hair again, and turned to leave. "You four need to fix whatever you broke with her. I'm not helping you."

My temples began to throb. "Thank you for the advice," I managed to say with the world's most rigid jaw. "Please take Willow and Winona and go home. Willow still doesn't have a moondamned shirt on, and she's lucky Wyatt's inside dealing with the bar's owner."

She was already walking away. "Fine, byeeeee."

The three girls climbed back into the car. Willow flipped us off before she peeled out of the parking lot, the screeching tires one last shot to my aching head.

"Did I suddenly sprout gray hair?" Aiden asked as we watched them go. "I feel like I did."

"You and me both." I straightened my spine as a sleek black van, sporting the Southeastern Council crest, pulled into the lot. It came to a stop, and then two burly men in dark jumpsuits exited.

They were here for the body.

As the investigators joined the team from the van, Ian and Brody came trotting out of the shadows near the building. Ian had managed to put his clothes back on, and the two of them were holding hands. All was forgiven, maybe, at least with respect to Brody.

If I knew my mate, she would make her brother sweat a bit longer.

Ian gave a cursory glance to the team loading Mahoney's wolf into the van, as if it was hardly interesting to him. Brody elbowed him, and after a put-upon sigh, he turned to me. "Thank you, Blackwell. Obviously I did not intend for my sister to get involved in this, and I don't regret breaking that motherfucker's face in four places before he lost it—" Brody cleared his throat. "—but in hindsight, it was rash. I appreciate you fixing this and covering for her." He looked at Aiden. "And I appreciate you taking the burden of the kill."

Aiden dipped his head. "I would kill an extraordinary number of people to keep Avery safe and not lose a bit of sleep over it."

Ian blinked at him.

"Well, if that isn't the most romantic thing I've ever heard," Brody said, sighing. He elbowed his boyfriend again. "Isn't it, Ian?"

The doors of the van slammed, and then its engine sparked to life. We were all quiet for a moment as we watched it slowly roll out of the parking lot.

"Sure," Ian replied. "But you know what would've been more romantic? If my sister's so-called mates had taken care of Mahoney the second he walked into the bar."

"You think we didn't want to?" I growled. "It took the full power of my wolf and seven shots of whiskey to keep Elijah's beast from erupting in the bar. Unlike you, we have to be more strategic about these kinds of things."

"And my dove had already left when Mahoney arrived," Elijah said. He flipped the dagger in his hand again. "We would've never allowed that wolf to breathe her air."

"How gallant," Ian said dryly.

The investigator from earlier strode over, closing the cover of his tablet and sticking it under his arm as he walked. "The Council should be able to close this one quickly enough," he reported. "Seems to me like a run-of-the-mill challenge between Primes. At any rate, a shifter who decides to challenge a quad with two Blackwells and a basilisk as members is going to get what's coming to him."

"On that, we agree," I replied. I held out a hand, and he shook it, his grip entirely too firm.

After he and his partner had loaded themselves into their nondescript SUV and left, I finally let myself slump under the weight of the events of the night. I raked a shaky hand through my hair and released all the air from my lungs. "*Fuck.*"

I didn't want to be here in this parking lot.

Staring at the pool of blood smeared on the asphalt.

Ignoring Ian's judgmental stare.

Worrying that my brother wasn't as okay as he seemed about the fact that he'd had to kill one of our peers.

Wondering what the hell was taking Wyatt so long.

All while bracing against the chill still emanating from Elijah.

The only thing I fucking wanted was to be somewhere quiet and safe, holding Avery in my arms.

And I wasn't going to get that tonight. There was a chance I wouldn't get that ever in my life. My wolf howled in agony at the thought.

"All right," I rasped. "Let's get the hell out of here—"

A small blue sedan stopped in front of the entrance to the lot. Drew—the lanky panther shifter who was part of Mahoney's trio—climbed out of the passenger seat. After a wink and a wave at the girl behind the wheel, he slammed the door and swaggered in our general direction, the car taking off behind him.

He reached the pool of blood, and his cocky gait came to an abrupt halt. His nostrils flared and his eyes widened. He looked around, harried, and he quickly zeroed in on Ian. His green eyes went nuclear, and black fur sprouted along his neck.

"You!" he bellowed. "What the fuck did you do?"

Before he could lunge for Ian, a dagger with an ornate floral hilt sprouted from his stomach. He staggered, falling to his knees on the pavement.

A weary sigh left me. This hellish night wasn't over yet.

21

ELIJAH

After being forced to sit on my hands while a dead man attacked my mate, it pleased me greatly to be able to mete out some violent retribution in her honor after all.

Pretty mate. Savage mate.

Yes, she's perfect, isn't she?

"What the fuck!" Drew bellowed. His knees hit the ground, and he grasped at the intricate hilt of the dagger that had killed my mother.

Blood seeped from the wound, but I hadn't hit anything that vital. A lick of my lips gave me a hint of his fury, heavily doused by quavering fear. Delightful.

I strolled over and kicked him in the chest. He flopped onto his back with another loud curse.

I heaved a sigh and ripped the knife from his stomach. "Sorry, can't let you keep this," I said. "It's very important to me."

Heath and Aiden joined me, both taking a moment to stare down at our unwelcome guest, Heath with his usual skull-boring intensity and Aiden in mild disgust.

I knelt and wiped the blood from my blade on the hem of Drew's shirt. My dove had taken off with mine, after all, wearing it as a sexy little skirt. *Mmm.* "It's been a bit of a trying night," I told him. "I suggest you don't push me further than I've already been pushed. The lesson I hope you'll have learned this evening is that you will not look at, talk to, threaten, or lay a single paw on anyone with the last name of Baxter."

"What the fuck, man?" he groaned, pressing a hand to his wound. "That little fox asshole started it with Kace. And I don't give a shit about his cursed skank of a sister."

"What—" I jammed the dagger through his hand where it lay on his stomach, and he roared another string of curses. "—did I *just* say?"

Ian snickered behind me.

Heath must have arrived at the end of his rope, because he let loose a tidal wave of his wolf's aggression. The basilisk bristled—respectfully. "Your friend Kace let the wolf take him," Heath spat, disgusted, "and he ended up challenging my brother to the death. As you've probably surmised, he lost."

Drew tried to formulate a response, sweat gathering on his pale brow from the pressure of Heath's wolf and possibly also the blood loss. He screeched when I once again plucked the dagger from where it impaled him.

"He wouldn't.... Why the fuck would he do that?"

Heath's unaffected shrug was a work of art. "Because he was a weak fucking Alpha. You knew that."

Drew shut his eyes and groaned. "The knife.... So fucking unnecessary."

"Would you rather the basilisk?" Aiden asked dryly. "Quit moaning. Just shift into your animal and walk it off."

Drew growled something unintelligible before quieting

to focus on the shift. His eyes sparked neon green and then faded out, like a candle failing to ignite.

He tried again. Same result.

"What the fuck?" he yelped, his voice jumping up an octave. "Why can't I feel my beast?"

Ian sucked in a startled breath.

Two puzzle pieces slammed together in my brain. The ground wobbled under my feet, and I gripped the dagger's hilt tighter. "Aiden," I said softly. "Will you please attempt a healing spell on this panther?"

Aiden frowned and bounced a troubled look between me and Ian, who was hovering over my shoulder. Ian tasted of horror and budding dread—a familiar flavor that I'd indulged in once before, back when I'd upset my dove during training and had been wholly unprepared for the basilisk's reaction to it.

"Okay," Aiden said slowly. "I won't be able to do much under a waxing crescent."

"Please try," I said with as much patience as I could muster. My beast slithered under my skin, coiled tight, anxious.

Aiden dug into his pocket and retrieved a pen. He knelt next to Drew, who was hyperventilating as he continued to attempt to shift without success. Aiden drew a few hasty runes on a clean patch of Drew's white T-shirt, and then he lay his fingers lightly across them. He began to channel what trickle of magic he could pull from our celestial source. Unlike Avery's friend Mallory, Aiden did not have a healing affinity and couldn't perform healing magic at will.

After a few seconds, Aiden swore and withdrew his hand like he'd been burned. "What in the wraith-infested hell?"

My heart beat harder against my ribs. "What is it?"

Aiden's eyes widened as he came to the same realization

I had. "His body is rejecting the magic. I can feel it pushing back."

Ian made a choking noise.

"What is it, babe?" Brody asked softly. Urgently. "What's wrong?"

My vision narrowed and the colors of the world slid into a monochromatic haze as my beast pushed to the surface. I climbed to my feet and turned to my mate's brother.

He was in my face in a flash, the fearless little fox. "Where the fuck did you get that dagger, Harrow?" he snarled. "What did you *do*?"

I held it out to him. "This is the dagger that was used to murder my mother, Little Baxter."

The rage melted from his body in a blink. He took the blade carefully from my hand. "Your mother. Whose body rejected the magic used in an attempt to heal her after she was attacked?"

So my dove had shared that bit of my mother's story with her brother, which confirmed the suspicion I was rapidly developing.

The symptom was familiar, which is why she'd become so upset when I'd mentioned it.

"Yes," I replied. "And tell me, Little Baxter—did your mother's body also resist magical attempts to heal her after whatever happened that caused her death?"

He continued to examine the knife, rubbing his thumb across the hilt's floral carvings, over the amethyst gems embedded in the bell-shaped blossoms and the large onyx pearls that looked like berries. "Yes."

"And from the way you reacted earlier, I'm guessing she was also unable to shift into her beast?"

"Yes."

He had Heath's and Aiden's full attention now. Drew,

unimportant to anything, continued to moan and writhe on the ground.

"Was your mother killed with a dagger?" Heath asked softly.

Ian shook his head. "She was shot by hunters while out on a walk in the woods with my dad. The hunters weren't shifters, just dumb humans who were supposedly aiming for my dad's wolf but hit my human mother on accident. The bullets weren't even silver, and they still killed her."

I frowned and looked at Aiden. "Could it be a coincidence?"

He stood up and wiped the sweat from his brow with his sleeve. That small bit of magic was unnatural to him and had taken some effort. "I really don't know," he replied, shaking his head.

"It's not the dagger," Ian said suddenly. "There must be something *on* the dagger. I can't.... Why didn't we think of this before?"

"Babe," Brody said gently. "What do you mean?"

"The hilt has a belladonna flower carved into it. It could be.... I mean, I'm not sure, it would be nearly impossible—"

"What?" I asked. "The design on the hilt is a belladonna?"

Ian gave me a droll look, so much more like his usual countenance that it loosened a knot of tension from my body. "You didn't know what was carved into the hilt of the instrument of your mother's death?"

I scowled. "Why would I know what that was?"

"Not everyone has an apothecary affinity, my love," Brody added.

Ian blew out a breath and looked me right in my beast eyes. "I'd like to borrow this, Harrow. I promise I'll take good care of it, and I'll return it to you after I've done some research. Maybe I can get some answers for both of us."

"Done." Even a far-fetched hunch was the biggest breakthrough we'd had in a long time. "Thank you."

"I'd prefer...." He frowned, like he was wrestling with something, and then he lifted his chin. "I'd prefer if we didn't mention this to my sister quite yet. She's dealing with enough shit right now, and I'd rather not open old wounds if it turns out I'm wrong."

Ah. None of us, including Ian, wanted to keep secrets from my dove, but I understood his hesitance. "You have my word," I said.

"Thank you." He carefully slid the knife through his belt and then grabbed his boyfriend's hand. "Oh, and the potency of whatever is on the dagger that may be cutting off access to the beast has to have faded in the decades since it was used on your mother. Try forcing the panther to shift."

With that, they left us.

As the most powerful feline present, Aiden did as Ian suggested. Using the force of his beast's dominance, he threw everything he had left at Drew and commanded him to shift. The telltale turquoise rings lit up around his irises, and his muscles bunched under his rumpled dress shirt.

Drew bellowed in pain, his voice cracking under the strain. Black fur sprouted along his face and neck.

"*Shift*," Aiden growled.

With one last hoarse shout, the panther emerged. The shift was slower than normal and looked painful as hell, but he managed to complete it, and he didn't waste time after that.

He sprinted out of the parking lot as fast as his panther legs could carry him.

Heath watched him go with a resigned look. "I'll have someone tap his phone, just in case."

"Good." I bounced on my toes, feeling lighter than I had in months. Handing the issue of my mother's death to someone else—someone who may have just as much interest in finding the truth as I did—was freeing, even if it would be short-lived. "Let's find our wayward bear and make sure our mate made it out of here safely."

"Damn, where the fuck *is* Wyatt?" Heath said with another frustrated rake of his hand through his hair. "Surely Bernard wasn't giving him trouble about what happened back here?"

"Unlikely," I agreed. The barkeeper was a good friend of my uncle, and as the proprietor of a shifter establishment in a shifter town, he was used to this kind of thing happening on his property. There were no cameras back here for a reason.

We made our way inside. As soon as we'd slammed the door and stepped into the dim staff hallway, it hit us.

Heath let out a menacing growl.

Aiden made a noise like he was choking.

And I tasted the most luscious, sinful, *decadent* thing to ever grace my lips.

My dove. Her lust. Her *pleasure*.

Heath shot forward and shoved his way into Bernard's office. Aiden and I jostled with each other to rush in behind him.

There, alone in the dark, sitting on the floor with his back propped against an old leather couch, was our fallen brother. He seemed dazed, like he wasn't sure where he was, and he was gripping what appeared to be his erection through his jeans.

I licked my lips again. Avery's deliciously amorous

pheromones were thick in the air, and Wyatt's earthy bear lust intermingled with them in such a harmonious way, I could only assume that was by the Moon's design.

I knelt next to him. "Hey there, buddy. You doing okay?"

He grinned lazily. "Fuck yeah, I am."

"Is this real?" Heath asked, his voice cracking, his nostrils flaring like a bull's. "She let you...?"

"Yeah." He sighed wistfully. "There were conditions."

He explained what happened and exactly what Avery had demanded of him.

I could only blink at him. Aiden gaped like a fish, and Heath had the look of someone who'd been punched in the stomach.

Finally, I barked a loud laugh. "That's our girl. I wouldn't have expected anything less."

"I'm just...." Heath blew out a breath. "Fuck, I'm ecstatic she let you take care of her, man. Deep down, she knows her body and her beast are only going to be satisfied if it's one of us. It's a start."

I stood up and held out a hand to Wyatt. He grabbed it reluctantly, grumbling irritably as I pulled him to his feet.

I tossed an arm around his broad shoulders, squeezing as I led him to the door. "Let's go, Casanova. We have a lot to talk about. You have until we get back to Gale Manor to will your cock to calm down."

His grin was smug. "I'm never showering again."

As we made our way to Heath's car, every beast in our quad thrummed with anticipation, eager for the thrill of the hunt.

There's more where that came from, Dove. Just you wait.

22

AVERY

Ian and I arrived back at camp a few hours before we had to report for Sunday night dinner. After a quick run around the perimeter of the grounds and a shower in the detached bathroom facilities I shared with the female staff, I spent fifteen minutes pacing the cramped space of my cabin.

There was something I needed to do, and I couldn't put it off much longer.

"Boys are so fucking *dumb,* George," I said to my serpentine friend, who was coiled up on the concrete floor, basking in the late-afternoon sun streaming through the window.

He made a soft hissing noise and unfurled slightly, shifting to catch the sun's rays on a different part of his shimmering purple scales.

"Yeah, you're right. It's in their DNA. That's not an excuse, though."

I'd slept damn near twelve hours last night, and I'd awoken feeling rejuvenated and full of energy. Unfortunately, it appeared that having transcendent sex with Wyatt had the same effect on my body as spending two straight days at a spa.

My beast flicked her tail and licked a claw at the thought.

Quit it.

Before we left home, Ian and I brought our dads up to speed regarding what had gone down with Mahoney, and they'd seemed equal parts concerned and proud. Ian, in a rare fit of charity toward my not-mates, had assured us all that he was extremely confident in Heath's ability to button up Mahoney's death and erase me from the scene.

Ian had delivered this news, apologized to me for his part in it all, and then disappeared into his room. He'd been acting shifty all day, but I couldn't muster the energy to get to the bottom of it.

I had other assholes to interrogate.

"Okay, George," I said, tossing my damp braid over my shoulder. I took a deep breath and squared up to the cabin's screen door. "Let's go."

We set off for the Guardian cabins. The July sun heated my exposed skin, and the warm breeze smelled of maple trees, mountain laurel, and musky shifter boys. Without all the bullshit, it might've been downright pleasant here.

Along the way, I ran into Kellan, who was sweaty and shirtless and coming from the direction of the outdoor pavilion that served as the camp's weight room.

"Hey, Baxter," he said, deploying his six-million-dollar golden-boy smile. "Out for a stroll?"

"Something like that."

"Where you headed? I can walk you—"

George, who had veered off the path twenty yards back to slither around in the thicker foliage that bordered it, sprang from the underbrush like a jack-in-the-box and latched his sharp teeth around Kellan's calf.

"Oh *fuck*," he barked, hopping on one foot and violently shaking the leg George was attached to. "Call him off, Avery!"

I sighed wearily. "Don't worry, he's not venomous. George, let go of him, please. We don't have time for this."

My python companion did as I asked. He released Kellan's leg, leaving behind a bloody mess of tissue damage. He blinked innocent snaky eyes as he slithered around my legs and then rose up to nose at the hem of my shorts.

I stroked a finger along his scaly head. "Sorry, Kellan. Nothing a quick shift won't heal, hopefully?"

He laughed, and it almost didn't sound forced. "I'll live, but if you wanted to swing by our cabin later to check on me, I wouldn't be opposed."

George hissed at him.

It was time to move on. I stepped around Kellan and continued down the path. "I'll see you at dinner," I said over my shoulder.

I waited until after I'd passed the Support Squadron cabins and had begun the march up the sloping hill that led to the Guardian cabins before addressing the naughty snake at my side. "Did you have to break the skin?"

He didn't answer.

"I know you think you're helping Elijah with all the hostility towards Kellan and his quad, but I promise it isn't necessary."

Still no response.

"You do realize that if you keep antagonizing Kellan, he could shift into his griffin and snap you up in his beak? It's a testament to his character that he hasn't."

That got me an irritated hiss.

I reached the first set of Guardian cabins. There were at least two dozen of them, set in several opposing semicircles with the bathroom facilities in the middle and the dense forest behind them. These cabins were twice the size of everyone else's, which was Prime shifter favoritism at its finest.

I let my beast float to the surface, where she simmered, thrumming with anticipation at our mates' nearness and incensed at the secrets they'd been keeping. It was the tiger that led me to the second set of cabins, and I stopped at the one right in the middle of the pack.

George departed, leaving me to my private business. Probably for the best.

Steeling myself, I stepped onto the small stoop and rapped my knuckles on the wooden frame of the screen door.

Heath appeared behind the screen. He was shirtless, all carved muscles under golden-tan skin, the wolf tattooed across his chest staring at me with a dominance that was almost palpable.

"Avery." The air left him, as if seeing me standing on his doorstep was the biggest relief he'd ever experienced.

"I need to talk to you," I said flatly.

He opened the door and beckoned me inside. In an effort to further delay the inevitable, I paused to examine the cabin's interior.

Four double beds, two on the left wall and two on the right, a small night table situated between each pair. One bed was unmade and covered in discarded clothing and what looked like a handheld gaming system—Wyatt's. The bed next to that one was made, had a worn paperback lying on the pillow, and looked as though it'd hardly been slept in at all during the month we'd been here—Elijah's. Across the room was another neatly made bed, though the covers were a little rumpled and smelled like wolf—Heath's. So the last bed was Aiden's—extra obvious because Aiden himself lay spread out on top of the covers, also shirtless, holding a tablet in his hand and staring at me with raised brows and wide eyes.

Heath stepped in front of me and searched my face, his hazel eyes burning bright. "What's wrong, Killer? Is everything okay?"

Fury scorched through my body as everything I'd been feeling in those final moments in the car with Clara and the Gale girls came crashing back. "No, everything is not fucking okay, Heath, as you well know."

He frowned, and his wolf reacted to my beast's aggression by bubbling into the space between us. "You're right," he growled. "Nothing will ever be fucking okay until you're ours."

"Avery," Aiden said carefully, sitting up on his bed and watching me like I was a ticking bomb. "What is this about?"

I clenched my fists, my blunt nails digging into my palms. The pinch of pain helped me focus. "I know," I said softly. "I know why you did what you did. Why you were suddenly in a rush to bond."

"Fuck." Heath sat down on the trunk that lay at the foot of his bed and buried his head in his hands. "Clara told you."

"She did. But I don't understand why *you* didn't tell me. I know that I wasn't receptive to hearing anything you had to say in the immediate aftermath of the night in the woods, but you've had ample fucking time to say something in the month we've been stuck together as a quintet."

Heath met my eyes, and the same despair I felt was reflected back at me. "Because we decided we couldn't put that kind of pressure on you or, Moon forbid, *guilt* you into bonding with us. I'm going to figure out another way to save my sister—"

"*Heath.*" The word came out an anguished plea. "I understand now. I understand why you all made the decision to pursue what you thought would get you the most power to face your dad. All you've ever been taught is that the strongest bonds are made with latent females from a Prime line, and I know that, even if I've always known that it's wrong. The fact that you as a Prime quad would be seeking a latent bond was the thing that kept us denying our attraction for each other from the jump. I'd started falling for each one of you, despite knowing I wasn't considered central bond material, just stupid, naive hope—"

"We would've chosen you in a heartbeat, Avery," Heath said. "In a fucking heartbeat if I hadn't planned to challenge my father—"

I let out a humorless laugh. "I almost believe you, Heath. You're so fucking noble, so *of course* you planned to fall on your sword to save your sister, and Aiden was going to have to stand by and watch his little brother put himself in danger, and the same for Elijah with the guy who's his rock and Wyatt with his best friend." I sucked in a breath and blinked back the tears that had welled in my eyes. "I could forgive you for that, Heath. I could forgive all of you for prioritizing Clara's and your safety over your little crush on me, or whatever it was—"

"It wasn't a fucking *little crush*, Avery," Heath barked, surging to his feet. "Every single one of us was *obsessed with you.* You were under our skin and the star of every dream for the future we couldn't have and the object of every dirty fucking fantasy."

"Then why didn't you just tell me!" I screamed. The tears

escaped and flowed freely down my cheeks. "You could've come to me and said, 'Avery, the worst has happened, Clara's in trouble, and we're so sorry, but we have to do something we don't want to do.' And you know what I would've said?"

"What, Dove?"

The cabin door clicked quietly shut, and then Elijah and Wyatt were there, standing in the tight space in front of the door with wet hair, wearing nothing but towels around their waists. Elijah was as somber as I'd ever seen him. Wyatt just looked stricken.

I scrubbed the tears from my face with the back of my hand. "I would've asked you if the custody challenge rules apply to bonded mates or legal spouses the same as they do to blood relatives."

Heath stared at me with a slack jaw.

"They do," Aiden said quietly.

I already knew that because I'd looked it up before I left home earlier today.

"And then I would've said, 'Pick me.'"

Heath sucked in a harsh breath, like a boulder had hit him in the chest.

I forged on. "Pick me. As your central, or even just as Aiden's or your legal spouse. Pick me, and I will challenge Holden Blackwell for custody of Clara because my beast is really fucking powerful, and I bet I can beat him. And the thing is, now I *know* I can beat him."

Heath was on me in a flash. He grasped my face, his handsome features terrified. "How, Avery? How could you know that?"

I held his wrists but didn't push him away. "Because he accosted me in the hall after the open SWIM challenges. He tried to force me to shift, and I broke his hold."

He paled and released my face. "Fuck," he said, beginning to pace, running his hand through his hair. "Fuck, this is bad."

"He can't know what she is," Aiden said, rising from the bed. "If he knew about her tiger, we'd have heard about it. And he certainly doesn't know she's our Fated."

"But he'll know she's a female with a powerful Prime animal," Elijah said. "One that's potentially more powerful than him."

"He'd feel threatened," Wyatt added. "Especially if he suspects she's also a feline."

Heath's gaze snagged on the tears rolling down my cheeks. He stopped pacing and cupped my face again, wiping my tears away with his thumbs. "Baby, you have to stay away from my father. I have no doubt that you are at least as powerful as he is, and as it stands, your tiger does have a better shot at him than my wolf does. But I need you to listen to me—I will *never* risk your life like that. He's too powerful, not just his beast but as a member of the regional Council, and he can't know what you are. I will die before I let him hurt you."

"You're not allowed to die," I hissed.

He shook his head sadly. "I'm going to try to find another way."

I finally mustered up the strength to shove him away. "None of this matters!" I shouted. "Because you *didn't* come to me. You didn't save even a sliver of decency for me when you decided to throw away anything we could've possibly had. I said I could've forgiven you for seeking what *you'd been taught* was the most stable and powerful bond to save Clara, but how am I supposed to forgive you for the way you treated me?"

The silence in the cabin was deafening.

"You made me feel this small," I said, holding my thumb

and pointer finger half an inch apart. "You ruined the best battle against the SWIM I'd ever had, in front of the entire school. You were dismissive, belittling, you left me in the woods—"

"*Avery*." Heath's voice was a tortured cry.

"—and you paraded *other fucking women* in front of me." I whirled and glared at Wyatt. "Including one who'd said horrible shit about *my dead mother*—"

"Wildcat," he said, the word scraping his throat like sandpaper. "I know, and I'm so sorry."

He looked so broken, so unlike the sexy confident guy who'd fucked my brains out less than twenty-four hours ago. It hurt to look at him.

I turned back to Heath and poked him right in his bare chest. "So you tell me, *Alpha*, how am I supposed to forgive you for *that*?"

My heart fell right out of my body when a tear leaked from Heath's eye. "I don't know, baby," he said softly. "I made the decision to treat you like that because I was selfish. Because I was fucking *weak*. I thought it would be easier if you hated us. Easier to keep our distance from you, easier for us not to long for a girl who despised us when we were planning to bond another. I know you don't want to hear it, but it was *agony*. The whole thing was my idea, so blame me, not the others. Especially not Elijah, he was so opposed to this—"

"No," Elijah said. "Don't do that. I went along with it, and I hurt the love of my life just as much as everyone else in this room."

"Don't call me that," I sniffed.

The quiet anguish in his yellow eyes pierced me like a bullet. "Dove, you'll always be the love of my life, even if you never love me back."

A sob escaped me. I was drowning. Tears blurred my vision and my hands shook.

Strong arms wrapped around me, and I caved to the urge to bury my face in that solid, naked chest because I wasn't sure I could remain standing otherwise.

"You're not, and you never were, *no one*," Aiden whispered into my hair. "Saying that about you made me want to vomit, and I didn't even know you were my Fated then. And I still have nightmares about sending you away in the woods. I thought I was protecting you. I'll be sorry for what I did for the rest of my life, Avery. I was scared shitless for Heath, but that's not an excuse."

Another hard body pressed in behind me. "All we can do," Heath said, his hands on my hips and his lips on the back of my neck, "is keep trying to show you how we feel. Keep trying to convince you that we'll never hurt you again and that you're the sun around which we all want to fucking orbit for the rest of our days."

My tiger purred so loudly in my chest at being sandwiched between the shirtless Blackwell brothers that it was a wonder I wasn't vibrating like a cellphone.

Everything was so muddled—my anger and resentment, the memories of all the qualities each of these men possessed that'd made me start falling for them in the first place, the way my body responded to them, the echoes of the feeling of bleeding out on the forest floor after they'd dismissed me for the last time.

The way they looked at me now as if they needed me more than air.

I shook myself loose from Heath and Aiden, and they released me without a fight. "I just.... I need some time to process this," I said. "Hearing about everything from Clara and then jumping straight into a fight where I essentially killed another shifter and *then* having sex with Wyatt was... a lot."

"Do you regret what we did?" Wyatt asked.

I'd never seen him look so vulnerable, and I found that I passionately hated it.

I looked him in his sad eyes. "No. Absolutely not."

That got me a sexy grin, and it loosened something in my chest.

"Good," he said. "Because it was the hottest and best thing to ever happen to me."

My face was already flushed, thank the Moon, disguising how my cheeks heated at those memories. "Well, um," I said, rubbing my eyes. "It's almost time for dinner, so I should let you all get dressed."

"I am dressed," Elijah said, stepping out from behind Aiden like the phantom he was. He wore our Guardian-issued black track pants and one of his loose tank tops that hardly qualified as a shirt. "I'll walk you to dinner."

"I don't think—"

A chill infused the air between us, his eyes two light-houses in a stormy sea. "*Please*, Dove."

"Okay," I whispered. This conversation had been a lot, and I wasn't callous enough to think I was the only one wrung dry.

Wyatt, Heath, and Aiden watched us go without a word.

Elijah slipped his hand into mine and threaded our fingers together, and I didn't protest because it felt good and right, the same way being wrapped up tight in Wyatt's arms while his dick was inside me had felt good and right.

We walked in silence to the chow hall. After a few minutes, George came slithering out of the forest and joined us. He rose up to nose at Elijah's hand, and Elijah stroked an affectionate thumb across George's shiny head.

The longer we walked, the more the chill dissipated.

At dinner, Elijah gathered a plate of my favorite foods from the buffet line and deposited me next to Ian and Brody without a fuss. He pressed a kiss to the top of my head, and then he disappeared into the kitchen to charm the cafeteria ladies into making him something special to eat, as usual.

Ian watched him go with a furrowed brow. "Are you okay?" he asked me.

"No," I replied. "But ask me again tomorrow."

23

WYATT

I waited with Heath and Aiden outside our cabin, dressed in my workout gear. Campers were beginning to emerge, most of them headed to breakfast, while others who had gotten a later start were scrambling around, rushing to and from the bathrooms and throwing clothes on.

The trees rustled behind us. Twigs cracked and branches swayed.

A few alarmed shouts sounded. Several half-naked guys bolted from the bathrooms and ducked back into their cabins.

The basilisk emerged from the forest.

"Fucking finally," I muttered.

Elijah slithered along, carving a path through grass, ignoring the gaping of our fellow trainees. His yellow eyes burned brighter as he passed the Crimson Quad, who were filing out of their cabin two doors down from ours.

The basilisk flicked his barbed tail at Ari as he slithered by. Ari shouted in alarm and jumped out of the way. Kellan's eyes went molten, but Teegan shoved him along.

Elijah melted smoothly back into human form as he reached us. I threw his clothes at him, and he pulled them on while Heath began the interrogation.

"She left for breakfast?"

He nodded. "George is with her. He returned from his nightly adventures about twenty minutes ago."

"Good. Anything to report?"

Elijah grinned, his canines extra sharp. "Ari tried to knock on her door fifteen minutes before lights out, but he changed his mind when he saw me wrapped around her tree."

Aiden's head snapped in the direction of the offending cat's back as he and his quad made their way down the path. "Sounds like I need to break more fingers."

"Later, man," I said. "Let's go. I want to see her."

The bear was pushing me harder than he had since the night we discovered Avery was our Fated. Thoughts of her played on loop in my hormone-addled brain, a goddess as she rode my cock and took what her body needed from me.

Warring with those memories were thoughts of her tear-streaked face as she finally wore her heartbreak for us to see.

I was being tortured by my own psyche with both my fantasy and my nightmare.

None of us could do this any longer without losing our fucking minds. All the cards were on the table. The idea that Avery might've agreed to be ours—our central, our *bonded mate*—had we simply gone with the novel approach of being honest with her about fucking everything last semester? That had left each of us more devastated than we already were.

But somehow, we also had a renewed determination, and I was so fucking *hungry* for my girl.

"Right," Heath said. "No more fucking around. Let's go."

We made it to breakfast just in time. Avery was seated in her usual spot in the middle of a table on the Support Squadron side, next to her brother and the cats.

The end of that table was still empty.

I set my tray down at the open seat next to Avery. Elijah sat down across from me, next to Joon the bobcat, who squeaked in alarm and jumped six inches out of his chair. Aiden and Heath filled in next to us.

"Hey, Wildcat," I said as I slid onto the bench beside her. Fuck, she smelled good. "Sleep okay?"

She stared at me, a forkful of waffle paused in front of her face. "I did," she said slowly. "Are you guys eating on the white-shirt side of the chow hall now? Cash's head is going to explode."

"One can only hope," Elijah said, smiling fondly at her.

"He can go fuck himself," Heath added, and then he jerked his chin at Avery's fork. "Eat, Killer. It's sprints this morning instead of the long run. You'll need your fuel."

She narrowed her gorgeous eyes at him, but she finished her bite without protest.

Heath grinned, the pleased look on his face and the heat blazing in his eyes practically screaming, "Good girl." Her cheeks flushed the slightest pink as she focused intently on her plate, and then I had to adjust myself in my shorts.

We settled into our meal. The cats struck up their usual energetic chatter, even including Aiden at one point as they debated the finer points of feline battle tactics. Ian and Elijah exchanged a few cryptic words, which did not go unnoticed by Avery. She frowned in confusion, but then Ian distracted her by regaling the table with the tale of Joon and Nico's antics during Avery's absence at the bar.

Shifters skewed a little slutty, but those two took it to the next level.

By the end of our meal, it dawned on me that something felt different.

Avery was *relaxed*.

In the weeks we'd been at camp, the open hostility and visceral hatred she'd arrived with had morphed into a sort of rigidity and cool politeness. It'd had to because my dad had forced her to work so closely with us and because she possessed an unwavering dedication to becoming a Guardian.

Her beast was always on the surface, but she'd become an impenetrable wall. Our mate worked tirelessly day after day, not just rising to meet every physical demand of this program, but to keep her tiger and her emotions locked down. She wore the strain on her face always, and it made my bear a raging lunatic.

But right now?

Her body lacked the tension our presence had always triggered in her ever since the day we returned to school from spring break and decided to ruin our fucking lives. Her beast was content, and she wore a soft smile on her beautiful face.

Heath's speculative look said he'd felt it too.

Aiden stared down at his omelette, failing to smother a grin.

And Elijah was about five seconds away from shifting, grabbing our mate, and disappearing into the forest with her.

I let my body relax into the narrow space between us. My thigh brushed against hers.

She sighed, resigned, maybe a little bit annoyed, but she

didn't move away. My bear crept forward and nosed her tiger.

The quiet purr we received in return shot so much dopamine through my body, it was damn near as euphoric as feeling her clench on my cock and drench it with her cum.

I wrapped my hand around her thigh and pressed my lips to her hair. "You're so fucking perfect, Wildcat," I murmured against the silky strands.

The purr intensified.

The cats smirked at her. Brody beamed a happy smile, and even Ian seemed weirdly content.

She grabbed my hand, slowly slid it back into my lap, and then she cleared her throat. "I'll see you guys out on the field," she said before picking up her tray and striding confidently away.

We watched her go like a bunch of lovesick idiots.

"What the hell is wrong with y'all?" Ian whispered aggressively across the table. "One of you go with her so she isn't alone, for fuck's sake."

Aiden was out of his chair before Ian had finished his sentence. He shot us a smug grin and took off after our girl.

I arched a brow at Ian across the empty bench space Avery had vacated.

He scowled. "I'm warming up to this."

I clapped him on the shoulder and got to my feet. "Best news I've heard all day."

CASH AND TRENT RAN OUR ASSES OFF LIKE THE SADISTS THEY were. After forty-five minutes of sprints with our weapons

STRAPPED TO OUR BACKS, WE TRUDGED BACK TO THE PICNIC area at the front of the campgrounds to chug water before we moved on to weapons drills.

Avery took her drink and sat down at the table farthest from the rest, as she usually did. She liked her quiet after a hard workout, and every day we would take up a post nearby—close enough to her table to scare off Crimson and anyone else who wanted to sniff around, but far enough away to give her the space she wanted.

Not anymore.

Heath and I squished ourselves onto the bench on either side of her. Aiden glowered at us before he sat down across the table. Elijah decided to just hop on top of the table right in front of where Avery was sitting.

She took us in with a look of mild surprise, but once again, I could detect nothing from her beast or her body that said she was uncomfortable, angry, or rebuilding her walls.

We all grinned at her and rehydrated in companionable silence.

"You should be nicer to Hank," she said to me after a minute. "You'd think a bear would have some sympathy for his fellow bears on sprints day."

"Baby, Hank is lucky I haven't ripped his entire head off. He managed to check out your ass exactly fifty times while he was huffing and puffing and trying not to pass out during all of that."

She rolled her eyes. "You can't kill everyone who looks at my ass."

"Is that a challenge, Dove?"

Avery looked Elijah right in those slit pupils and pointed a finger in his face. "Behave," she commanded in a husky voice.

The chill that engulfed the table wasn't Elijah's usual sharp prick of ice but more a caress of cool fingers on my skin.

So that was what it felt like when the basilisk was super fucking horny.

Elijah nipped at Avery's finger and gave her a silky smile. "No."

During all of this, Heath's beast radiated primal satisfaction. Our quintet suddenly felt real and whole, with our mate in the center where she belonged.

That cute little bubble burst when my dad stormed up to us.

He slammed his palms on the table and asked in a menacing whisper, "Why the hell is a Council investigator calling me about this quad's involvement in a death challenge in a fucking bar parking lot?"

Ah, damn it.

Heath cleared his throat. "Well, as I'm sure you were told, Ward, the challenger was an ex-Guardian trainee."

"Mahoney," he growled. "Who the investigator seems to be under the impression had a vendetta against this quad that warped his lupine brain so badly that he would challenge Aiden Blackwell to the death."

"Who knows why a feral Alpha does the insane things he does?" Aiden asked evenly.

Dad cut him a look. "Spare me. I gave the investigator the bare minimum of details to confirm whatever bullshit you all told him, but something is not adding up. I've known the three of you who are not my son since you were preteens. This quad does not just kill their peers in parking lots, challenged to the death or not. You all have more power, sense, and finesse than that. It is out of character for Aiden in particular, which is why I am baffled as to the reason you picked him to sell this truckload of horseshit to the Council."

"Dad—"

He held up a hand.

"Ward, there were circumstances," Heath said carefully.

The air became oppressive with the dominance of my dad's bear. Elijah shifted uncomfortably. Avery reacted instantly, running a soothing hand down his thigh.

"They had better have been some dire fucking circumstances," Dad snarled under his breath.

I tried again. "Dad, it's better if you don't ask questions—"

"It was my fault," Avery announced.

The pressure of Dad's bear fell away, and he looked at Avery curiously. "Oh?"

"The fight was with me, not Aiden," she went on. "We —Aiden and I both—killed Mahoney to protect my secret."

"Killer, you don't have to—"

She shook her head. "No, Heath. You've done so much already. I can't let it all fall on you." With a deep breath, she straightened her spine and looked at me. "You trust your dad implicitly?"

"Of course."

She stood up and took one last swig of water. "Okay. Ward, please come with me. Wyatt, you can come too. Heath, can you keep everyone away from those woods until we get back?"

She pointed at the tree line twenty-five yards behind us.

Heath frowned but nodded slowly. "Anything you need."

"Thank you." She turned and marched toward the woods.

I scrambled out of my seat. "Come on, Dad."

Curiosity got the better of Ward Gale, and we followed her into the forest.

Avery led us deeper into the woods until she found a clear patch of grass. "Wait here, please."

She disappeared behind a cluster of trees, ripping her shirt off as she went.

My heart kicked into my throat.

"Dad, for the love of the fucking Moon, do not react in any way but positively to what is about to happen."

"Wyatt, what in the world—"

A glorious silver tiger emerged from the trees.

Dad's jaw fell open, and the force of his bear punched the air, a knee-jerk reaction to the shock of a huge Prime beast appearing out of nowhere.

Avery growled a warning.

"Get it together, Dad," I hissed, and then I approached my mate. "Hey, beautiful," I murmured, stroking a hand down her neck. "You're the most gorgeous and fearsome beast I've ever seen."

A purr erupted from her, and she rubbed her huge head on my chest. I laughed and began to scratch her ears.

"Wyatt," Dad finally managed to rasp. He crept closer. "This is Avery?"

"Yeah. Isn't she beautiful? Tell her she's beautiful, damn it."

"She sure is. By the Moon...." He reached out a tentative hand. The tiger took a delicate sniff, and then she let him pet her head for three seconds before she went back to rubbing it on my shirt.

My bear had never been so smug.

"She's enormous," Dad said, sounding awed. "Is she as good a fighter as she looks?"

"Better," I replied, and the tiger licked my face. "And she can break Heath's wolf's hold."

"You're shitting me."

"Nope."

Dad finally overcame his shock, and a smile creeped onto his face. "She's going to be one of our best warriors."

"She already is."

That earned me another lick. I grabbed her head and started rubbing her ears again. She rumbled happily.

Dad became thoughtful. "There are people in our world who would certainly get... weird about a female tiger. Especially one who looks like her. She's not white but she's damn close."

"Right."

"And Mahoney saw her?"

I nodded. "She destroyed him, Dad. Aiden only finished it so we could sell it as a jaguar kill."

He beamed at the tiger. "Of course she did."

"Dad." I let all mirth drain from my expression. "I need you to understand something. Avery's mother was also a silver tiger, and she was murdered."

He jerked an alarmed look at me. "What?"

I explained what little we knew about Avery's mother, mostly gleaned from Ian, and Avery declined to shift back to add to the story.

She'd tell us when she was ready.

"You see now?" I asked. "You see why we couldn't let Mahoney walk away? You see why she needs to be a Guardian?"

He nodded solemnly. "She will be one, Wyatt. And the force will have her back, especially when they see what she can really do. All she has to do is survive out there, and with your quad at her back, I have all the faith in her."

That must've satisfied my wildcat, because she decided this little interlude was over. She trotted back behind the trees and emerged a minute later, fully dressed again. She pulled her hair back into its ponytail as she made her way over to us.

"Thank you, Ward," she said. "I appreciate your discretion and your support in... all of this."

"You'd have it even if you weren't my son's Fated, Avery. You're a damn good soldier and an asset to the cause."

She practically glowed at his praise. My dad deserved ten bottles of the expensive scotch he liked for saying the exact right thing to please my mate.

I'd make Heath pony up some Blackwell trust fund money for those later.

As we walked out of the woods, I ached to hold Avery's hand, but I managed to refrain. I wouldn't push my luck after all the loving she'd allowed her tiger to get from me.

When we arrived back at the table where the guys waited, Heath rose and greeted my dad.

"I'm satisfied," Dad said, shaking Heath's hand. "I'll handle the Council investigators from here. You boys just keep taking good care of Avery, and we won't have a problem."

"Thanks, Ward," Heath replied, blowing out a breath, and then he grinned at our girl. "And of course we will."

Avery rolled her eyes at him but didn't protest.

"By the way, Dad." I propped my ass on the table and gave him an exasperated look. "Willow and Winona also happen to be *aware* of what Avery just disclosed to you because they were *at the bar* that night and witnessed the entire thing. They're out of control, and you guys just keep letting them act up."

Dad scowled and pointed a stern finger in my face. "Your sisters, like your mother, are perfect."

I sighed, defeated yet again.

Avery bit her lip to keep from laughing.

Dad sent one last look of warning around the group of us, and then he strode away.

24

AVERY

I gave my sword a few hard shakes, and the blood lingering on the blade spattered on the nearby grass.

The members of a moderately talented gold-shirted quad limped away from us, cursing and arguing with each other, two in human form, the others a panther and a rather terrifying gorilla. Commander Moss barked orders from somewhere in the distance, hidden by the thick foliage. He was wandering around the woods, observing today's combat tactics session. We'd been assigned a game of Capture the Flag, black versus gold, and my quintet had been working our way into enemy territory for over an hour.

"Nice work, Killer," Heath said, sheathing his saber on his back. "That gorilla underestimated your strength and the reach of your little blade."

"He did," I agreed. "You'd think after over a month of this, they'd have learned."

"They will, sweetheart," Aiden said, giving me an indulgent smile that got my beast's tail flicking, and then he turned to frown at Heath. "We're still clunky, though. We should've eliminated that group in half the time it took us."

Wyatt, a bear, grunted in agreement.

"I suggest we come up with a new plan, then," Elijah hollered down at us. He'd climbed the tallest tree in the vicinity like the dexterous monkey he was to scope out the rest of our path toward the enemy flag. "Because the flag is flying from the top of an old hunting cabin a hundred yards ahead, guarded by one last quad."

"Is it Crimson?" Heath shouted up at him.

"No, Yang. Crimson was probably sent to attack our base like we were nominated to attack theirs."

The Yang Quad were all Prime leopards. Not the biggest cats in camp—that would be Aiden, Cash, and, unbeknownst to everyone, me—but they were vicious fighters and slightly insane.

"Are they all in beast form?" Aiden yelled up the tree.

"Yes."

Heath swore. "Team Gold is not as dumb as we'd hoped."

Elijah came down from his perch, swinging on branches and jumping from limb to limb before he dropped and landed on light feet. He winked at me, and I smothered a grin.

I'd... had fun today.

It wasn't that I'd had zero fun since I'd come to camp. There'd been plenty of moments with Ian and the Support Squadron guys, and swinging my swords in the heat of battle, even when it was just practice, was always fun for me.

But I always came crashing back down when reality intruded. I spent most of my time here fighting my beast and locking away every errant emotion that plagued me.

Today I stopped fighting.

And so far, today had been a good day.

Heath studied the group of us, his shapely arms folded across his chest, his blond brows furrowed. "It's our formation," he said after a moment.

"What?" Aiden asked.

"Our formation," he said again. "When Ward assigned Avery to us, we decided to keep the normal square of the Guardian Unit and just stick her in the middle. I didn't see the need to make drastic changes to what's worked for the Guardians for decades, and we all felt that it made sense that the four of us who were going to be shifting at will to be on the edges, with our full-time blade wielder in the center."

Aiden pursed his lips. "You want to move Avery out of the center."

Wyatt the bear growled his disagreement.

Elijah only studied Heath with a quiet, unsettling intensity.

I shrugged. "I don't have a problem with where you put me, Heath. It made sense to me at the time."

"That's the thing, Killer. It might've made sense with any other trainee assigned to us with the instructions to make it work with a quintet. But anyone else is not our Fated." He shook his head, and his frown said he was reluctant to admit what came out of his mouth next. "I think we're hampering you."

"You do?"

And you care?

"Yes. Not on purpose, but it's natural that we're going to want to protect our mate from all sides. That's why we're sluggish. We've all done our best over the past month to treat you like another soldier at our side, but that's just not reality. We're constraining you, and we can't have that."

"Heath," Aiden growled. "I don't like this."

Wyatt the bear grunted in agreement.

"I don't like it either," Heath snapped at his brother. "You think my wolf wants to do anything except stand between his mate and anything that remotely smells like danger?" He looked at me, and my cheeks heated under his assessing gaze. It was somehow the look of both a commander at his soldier and an Alpha at his mate. "But I can't do that. Avery's as good of a fighter as anyone in our quad, and someday, hopefully very soon, she'll be shifting into her beast just as freely as the rest of us."

My heart thudded against my rib cage, and my beast released a savage growl of triumph within me. That was my dream, the ability to shift without worry, and Heath hadn't forgotten that.

Aiden sighed. "You're right. Her beast will be such an asset in the field. It frustrates the absolute shit out of me that we can't just run her right at the Yangs and watch them lose their minds."

"And securing Avery's ability to shift without fear for her safety is why we're all here, isn't it?" Elijah added in his silky soft tenor. "We're going to be the most powerful and feared Guardian quintet in history, such that no one would ever dream of crossing any one of us, especially our mate."

I could only stand there in stunned silence.

Wyatt nudged my hand, and I scratched his ear while I attempted to gather my thoughts and also not cry.

I cleared my throat. "I'll, um.... I'll take whatever position in our formation that you decide works best, Heath."

He smiled at me, and it was tender and fond. "How about the point of the spear, Killer? Let's try a pentagon formation with you at the front."

Aiden blew out a breath, Wyatt growled, and even Elijah rolled his shoulders and cracked his neck.

But none of them protested.

Adrenaline raced through my body. I marched forward, twirling my blade in my hand as I went. "Sounds good to me."

With that, we began our attack on the gold team base. Wyatt and Heath lined up behind me, with Aiden and Elijah behind them. We always kept our shape fluid, but as we made our way stealthily through the trees, I realized immediately that Heath was right.

I had been constrained. Now, I was in the lead and could move however I needed, with the might of my quintet at my back. This already felt easier.

We approached the hunting cabin Elijah had spotted, situated on a small hill with a gold flag flying from its roof. Heath's wolf pulsed a command to slow. We took cover in the thick brush, and Elijah activated his beast's vision, which was far more powerful than the average binoculars.

"There's only one clear path to the cabin, and the leopards are covering it four across," he reported.

Heath nodded. "We'll hit them head-on. They'll be expecting Aiden to shift, but it's easier to draw blood with blades than claws. Elijah, peel off and get on that roof."

I drew my second sword from the sheath on my back and waited.

Heath's wolf punched us with another command, and then we bolted from the trees. Elijah disappeared, and the rest of us ran straight at the leopards.

Four huge cats snarled in unison. Three of them were the light orange of African leopards with dark brown rosettes, while the fourth was a thicker-coated white snow leopard. Their frames were only slightly smaller than Aiden's jaguar, but they were much lighter in weight.

The problem was that they were crazy.

The first leopard charged me at the head of our group. No hesitation, no finesse, he just leapt for me, soaring through the air and hissing up a storm.

Instead of waiting for my team to engage and then reacting to the fight as the center, I moved without thought, muscle memory and years of honed instinct in the driver's seat.

I ducked under the flying leopard and rammed both swords straight up into his belly. He yelped and fell to the ground.

"One down!" I shouted. Those were the rules—if your opponent drew blood, you were out of the game.

Wyatt had tackled the second leopard out of the air as it, too, had flown at my head. He held it down with his giant body, grinning his bear teeth at the cat. I sliced the leopard across the shoulder.

"Two down!" I yelled.

"Three!" Aiden shouted back, yanking his saber from the snow leopard's flank.

Wyatt released his leopard and shot across the grass, faster than an enormous bear had any business being. He aimed right for the last leopard, who was playing cat and mouse with an irritated Heath twenty-five yards away. Snarling, leaping, ducking, hissing, swatting—all while Heath brandished his sword and invited the cat to stop fucking around.

Sensing what was coming, Heath grinned, ducked, and rolled away as Wyatt hit the leopard like a wrecking ball. Aiden arrived to stab the leopard before he'd even registered that there was a bear on top of him.

The rest of the leopards limped off to the side, defeated. They'd hang out and heal before shifting back to their human forms.

Elijah whistled.

I craned my neck to take in the cabin at the top of the hill. Elijah sat on the roof, waving the gold flag.

I laughed and waved back. We'd won the game for Team Black.

Suddenly, Elijah's smug smile vanished and his eyes widened in horror.

Two Alpha wolves leapt from the thick foliage near the base of the hill and ran straight at me.

While the others were still standing by the final "kill," twenty-five yards away.

I dodged a snap of the first wolf's jaws, ducking and rolling away. I surged to my feet and ripped my swords from their sheaths just in time to meet both wolves head-on. I struck as fast as I could move, spinning in a circle and slicing my blades one after the other again and again as my tiger shot speed and strength into my limbs. I opened deep gashes on each wolf's head, neck, or shoulders, and still they didn't relent.

Through it all, they pressed suffocating dominance on me, trying to force their will, commanding me to shift, to cower, to *obey.*

My beast raged. We resisted, but we couldn't return the favor, or it would blow our cover.

Because I recognized these two assholes.

These wolves were Alex and Jared from Cash's quad.

The shouts of my quintet rang in my ears. A bear roared. Feet pounded the grass behind me.

"Avery, bail out!"

I followed Heath's command without question. I whipped my blades like a blender one last time before I dove clear of the wolves.

I hit the ground and flipped to my stomach just in time

to witness Heath's enormous golden wolf burst from his body. He blasted Alex and Jared with so much dominance that both wolves winced and lost focus for the briefest moment.

They shook it off, but the delay was enough for Heath.

He grabbed Alex by the neck and used those truly terrifying wolf muscles to shake him violently, the crack of his spine piercing the air. Heath spat him out, and he dropped to the ground like a discarded sack of trash.

Heath attacked Jared next. The wolves snarled and growled and snapped their jaws, chasing each other in a whirlwind until Heath let loose another wave of dominance so powerful, even my tiger shivered under its force.

Jared yelped, and then Heath's jaws were in his throat.

In a flash, fur retreated and bones collapsed until Jared the man dropped from Heath's clutches to the ground, nude and bleeding. "I yield," he snapped, crawling to his feet.

Wyatt, now a naked man, was in his face in an instant. "What the fuck was that, asshole? Are our trainers attacking students now?"

Jared's face had reset to its usual bored indifference, no matter the blood pouring from an open gash in his jaw. "It was a surprise final challenge. Cash and Trent are hiding at the Black Team base."

Aiden stepped to Wyatt's side and gave Jared a look that said he was two seconds from choking him to death. "You singled out Avery when there are five of us in this group, and you continued to attack her even after she drew blood. There is no chance that was sanctioned by Commander Moss."

Jared shrugged and answered in his monotone. "The bitch has been told repeatedly that if she can't handle it, she doesn't belong in the fucking Guardians."

Heath's wolf growled, liquid gold starbursts in his eyes.

Jared clenched his bloody jaw. "Stand down, trainee," he ordered Heath.

The golden wolf snorted in derision, and we all laughed.

Jared went red in the face. "I'll have you tossed, Blackwell—"

The air turned frigid. A July blizzard was coming down the mountain and bringing an avalanche with it.

Elijah stalked down the hill. Green-gray scales ghosted along his neck and arms. The glowing eyes and slit pupils of his beast zeroed in on Jared.

"Come anywhere near Avery again, and you will be dead," he said, his voice a serpentine hiss. "Is that understood?"

Jared blanched but didn't respond. He stalked away, retrieved some clothes he'd stashed behind a bush, and hastily put them on. Still not looking at any of us, he marched over to where Alex lay recovering from Heath cracking his spine in half. He kicked him irritably, and the dark gray wolf got slowly to his feet.

Elijah's cold fingers caressed the back of my neck, and I shivered.

Alex and Jared trudged away. The five of us, along with four wounded leopards, watched them go.

We'd been walking through the woods for about fifteen minutes, headed back to camp, when I decided I'd stewed enough on today's events and the conversation in the guys' cabin and couldn't take it anymore.

My tiger's ire leaked from my pores as I grabbed Heath

by the shorts—those had survived his unplanned shift—and dragged him to the nearest tree.

"Killer, what—"

I put both hands on his bare chest, right on top of his wolf tattoo, and shoved him against the trunk. "You are not *weak*, Heath Blackwell," I growled in his face. "I *never* want to hear you say that about yourself again. You got that?"

He blinked in shock for exactly one second before he grabbed me by the waist, flipped me around, and pressed his entire body up against me, trapping me between his hot, hard chest and the tree. With a snarl, he grasped my face and slammed his lips against mine.

My tiger's agitation turned instantly to a pleased purr, and I moaned against his lips.

He held my face in an unyielding grip and took what he wanted. He wasn't sweet or gentle. He was demanding and firm, like I was his and he was mine and he had every right to press his hard dick between my thighs while he stroked my tongue with his.

Heat pooled in my belly, and lower, and I gasped when he ripped his mouth from mine. "I'll agree to that, baby," he said softly, resting his forehead against mine. "I won't ever say that about myself again, but you have to do something for me in return."

"What?" I asked breathlessly.

"Tell me what happened before you came to school," he said, his voice velvet. "I know you, Killer. You would've been happy staying home in the city, slaying wraiths with your family instead of facing all the bullshit of being someone like you at a shifter school and in this program." He gripped my chin and tilted my face to ensure I was looking him right in his glowing hazel eyes. "Tell me what scared you enough that you ran off to join the Guardians?"

I shut my eyes and reveled in the feel of him. I was getting lost. I hadn't forgiven him, not yet, but I'd decided to stop the constant battle I was waging against them, my beast, and myself.

I *wanted* to trust Heath. So, I did.

"Right before Christmas last year, a few Rippers and a Giant made it into our neighborhood."

Heath sucked in a breath. The others were nearby, listening, the pheromones of the jaguar, the bear, and the basilisk mingling in the air around us.

I told them about the wraiths, how they'd surprised me, how I'd gotten torn up enough that I'd had to shift to save my own life, and how a couple of our shifter neighbors had seen my tiger.

"And their names?" Heath asked innocently, peering down at me, our noses almost touching.

I narrowed my eyes at him. "You can't kill them. They're minor shifters who live as humans. They're harmless."

"I'm sure they are, baby. But if your dad says they have relatives in the Hills, and if there's any chance whatsoever that a whisper of a female tiger is going around our community, I want to know about it."

I relented and gave him the Martins' names. Heath shot Elijah a pointed glance over his shoulder, and Elijah responded with the barest of nods.

"Okay, Killer, we have a deal," Heath said, grinning triumphantly at me. He pressed one more slow, sensual kiss to my lips, and then he released me from the tree.

Wyatt and Elijah rose from where they'd been sitting on the trunk of a fallen tree, both of them grinning knowingly at me. Aiden stood nearby, his eyes heated as he gave me a chastising sort of look, like I was in trouble for turning him on.

I gathered my bearings, stuffed my lusty tiger back into her cage, and continued the march back to camp. The guys fell in behind me without another word.

A smile crept onto my face.

It had been a good day.

For the rest of the week, I didn't see Cash or anyone in his quad. Commander Moss or Ward Gale himself covered most of our training sessions, and they even sent Kit out to lead a few of our morning runs.

Our trainers were allowed time off over the long summer, but the timing was suspicious. The Blackwell Quad didn't tend to use their relationship with Ward to curry favor in the program—they wanted to be at the top because they'd earned it, something I'd known about them from the beginning—but when it came to *me*, I didn't doubt they'd stooped to tattling to Ward about what Alex and Jared had pulled.

When I asked Heath about it, he just smiled innocently, dropped a kiss on my hair, then went right back to expertly slashing his saber at the pell in front of him.

We also continued to play with our formation as a quintet unit. Heath ensured that no matter the shape, I was on an edge, whether it be leading the charge or working from an outside corner. We even tried our old rectangle, but instead of me, Heath stuck Elijah in the middle, where he spent most of his time just looking pretty and throwing the occasional dagger. If his beast was ever to erupt from the center of our group, it meant things had already gone to shit and the formation was out the window anyway. It would be a fun surprise for all involved.

Things were coming together. Heath tried not to act smug about it, and I tried to allow myself to genuinely enjoy being a part of this particular quintet without guilt or resentment.

Ward had all but guaranteed my spot in the Guardians when I graduated from Proteus. All I had to do, as he'd said, was survive, and my odds of doing so were astronomically higher with Heath, Aiden, Wyatt, and Elijah by my side.

They were the best in our class by a mile, and they cared very much whether I lived or died.

Once I'd decided to let go of the anger, it was easier to be pragmatic about it all.

As I contemplated all of this, my tiger flicked her tail, radiating a rather obnoxious *I told you so*. I'd found a peaceful spot on the little beach on the lakeshore and was setting out my supplies for the Moon blessing. The July Full Moon fell on a Tuesday, so I had to handle this one at camp rather than from the comfort of home.

Ward had given me special dispensation to be out of bed after lights out. The man had slotted me into the "females he didn't say no to" column, and I wasn't going to complain.

The Moon was big and gorgeous tonight, her brilliance reflected in the dark, glassy surface of the lake, as though our celestial goddess was blessing me with double the love. I took a moment to soak in the frothing river of magic as I sat in a meditative position on my beach towel, both my swords and Ian's katana laid out in front of me.

Ian had arranged himself in a similar position ten feet to

my right, his apothecary supplies scattered around his towel. I had no idea what he was up to, but he'd brought a ceramic mixing bowl, a mortar and pestle, pouches full of herbs and powders, and who knew what else. Brody perched on a nearby rock, an adoring smile on his face as he watched Ian work.

I pushed my hair out of my face, then closed my eyes and hummed softly, twirling my etching needle between my fingers. There was the Moon's magic, swirling brightly alongside the beast soul within me. In my mind, I dipped my fingers into the current and prepared to channel that power into blessing my blades to kill wraiths.

Soft footsteps padded though the sand behind me. A gentle breeze caressed my face, and I cracked an eye open to find Aiden laying his own towel down next to mine.

He grinned, the neon turquoise that ringed his irises flashing briefly before his beast faded away. He sat down on the towel and set his saber in the sand in front of him. "Hi," he whispered.

"Hi," I replied dumbly. Aiden wore dark joggers and a white long-sleeved T-shirt with the sleeves shoved up to his elbows, which meant I was going to have to exert extra effort not to be distracted by his veiny, corded forearms while I worked. "What are you doing?"

"Joining you, if that's okay? I took over the blessing of our quad's blades a few months ago."

Heath and Wyatt arrived next, barefoot, carving their way through the sand with much less stealth than Aiden's feline prowling. Heath produced his own saber and laid it next to Aiden's, and then he pulled three different daggers from his backpack and set them down as well. Elijah's blades, though Elijah himself was conspicuously absent.

Wyatt spun his big battle-ax like a baton and ran his hot

green gaze up and down my body. He was wearing nothing but tight swim trunks, his pale skin iridescent beneath those tattoos, the moonlight caressing his body. Our celestial goddess was sure proud of her handiwork.

Or she was torturing me. I was subverting her will by refusing my Fated, after all, so I wouldn't put it past her.

"Hey, Wildcat," he purred. "I'm disappointed you didn't use this extra beach time to wear your sexy little bikini."

I squinted at him. "How are you all out after lights out? Did you get permission from Ward too?"

Wyatt chuckled. "I prefer to ask for forgiveness instead. It'll be fine, baby. Dad knows Aiden's doing this for us now."

Aiden had an etching needle pinched between his long fingers that looked suspiciously like an exact copy of mine, and he was laying Elijah's daggers out in meticulous order. "I grew more confident after we successfully used my saber to kill the L4s that breached the school walls," he said softly.

Guilt shone in his eyes, and my stomach soured at the reminder of that horrible night.

I let it pass. After a moment, I held out my hand to Wyatt. "Let me do yours, since Aiden has five already."

He stopped twirling his ax, and his sexy smile softened into something so adoring that it made my chest ache. He gingerly laid his ax next to me, its blade nestled in the sand next to my swords. "Thank you, Wildcat. I'd be honored to carry a weapon with your blessing."

"Can you four pipe down?" Ian said drolly. He'd put gloves on and was stirring something in his bowl in a slow, careful circle. "Some of us are trying to work magic out here."

"Sorry," Heath replied, and he actually sounded contrite. "We'll let Avery and Aiden get started."

Aiden laughed softly, and then he pulled something from his wrist and handed it to me. "Here, sweetheart."

I took it from him. It was a hair tie—a sturdy purple band like the ones I used to pull my hair back.

"Not that you aren't fucking gorgeous with your hair down," he said, his turquoise rings sparking behind his glasses, "but blessing four blades is tough, and I know you like your hair out of your face when you're working."

He was right, but I'd wandered out of my cabin without my usual ponytail or braid because my hair was damp from the shower, and I was letting it air dry.

I swallowed the lump in my throat and tied my hair back. "Thank you," I whispered.

He looked so pleased. "You're welcome. Now show me why you're the best Runes student I've had in my short teaching career."

My beast preened, as if she had anything to do with my ability to work a secondary affinity. I mentally swatted her nose and returned to the potent magical current flowing through my body before I did something rash, such as rub myself all over Aiden like the oversized cat I harbored in my soul wanted to.

I let the Moon's gift suffuse me, and then I went to work, etching over the runes on each blade and whispering my prayer.

Aiden worked quietly next to me. His smooth, deep voice was as relaxing as the gentle break of the water against the sandy shore. The feel of our magics mingled in the air between us. The harmony struck me, much more so than when we'd blessed blades together at school, back before everything went to shit. It was as if the Moon had deemed those parts of us as compatible as our beasts.

Figures, I thought at the beautiful yellow orb in the sky. *You really are torturing me.*

Heath and Wyatt sat quietly nearby and watched. Wyatt wore a look of quiet wonder, and starbursts sparked in Heath's gaze, his wolf's sturdy presence a possessive hand on the back of my neck.

As I finished up the last rune on Wyatt's ax—inverted *Lifeforce,* just as it was on my blades, because Aiden had copied my preferred sequence exactly in the original etching of Wyatt's ax—Elijah came strolling down the beach.

Unlike the rest of us, who were in some form of training clothes or a swimsuit, Elijah wore tight ripped jeans and one of his linen shirts, buttoned only about as high as the bottom of his sternum, the tails of the shirt fluttering in the breeze. He had a plastic bottle in one hand and a popsicle in the other. As he neared, he took an obscene lick of the popsicle with his long tongue, locking eyes with me as he did.

It took everything I had not to squirm on my towel.

"Here you are, Dove," he said, holding out the bottle. It was blue Gatorade, which I drank at nearly every meal since coming to camp. "I had to snoop through several of the cafeteria fridges to find a cold one."

"Oh, um." It occurred to me that I was indeed very thirsty. I was used to blessing two blades, not four, not to mention Wyatt's was enormous and had taken some extra juice. I took the drink from him, twisted the top off, and took a big gulp. "Thank you, Elijah."

"Anytime, my love."

I'd given up on trying to get him to stop calling me that. At least the words felt less like a hot poker jammed through my ribs than they once did. Lately, they hit gentler, more like the icy caress of the basilisk.

Aiden finished up his blessings and wiped a bead of sweat from his brow. "If you're going to pilfer from the kitchens, you could have brought the rest of us something."

Elijah shrugged. "It was a quick dash in and out, and as always, Avery is my priority."

I took pity on Aiden and passed over my open bottle. His smile was grateful, and then I was subjected to the lewd movement of his Adam's apple as he took several big swallows of the drink.

"Plus," Elijah went on, "I didn't want to linger too long in my pilfering. I figured you might all like an update on my little field trip down to Fulton City as soon as possible."

I snapped my head in his direction like a Doberman. "Your *what?*"

My ire only excited him. He beamed a big smile at me and then nudged the handle of Wyatt's ax out of the way. He flopped down onto the sand next to me, his long legs splayed out in front of him.

"I sent Elijah to visit the Martins," Heath said in the matter-of-fact *don't argue with me* tone of a quad leader.

"You *what?*"

"Don't worry, Dove," Elijah said smoothly. "Your neighbors are just fine. Minor shifters are incredibly susceptible to the basilisk's hypnosis. It took only the lightest touch to get them to forget they ever saw a beautiful silver tiger tearing apart a Giant wraith last December."

"More like it was tearing me apart," I muttered, and Aiden made a pained noise. "Wait, your beast can hypnotize?"

Elijah's grin was sly. "He can lull or stun all but the most powerful shifters. I learned the art of hypnosis myself to... complement the power."

I blinked at him. Elijah really was an *incredibly* dangerous shifter. He needed to become a Guardian as much as I did—before he became a target.

"Fine. If you're sure you didn't do any permanent damage to them."

"I'm sure, love."

Heath speared him with a serious look. "And before you wiped their memories, were you able to discern whether they told anyone about Avery's tiger? In particular anyone within our parents' social circle or with even loose ties to the Council?"

"Mr. Martin was adamant that neither he nor his wife told anyone," Elijah replied. "He doesn't talk to his brother or the rest of his family, who are all Prime felines of some sort. I didn't want to pry as to his beast, but his pheromones tasted like rodent—squirrel if I had to guess."

Ah. Poor Mr. Martin. While it wasn't a given that Prime families would produce children who manifested with a Prime beast soul, it was likely that anyone who didn't would be latent. It was expected—*prized*—in females, but it could also happen in males, and they often went on to excel in secondary affinities because their magical abilities were strong. It might be unfortunate in the eyes of some, but it was also expected and normal.

But to pull a random minor beast from the genetic deck of cards in a family full of Primes? That was rough, and I understood now more than ever why Mr. Martin and his wife chose to live as humans in the city.

Heath blew out a breath, the tension bleeding from his shoulders. "Thank the Moon. I mean, it's been seven months, so you would think we'd have heard by now if there was a rumor flying around our community about the appearance of a white or silver female tiger, but I just...." He looked at me, a worried frown marring his stunning face. "I had to be sure."

"We all did," Aiden agreed.

I let their words hang in the air, taking a moment to look up at the sky. The Moon was almost directly overhead, still big and luminous and thrumming with power.

Still not imparting any sage wisdom either.

These men, my Fated, had been so concerned by the event—the sheer bad luck—that'd sent me on my quest to become a Guardian that Elijah had snuck out of camp, driven two hours, tracked down the Martins, and used his unnerving basilisk talents to (gently) warp their minds.

It was a lot to take in, even if it didn't exactly surprise me.

"Thank you," I said, taking care to look each of them in the eyes. "The fact that there were two people I don't exactly trust out there with the knowledge of my beast was weighing on my family, and I appreciate you all helping me lift that weight."

Aiden reached over and squeezed my knee. "There's nothing more important to us than your safety, sweetheart."

"That's just it," I said. "You guys have had this awful shit with Clara hanging over you. I don't want you to have to keep cleaning up my messes. I don't want to add to your burden."

"You are *never* a burden," Heath growled. "Not to us. You're our mate."

"We're gonna keep you safe, Wildcat," Wyatt added. "Get fucking used to it."

My throat was dry, despite all the Gatorade I'd chugged, but for some reason, I kept talking. "Deep down, this wasn't really all about the Martins. My dads were right when they pushed me to find a way to stop hiding if I ever want to really live my life. Becoming a Guardian is the way I chose to do that." I locked eyes with Heath and let my beast shine through. "And being a part of this group, this quintet, is the right thing for me to accomplish that goal. I know it is. It doesn't mean I've agreed to be your mate or your central, but I am agreeing, wholeheartedly and no longer under protest, to be a part of this team."

Heath beamed the most beautiful smile I'd ever beheld. "I'll take it, Killer."

Elijah pulled my hand from my lap and brought it to his lips, pressing a soft kiss to my inner wrist. "We're better when you're with us, Dove." He rolled gracefully to his feet and offered me a hand up.

I accepted, and then I dug my feet into the sand and stretched my sore limbs. While I did that, Elijah gathered my swords and handed them over.

Wyatt scooped his ax off the ground and then dropped a kiss on top of my head. "Thanks again, baby. I love watching you work." He tossed his ax onto his shoulder and sauntered off. I didn't *not* stare at his round, muscular ass as he went.

Elijah exchanged a knowing look with Ian, which was weird, but then he winked at me and trailed after Wyatt.

Heath took his newly blessed saber from Aiden, threaded it through his belt, and gave me one last heated glance before he strode away.

Aiden packed up Elijah's knives, then slid his saber into the sheath on his back. In a few strides, he was in front of me, peering down into my face, his expression tender. "Best rune student I've ever had," he whispered, lifting a hand to caress my cheek softly. "The most beautiful too."

And then he kissed me.

His kiss was soft but insistent, and entirely too brief. My

brain shut down, and my tiger purred happily as he stroked my tongue with his before pressing his lips one last time to mine, then to my nose, then to my forehead.

"Thank you for allowing yourself to trust us," he murmured. "We're going to show you that trust is not misplaced."

With those parting words, he left, jogging down the beach to catch up with the others.

A throat cleared behind me. I whirled to find Ian smirking at me, his towel balled under his arm and all his potion-making supplies packed away in his backpack. Brody had come down from his rock, his arm thrown around Ian's shoulders and a knowing smile on his face.

I sighed. "Shut up, both of you."

"Come on, Aves," Ian said, laughing. "We'll walk you back."

I pointed his katana at him. "Not a word. I mean it."

"Sure thing. Neither Brody nor I have any comment whatsoever on your doting mates running around and fixing all our problems."

I grumbled at them, but they were both mercifully silent as they led me back to my cabin and tucked me into bed.

26

ELIJAH

Mate, my beast hissed in my head.

Yes, I replied. *Patience.*

Mine. Ours.

Yes, ours. Soon.

This was my fault for bringing the basilisk to the surface so I could track my dove's every move. It was Friday, so we'd been excused from combat tactics class in the afternoon and sent off to play sports like real summer campers. Avery had been whisked away by her brother and the cats to play flag football with the Support Squadron trainees, while my quad had been left at the sand volleyball courts with the rest of our Guardian class.

We won every game. Boring.

So boring that I'd resorted to engaging in my favorite activity—watching my dove.

She was a speedy little blonde demon out there, her long legs on display under her tiny shorts, her ponytail whipping with her every move.

I was salivating.

So was the beast.

Mate.

Wyatt nudged me. "Anyone touched her in a way that means I should beat the shit out of them?"

"So far, no," I replied. "If it happens, you'll have to beat me over there."

"Behave, both of you," Heath said, sounding grouchy. His wolf had really been riding him these past few weeks. The revelation that Avery knew everything about Clara had sucker punched him hard.

So had finally tasting her sweet lips, I would imagine.

And I sympathized because the basilisk had decided that Avery's tentative new openness to us meant that it was time to bond.

To burrow under her skin and become one with her.

To follow her around forever, whether she wanted us or not.

A thrilling, tantalizing fantasy.

"We're finally making progress with her," Heath went on. "Don't fuck it up by maiming one of her Support Squadron friends."

"Spoilsport," I said, grinning. He rolled his eyes, but he couldn't hide his enjoyment of my thirst for violence. "Fine. I'll save it for Cash and the cowards he calls his quadmates."

Aiden stepped off the court and joined us on the sidelines. He grabbed one of our assigned sport bottles, squirted water into his mouth, and wiped the sweat from his face with the hem of his shirt. He was excellent at volleyball and had subbed in for a trio who'd needed a fourth. "Ward is doing the best he can," he said, "but unless the higher-ups in the Guardians remove Cash's quad from the training program entirely, it'll be impossible to keep them from interacting with Avery eventually."

"Fuck them and their 'best in class' wraith kill count,"

Wyatt muttered. "They'd have been tossed to the curb a long time ago if it wasn't for that."

Indeed, and Cash and crew were back at camp after a week of mandated vacation. At least Ward had rearranged training assignments so that they were working with the gold shirts, while Ward and Commander Moss were stuck with our class.

I, for one, was nearing the end of my restraint. Plenty of our fellow Guardians weren't fans of Avery's presence here, but most of them had grown to at least begrudgingly accept her if not been won over completely by her stellar performance.

But there was something more insidious about Cash's quad and their hatred of her.

The basilisk had marked them for death.

One more wrong move, and I'd let him have it.

The beast nudged me.

Yes, back to our dove.

Avery had finished up her game and was standing on the sidelines, drinking her water and chatting amiably with Brody and one of the avians.

A wave of gold shirts crested the hill behind them, returning from their water sports activities on the lake.

Kellan Crimson sighted Avery immediately, and a hungry smile crept onto his face. It was rare that my dove was without us hovering nearby, and Kellan was no fool.

His quad veered away from the pack and marched straight toward her.

"We're done here," I snapped at my quad. "Crimson is going for it."

"Damn it," Heath growled. "I'm about to let you kill him."

I whistled. George unfurled from where he'd been

sunning himself on a nearby rock. The basilisk radiated possessive violence, and my python caught on instantly.

He zipped away, winding down the sloping grass and across the athletic field, amethyst scales glimmering in the afternoon sun, eager to be reunited with Avery. Campers in his path shouted in alarm and sprinted as fast as they could in the other direction.

I jogged after him, the rest of my quad at my back.

We arrived to find Kellan and Ari not so subtly chatting up Ian and Brody while Teegan looked on stoically. It was Hank the jolly bear shifter who had the death wish today as he sidled up to my dove, making sure he took a long, hard look at her ass before he got her attention.

"—were wondering if you wanted to go out on the boat with us," he was saying, beaming a big hapless smile down at her. He reached for her hand. "Come on. We just took one of the ski boats for a spin. You'd love—"

George shot forward, reared up, and struck.

Hank hardly had time to register the open jaw headed for his throat. "What the f—"

George sank his teeth into Hank's thick neck and whipped his long body around Hank's rotund frame. The momentum knocked Hank over, and he hit the ground like a felled tree, shouting expletives as George constricted around him.

"George, come on," Avery said with a sigh that was equal parts exasperated and affectionate.

Kellan stormed up to me. "Get that snake the fuck off Hank, or I'll finally fucking kill it."

The basilisk shot to the surface. Scales bloomed on my arms, and my vision sharpened into monochrome. "Try it," I hissed.

Heath was engaged in a similar standoff with Teegan and Aiden with Ari.

Hank's huge bear burst from his struggling body, but George adjusted, still wrapped around that big furry neck. The bear lumbered off, roaring and tossing his head around.

Wyatt barked a laugh, let his own bear out, and ran after Hank. That would be fun for him.

Kellan jabbed me in the chest with his finger. "I've had enough of this, Harrow. You don't have any fucking claim on Avery beyond the fact that Gale is playing favorites by sticking her with your unit."

"Wrong," I hissed. "So unbelievably fucking wrong."

Kellan's eyes flashed orange, and whispers of feathers appeared along his neck. Beastly aggression saturated the air, coming from all directions.

I prepared the basilisk for battle.

"Hey, that's enough," Avery snapped. "All of you—"

"Harrow, I need to talk to you," Ian said suddenly.

I stuffed the beast back inside and turned to face him. He had his phone pressed to his ear, and he looked grim.

"About?" I asked cautiously.

"You know." He looked at his sister. "You need to come with us, Aves."

Everyone deflated. Ian didn't often look so serious, and it had apparently thrown even the Crimsons.

"What?" Avery looked between Ian and me. "Is this about whatever has had you two acting weird with each other?"

Had we? "I suspect so, Dove."

Brody wrapped his arms around Ian and whispered something in his ear. Ian nodded and straightened his spine. "Let's go, both of you," he said to me and Avery.

Heath clapped me on the shoulder. "Go. Aiden will retrieve George, and I'll get control of everything else here."

My quad leader was a saint. "Thank you."

I reached for Avery's hand and threaded my fingers through hers. She wore her swords and a look of confusion, but she didn't pull away.

Maybe she could tell that I needed her.

The taste of her trepidation was bittersweet on my lips, so maybe she needed me too.

I squeezed her hand, and then we followed silently after Ian.

IAN LED US TO THE FRONT OF THE CAMPGROUNDS. WE rounded the side of the main building, where Ward had his office and we our classroom sessions, and then we stopped on a small covered patio attached to the back of the building. The patio contained a single long picnic table and several circular metal tables and had a view of an idyllic meadow, the tree line, and the mountains in the distance.

"Ian, what is going on?" Avery asked, her voice full of concern.

She still held my hand, and I relished it.

"I promise I'll explain, Aves," he replied gently.

I certainly had an idea of what our fox might have to discuss with us, and the basilisk slithered under my skin, agitated and bloodthirsty.

The door to the building opened, and Ward stepped out.

He was followed by Joseph, Avery and Ian's fox father.

The pharmacist. The one with the apothecary affinity, like his son. He had kind green eyes, and his long golden hair was tied in a messy knot on the back of his head. He was about Avery's height and had the same leanly muscled body as Ian.

The basilisk coiled tight at his presence. Bracing. Avery's father didn't travel all the way here for no reason.

Avery gasped. "J? What in the world—"

He smiled at his daughter, pausing his lively conversation with Ward. The two of them were friends already, it seemed. "Hi, sweetheart. How are... things?" His eyes twinkled as he cast a pointed glance at where Avery's hand was in mine.

She didn't seem to notice, releasing me to go throw her arms around his neck. "Is everything okay?" she asked him. "Is something wrong? Why are you here?"

He patted her back and gestured for her to sit down at the table. She set her sword harness on the ground and then did as he asked. I slid onto the bench next to her and made sure our thighs were touching. I pulled her hand into my lap under the table, and she didn't protest.

"Everything is fine, Aves," Joseph said. "As fine as ever, anyway. I'm here because Ian asked for my help with something that affects both our family and Elijah's." His kind gaze slid to me. "Hello, Elijah. It's nice to see you again."

"You as well, sir," I replied, forcing a smile through the tension in my chest.

"Well," Ward said, frowning at the scene. He turned to head back inside. "I'll leave you all to it—"

"Wait," I said. Even with Avery's hand in mine, I was suddenly drowning. I looked imploringly at Wyatt's dad, the closest person I had to a father besides Uncle Horatio. "Ward, would you mind... staying?"

Avery squeezed my hand.

His bushy red brows crept up his forehead, and then his expression softened. "Sure, son."

He grabbed one of the metal chairs from an adjacent table and pulled it up to the end of ours. He sat down, his enormous body challenging the chair's frame, and crossed his burly arms over his chest.

Ian and Joseph sat down on the bench across from Avery and me. Ian reached into his backpack and extracted the belladonna knife. He set it gingerly on the table.

Ward went eerily still.

"Ian, what is that?" Avery asked slowly.

Her brother looked at me expectantly.

"Dove, I believe this is the weapon that killed my mother."

She blinked at me, her confusion growing. "And why does Ian have it?"

"I, uh, saw this knife in action recently," Ian said, darting a furtive look at Ward, who caught on immediately and sent an exasperated look my way. "And it caused the, um, stab-ee to experience certain symptoms." He paused, his expression turning grave. "Symptoms I recognized."

Avery gasped.

"I asked Elijah if I could take the dagger and study it," Ian went on. "And, obviously, I went to J for help. The reason we're all sitting here is that J and I both believe, without a doubt, that Elijah's mother's murder and our mother's murder are connected."

My dove went rigid next to me, her horror palpable and bitter on my lips. The basilisk hissed angrily—at my distress and hers. My fangs lengthened and my vision slid into the sharpened colorless focus of my beast before I blinked it away.

"For the benefit of everyone at this table," Joseph said, "let's start at the beginning. We are all aware of what Avery's beast is."

"A magnificent animal," Ward declared, and Avery softened slightly, her cheeks pinking.

My adorable, savage girl.

"Avery and Ian's mother, Gwen, had a nearly identical beast," Joseph went on. "And like Avery, she kept it a secret. Gwen only shifted when we were in the remote wilderness or in emergency situations. Nineteen years ago, we had a rare wraith incursion in the small Colorado mountain town we lived in. The shifter population was minimal there, so we saw wraiths once a year or so and rarely above the power level of a small Ripper. But that night, Gwen and Rand got tangled with a Giant, and Gwen was injured enough that she shifted."

An eerily familiar story. No wonder Avery's fathers shoved her straight into the powerful embrace of the Guardians.

"We did not think anyone saw her. We were in the woods, and no one else in our community was out that night." He sighed, the grief he still felt a visible weight on his shoulders. "But I suppose we were wrong. Several weeks later, when Gwen and Rand were out walking in broad daylight, she was shot multiple times by human hunters in a supposed accident."

Avery was silent. Her beast reached for mine. She was sorrowful, mourning her mother as I was sure she did nearly every day of her life.

"Naturally, Gwen tried to shift immediately after she was shot," Joseph said. "Even silver bullets would not have cut off access to a beast as powerful as hers, and we later found out the bullets were not silver. But she was unable to access her animal. Rand rushed her to the local healer—a latent man from a wolf family who was quite adept with his healing affinity."

"But her body rejected the magic," I finished for him in a low voice. "Aiden said he could feel it pushing back when he tried the same thing himself."

Joseph nodded grimly.

"What?" Avery said. "You stabbed someone with this dagger, and Aiden tried to heal him? When did this happen?"

While you were using Wyatt for your pleasure, my love.

"Don't worry about that, Dove."

Ian looked at me. "And your mother's story is similar enough, correct?"

I nodded. "She was murdered twenty years ago, about six months after my fathers were killed by wraiths, in an alleged mugging at a farmers' market." Avery squeezed my hand again, and I found there wasn't so much pain in retelling this story when her hand was in mine. "She was stabbed with this dagger, which I only recovered last fall. My mom didn't have a beast, but her body similarly rejected all magical attempts to heal her."

Joseph smiled encouragingly at me. "And her tox screen showed no substances poisonous to humans or shifters."

It wasn't a question. "Yes."

"I took the liberty of contacting your uncle," he explained. "I hope you don't mind."

I certainly did not mind. If my dreams came true, we'd all be one big happy family in the near future.

"Mom's tox screen was the same," Ian told the group. "But my family obviously suspected foul play, and Dad saved the bullets. Don't worry," he added at Avery's stricken look, "we didn't bring them here."

Ward had been taking this all in like we were combatants on the battlefield and our enemy was afoot. The red sheen of a murderous bear glinted in his eyes. "So aside from the deliberate attacks and strange symptoms," he said, "what makes you think these tragedies are connected?"

Ian gestured at the dagger. "Seeing this dagger in action, along with the belladonna flower carved into the hilt, gave me a bit of a lightbulb moment. There were clearly trace amounts of *some* kind of substance on the blade, given that it was still able to affect the, ah, person Elijah stabbed. Maybe the same was true of the bullets. So, I developed some theories and ran some tests. With my dad's help, of course."

"What is it about the belladonna specifically?" I asked. I was kicking myself for not identifying the design earlier, but then again, I wouldn't have known the first thing about what it could have possibly meant.

Joseph propped his elbows on the table and steepled his fingers in front of his face. "*Atropa belladonna* is one of the more toxic plants on earth—to humans. Its roots, stalk, flowers, and berries all contain a compound that, when ingested, can cause maladies like blurred vision, tachycardia, rashes, hallucinations, delirium, all kinds of nasty stuff."

"It also has a kind of mythical status in human lore," Ian added. "Supposedly used by the Romans as biological weapons. Some theorize it was the poison Romeo and Juliet used to end their lives. A symbol of both the beautiful and deadly, that kind of thing."

Like our mate, said the basilisk.

Yes, indeed. Pay attention, this is important.

"But the toxin wouldn't necessarily be poisonous to shifters," I said, following the natural logic. "The magic in our bodies makes us more resistant to such things."

"Correct," Joseph replied. "Ingesting belladonna toxin might give a shifter a stomachache, but that's about the extent of it. Still, it's the closest thing we have to a controlled substance in our practice, mostly because the toxic effects can be worsened via lunar magic infusion, which would be fatal to humans. We still exist in their world, after all, and we can't have that kind of thing just laying around."

"But from what you're saying," Avery said, "there's no way our mom or Elijah's mom died from being poisoned with belladonna toxin. It couldn't have killed them."

"Right," Ian replied. "And there was nothing in Mom or Elijah's mother's bloodwork to indicate poison, belladonna toxin or otherwise."

"But it was the key to figuring this out?" I asked.

"The thing about the belladonna," Joseph said, "is that, while it isn't necessarily poisonous to us, it is one of the most magically potent plants known to shifterkind. Under a Full Moon, it can absorb so much magic that it makes the plant incredibly unstable and nearly impossible to work with, even for those of us with a strong apothecary affinity."

"Very few of us mess with it," Ian added. "It's a pain in the ass, and all the potential uses for it are theoretical."

"But some of those theories," Joseph said, "posit powerful and frankly horrifying uses for super-charged belladonna extract, made from the plant's roots, stalk, and leaves. A shifter with extraordinary talent and control in this affinity could, *in theory*, use the magic-absorbing potential of the plant to create a substance that cloaks or conceals everything within it. It could also, *in theory*, amplify the effects of the concealed substance."

Ward swore.

Ian looked at me, probably because it was too difficult for him to look at his sister, who was taking this all in with a bone-chilling calm that said she'd gone to her numb place. "What is the one substance that could both cut off access to our beast and make our bodies repel healing magic?"

I knew immediately. "Silver."

Joseph smiled sadly. "Exactly. More specifically, colloidal silver that has been infused with a magic repelling spell, rather than a magic absorbing one, like what is used to create the anti-wraith wards around Proteus College."

Ward frowned deeply. "But the presence of silver in the body would've been the first thing a shifter physician would've tested for, given the symptoms."

"Exactly," Joseph said. "They did, in both cases, and found nothing. For Gwen, they ruled her cause of death inconclusive but still an accident. For Elijah's mother, there was some nonsense about her body giving up. Her magical soul rejecting the will to live because of the loss of her bonded quad."

"She would never," I hissed. I hated that bullshit the doctors concocted about my mother.

"Of course not," Joseph said gently. "She had you."

"The point of all of this," Ian said, "is that the belladonna could be used, *in theory*, to create a poison that would deliver a small amount of colloidal silver into the blood and both amplify its effects on the body and conceal it so that it is completely untraceable." He leaned forward, and the electric sheen of his beast gleamed in his eyes. "And if you go into this knowing exactly what you're looking for, you can reveal the presence of the belladonna. Which we did, in trace amounts, on both the dagger and the bullets."

Avery sucked in a harsh breath.

I wrapped my arm around her and pulled her tight into my side. "I'm sorry, Dove," I whispered, my lips pressed to her hair. "I'm so sorry this is happening."

I'd had many months to come to terms with the hunt for this murderer. Avery was having to absorb right here, right now, that her mother did not die in a tragic accident—something she'd always suspected but hadn't known for sure—and that we were looking for the same killer.

She snuggled tight against me, and it was a wonderful feeling, despite the circumstances. If she let me, I would share this and every other burden of hers until the end of time.

"Nothing to be sorry for, Elijah," she said. "We're all in this with you now."

Ward glared at the mountains in the distance before he asked the table the million-dollar question. "But *why*? Gwen was a powerful Prime female and a tiger to boot, and there are zealot-types out there that would target her for that. But Amara was a latent war widow. Why was she targeted? It makes no sense."

Joseph blew out a resigned breath, and then he looked at me, sympathy and curiosity both clear in his gaze. "It might if Elijah's mother was not actually latent."

27

AVERY

Elijah's body went rigid against mine. "What?" he rasped. "Of course she was latent."

I rubbed a soothing hand over his thigh. "Maybe. Or she might've been hiding a powerful animal. It would make sense."

He shook his head. "I.... Would she have lied to my uncle?"

My dad's smile was full of empathy. "We don't know anything for sure, but if she was some kind of powerful Prime, she likely hid it from everyone who wasn't your fathers. Gwen did, and as did her grandmother before her. And, of course, you understand how hard Avery works to keep her own beast a secret."

Elijah nodded. He'd seen me take enough hits without shifting to know how much someone like me didn't trust the shifter population at large.

"Do you have any other family members on your mother's side you could contact?" Ian asked.

He shook his head. "I don't think so. My mother was an only child, and my grandparents on that side are long dead."

I rubbed his thigh again. The thought of little orphan Elijah made my heart pinch, but he had his aunt and uncle, and Ward, and his quad brothers. Also a gaggle of teenage sisters. He wasn't alone.

"Elijah," Ward said, "why don't you bring Avery's family up to speed on what your investigation has revealed in the months since you discovered that dagger. Then we can all be on the same page and move forward together."

I sat up straighter. I hadn't known until today that Elijah had recovered his mother's murder weapon. It was just like him to immediately throw himself into finding answers, and it explained his lengthy absences from school last semester.

I listened, riveted, as he walked us through everything he'd learned, absently playing with the ends of my hair as he spoke. He told us how he'd come across the dagger while out in a bar with Wyatt last fall, how he'd traced it to a scummy shifter motorcycle club in South Fulton, how he'd discovered the old President and VP had been doing jobs for some unknown rich Primes and that their contact went by the name of "Archprime."

How he suspected that the President and VP had been the ones to kill his mom.

And how the President's widow had given him a name from a bank statement.

Lunar Heritage.

"Horatio's looked into this company," Elijah said, "and so far hasn't been able to find anything."

"It is probably not a normal law-abiding, tax-paying business that would be on the government's books," Joseph mused. "And it's entirely possible it no longer exists or has changed its name. That was twenty years ago."

I rolled all the horrifying, tragic things I'd learned while sitting at this table around in my head. My beast paced her cage, her thirst for violence spurred by Elijah's beast doing the same. My family had always believed my mother's death was no accident, but for damn near two decades, there'd been nothing but dead ends when we'd tried to figure out more. My dads had to tread so lightly, always terrified that their poking around could result in someone asking questions about my mother's beast. They'd never even been able to get the identities of the hunters out of the human authorities.

Elijah's discovery of the dagger and the subsequent intertwining of our lives—both by happenstance and divine will—had changed *everything*.

A focused calm descended. This was another battle to fight, another enemy to slay.

"Okay," I said. "Here's what we think we know: Both our mothers were killed by the same untraceable poison—"

"It was their injuries that killed them," my dad said gently. "The poison prevented them from being able to heal or be healed."

"Right," I said. "And it was made with belladonna extract that both masked and amplified the effects of silver as it entered their bloodstreams via the bullets or the dagger. This substance could only have been made by a shifter with an apothecary affinity so powerful that they were able to successfully create something that is still, to this day, considered theoretical. How am I doing?"

"Wonderfully," Joseph replied. "That's another head-scratching aspect of this. Whoever created this poison has not gone public with their skill. They would be printing money. The absolute top of the profession."

"Obviously they prefer to use their powers for evil, J," Ian said.

"And it seems odd," Elijah mused, "that they'd broadcast

the key to their special poison by using a dagger with the secret ingredient carved into the hilt."

"I suspect they thought it was poetic," Joseph said wryly. "A deadly flower with rich human lore behind it."

"And they think they're smarter than we are," Ian said derisively. "Joke's on them."

"And we also know," I went on, "that, at least back then, the people behind this were rich Primes with evil genius apothecary talents on their payroll and a penchant for paying motorcycle clubs to do their dirty work."

"And they were going by the dumb moniker 'Lunar Heritage,'" Ian added with a roll of his eyes. "And were possibly being led by someone using the even dumber moniker 'Archprime.'"

My tiger bristled. Some asshole had anointed himself king of the jungle.

"And lastly," I went on, "both of our mothers were killed in the wake of wraith attacks. My mom after she shifted to fight a Giant, Elijah's mom after she survived the attack on their home by Giants and an Apex wraith during a lunar eclipse."

"Do you think someone was there the night my parents died?" Elijah asked. "Maybe my mother saw something she wasn't supposed to see?"

"We're going to find out," I told him.

Ward slapped his meaty hand on the table. "Damn right we are. I have a few ideas." He stood up and pointed at my dad. "How about a scotch, J? It's happy hour in my office, and these young people tire me."

Joseph jumped to his feet and winked at me. I tamped down my scowl. My dad had gotten chummy very fast with one of my *Fated's* fathers. I'd call him a turncoat, but I also happened to like Ward Gale. *He'd* never been anything but awesome to me.

"Sure," he said to Ward. "We can finish our chat about the various remedies I can whip up for your back pain."

"My man," Ward replied, grinning.

And then the old bear and the kind fox disappeared inside the building without a backwards glance.

Ian smothered a smile when I glared at him. He rose and shrugged on his backpack. "Well, I'm off. Brody and I are having a picnic by the campfire."

"Oh, is that what we're calling it now?" I asked, snorting. "No one wants to see that, Ian."

He gave me a droll look. "Not everything is about sex, Aves. Just because Gale flipped the hornball switch in your brain by busting your dry spell—"

"Stop talking," I snapped.

He grinned triumphantly.

Elijah squeezed me affectionately and cleared his throat. "Thank you, Little Baxter. For everything."

Ian saluted him. "I should be thanking you. Your penchant for stabbing people when they insult my sister is what brought us all here."

With that, he strode away.

"*Elijah*," I growled. "Who did you stab?"

He chuckled. "Just a little cleaning up after the Mahoney incident." He threw one of his long legs over the side of the bench to straddle it, turning to face me where I sat next to him. His sly grin faded, and he sighed heavily. "Are you okay, love?"

I arranged myself on the bench to face him. Our knees touched, my face mere inches from his. He smelled like mint and citrus and the lingering musk of a man who'd spent the afternoon sweating in the sun. His yellow-gold eyes were sorrowful, devoid of his usual mischief and danger.

"I'm okay," I assured him. "That was a lot to take in, and I'm not exactly sure how I feel about being left in the dark while Ian and J were running down their theory. I'm sure my other dads knew too. I guess Ian probably didn't want to worry me until he had something."

"Yes," Elijah agreed. "I'm sorry I didn't mention it, Dove, but I actually had very little idea about what your brother was up to. I assumed he'd tell us both when he was ready." He was quiet for a moment, deep in thought while he absently stroked the back of my hand with his thumb. "I'm still just... astounded at what he and your dad were able to figure out. It is beyond my wildest dreams to have made such a breakthrough in the hunt for my mother's killer."

Pride buoyed me. "Ian can be focused and relentless when he wants to be."

He nodded and tucked a finger under my chin, lifting so that I was looking him right in those mesmerizing eyes. "But I wish this wasn't happening to you and your family too. I'm glad you're getting answers, but hate that those answers involve some secret cabal that's hunting female shifters, and I'm terrified we may find it still exists and is a danger to you."

I had a strong suspicion that these killers did still exist in some form, but that wasn't news. I'd been living my life under that assumption since I'd gotten my beast as a preteen.

But this pain and worry on Elijah's face? This was new. He'd been after his mother's murderer for months and had taken it in stride like the focused, cold-blooded killer he was in his own right.

What was new was that it was all connected to my family.

To me.

And that threat, that nebulous danger that had me hiding for the past ten years of my life, that had sent me to the Guardians—it had become all too real.

And it scared him because I was his Fated.

I grasped his face. He was so hauntingly beautiful. "I won't let them get me, Elijah. We're going to find them, and we're going to destroy them."

His eyes hooded, and his sinful smile returned. "I look forward to ripping their hearts from their chests and bathing in their blood with you, my love."

I couldn't help my amused grin. "You had to go there."

"Of course. I don't lie to you."

The chill of the basilisk licked my skin, and my tiger purred and flicked her tail in return. Elijah wrapped his hands around my hips and pulled me into his lap, maneuvering my legs snuggly around him. He was hot and hard and smelled really good. My heart thudded against my ribs, and an ache bloomed between my thighs.

Elijah licked his lips, and his golden eyes began to glow. "You tempt me, Dove. I want to sit you on my cock, right here on this bench, and drive you mad with pleasure. I want to be inside you, to become a part of you, and to never fucking be away from you ever again."

I sucked in a breath. His luminous eyes had me ensnared, and it wasn't the basilisk. It was all Elijah.

The ache intensified.

"But I won't," he murmured. "Not now. You're not ready for me yet. You can have my cock when you decide to let yourself love me back. When you decide I've earned it. Then

I'll fuck you, and love you, and never leave your side for the rest of our long shifter lives."

"*Elijah—*"

"For now," he went on, "we're a team. You and me. The others, too, if you want them. We fight together, and we're going to find out who did such irreparable harm to our families and wipe them from the face of the earth."

It was heady, the power of having this terrifying monster on my side as well as underneath me and between my legs.

I slid my fingers through his silky hair and down the back of his neck. He shivered ever so slightly underneath me, and I almost broke right there. I almost begged him to do exactly as he'd said and bury his cock in me until I fell apart, and I didn't have beastly post-fight urges to blame this time.

"Okay," I whispered. "A team. You and me."

"Perfect," he purred. "My perfect mate."

He closed the distance between us and kissed me. My entire body melted into a gooey puddle, and I moaned against his lips.

He took his time, exploring, nipping, stroking my tongue with his. His hands wandered up my back, and he skimmed his fingertips along my shirt and my exposed skin, sending chills through my entire body.

After a few minutes, he nipped my lip one last time and pressed his forehead to mine. "I need to take you to get some dinner, Dove, or Heath will have my head."

I snorted. "He's so bossy."

"Indeed," Elijah replied with a suggestive grin. "And you haven't even been naked in his bed yet."

I bit the inside of my cheek and batted that image away. It was not what I needed when I was straddling this gorgeous man while he was hard underneath me and my tiger was ready to roll over and show him her belly.

With a reluctant sigh, I climbed off him and put myself back together. I smoothed my clothes, tightened my ponytail, and strapped my blades to my back where they belonged.

We set off for dinner, and I shored up my resolve.

There was so much work to do, and we still had to survive the rest of camp and whatever the wraiths had in store for us when we finally went out on patrol.

28

AIDEN

When we reached the second-to-last week of camp, Ward announced that we'd be getting a break from mandatory classroom sessions, at least until the end of the following week. On those days, we'd be required to receive briefings on strategy and wraith activity before we went out on patrol for the August cycle.

This left our esteemed professor Kit with too much time on his hands, apparently, because he decided to hold office hours during our regularly scheduled classroom time, just in case any of us couldn't resist the urge to seek his knowledge instead of spending extra time at the lake or the archery range or doing any other activity that didn't involve being pleasantly condescended to.

It'd been five days since Elijah had learned that Ian and his father had cracked the code on the belladonna dagger. Unfortunately, the time I'd spent digging through the Gales' resources at their estate over the weekend and whatever I could get my hands on with both my Proteus College faculty and Guardian trainee credentials had yielded nothing particularly helpful.

The urgency of the situation beat an endless drum through my body.

Look harder, solve the puzzle, protect your family.

It'd wrecked my sleep and driven my jaguar to constant pacing in my chest.

Because this involved Avery now. There was quite possibly some powerful underground organization out there that would kill her if they had the chance.

I was going to figure this out.

So here I was, barging into Kit's office with my laptop tucked under my arm. His assigned office was a smaller version of Ward's—the same utilitarian gray carpet, same simple wooden bookshelves, same sturdy desk, same small window, its blinds closed to the bright afternoon sun.

Kit looked up from his computer, his brows bouncing behind the stupid wire frames of his glasses. "Aiden, what—"

I made myself comfortable in one of the two chairs that faced his desk, shoved aside his neat stack of papers, and set my laptop on the desk. "As much as it pains me, Kit, I need your help."

He leaned back in his chair, his surprise morphing into smug satisfaction. "Oh, do you?"

I clenched my jaw and bit back a scathing reply. For Elijah. For Avery.

"Yes," I growled. My jaguar noted my annoyance, but he couldn't be bothered with Kit. That was all me. "Ward informed you that we'd need your assistance with some research into the Guardian archives for a very important and very confidential purpose. You have access to things as a counterinsurgency analyst that he does not as a training officer."

He crossed his arms and frowned. "He did, but I wasn't

informed I'd be working with *you*. I agreed because it was supposed to be a discreet project for Avery—"

"Knock, knock."

At the sound of my mate's beautiful voice in the doorway, Kit lost his scowl and perked up like an excited fucking puppy. "Avery? Come in, please."

Her ethereal blue gaze ping-ponged inquisitively between Kit and me. "Are you two playing nice with each other?"

"Always, sweetheart," I replied, and Kit blew out an annoyed breath. "Thanks for agreeing to meet me here."

"Of course."

She sat down in the chair next to me, her hair damp from her post-lunch shower and braided over her shoulder. She smelled of lavender and jasmine, and suddenly my jaguar cared very much that Kit was in her vicinity, gazing upon her lovely splendor like a smitten asshole.

I'd invited Avery here instead of Elijah because her presence would make Kit more amenable, but I was having second thoughts.

Kit rolled his eyes at my murderous glare and then gave Avery his full attention. "I'm glad you stopped by because I wanted to update you on the progress I've made with headquarters after chatting with you and your brother."

Avery sat up straighter. "Oh? Is it good news?"

He shrugged nonchalantly. "Things are at least moving in the right direction. Leadership is going to send some scouts down to Fulton City during the next few cycles to get a sense of what kind of reinforcements might be needed. The logistics are more complicated, of course, since we'll need to send a team that's a bit more incognito. Need to blend in amongst the humans, so—"

"Kit, we don't have all day," I snapped. After a calming

breath, I softened my expression and smiled fondly at Avery. "Not that it isn't fantastic news that the shifters in the city are finally going to get the help they need."

She managed not to roll her eyes at me.

Kit cleared his throat. "So, Avery, this research you need help with is a project you're working on with Aiden?"

"Yes. It's for me and Elijah, so naturally Elijah's quad is involved."

"I see."

I thumped an impatient finger on his desk. "I'm going to be asking the questions, Kit. Your eyes better be on me or your computer for the rest of this meeting."

He shot Avery a conspiratorial smile. "Primes. So over-bearing, aren't they?"

She chuckled and sent a teasing smirk my way. "They really are."

Brat.

My jaguar rumbled a pleased purr.

Back to business. "Kit, we need everything you can possibly find on the deaths of the Harrow Quad that occurred in Zone 3 during the lunar eclipse on March 6, 2006. Surely there was an incident report filed by the Guardians."

He lost his mirth entirely. It was common knowledge that Elijah was an orphan, but how his parents died was not. "Ah. Let me see what I can find."

His fingers flew over his keyboard.

Avery leaned closer to me. "You're thinking that some-thing happened that night that put Elijah's mom on the radar of the killers?"

"It's the theory that makes the most sense," I replied in a low voice.

"It is true that in the case of wraith casualties, there

should be an incident report on file," Kit said distractedly as he typed. "Those are usually classified for the privacy of the deceased and other community security concerns, but we should have no issues given my clearance. In a lunar eclipse situation, there should also be nonclassified, detailed reports on the locations of all wraiths, but especially all L4s and any L5 that manage to break out of the realm."

It occurred to me that all the information we had on the night Elijah's fathers died came from his mother. She'd told Horatio and Kat that her bonded quad had been killed fighting half a dozen Giants and an Apex and that she'd only just managed to escape with toddler Elijah in her arms. She'd never mentioned any Guardians making it to the scene before she'd fled.

Would the official report show something different?

"Huh." Kit leaned back in his chair and studied whatever was on his screen. "That's weird."

"What is?" Avery asked.

"Well, the Zone 3 report from that night is... a little sparse." He typed some more. "In the case of the deaths of an entire quad of Primes, we should have names, descriptions of injuries, detailed medical examiner reports, names of any survivors or witnesses, and a cataloging of the wraiths involved, including not just the power level but physical descriptions, if available. It's important for the defense strategy of that particular zone in the future. But...."

He frowned at his computer. We waited.

"All that's available in our archive is an entry stating that there were four male shifters killed on a remote ranch property in the northeast quadrant of Zone 3 on March 6, 2006. That's it."

Avery and I exchanged a look. Had that entry been scrubbed?

Kit's gaze bounced between the two of us. "What do you know about what happened to Elijah's parents?"

I told him. A gang of Giants. An Apex. His mother's escape and subsequent suspicious death, though I went lighter on those details. Avery added a vague mention that her mother had also died under mysterious circumstances and that we were working under a theory that they were connected.

Kit gaped at us. "There was an Apex in Zone 3 that night?"

"I don't think Elijah's mother would lie about that," I replied tersely.

He went back to his computer. "We absolutely have reports of an Apex wraith appearance during that particular eclipse event. But it was in Zone 13, which is on the complete opposite side of the map. Because an L5 cannot be killed, only outlasted, we have detailed reports of its path from the moment it broke through the veil until the first hint of daybreak, when it disappeared back into its realm. It killed ten shifters and injured two dozen more. It went nowhere near Zone 3, so it cannot be the same Apex wraith."

I chewed on that. "According to Elijah's mother, it was around 1:00 a.m. when she and Elijah escaped. In theory, the L5 should've had two or three more hours to rampage around, and while Zone 3 is sparsely populated, there is a wealthy gated community in neighboring Zone 4 that contains at least one cluster of higher-powered shifter souls. It should've tracked that way, and someone else would've seen it. There should be a record of it *somewhere*."

"Yes," Kit agreed. "Something is not adding up. I don't like it. Not just for the sake of Elijah's family, but for the entire Guardian project. We can't have these sorts of holes in our records."

"Kit," Avery said softly, "do you remember how on our first day of class you told us that Zone 3 is marked as dormant on our map because there haven't been any wraith sightings there for quite some time. Can you check and see when the last recorded sighting occurred for that zone?"

Brilliant, my mate. We'd all thought that was odd, but was that night truly the moment that switch flipped?

He stared at her, his frown deepening. "Shit." A few more seconds of frenzied typing. "Shit," he said again.

Avery's smile was knowing and sad. "Nothing since the cycle before the eclipse, I bet?"

"Correct. And as we discussed in class, I suspect the neighboring zones are actually dormant as well, though there are sparse sightings from over the years, likely from wraiths that spawned in other zones and drifted into those." He banged his fist on the desk. "Shit. We could've been studying this for *decades* if these records hadn't been... incomplete."

"Tampered with, Kit," I said. "Or deliberately *underreported*. I know that's hard to believe, given the Guardians are, for the most part, an organization of honest and noble shifters. But there are always bad apples, and there are people out there with agendas that don't align with our mission."

"Is there a way to look at who's accessed this entry in your system?" Avery asked him.

Kit's distress morphed into pissed-off determination. He cracked his knuckles. "Indirectly. I had a hand in designing the latest version of our electronic records system, so if someone tampered with this entry and tried to hide it, even twenty years ago, they weren't accounting for *me*."

I smothered my eye roll. At least Kit's arrogance was making itself useful.

As he set out typing and clicking and scrolling, I let my beast nose at Avery's. She hadn't moved a muscle in several minutes, and while she appeared calm, her gaze was boring into Kit's computer like she could break it open and make it reveal all the secrets we sought. Her tiger was agitated, pacing, incensed at the hurt these nefarious forces had caused to her basilisk's family as well as her own.

I pulled Avery's hand into my lap and then began to rub little soothing circles on her palm with my thumb.

The tiger quieted. Avery sighed and gave me a small, grateful smile.

I felt like I could fly.

"Motherf—I've got you." Kit banged on a few more keys and then looked up at us. "Access log, twenty-four hours after the incident. A log-in linked to a Franklin Fordham. A Prime panther, twenty-five years old and two-year veteran of the Guardian force at the time. The system only recorded a single access to log this report, which means it wasn't altered. It was, as Aiden said, underreported."

I swore. "So there never was a true record of what happened?"

He shook his head. "Not officially in the Guardian system, it appears. But the patrol logs for Zone 3 that night were easier to locate. Franklin wasn't in a bonded quad, but he'd been assigned to a unit that was covering the entire eastern half of the zone. It wasn't a high priority area, even during the eclipse, because it was so sparsely populated."

Reluctantly, I released Avery's hand. I flipped my laptop open and went immediately into one of the databases I had access to via my Proteus faculty credentials.

"Do you know any of the shifters in that unit?" Avery asked Kit. "Are they still Guardians?"

"It appears not," he replied. "Franklin separated from

the force a year later. Two others were assigned to different unit and were killed in the field in a particularly bad wraith event a year later. The last member of the unit went AWOL and hasn't been heard from since."

"Convenient," Avery murmured.

"Sure is," Kit replied.

I clicked rapidly through the public records I'd found for the name Fordham until one snagged my attention. I pulled the only property record with an address in Georgia, registered to a Franklin Fordham. I located an expired driver's license photo, and it showed an elderly man—too old to be our Franklin Fordham.

Going off a hunch, I entered the address into an online real estate marketplace. I studied the photo in front of me.

My throat went dry. Avery wrapped a hand gently around my bicep. "Kit," I said slowly, "was our Franklin Fordham actually Franklin Fordham Junior or even the third, by chance?"

"Hmm." He typed and scrolled some more. "Yeah, he's got Franklin Fordham III listed on his intake questionnaire."

I tilted my laptop screen toward Avery. On it was a photo of a historic mansion located in a remote area of the state and visible atop a sloping hill beyond a stone wall and a wrought iron gate. Ward runes had been etched into that stone, shining in the sun, likely coated in liquid silver. I pointed at the greenery that bordered the gate—two lush bushes containing purple flowers and dotted with onyx berries. "What does that look like to you?"

She gasped. "Belladonna."

29

AVERY

"What?" Kit was on his feet and striding around to the front of his desk before I could fully process what I was seeing. He leaned over my shoulder to stare at Aiden's screen. "Like the plant? The deadly nightshade?"

"Too close, Kit," Aiden growled.

I managed the wherewithal to punch Aiden in the arm. "Quit it. He's fine."

Kit chuckled under his breath and leaned in further, studying the photo. "Fascinating. A potent magical conductor, though it has little utility in modern shifter apothecary practice. Did you know, Avery, that some literary scholars theorize the deadly nightshade is what Romeo and Juliet used to shuffle off this mortal coil?"

"Way to mix your Shakespeare," Aiden muttered.

"I did, in fact," I replied diplomatically. "I've recently learned quite a bit about this plant, actually."

Kit shifted from hovering over my shoulder to leaning against the edge of his desk, facing me, his legs crossed casually and splayed out next to mine. He folded his arms over his chest and narrowed his eyes at me. "What is the significance of the belladonna to all of this?"

Aiden vibrated next to me. He glared at Kit, as was his usual setting in our instructor's presence, but behind those softly glowing hazel eyes there was... pain?

Despair?

I shook off my concern, at least for the moment. The discovery Aiden had just made with Kit's assistance was monumental. "The belladonna is a symbol tied to the group of people responsible for the murder of my mother and Elijah's," I replied. Kit didn't need to know the finer details. "And, thanks to you, we now know that what happened to Elijah's mom is connected to what happened the night his fathers died. And we have a family name to look into. We really appreciate your help, Kit."

I elbowed Aiden.

He cleared his throat. "Right. Yes. This was extremely helpful. Thank you."

"Of course," Kit said, smiling at me. "I'm happy to continue assisting with anything you need as you investigate. For my part, I'll work on tracking down any other records from that 2006 lunar eclipse in our archives to see if there is anything that *respectable* Guardians of the time left for us that may shed some light on things."

"That would be great," I said.

He reached out and gave my shoulder an affectionate squeeze. "I look forward to working with you once you become a Guardian, Avery. You're exceptionally talented."

Heat crept into my cheeks at the compliment, but I managed a professional smile. Aiden remained silent, but the sharp bite of his jaguar pulsed, saturating the air. He was holding on by a thread, on the edge of violence, which was entirely unnecessary for the noncombative situation in this office and inappropriately directed at Kit given the vast power imbalance between the two of them.

It was time to go.

Kit had taken the hint and returned to his side of the desk, looking both annoyed and resigned. I stood up and grabbed Aiden by the arm. "Thanks again, Kit!" I waved at him over my shoulder as I dragged a stone-faced Professor Blackwell out of the room.

WARD'S OFFICE, A FEW DOORS DOWN FROM KIT'S, WAS EMPTY. We had about half an hour before we had to report to our afternoon combat session, so he was probably out on the field with Commander Moss, prepping for whatever they had in store for the day.

I shoved Aiden inside the office, shut the door with a firm click, then lifted my chin to stare him down. "What is your problem?"

He appeared more bemused than murderous now. He sat down on Ward's desk and leaned back on his hands. His taut forearms flexed. My tiger purred, and I mentally swatted her on the nose.

Don't get distracted.

"What do you mean?" he asked innocently.

"Kit was helping us. *You* asked him to help us. And we discovered something crucial to solving this mystery. We are *light-years* ahead of where we were even a week ago. I can't wait to tell Elijah, and I know you feel the same."

"Of course I do—"

"And *yet*," I went on, "after all that, you looked like you couldn't decide whether you wanted to tear Kit's head off, which is not okay, or jump off a cliff, which is even *more* not okay. I get that you two were academic rivals of sorts, and I get that he's a little flirtatious, but you guys have been *mostly* better about all that cave-beast possessive shit, except around the Crimsons, which I also kind of get, but Kit's not—"

He shoved off the desk, and in two strides of his long legs, he was on me, pressing my back against the door and obliterating the rest of my thought.

"Were you trying to torture me?" he growled, caging me with his strong arms, his eyes ringed in turquoise. "By letting Kit be that close to you? By letting him touch you?"

I bared my teeth at him even as his fresh woodsy smell and his nearness had heat pooling between my legs. "You're being ridiculous—"

"I deserve it," he rasped. "But I don't have to like it. Maybe you like it, though, just a little bit. Tell me, sweetheart, do you like that Kit thinks he has a shot with you? That he thinks you're just an ordinary female, destined for an ordinary mate bond with a guy like him, and not one of the most powerful Prime shifters alive, destined to be the *beating-fucking-heart* of my quad?"

I gasped as he pressed his hard body fully against mine and wrapped my ponytail around his hand. "*Aiden.*"

He ran his nose from my collarbone to my ear, his voice a vicious whisper. "You like driving me mad. You always have, even before we fucked everything up. Sitting in my office with your big, beautiful eyes and your tight little body and your dazzling fucking *mind*. Kit sees it, baby. He wants it, and he thinks he can have it."

"Aiden, that's not—*ah*." I bit off a moan as he nipped my earlobe with his teeth. My tiger was off her leash completely, seeding the air with unadulterated beastly lust, impossible to resist for the jaguar who'd cornered his prey.

"He can't have you," he growled against my ear. "I'll do whatever it takes to be worthy of you, Avery. You are *my* mate, and I can't stand the fact that Kit's the kind of male who's already worthy of you. One who's never hurt you like I have."

The room lost its edges. The only tangible things were Aiden's body enveloping mine, his lips pressed to my jaw, and his hand in my hair. I grasped at his back, and his tight muscles danced under my fingers. "It's not.... I don't feel that way about Kit," I whispered.

It was the truth. Maybe in another life, he would've been the ideal man. Attractive, wildly intelligent, combat trained, and dedicated to service in the Guardians. He'd treated me with respect and admiration since the day we met. A fox, like my brother and dad, and the kind of male that was much less likely to care that I was a female with a beast.

But this was not that life.

Kit would never be able to stoke the fire in me that the man in my arms could.

Aiden dipped his nose into the crook of my neck. "Fuck, you smell good."

"Aiden," I whined.

"I know, baby. I've got you."

The hand that was not fisting my ponytail dipped under the waistband of my shorts, slid down my heated skin, and skimmed a fingertip over my clit. I moaned into his shoulder, and he increased the pressure, making tight circles on that sensitive spot, enough to send me skating along the edge but not enough to push me over.

"Feel good, sweetheart?"

"Yes," I hissed.

"Want more?"

"*Please*, Aiden."

He plunged two fingers inside me and let out an obscene groan at the wet mess he found there. "Fuck. Is this all for me?"

"You know it is," I ground out. "Move, please."

He sank his teeth into the crook of my neck. "No. I'll give you what you want if you make me a promise."

Don't like that. I worked my hips on his hand, chasing the relief I was desperate for.

He yanked firmly on my ponytail, tilting my head so that I was looking him directly in his shining hazel eyes. "Behave. I said I would take care of you. I'll *always* take care of you. Do you understand me?"

He looked like he'd set fire to the entire camp if I asked him to. "Yes," I whispered.

"Good." He moved the fingers inside me lazily, the heel of his hand pressed against my clit. "Promise me that you'll wait for me, baby, and I'll make you come."

I frowned. "Wait for you—*oh.*"

He moved his hand faster, hammering into me, and the knot of pleasure coiled tighter and tighter. "Promise me that you won't go to Kit or someone like him. I know I hurt you, sweetheart, but promise me you'll give me a chance to earn your forgiveness."

"I—oh shit—I...."

He stopped, and I let out a frustrated cry. "Say it," he growled.

Through the fog of lust, I grasped for my reasonable mind. Was there a chance I'd want to date someone else? Someone who hadn't hurt me like my Fated had? I'd come to camp determined to hate them, but desire for other men had never entered my brain.

And after all these weeks, I didn't hate them anymore. I

trusted them, as partners on the battlefield and now partners in the hunt for my mother's killer.

I trusted them with my safety. Aiden had *killed* someone to protect me.

Did I trust them with... all of me?

That was something to ruminate on later. Right now, I only wanted Aiden to do what he promised and release me from this delicious torture.

"I promise," I said hoarsely. "No other men. I don't want other men."

That, at least, was the Moon's honest truth.

"Good girl," he purred, and then he hammered his fingers into me again, sending me into the stratosphere.

I screamed as my climax shot through me, and he smothered the noise by slamming his mouth onto mine, consuming my every moan and whimper until I was boneless in his arms.

His kiss gentled. His grip on my hair remained firm and bossy, but the way he angled my face where he wanted it as we lazily made out was soft.

Reverent, even.

With one last kiss, he withdrew his fingers from my body and let go of my hair.

And then he looked me in the eyes, neon ringing his irises, as he sucked the taste of me right off his fingers.

I smothered a tortured moan.

He grinned wickedly and then went right back to business. He straightened my shorts, smoothed my shirt, and tucked a stray lock of my hair behind my ear, all while I stood there in stunned silence. "Ready to run around a field in formation while Commander Moss yells at us?" he asked.

I sighed. "Yeah. I hope Ward isn't planning on using his office anytime soon. It needs time to... air out."

Aiden chuckled, his eyes dancing behind his sexy glasses. "Do you think Ward would be anything other than thrilled that you'd allowed yourself to indulge in one of us in that way?"

"No," I said with a huff. "I suppose not."

Ward was ready to add me to his pack of daughters at my earliest convenience.

We left the building and headed out to our combat session. Aiden held my hand until we crested the small hill and came into the line of sight of the trainees gathered on the field. Then, he dropped my hand and positioned himself off my right shoulder and just behind me, as if I were his quad leader.

I smothered the smile that pulled at my lips. *Game face, Avery.*

We located the others milling around amongst the herd. Heath was warming up his sword arm, swinging his saber in fast, precise strokes. Wyatt was stretching, his long legs spread and his shorts riding indecently up his thick thighs as he bent over to touch the grass. Elijah idled on a nearby bench, his face tipped up and his eyes closed as he sunned himself, reminiscent of another snake I knew.

Heath's face lit up as we approached, and then his nostrils flared. His grin turned lascivious. "Did you two have a private meeting after you met with Kit?" he asked, handing me my sword harness.

I took it from him and stuck my nose in the air. "Maybe."

"It was a negotiation," Aiden added, a smug grin directed at his brother. "We came to an acceptable agreement."

Wyatt ambled over, his ax resting on his shoulder. He ran a hand down my back and stuck his nose in my hair. "Fuck me," he groaned. "That's the stuff right there."

And, of course, Elijah was now alert. He licked his lips and shot me a wicked smile. "There is nothing more divine than the taste of your pleasure, Dove."

I huffed and shook Wyatt off. "Cut it out, all of you. Aiden and I have something really important to tell you."

They sobered immediately. Aiden and I relayed what we'd learned in Kit's office. The temperature of the air around us had dropped ten degrees by the time we got to the belladonna boldly growing at the gates of the Fordham family compound.

I reached for my beast and sent soothing energy toward Elijah, the equivalent of her licking him in the face. He blinked away the slitted pupils of the basilisk and grinned at me.

Heath's brow was so furrowed, I worried he'd get premature wrinkles—difficult to do for a shifter. "Shit. I don't know that name. Clearly a shifter family of wealth, but not part of my parents' loose social circle. What in the world is going on here?"

"We'll figure it out," Aiden said with finality. "Camp ends a week from Sunday, and then we have a few weeks before school begins. We'll get through patrol, and then we'll give this the focus it requires."

On cue, Commander Moss's voice boomed across the field. "Trainees, you better be in unit formation and on the field in the next fifteen seconds!"

I sucked in a breath and tightened the straps of my harness.

A week from Sunday.

We were almost there. Camp would be over, and then I'd get to spend a few weeks at home, away from the Guardians.

Away from my Fated.

For the first time, I found that I wasn't particularly excited by the thought.

30

AVERY

For the next week, my quintet put our heads down and trained relentlessly. We were going to go into the August patrol ready for anything, and we'd finally clicked as a group of five, our fighting styles, both beast and blade, melding into a seamless machine.

I'd updated Ian and my dads on what Kit had helped us uncover, and they agreed that Elijah's pursuit of what happened the night his fathers died would almost certainly lead us to more answers about Mom. It didn't matter that she was killed a year later in a completely different state. Following the belladonna was the key.

We'd get through camp, and then we'd find a way to bring justice to our families.

And I hadn't forgotten that we also had to find a way to protect Clara. I was leaning towards just slicing her betrotheds to ribbons the second they set foot on the Proteus campus.

I said as much to Elijah as we stood in the parking lot of Peachtree State Park, surveying the staging of our base of operations for the first night of patrol.

"As if you could be any more perfect, Dove," he purred. "I, too, have offered to introduce those mangy little felines to a violent end, but Heath won't allow it. Maybe if you bat your eyelashes at him, he'll change his mind and let us do it together."

That little fantasy pleased me, and I hummed happily.

The Moon was a mere sliver tonight, and the cloud cover was thick. In our briefing with Kit earlier today, he'd told us that the Guardians' scouting drones had picked up high wisp activity in this zone, which meant that we might have a large number of active rifts to contend with.

Our staging area was busy, packed full of tents and equipment. Guardians strode purposefully around the parking lot. The largest tent was our makeshift medical bay for the night. Dr. Lee was on hand, as were several field medics, both professional Guardians and trainees. Aisha, Dr. Lee's student assistant, was crouched outside the medical tent, meticulously loading supplies into her pack, a large golden M stitched into her black uniform shirt.

Another large tent contained the command center, where computer screens and other communications equipment had been assembled on rickety-looking tables, tangles of cords and cables running in all directions. Commander Moss stood at the entrance, arms crossed over his barrel chest, engrossed in a serious conversation with Cash and another professional Guardian I didn't know.

A half mile to the west of our location lay the picturesque shifter town whose inhabitants we were tasked with protecting tonight. A tall concrete wall marked its borders, the roads in and out blocked by wide iron gates that had been closed and locked for curfew. Under the last Full Moon, ward security experts who worked for local law enforcement would've recharged the runes etched into the concrete and the gates.

It was because of those wards—and us—that everyone behind that wall was able to sleep peacefully in their beds.

Heath strode over, fiddling with the comms earpiece he'd been issued as our unit's leader. It was designed to remain lodged in his ear even with a shift to his wolf.

He certainly looked at home in the Guardian uniform we all wore—the breathable black shirt that molded to his chest, the dark cargo pants and flexible combat boots, the leather strap of the harness that kept his saber on his back. The seams of our uniforms were designed to split with a shift and could be stuck back together with some kind of magically enhanced Velcro—a rare and expensive perk for risking our lives for the good of our kind.

"Okay, gather 'round," Heath barked at our group.

Aiden came to stand at my other side, and Wyatt's big hand landed on the back of my neck. He dug his thumb into a knot there, and it took an enormous amount of self-control to bite back a shameless moan.

Our assigned Support Squadron spread out around us. As a part of Ward's ongoing campaign to butter me up, he'd given us Ian's group. Or Brody's group, rather, as he was the highest-ranked trainee coming out of the semester behind Ian. As a rising junior—one who wasn't even supposed to be at camp—Ian didn't get to wear the leader mantle. He was unbothered by this.

Brody's group consisted of himself, Ian, Joon, Nico, Matt the hawk, and Andre the wolf. The guys had worked with a lot of the Support Squadron trainees over the spring and summer, and their leadership had decided to give Matt and Andre a try with our unit tonight to see how they meshed.

Their group wore uniforms nearly identical to ours, though their shirts were gray with a black "S" embroidered over the chest where ours had a large golden "G."

"We're part of a four-unit group being sent to cover the south end of the zone," Heath announced. "Twenty square miles, mostly within the state park, including the family camping area."

A drone whizzed by overhead and disappeared into the trees.

Heath watched it go and then continued. "We head out at 11:00 p.m. on the dot. As a reminder, the most active time for wraiths is between midnight and 3:00 a.m. We report back here at 4:00 a.m. unless we have injuries and need to return earlier. As usual, Wyatt will be our primary beast combatant, with Aiden and I shifting as needed. Avery will fight in human form, and Support Squadron can also shift as needed. I don't care that leadership discourages it outside of healing. Follow your beast's instincts."

Andre the wolf gazed at Heath with stars in his eyes.

"And a final reminder that Elijah will not be shifting unless things get out of hand, in which case, you need to stab whatever is in front of you and then get the fuck out of Dodge."

Andre went a little pale at that, and Matt swallowed audibly. Even Nico and Joon shifted on their feet, looking uneasy.

Elijah chuckled. "Don't worry, friends. I'm sure we will have things well *in* hand tonight."

On cue, a chorus of high-pitched screeches and chitters echoed from deep in the woods. Swarmers, always the front-line attack, climbing their way through the thin veil between our realms.

A shiver hit my spine, as it always did at the first sign of wraiths. Wyatt gave my neck a comforting little squeeze. The tiger flicked her tail, somehow both keyed up for some killing but also luxuriating in Wyatt's hold. She was a multifaceted beast.

The golden starbursts in Heath's eyes flashed as his wolf was called to battle.

Another shiver, another flick of the tail.

"All right, you have one minute to get your asses out into the field!" Commander Moss shouted through the bullhorn he held in front of his face. "Make me proud and do not die!"

"Motivational," Aiden said dryly.

"Let's do this," Heath said, clapping his hands. "Loose formation."

Brody's group quickly spread out, forming a wide, arching semicircle facing south. Heath stepped into place about ten feet behind Brody in the center, and the rest of us took our posts at the four corners behind him, creating a loose pentagon shape.

More screeching sounded in the distance. I hopped on my toes, cinched the straps of my harness tighter across my chest, then unsheathed my swords and twirled them quickly, loosening my wrists.

It'd been far too long since I'd hacked the head off a live wraith and watched it ooze into the ground. There was a *rightness* to this that burned deep within my soul—the beast and the human. I knew with some mysterious, unwavering certainty that I was meant to be here, doing exactly this.

With these men, I admitted to myself. The Moon had all but slapped me in the face with it.

On Heath's command, we took off running into the woods.

OVER THE NEXT FEW HOURS, OUR SUPPORT SQUADRON HAD most of the fun. We'd run into several dozen swarmers as we traipsed along hiking paths, waded through the ankle-deep water of a creek, and clambered up a steep rocky hill, all in the near pitch-black, aided by the sharpened night vision of our beasts.

A pair of Rippers had surprised us at the top of that hill, but Heath, Aiden, Wyatt, and I were able to put them down without anyone having to shift.

Masculine shouts and eerie screeches echoed all around us. Our fellow campers were keeping busy.

After we traversed the top of the hill for fifteen minutes, Heath touched a finger to the comm in his ear.

"Shit," he barked. "We've got a new rift opening near the family camping area. Half a mile up ahead."

We scrambled down the rocky slope in an unorganized fashion, reformed our group, then sprinted through the trees. Minutes later, we emerged onto the campgrounds.

Dozens of picnic tables sat under a large open-air pavilion. A nearby rectangular concrete building contained the bathrooms and showers. In the distance, the spacious RV park was deserted, a single chain draped across the entrance to the gravel parking lot. Looming in front of us was a huge playground, its multicolored towers and slides muted and sad under the cloudy dark sky.

Floating right behind the playground, as high as the tallest slide, was a rift.

"Fuck me," Ian whispered.

Our entire unit slowed to a stop for a moment, taking it in.

As many times as I'd been out during curfew, as many

wraiths as I'd killed, I'd never seen a live rift. It was something the Guardians assumed correctly—wraiths didn't tend to spawn in the city. There weren't enough shifter souls there to draw them out of their realm, and the ones that did rampage through our streets usually came from the more active neighboring zones.

From the looks on the faces of my unit, this was a first for all of us.

The rift was a horizontal slit in our reality, ten feet wide and blurry, like someone had smudged the scene with a paintbrush. A faint violet glow emanated from it, the same color of the wraiths' eerie, poisonous magic. Seeping from the rift were wisps—the Li wraith, vaguely beast-shaped clouds, harmless to us but harbingers of something much worse.

There were *so* many wisps, though. The fog of them blanketed the campground, challenging even my beast's sharp night vision. I'd never seen anything like it.

"Get ready," Heath breathed.

The rift *yawned*.

Swarmers crawled out of the void and spilled onto the playground. They had the fat bodies of boars, the more agile legs of a dog or wolf, and vaguely canine heads, their jaws sagging and unhinged, needle teeth lit by the violet glow leaking from all the holes in their gray skulls.

There were at least a dozen, and they crawled over the playground equipment like demonic ants. They chittered and screeched, their claws scraping over the plastic.

"Support, let's go!" Brody shouted, ripping his sword from his back.

Our front-line team went to work. They sprinted in arrow formation toward the playground. Brody ducked the first swarmer that leapt from the railing of the merry-go-round, spun in his crouch, and sliced the back legs off the monster. Ian was there a second later to cleave the head from the body with one smooth upward strike of his katana.

Nico batted another wraith out of the air with a vicious backhand of his tactical tomahawk right to its head. He whipped around, spinning the small axes in both hands and mincing another attacking wraith to pieces. Joon cleaned up behind him, slicing the heads off each of Nico's battered wraiths with his sword.

Matt and Andre ran right up into the playscape, hacking away, conducting a symphony of death screeches.

We'd jogged closer, ready for whatever else was about to come out of that rift.

"We lost one!" Ian yelled. "Incoming, Blackwell!"

One of the wolf-boars streaked our way, its lifeless gray flesh peeling from its body and exposing its rotting rib cage as it ran.

Wyatt spun his battle-ax in one hand before he stepped into its path. He swung the ax like a baseball bat and hit the wraith square in the neck. It split apart, exploding against his blade, body parts hitting the grass and melting into gray sludge.

More screeching sounded, this time a deeper pitch.

Two Rippers crawled from the rift and hit the grass on four grotesque feet.

These were hellhounds as big as Heath's wolf, the molting gray flesh of their bodies hairless, their legs covered in flaking scales and ending in three-toed talons. One of them was missing a chunk of its skull entirely, and both glowed with sickly violet magic.

Before we could attack, two more leapt from the rift. Also hellhounds, but instead of scaled legs and talons, these had a row of vicious spikes down their backs and tails that looked like machetes.

I ripped my swords from their sheaths. Wyatt tossed his ax to Elijah, yanked his shirt off, and then shifted into his bear. Aiden unsheathed his saber and handed it to Heath before his jaguar burst from his body.

"We're on!" Heath shouted.

Wyatt ran for one of the talon-hellhounds while Aiden attacked one with spikes. Wyatt's bear hit the wraith with the force of a tank and knocked it straight into the cement wall of the bathroom complex. Heath ran up behind him, both his and Aiden's sabers in hand, and slashed the head clean off.

I sprinted after Aiden, my assigned side of our formation. The spike-hound jumped into the air, and Aiden's jaguar followed suit. They clashed like cymbals, and the wraith hit the ground on its back, while Aiden twisted and landed with feline grace on his paws. He snarled and dropped to his belly as I took a running leap over his back, my swords raised high.

Just as the wraith hound flipped to its feet, I was there to drive my swords into its back. Wraith guts splattered, and it screeched at a decibel level that would've made human ears bleed.

Aiden snarled again and pounced. As he sank his incredibly strong jaws into the wraith's skull, I yanked my swords from the body and hacked through the neck in two fast strokes.

Then we ran for Elijah.

He'd drawn both the remaining Rippers, his brilliant mythic soul too juicy for them to resist. With a look of only mild exertion on his face, he swung Wyatt's ax at the talon-hound as it bore down on him, its jaw unhinged and its mouthful of jagged teeth aimed at Elijah's face. Elijah took its head off on the first swing, spun, and then rammed the butt of the ax into the chest of the spike-hound, impaling it there.

Wyatt arrived just in time to smash the impaled hound, taking it to the ground. It thrashed under our bear, but it went still after I drove one sword through its glowing violet eye socket. I quickly chopped off its head with my other sword.

More swarmers crawled out of the rift. Cat bodies, eight hairy spider legs, four glowing eyes. Seven, eight, nine....

Heath began to swing his sword at them, calmly and methodically. Ian and Brody rushed in to help, leaving our other Support Squadron members to clear the last round of swarmers.

Two more Rippers climbed through the rift. Gorilla bodies with reptile heads, mottled flesh, exposed bones, glowing eyes.

Masculine shouting sounded from behind the playground. Kellan's unit had arrived on the scene. Their six Support Squadron trainees joined ours in clearing out the swarmers. They chased them off the playground and into the pavilion, jumping on top of picnic tables and hacking at limbs.

Kellan and Hank the bear attacked one gorilla wraith. Ari the orange tiger and Teegan the man took the other.

A jarring bellow shook the ground, and a Giant vaulted from the rift. Taller than a house, humanoid like Giants often were, it had a lion head with a horrifying clown mouth full of teeth. Gray skin stretched over knotty muscle, its clawed hands too large for even that enormous body.

I exchanged a look with Aiden's jaguar. His eyes glowed turquoise, wary but confident. We could do this.

We ran toward the Giant but pulled up short when its twin jumped through the rift and hit the ground next to it.

"Elijah!" Heath bellowed.

The basilisk poured from Elijah's body, its roar somehow louder and more frightening than the Giant's.

More than a few of the trainees shouted in alarm.

"Herd the remaining swarmers east!" Brody shouted. "Get out of his path!"

The Giants leapt on top of the pavilion, one right after the other. The metal roof creaked and sagged under their enormous bodies. Void eyes surveyed the carnage below, and then they turned, zeroing in on the neighboring shifter town in the distance like they'd decided to pass on the buffet of Prime souls here and look for easier prey.

"Fuck," I spat. "That's high intelligence."

Aiden rumbled a noise of agreement. I stroked the soft fur on his muscular shoulder to center myself as I planned my attack.

One of the Giants lost patience and leapt from the roof, landing on all fours, ready to sprint down the road toward town.

The basilisk was on it before it could move. Elijah sank his teeth into the thing's neck and whipped his thick serpent body around it. Heath ran for them, sword raised.

The remaining Giant screeched from the roof. Wyatt the bear appeared on my other side and huffed in annoyance.

"I know," I said, scratching his ear. There was blood matted along a shallow gash on the side of his head, and the ire I felt over that minor injury almost set my beast loose. I shook it off. "We could climb up there," I went on, "but it seems like a waste of effort when it'll just jump down—"

Kellan's griffin bounded over and took a running leap into the air. He batted his enormous wings and landed on the roof, screeching his bird head off and flapping his wings menacingly at the Giant.

The Giant took the bait and charged. They smashed together and tumbled off the roof. Wyatt, Aiden, and I were there when they hit the ground.

As Kellan flapped his wings and pecked that razor-sharp beak at the Giant's head, Aiden clamped his teeth around one arm, and Wyatt got the other. They pulled with their strong jaws and managed to pin it. I scrambled onto its back and stabbed one blade straight through the base of its skull. I reached for my beast, digging for the strength to hack through its thick neck with the other while the animals around me tore at its limbs.

I didn't stick around after I severed the head and the wraith's flesh began to ooze into the grass. More Rippers had found their way out of the rift, and while Kellan's quad was dealing with some, two were headed straight for where Elijah and Heath wrestled with the other Giant.

I sprinted, my beast pumping energy into my limbs. I would get to those hellhounds before they got to my Fated. Before they could sink their teeth into my basilisk's smooth, scaled flesh. Before they could hurt Heath while he swung his sword at the Giant thrashing in Elijah's hold.

More Guardians poured out of the woods. As their boots hit the pavement, their shouts grew loud and alarmed. This rift was spitting wraiths at an alarming rate, so leadership must've sent as many units as they could spare.

Wyatt roared, waylaid by another Ripper in the pavilion. Ian jumped in beside him, lending his sword.

The thud of feline paws behind me said Aiden was hot on my heels.

Heath stabbed the Giant through the throat. It shrieked.

The Rippers were nearly to them, but then they registered my beast soul, shiny jewel that it was, and whirled to face me.

I lifted my swords, ready to disembowel the first one that tried to jump on me.

Then I froze, locked in place as the force of aggressive shifter dominance clamped down around me.

31

HEATH

I looked up from where I'd lodged Aiden's saber in the Giant's throat just in time to see the love of my life, her blue eyes blazing, freeze like she'd just slammed into a brick wall.

While two Rippers bore down on her.

The heavy, oppressive weight of *feline* dominance saturated the air. A huge lion prowled nearby, at the edge of the chaos by the pavilion.

Fucking *Cash*.

My beast thrashed in my chest, panic like I'd experienced only once before choking me.

I couldn't get to the Rippers in time. I couldn't get to Cash in time.

Those hellhounds were going to kill *my mate*.

Elijah bellowed and hissed, but the Giant in his hold wasn't dead yet. He couldn't let go.

Aiden's jaguar roared and sprinted faster.

But we shouldn't have worried.

Avery released the loudest, most frustrated scream I'd ever heard come out of her mouth, and she broke the lion's will seconds after he'd clamped her down. Her beast's fury shot clear across the field, blanketing us all.

The lion's eyes widened, and he couldn't suppress his shiver as the powerful pulse of Avery's beast hit him.

Freed, Avery ducked under the attacking wraith and thrust her swords upwards, impaling it with a roar. Aiden slammed into the other one, and together they made quick work of the monsters.

Releasing my own bellow of rage, I brought my saber down on the Giant's thick neck, finally removing the head. Elijah uncoiled from the body as it began to disintegrate.

An icy wind whipped around me. The basilisk roared, his yellow eyes blazing hotter than I'd ever seen them as he zeroed in on Cash's lion.

"No," I barked, sinking all my wolf's power into the command. "Aiden has it."

Our jaguar was already streaking across the grass, his bloodthirst a surging river around him. Avery watched him run, her spine straight and her face hard. She was so beauti-ful, splattered in gray guts, her chest heaving as she caught her breath, blue fireworks sparking in her eyes.

The lion turned and sprinted back into the thick trees at the edge of the campground.

Aiden chased after him.

"Son of a bitch," I said. "That fucking *coward*."

Elijah returned to human form, the basilisk falling away easier than I'd expected. Avery was safe for now, and the activity from the rift had finally died down. There were only a few swarmers loose, and Kellan's team had them covered.

"Did he just do what I think he did?" Elijah hissed.

Maybe the basilisk hadn't fallen completely away.

Wyatt, no longer a bear, jogged over. He'd managed to

get his uniform back on, and he carried Elijah's and Aiden's clothes.

"What the fuck is going on?" he asked, coming to stop next to Avery. He threw the pile of clothes at Elijah, and then he turned to Avery, cupping her face in his hands and lowering his voice. "Why does it feel like our beautiful tiger is about to go on a murder spree, hmm?"

"I was, but Aiden beat me to it," she murmured.

"Cash just popped out of the woods and tried to kill Avery, just bold as fucking brass," I said through gritted teeth.

Wyatt's eyes went an angry red. "He *what?*"

The tiger's aura changed instantly. Gone was the ferocious aggression, replaced by a soothing purr. She was practically stroking Wyatt's bear down his back.

Wyatt groaned and cracked his neck. "That feels nice, baby. Keep doing it."

"That's what Cash did, right, Killer?" I asked. "He tried to lock you up in front of that Ripper?"

She nodded. "It was definitely him. He doesn't pack the punch of your dad, but the flavor is similar."

I blew out a breath and tried to relax my jaw before I cracked a molar. The reminder that my dad had attacked Avery, while she was alone and reeling from us being total fucking assholes to her, made me want to impale myself on my sword.

The tiger nudged at me with a playful lick. My wolf's self-loathing evaporated instantly, and he wagged his tail like an excited puppy.

Elijah, now dressed, slinked over to Avery and pressed his body up against her back. "Cash got a nice little surprise, didn't he, Dove?"

She sighed. "Yeah. Now he'll at least have a sense that

I'm stronger than he thought. I don't know if that's a good thing or a bad thing."

Unease trickled through my body. Cash was a problem that needed solving yesterday. He'd targeted my mate too many times, and I took the fact that he was still breathing as a personal failure as the leader of this quad.

He was now on the list—the one with all the problems we had to deal with once we survived camp. There was no chance I'd allow him to be in a position of authority over Avery once we returned to the program at school.

Aiden's jaguar came loping out of the woods. He shifted back into a man as he approached us, his body glistening with sweat and his chest heaving as he caught his breath.

"He fucking got away," he spat. "I couldn't find Cash or any of the other assholes in his quad either."

Elijah threw Aiden's uniform at him. He wiped his brow with his shirt and dressed hurriedly, finishing by pulling his glasses from his pants pocket and sliding them onto his face.

"It's okay, Aiden," Avery said, her voice serene. "Cash's day will come. He's pushed me too far now."

Aiden nudged Wyatt out of the way and pulled Avery into his chest. "Fuck, sweetheart. I thought I was going to choke on my own lungs when I saw you freeze. But my jaguar knew better. He knew his mate could handle that weak fucking lion."

The tiger's preen in response to Aiden's praise was immediate and palpable. I shared a smug smile with the others.

"Hey, lovebirds," Ian barked, jogging up to us. "We've cleared the area, and the rift is dissipating, but Matt's injured."

Shit. "How bad?" I asked, striding immediately in the direction of the playground.

Ian fell into step next to me. "He'll live. One of the Rippers Crimson's unit was handling got away from them, and it took a bite out of Matt's arm while he was finishing one of our swarmers. He shifted, but his wing looks all fucked up."

I hurried over to where the hawk was perched on the railing of the merry-go-round. His fluffy body was marred with wraith guts, and his left wing was clearly broken, hanging at an awkward angle. Brody sat with him while the rest of our support team stood guard.

"Hang on, Matt," I said, bringing my finger to the comm device in my ear. "I'm calling for medical."

It was needed, as we weren't the only unit with injuries. At least a dozen trainees were scattered around the campground in their beast forms, healing from gashes and broken bones.

I tried not to delight in the sight of a puffy purple bruise on Teegan's human face. Something had given him a shiner, and he looked even more put out than usual.

"Blackwell to base," I said through comms. "The rift at the family campground has dissipated, but we have units with injuries that need medical attention."

"*Tracking,*" Commander Moss replied. "*Any wraith activity in the vicinity? Our drones aren't picking up anything except around a smaller rift on the opposite side of the state park.*"

I let my wolf surface and listened to my surroundings. Past the low murmur of voices around us—unit leaders concerned for their injured, trainees recounting their kills, others calling in their own requests for aid. Past Avery's husky, hypnotic voice, repeatedly assuring Wyatt and Elijah that she didn't have a scratch on her, the sound like gentle fingertips dragging down my spine. Past the soft rustling of leaves and the distant sounds of cars on the highway.

No screeches or unnatural gaits crawling through the woods. No claws scraping tree bark or fucked-up insect noises.

"Nothing in range," I reported.

"Then hold your position for now. I'll send a team your way."

"Thank you, sir."

It took ten minutes for the two black SUVs to whip into the nearby parking lot and eject four medics a piece.

Matt was seen to right away, and he was able to shift back to human after his wing was reset. He'd endured it with minimal squawking.

My brother joined me. He surveyed the other units as they put themselves back together, and then he shifted his gaze to where Avery sat on the merry-go-round next to Brody and Ian, chatting quietly with them. Wyatt and Elijah didn't try to pretend they weren't hovering over her.

"Night one in the books," Aiden murmured.

"A fucking bad one," I added.

He nodded, still watching our mate. "Tomorrow is going to be worse."

"I expect so."

He finally looked at me, brilliant turquoise ringing his irises and shining behind his glasses. "We have to be ready. We can't let anything happen to her."

I swallowed roughly. "I know."

"You sure it's not my turn?" Wyatt asked me as he scrubbed his wet hair with a towel. "It feels like I haven't been on duty in forever."

I sighed wearily and pointed to the makeshift calendar I'd scrawled on the back of a menu I'd stolen from the chow hall and taped to the wall of our cabin. "It is very clearly my turn. We hashed this out and put it on paper for a reason, and yet you all insist on arguing with me about it every night."

"You can't fault us for sleeping better near our dove," Elijah said lazily. He was sprawled on his bed, wearing flannel pajama pants and nothing else, flicking idly through the pages of a paperback. "Especially after the events of tonight."

I rolled my eyes. "Like you won't be lurking in the woods anyway."

"Maybe," he replied with a fangy grin. "After a little nap."

"Just go, Heath," Aiden said, yanking on his own pajama pants. "There's barely any night left. Harder to be sneaky when the sun comes up."

He was right. It was damn near 5:00 a.m. We were allowed to sleep until lunchtime after patrol, and we needed it badly.

I tossed the towel that I'd tied around my waist onto my bed and strode out of the cabin in the nude. As my bare feet hit the grass, I released my wolf.

The sting of the shift hardly registered, my wolf elated to be let out and on a journey toward his mate.

I trotted along the worn path that led away from our cluster of cabins. At the bottom of the hill, I picked up the pace, making my way past the Support Squadron cabins and around the lake. The buzz of the night insects filled my sensitive ears, and a barrage of scents assaulted my canine nose. Wet sand, maple trees, shifter pheromones, and soap that smelled like sandalwood and sage. I looked forward to a night—or a morning, really—of dozing to the smell of Avery's jasmine and lavender on the breeze.

I veered off the main path and took a circuitous route so that I could sneak into my usual cluster of trees near Avery's cabin. It had an unobstructed view and room for a beast of my size to sleep comfortably.

As I approached my hiding spot, the low murmur of deep voices sent my hackles straight up.

"—not sure this is the time," Teegan said in his usual monotone.

"I'm aware it's not ideal," Kellan replied. "But fuck, man. Did you see her tonight? She's amazing. We have to shoot our shot. Camp is about to be over, and who knows what the hell is going to happen tomorrow night."

Teegan grunted. "She's softening toward Blackwell and the rest of them."

I crept closer, lying low in the shadows and avoiding the soft light emitted from the cabin.

"I know," Kellan replied. "It's now or never."

He stepped onto the little stoop in front of Avery's screen door and rapped his knuckles on the wooden frame.

Light footsteps sounded inside as Avery approached the door. She didn't open it or step outside, instead staring at those two presumptuous assholes through the screen. "Uh, hey, Kellan. Teegan." She sounded tired, and my wolf wanted to rip their throats out for keeping her awake. "What's up?"

Kellan propped an arm against her doorframe and hit her with his blinding white smile. It pained me to admit it, but he truly was a handsome bastard, with his blond beach waves and perfect face. He never wanted for female attention at school, especially from the girls from Prime families who circled the power quads like glittery vultures.

But here he fucking was, *shooting his shot* with my mate.

Still, I lay there, not making a sound. Kellan was real fucking lucky it was my night on duty and not Elijah's.

"You were spectacular tonight," he said to Avery. "I promise we won't keep you up, but Teegan and I wanted to drop by, first and foremost to just make sure you were okay. No lasting injuries, anything like that."

"Oh," she replied. "Um, thank you for your concern, but I'm fine. Our kills tonight were pretty textbook, despite the very active rift and the, uh, Giants."

"Good to hear," Kellan said. "My beast wouldn't settle until we knew you were unharmed."

I smothered a snort. What bullshit.

"We had another question," Teegan announced, nudging Kellan. "If we could just have one more minute of your time."

"Yes." Kellan's expression turned serious. "We—all of us, my whole quad—were wondering if we could spend a little time with you when camp is over? You have a few weeks before school starts, and we'll have about the same amount of time before we have to report to active duty with the Guardians—"

"You mean like a date?" Avery asked.

Kellan's slick smile was back. "I mean exactly like a date."

Kill, my wolf snarled.

No, I said, even though it went against every instinct I had. *We have to trust in what we've been building with her. What's been growing between us.*

Avery didn't answer right away, and I could *feel* her scrutinizing Kellan. His smile slipped, and he shuffled his feet.

"You're aware that I have a beast?" she finally asked. "I'm not playing coy about it anymore. She's real."

"And I bet she's a Prime," Kellan replied silkily. "I wasn't lying when we spoke at the beginning of camp, Avery. Our quad is *very* interested in a central bond with a beast, especially one of substantial power. You ladies don't exactly grow on trees."

"Why?" she countered.

"Why, what?"

"What is it about bonding with a beast soul that has you so interested? What do you think you know that the rest of Prime society doesn't? What are you hoping to gain with a bond like that?"

Kellan's smile faltered again. "I—" Teegan elbowed him, and he sighed. "Listen, Avery. It isn't just that. You're also gorgeous, funny, and so fucking talented. Let us take you out, and we can answer all of your questions."

Kill.

We can't.

"It's late, Kellan," Avery said wearily. "I'm... flattered, but I don't think a date is in the cards."

The knot of pressure in my chest released.

Kellan did not appear deterred. He grinned, leaning in as far as he could, and his eyes blazed a warm amber color. "We still have plenty of time to change your mind, gorgeous. Maybe we *do* know something the others don't. Whenever you want answers to your questions, we'll be waiting. Have a good night."

The two of them strode off, Prime swagger in full force like they hadn't just been shot down by the only female in camp.

I remained still, my chin on the ground, my breath stirring the blades of grass in front of me. At some point, I would need to relocate to my trees, but for now, my wolf could only lie here, huffing the tantalizing hint of jasmine and lavender on the breeze, feeling relieved and morose all at once.

How many more times would we have to watch hungry men make a move on our mate?

Avery's beautiful face appeared in the window facing my wallowing spot. Her hair was damp from her shower, hanging in waves around her shoulders. She wore a tiny little tank top, her nipples peeking at me even in the fucking dark, and now I really would have to murder Kellan and Teegan.

Elijah would help, no question.

She propped her forearms in the windowsill and arched a brow, staring at me through the screen. "I take it you heard all of that, huh?"

I snorted irritably.

"You managed to behave yourself."

I rumbled another annoyed noise.

"Is it your night to pretend you aren't sleeping outside my cabin?"

I snorted again.

She sighed, and a soft smile pulled at her lips. I nearly melted into the ground. My mate smiled for me, and I could die happy.

"Just... come inside, Heath."

32

AVERY

I wasn't sure what I expected when I invited Heath into my cabin at five o'clock in the morning, but he did not shift back into a naked man outside my door. No, he managed to squeeze his giant furry body through the door as I held it open for him, fighting a bemused smile.

"Oh, okay," I said as he did a few circles in the tight space between the two beds and sniffed my things. "Make yourself at home, then."

He sent an aggressive snort at George, who was curled up in the middle of the piles of clothes on my extra bed. Heath was probably unhappy that my python pal did not attempt to strangle either of the men who'd decided to knock on my door and ask me out at this unholy hour.

George returned Heath's snort with a sassy hiss and went back to ignoring us both.

Heath proceeded to rub his giant wolf head all over me, and I laughed, scratching his ears. "Yes, hello. Are you happy to be out? You had to sit on the sidelines tonight, like my girl does pretty much every time."

He huffed and nudged me toward my bed.

"Fine, I'm going. Bossy."

I climbed into bed and pulled the covers up to my chin. The exhaustion sank into my bones, and my eyelids fluttered, sleep coming for me almost immediately.

The large wolf curled up beside my bed was a safety blanket I didn't exactly need, but my body and beast appreciated it nonetheless. My tiger purred contentedly—another thing that was going to lull me to sleep in short order.

I reached over to rub the soft fur on top of his head. He rumbled a happy noise. "Tonight was... good, Heath. It felt right."

He huffed and licked my arm.

"You're a good leader," I said sleepily. "A good brother. A good... friend."

A good man that will make a good mate.

I batted that pesky thought away as I let sleep take me.

"WELL, ISN'T THIS COZY?"

I blinked awake, slowly and reluctantly. The sun was blazing high in the sky, and I hissed like a vampire as it assaulted me through the windows.

Heath let out a big wolf yawn and flopped over on my floor, also in no hurry to get up.

Wyatt stood at my door, smirking at us through the screen. "Can I come in, Wildcat?"

I sat up and swung my legs over the side of my bed. "Yeah," I croaked, rubbing my eyes. "Watch where you walk. Don't step on my snake or my wolf."

Heath chuffed and licked my leg. George had already made his way down from my spare bed and was making his escape.

Wyatt shoved the door open, waited a beat for George to slither past him, then stepped inside. He wore black joggers and the world's tightest white T-shirt, and he had a backpack slung over one shoulder.

He grinned at me, his emerald eyes bright as he took in my silky tank top and tiny pajama shorts. "Heath's a better man than I am, baby. There's no way I could've stayed a beast and slept anywhere but in your bed with you if I'd been invited in here, not with you looking like that."

My tiger preened. I did my best to look unaffected, even as the idea of naked Wyatt pressed up against me in my bed, even just to hold me while I slept, made my entire body tingle. I squinted at him. "Are you here to retrieve your fearless leader?"

"Yes, but I also came to talk to you." He sobered and reached into his backpack. He tossed a pair of shorts and a T-shirt at Heath. "Shift and get dressed, man."

Heath growled irritably then stood up and shook out his sandy-blond coat. He nosed at me one more time for some pets, which I gave to him, and then his body morphed into a naked man, all tan skin stretched over taut, hard muscle.

He yawned and raked his fingers through his disheveled hair. I stared unabashedly at him, though I was demure enough to keep my gaze above his waist. He winked at me, then turned around to pull on his shorts, which only gave me a view of his award-winning ass.

My beast flicked her tail with great interest.

I know. I won't even argue with you anymore.

"Good morning, Killer," Heath said, turning back to face me as he pulled on his shirt. "Did you get enough sleep? Feeling rested?"

"I think so." I stretched my arms over my head and pretended my entire body didn't warm when both of their gazes went straight to the sliver of my stomach that peeked out. "I'm used to the late-night patrols, Heath. Been doing them since I was fourteen."

"Don't remind me," he growled.

"But last night was a lot," I added. "I'll admit that. Killing wraiths that wander into the shifter neighborhoods in the city isn't like taking them on directly from the rifts up here."

"They've already coded our zone red for this cycle," Wyatt said. "Dad told me. The Guardians are considering sending in non-trainee backup for the New Moon tonight. It could get nasty."

The thought stirred nervous excitement within me.

I'm finally doing it.

"What's the update from Ward?" Heath asked, giving Wyatt a pointed look.

"That's what I came to talk to you about, Wildcat." He sat down next to me on my bed and wrapped his big hand around my thigh. "Aiden and I went to my dad earlier this morning. We told him exactly what Cash tried to do, and we told him we were walking if he didn't remove Cash and his quad from the program."

"You what?" I asked, incredulous. "You'd leave the Guardians?"

He nodded. "We know becoming a Guardian is important to you, baby, but it's not worth the danger our own fucking trainers are putting you in. We figure we can all just move to your neighborhood and kill wraiths in the streets. You'd be safer with us around, even if we weren't Guardians."

I blinked at him, stunned, then I looked at Heath. "You sanctioned that?"

He shrugged. "The vote was unanimous."

Wyatt squeezed my thigh. "But it won't come to that

because Dad's finally had enough. Cash and his quad are out. Not out of the Guardians, unfortunately, but out of the training program. He's going to find someone else to take over at school."

"What about in the field the next two nights?" Heath asked.

"It's all hands, as you know," Wyatt replied. "But Dad is going to try to ensure that our units are sent to the opposite ends of the zone."

I waved a hand. "Cash doesn't scare me. I appreciate that I won't be watching my back for the entirety of our senior year, but I hate that it was necessary. I joined the Guardians with every intention of handling this sort of shit myself."

Heath knelt in front of me and wrapped his hands around my calves. I suppressed a shiver. The feel of his and Wyatt's hands on my skin was like slipping into a hot bath. He regarded me with his familiar intensity, his hazel eyes soft. "Let us take care of you, please, Killer. You don't have to face any of this alone. Not ever."

"We're not fucking around with your safety, baby," Wyatt added. "I don't think you'd fuck around with ours either."

"No," I growled, my beast showing herself before I could stop her. "I wouldn't."

"That's good to hear," Heath said softly. His hand began a slow journey up my leg and onto my inner thigh. "Because there's nothing on earth more important to us than you."

Wyatt, always the most brash and untoward of the bunch, took the hand he already had on my thigh and slid it under my shorts to tease at the edge of my panties. He put his lips to my ear. "You gonna let us take care of you, Wildcat?"

I bit my lower lip and braced against a heady wave of lust. We were in my cabin, its screen doors and windows open to the air, and anyone could just *walk by*. "It's probably not a good idea—"

"Hey, assholes," Ian barked from outside my door. "Unhand my sister. She needs to eat."

My lust haze evaporated instantly.

Heath dropped his head into my lap and groaned. Wyatt threw his hands into the air and flopped backwards onto my bed.

Ian crossed his arms and quirked a brow at me. Brody stood behind him, wearing an enormous grin.

I looked over my shoulder at Wyatt as I stroked Heath's thick, silky hair. "I am pretty hungry," I said.

"Me too," he mumbled into my pillow.

I nudged them both. "Go wait outside while I get changed. And don't antagonize Ian. He fights dirty."

They grumbled but didn't argue. Wyatt peeled himself off my bed and trudged to the door. Heath climbed to his feet, dropped a kiss on top of my head, and followed.

My stomach growled. It was time to fuel up then get my mind right for whatever awaited us tonight in the field.

WHAT AWAITED US TURNED OUT TO BE PURE FUCKING CHAOS.

"Avery, with Wyatt!" Heath shouted. "Aiden and Elijah, with me!"

Wyatt the bear and I darted left while the other three veered right. Ian and his team had just plowed through a bunch of disgusting rodent-shaped swarmers, and three Rippers had jumped out of the trees on their heels. Vaguely feline-shaped, they were the size of a Prime lion, grotesque teeth visible in their long snouts where their gray flesh was melting away from their skulls.

Wyatt and I peeled one off, attacking its flank, while Heath's team dealt with the other two. I slashed its front leg, severing it from its body, and then Wyatt rammed it, knocking it to the ground before tearing its throat out. With two hard strikes, I hacked off its head, then whirled to face north again, tense and ready.

Screams echoed throughout the woods, both the high-pitched wailing of wraiths and what sounded like screams of pain from our fellow Guardians. Heath already had to call for medical assistance when we happened across a unit who'd been badly torn up by an unknown number of wraiths, and we hadn't even been out here for an hour yet.

We and a dozen other units had been sent to the northeast side of the state park tonight. Heath had us following the path of one of many mountain-biking and hiking trails, and we'd already killed six Rippers and one Giant. I'd lost track of how many swarmers Ian and his team had killed, but they hadn't stopped swinging their blades for more than sixty seconds at a time.

The tortured screeches of Rippers in their last throes sounded behind me. In my periphery, Joon and Nico spun, hacking and slashing at the rodents, both bleeding from cuts to their arms and face.

More Rippers—hellhounds and some kind of horse-bodied creatures with jackal heads and taloned feet—burst through the trees. *Six, seven, eight, nine, shit, shit....*

I backed up to Wyatt's rump, swords raised. Wyatt growled menacingly as three Rippers surrounded us. They began to attack, first one, then another, then all three. I spun my swords in my hands, slashing at them, Wyatt doing the same with his big bear teeth and claws. We sliced and stabbed and bit, and guts and flesh rained onto the ground as we did our damnedest to weaken them little by little until I could manage to cut off heads.

Heath shouted more orders somewhere nearby. Aiden shouted back, which meant he was also alive and unharmed. And Elijah was basically unkillable. Everyone was fine.

Everyone would be *fine.*

Ian and Brody stumbled into my line of sight, fighting with a stray swarmer and one of the jackal-horse Rippers. Brody ducked a swipe of a huge taloned foot aimed at his head. Ian shouted in alarm and stabbed it in the throat. He had a large tear in his shirt, the gray material dark and wet on his side.

Worry choked me. When had that happened?

Horrendous shrieks sounded, and the trees in front of me were torn from their roots. *Three* serpent wraiths, Giants the size of a fucking house, careened onto our path, their spiked tails whipping like blender blades.

Elijah's basilisk erupted from his body. He launched himself at one of the serpents. Their long bodies wound together and tumbled out of sight.

Another of the serpents whipped its tail straight at Matt, who was trying to hack through the thick neck of a nearly dead croc swarmer. He cursed and jumped away, shifting into his hawk and flapping frantically to evade the wraith. The tail snapped again and connected with the hawk. I bit off a scream as he dropped out of the air, landing somewhere in the trees.

There was no time to panic. Wyatt jerked a Ripper by its neck and tossed it against a tree. I hacked its head off, stabbed another one through the throat, whirled, and did the same to another. Wyatt ripped out throats, and I finished the job.

When the last hellhound began to fizzle into gray goo, I darted a frantic look around.

Ian and Brody were now holding off two jackal-horse Rippers. Andre had shifted into his small wolf and was lending his teeth to the fight, snarling and ripping at the oozing flesh of the wraiths while Ian and Brody swung their swords.

Heath and Aiden the jaguar were busy with one of the two remaining Giant serpents.

The last Giant screeched as Nico and Joon made harried slashes at its face. It swiped at them with its enormous tail, and they dove out of the way.

It spun wildly, screeching and shaking its head, and then it darted toward Ian and Brody.

Fear choked me. "Wyatt!"

I sprinted for the Giant.

Wyatt roared and chased after me.

A stray Ripper leapt from the trees. A new one, with a hyena head and a tail like a scorpion's.

It jumped straight at Brody, whose back was to it as he stabbed at a hellhound.

Ian shouted in alarm and threw himself at his boyfriend, shoving him to the ground and out of the way.

Time slowed.

The Ripper's scorpion tail impaled Ian right through his stomach. Ian fell to his knees.

I screamed.

Brody rolled onto his hands and knees. His mouth was open like he was also screaming, but I couldn't hear him.

The Ripper whipped its tail again, and the knotty part below the stinger hit Ian in the head, knocking him out cold.

The wraith jumped on top of Ian's prone body. The eerie

violet light that leaked through its torn flesh and exposed bones glowed brighter.

It was trying to eat my brother's soul.

No!

I screamed again. Tears streamed down my face, clouding my vision. I veered away from the Giant and ran for Ian faster than I ever had in my life.

He cannot die. He's not allowed to die.

Before I could get there, Heath's enormous golden wolf flew through the air and slammed into the wraith standing over Ian. He snarled and sank his teeth into its thick hyena neck. He shook it violently until he tore a huge chunk from its throat.

It dropped. Brody stumbled over to it, sobbing, screaming, and he hacked its head off with Ian's katana.

Heath shifted back into a nude man, stooped to pick up Ian's bleeding, unconscious body, and then he sprinted away, shouting something into his comm as he ran.

Brody was now shouting at me too. His lips were moving, his face terrible, but I couldn't hear anything over the ringing in my ears.

Something crashed into my side. My ribs cracked under the hit, and I went flying.

33

AVERY

I rolled like a log, off the trail and down into the ravine where a shallow creek wound its way through the park.

Wyatt's agonized roar sounded above me.

My spine snapped against a huge rock as I came to a stop. I sucked in a breath that wouldn't come. I brought my tiger as close to the surface as I could, pushing all the power I possessed into my limbs.

"Avery!"

Wyatt's panicked voice echoed above the ravine.

I rolled onto my hands and knees in the ankle-deep water. "Wyatt!" I shouted hoarsely.

"Avery!"

He appeared at the edge of the ravine a ways downstream from me, just beyond where an old footbridge arched over the creek bed. He was naked, streaked with dirt and wraith guts, and so beautiful. His eyes glowed red as he scanned the area below. I'd never seen him look so terrified.

"Wyatt! I'm over here!"

The serpent Giant tore through the trees. With a

screech, it launched itself onto the footbridge and turned its unsettling void eyes on me.

Shit. I began to move, crawling my way out of the creek while every breath felt like I was being stabbed by a hundred tiny knives. My swords were still on my back. My tiger directed every ounce of power she had into healing my wounds.

I tried to stand and stumbled on the slippery rocks.

The Giant coiled. It was going to jump straight on top of me.

Move.

I slipped again and fell to my knees. My beast roared within me.

Wyatt ran for the bridge, shifting back into his bear mid-stride. He slammed into the wraith, knocking it off the other side. It thrashed and shrieked and swiped at Wyatt with its deadly tail, pulling him over the edge with it.

They landed hard in the creek bed just beyond the bridge, rolling and snarling and screeching and grappling.

My insides went cold as that sharp tail sliced straight through Wyatt's belly, opening him up from hip to hip. He roared in agony.

"No!" I screamed, but hardly any sound came out.

My tiger cut off her healing attempts and surged all of her energy into my limbs. I pushed to my feet and ran.

Wyatt rolled sluggishly to his bear feet, blood gushing from his stomach. He dodged the Giant's next strike, its grotesque jaw unhinged and rows of needle teeth aimed at his head.

I reached the footbridge and jumped up to grab the bottom of its iron railing, ignoring my screaming ribs and aching back. I pulled myself up and onto the bridge, and then I leapt from the railing, ripping my swords from their sheaths as I fell.

I landed on top of the wraith's head, using my momentum to plunge both swords straight through its skull, impaling whatever foul thing functioned as its brain.

It screeched and shrieked and thrashed. I held on, my swords my only grip, but it bucked me off and sent me flying, one sword dislodging and the other still stuck in its skull.

I collided with the side of the ravine, hitting packed dirt, roots, and rocks, and then I slid back down into the creek.

Sucking in an excruciating breath, I rolled onto my hands and knees once again.

"Wyatt," I croaked.

He wasn't moving. His bear body lay in the creek bed, at least twenty yards from me.

The wraith had collapsed nearby, twitching, my sword still lodged in its skull, its violet glow sputtering like it was short-circuiting.

I knew better. The head was still attached. It would regenerate whatever I'd fucked up in its brain, and then it would go straight for Wyatt, who lay only a few feet away.

I tried to stand, but my legs weren't working. My tiger was putting everything she had into healing me, and shifting from human to beast and back to human so that I could swing my sword was an expenditure of power and magic I could not currently afford.

I sheathed my blade and began to crawl.

The wraith twitched.

"Wyatt," I called, a little louder, my voice cracking.

The bear twitched. His eyes opened.

The wraith began to curl up, winding its thick, decaying body around itself, hissing.

The bear collapsed into Wyatt the man. He groaned, his hands going to the gaping wound in his abdomen. Blood ran into the shallow water around him.

"No, Wildcat," he shouted, his voice as hoarse as mine. "Stay back. It's not dead."

He'd shifted to talk to me. He was injured and depleted, having shifted too many times back and forth in the past few minutes, and now he'd be hard-pressed to pull enough energy together to shift *again* to heal faster. *You stupid, gorgeous, infuriating man.*

"Don't worry," I rasped. "I'm going to kill it."

"Avery." He shook his head, a tear leaking from his eye. "You can't even stand, baby."

"No," I said, and I kept crawling.

I had to get to him before the wraith did. His bear soul was a brilliant supernova that the monster wouldn't be able to resist.

I refused to lose Wyatt, just like I refused to lose Ian.

The wraith began to unfurl, its exposed bones scraping against the river rocks.

I crawled faster. Pain warred with the fierce will of my tiger, who was digging for everything she fucking had, pushing me to her mate.

"Avery, *please*," Wyatt croaked. "I can't watch it kill you."

"*No*," I said again, and it came out as a sob. My vision blurred. "I can't watch it kill you either. I won't, Wyatt."

The wraith screeched, tossing its head violently. My sword rattled in its skull. It was loosening.

Rocks scraped my knees and hands, but I didn't care. Wyatt tried and failed to sit up, letting out a pained shout.

My own pain had melted into throbbing numbness. There was nothing except getting to Wyatt.

He reached for me.

I tried to stand, stumbled, and fell to my knees next to him.

The wraith turned its glowing void eyes on us.

I brushed Wyatt's hair out of his eyes with a shaky hand and kissed his forehead. "I've got this."

Wyatt cupped my cheek, brushing away my tears with his thumb. "Baby, please try to shift into your tiger and get away from here. Get to the others."

The wraith shot toward us.

My tiger's vicious roar erupted from my mouth as I surged to my feet. I stood over Wyatt, drawing my sword.

The wraith struck, its jaw unhinged, deadly teeth aimed at my face. I jammed my sword through the roof of its open mouth, a move I'd never have attempted if I hadn't pulled it off against a simulation in the arena once upon a time.

The wraith shrieked and flailed, and my other sword fell from its skull. I caught it before it hit the ground. I wrapped both hands around the hilt and wound up.

With everything I had, I swung my sword right at the wraith's neck, catching it as it flung its head violently in my direction. The blade met rotten flesh and bone, the runes etched into the steel glowing softly, and sliced straight through.

The body flopped into the creek with a loud splash, and the head hit the water a second later.

I screamed.

In victory.

In rage.

In *despair*.

I fell to my knees again next to Wyatt. He was so pale, his teeth clenched, the red sheen of his bear pulsing in his eyes like a sputtering car engine.

"You're such a goddess, baby," he said softly. "I'm sorry I doubted you, but I was so fucking scared."

"You have to hold on," I whispered, grabbing his hand. "Please, Wyatt. Don't leave me."

He managed a weak smile. "I don't deserve you."

I shook my head. "Yes, you do. You saved me first."

His smile grew just a little more. "I did, didn't I?"

"And then you got yourself hurt," I said, choking on a sob. "I'm so mad at you."

"Good. You're fucking hot when you're mad at me."

I hiccuped a laugh. "What am I going to do with you?"

"Avery!"

Relief flooded me. "Aiden!" I shouted. "Down here!"

Aiden ran out onto the footbridge, stopping dead in his tracks when he spotted us in the creek below. He appeared to be in one piece, though he hadn't quite gotten his uniform shirt seam closed on one side, the tails flapping as he moved. He did have pants and boots on, and his glasses had survived the night.

"Shit," he swore, and then he vaulted over the bridge railing and landed on light feet like the cat he was. He knelt on Wyatt's other side and began to carefully examine his wound. "Fuck, man, what happened?"

I squeezed Wyatt's hand. "We had a little trouble putting down that last Giant."

"Wildcat killed that bastard," Wyatt said, sounding drowsy. "She didn't even have to shift. She's hurt, though. Make sure she gets fixed."

I shook my head vehemently. "No. Aiden, we have to get him help. He's shifted too many times, and now he's injured. We need to get a medic here right now."

Aiden stripped his shirt off and pressed it to Wyatt's

wound. "We'll get him help, Avery. I'll try to work a few healing spells to keep him stable in the meantime."

"Okay," I said, sniffling, and then I gasped. "What about Ian? Have you heard anything?"

"Yes, Heath got him to Dr. Lee in the med tent, and he's being stabilized—"

I groped for Aiden with the hand that wasn't clutching Wyatt's. "And you? Are you hurt?"

Aiden grabbed my hand and pressed it to his chest. "A few scratches, sweetheart. Nothing that won't heal in a few hours."

"And Elijah?"

"The basilisk took a few hits, but he heals very quickly. We finally managed to kill both the other L4s, and he's still in beast form, clearing out what's left of the wraiths. Kellan's unit chased some this way, so with his quad's extra help, they should have it handled."

Wyatt gripped my hand tighter and groaned.

My pulse began to pound in my ears again. "Aiden, we have to get him to a healer. *Please.*"

"We will, sweetheart, I promise." He said it confidently, but he couldn't hide the concern weighing on his face. "Kellan already called back to base for medical support. Hank and Teegan were both pretty banged up." He took my hand and placed it on Wyatt's forehead. "And look, feel Wyatt's bear."

I did, stuffing my fear down and letting my tiger reach for the bear. He was there, simmering, weak but holding. He wasn't fading. Not yet.

"Okay, good." I stroked Wyatt's hair. "You just hang on. We'll get you help soon."

He forced a smile for me. "Yeah, baby. Don't worry about me."

I tried to smile back, but I couldn't keep my lip from trembling.

"Hey." Aiden tilted my chin so that I was looking him right in his turquoise-ringed eyes. "I will stay right here with Wyatt and use my basic skills with medical runes. I think I can keep him stable for the time being, okay?"

I nodded and wiped my eye. "Okay."

He swallowed, glanced up out of the ravine, and then he blew out a breath. "But I need you to go get Heath," he said, the fear and reluctance at the idea of us parting clear in his voice. "We're only about half a mile from base, and Kellan reported that the wraith activity has died down after what was a very intense early surge. Grab Brody and get to base so you can both be with Ian while Dr. Lee works on him. Send Heath back out here with a medic. He will move heaven and earth to bring that medic straight to Wyatt."

Yes. Heath would take care of everything.

Nodding, I set my shoulders and scrubbed the tears off my cheeks. My future colleagues couldn't see me like this. "Okay. Yes, I can do that. Don't worry. I'll go right now."

I stood up on shaky legs. My entire body was one giant bruise, and I was exhausted, but I was in better shape than I was earlier. Sort of. Adrenaline and the power of my beast would get me through the rest of the night.

"Please keep him alive," I whispered.

"I will. You have my word."

I dusted myself off—futile for my wet, mud-and-guts-caked uniform. I retrieved my other sword from where it'd fallen into the creek, sheathed it next to its sister, then climbed out of the ravine and went in search of Brody.

THE PART OF THE HIKING TRAIL WHERE WE'D FACED THE SURGE looked like someone had driven several bulldozers through it. Trees had been uprooted and tossed across the trail. Dirt, leaves, and the last remnants of wraith guts that hadn't melted away covered everything.

Joon informed me that Elijah was still a basilisk and had disappeared into the woods, and apparently Brody had taken off for base the second the last wraith had been put down.

I didn't blame him.

Matt the hawk was awake, in human form, and in one piece, the entire left side of his face a puffy purpling bruise. He was sitting on a felled tree, looking sullen, Andre perched next to him. Nico stood over Andre, tying a makeshift bandage around his arm.

I waved to them as I strode past, trying my best to look like a person who was not hurting all over, especially in my fucking chest at the thought of the precarious states of both Ian and Wyatt.

"Hey, Avery, where are you—"

"Can't talk now, Kellan," I clipped as I marched past him. Teegan's wolf lay quietly at Kellan's feet, a nasty wound gaping in his hip. Hank sat on the ground next to him in human form, his uniform shirt balled up and pressed to a bloody gash in his face.

Get to Ian. Find Heath. Save Wyatt.

When I entered the non-demolished section of the woods, I increased my pace, testing my body with a slow jog along the trail. It did not feel good, but at least I'd regained the strength to remain on my feet. My beast would let me sleep when I was dead.

I jogged for what felt like hours but was probably only a minute or two. The packed dirt felt like cement under my aching feet. The trail wound around a bend, and I reached the intersection with a wider trail. Here, the path had been cleared so that a vehicle could traverse it, and I breathed a sigh of relief. It would be a straight shot down that trail back to the base parking lot.

And Ian.

And Heath.

As I stepped out onto the wider trail, two Alpha wolves prowled out of the trees that lined the other side of the trail.

I froze.

Those wolves were Jared and Alex.

Cash appeared out of the woods behind them, Trent on his heels. Wraith guts spackled their uniforms and exposed skin. Cash had a deep laceration above his eyebrow and claw marks raked into the skin of his forearm. Trent's white hair was matted with dark-red blood, and he was failing to conceal a limp in his right leg. They both gripped their swords.

They surrounded me.

My tiger took me to my coldest, quietest place. I reached behind my head and slowly drew my blades.

Cash's eyes were wild. I was used to his disdain, his hatred, his cold cruelty.

This was something different, and for the first time, I found him truly alarming.

"Finally," he spat. "We're going to take care of the fucking cancer that you are."

34

AVERY

"Come to kill me?" I asked lightly, though I already knew the answer. Cold fury washed through me, numbing me to anything resembling fear.

Ian.

Heath.

Wyatt.

Cash chuckled. "You've pissed off some powerful people. You could've just stayed in the city, hiding from shifter society with the rest of the cowards in your family, but *no*, you had to butt your way into the Guardians, and now everyone knows you're an abomination that needs to be put down."

Jared's wolf snapped his jaws at me. I sliced at his face with my sword, and he danced away.

"Who exactly have I pissed off?" I asked even though I had a sneaking suspicion that I already knew that answer too.

"Don't play fucking dumb," Cash spat. "If you would've just died like you were supposed to when the wards were down on campus, we wouldn't be here right now. It would've saved us all so much *fucking* trouble."

The cold turned to ice. "The breach of the campus wards was targeted at me?"

Cash rolled his eyes. "Your pathetic little perimeter walks were easy enough to track on the security cameras. Do you know the skill this quad had to possess to herd a group of wraiths of that size and power at the exact section of the wall where the wards were down right as you were walking past?"

I blinked at him. I'd known Cash had it out for me, and I'd definitely thought the failure of the wards had been deliberate, but I'd assumed my presence out in the campus woods when the wraiths had come over the wall had been an unfortunate coincidence.

Of all the shit Cash had tried with me, I had not suspected *that*. It *had* taken an incredible amount of planning and skill.

An overt and coordinated sabotage of the campus wards.

The regional Council was in charge of those wards.

And there was at least one member of our regional Council who was aware I was harboring a particularly powerful beast.

That fucking *asshole*.

Jared snapped at me again, and I opened a cut right across his nose.

I didn't have time for this.

I needed to get to my brother.

I needed to find Heath.

I needed to help Aiden save Wyatt.

And I needed to find Elijah and bring him back from the basilisk.

"And it almost worked," Trent added, sneering at me. "If it hadn't been for those sorry-ass excuses for Primes, who decided to start caring about you again for some fucking reason, you would've fucking bled out in the woods, just another casualty of the war against the plague on our kind."

"Those pathetic little shitheads have been such a fucking pain in the ass," Cash said. He flicked away a stream of blood that'd dripped into his eye. "Traitors to their bloodlines, that's what they are. They'd clearly gotten over their fascination with you, but then they show up to fucking camp acting like they might actually want to *bond* you. Can you fucking imagine?"

Trent scoffed. "Fucking messed up."

"What's up with that, Baxter? Your pussy just that tight?"

I gave him the coldest, blankest stare I could muster.

His eyes blazed with the molten amber of his lion. "Whatever their deal is with you, I'm tired of it fucking up my plans. So many opportunities for fatal accidents at training camp, and yet, here you still fucking are, standing upright and breathing my *fucking* air."

"It sure sounds like you and those powerful shifters who gave you this murder assignment went through a whole lot of trouble," I said evenly. "It would've been easier to just sneak into my cabin and slit my throat."

Cash pointed his sword at me. "You're so fucking right, and I would've relished taking the opportunity if there hadn't been a moondamned basilisk in your tree every fucking night. But unfortunately, we were under strict instructions to make it look like a tragic accident. Wraith death, training mishap, anything to prove that female abominations don't belong fighting shoulder-to-shoulder with men in the Guardians."

Ah. "Men die all the time in the field," I pointed out.

"For the love of the Moon, shut the fuck *up*." He began to pace. "I am so fucking sick of you, and your inability to just *die* already has been laid at my feet like I'm a failure. *Me*. Son of Northeastern Council members and leader of the most successful Guardian quad in a generation."

I held my swords aloft and tracked his movements. He seemed one last frayed string away from losing it completely.

He stopped pacing and smiled. "Lucky for us, there's been so much carnage tonight, and no one will think twice when we tell them the claws and teeth that ripped you apart were wraiths, not beasts."

I bared my teeth at him. "You're still so sure I'm weak."

"I don't know what the fuck you are," he barked. "But the powers that be want you put down, and I am happy to oblige." He looked at the wolves and threw a punch of dominance into his command. "Get it done."

As if struck with a whip, they snarled and attacked me.

I screamed, my rage burning me from the inside out. I *pulled* from the Moon, begging for help. Her power was a weak trickle, but I was desperate.

Desperate to get back to the men who would both kill and die for me.

Just as I would for them. I knew it now, as sure as if it'd been inscribed on my skin.

The bear with a cocky smirk and a heart of gold. The professor whose mind was as sharp as his sword. The Alpha who lived his life to care for those he loved. And the cunning, ruthless basilisk, my sunshine, who'd never left me, even when he did.

How dare Cash and these assholes keep me from my *mates*?

STOP.

The tiger's will exploded from me like a bomb. The blast hit Jared and Alex as their teeth and claws were inches from my body. They yelped, freezing for only a second, but it was enough.

I twisted my body hard to the left and slashed the blade in my right hand down over Alex's neck. Blood sprayed, coating my face, and his severed head fell to the ground.

Jared's wolf unfroze and pounced, jaws snapping and aimed at my face.

I dropped and twisted again, stabbing the wolf in the belly and then jerking my blade in a vicious upward strike. I disemboweled him before his paws hit the ground.

He crumpled at my feet.

I flipped the hilt of my blade in my other hand and dropped to one knee, stabbing wolf Jared in the heart, just be real fucking sure.

Cash gaped at me, blessedly speechless in my presence for the first time ever.

Trent roared, burst into his snow leopard, and charged me from the left.

Cash blinked away his shock, and his face flushed the deep maroon of pure unadulterated rage.

Of deep, visceral hatred.

He shifted into his lion and attacked from my right.

I dropped my blades next to the bloody carcass that was Jared and threw open the door to my tiger's cage. She had clearly reached into some deep reservoir within our shared soul because she came out brimming with power that should've been depleted long ago.

Trent didn't have time to adjust to the shock of the much larger Prime feline that'd appeared in front of him. I slapped him in the head with my giant paw and sent him staggering away.

Cash managed to halt his assault out of reach of my paws. He growled menacingly and prowled around me, taking my measure.

Yeah, look your fucking fill, asshole.

His oppressive dominance fanned out in front him. Just as I had last night, I flicked it away like it was a fucking gnat.

His lion eyes widened again. He growled, but there was uncertainly growing in those liquid brown eyes.

Finally, he lunged for me, snarling and snapping his jaws.

I met him with everything I had. We grappled, raking claws across fur, tearing chunks of skin and muscle with powerful jaws.

Trent recovered and attacked my hindquarters. I jerked my body violently and threw him off. Cash barreled into my side and knocked me to the ground.

Claws pierced my flesh from all directions. I let out an angry roar and tossed Cash off me. Trent was there again, sinking his teeth into my left flank. I twisted and locked my jaws around his neck and yanked *hard*, the way I'd seen Heath do with his absurdly strong wolf muscles. Trent flopped in my hold like a rag doll as I shook him savagely. His spine cracked, and I tore his throat out with one final jerk of my head.

He dropped to the ground, unmoving.

I didn't have time to contemplate whether I'd managed to kill him. Cash was on me again, bleeding profusely, but the wounds I'd made with my claws and teeth had only slowed him down a little bit.

We clashed again, tearing at flesh, snarling, drooling, bleeding.

I ripped a huge chunk from his shoulder, and he stumbled, finally giving me an opening.

I roared and pounced, ready to pin him under my bigger bulk and end this once and fucking for all.

His lion eyes widened. He knew this was going to be the killing blow.

In a blink, the lion disappeared and morphed into Cash the man, crouched low.

He grabbed a blade from the ground.

My fucking blade.

Cash thrust the blade up, aiming for my belly.

I threw my weight to the left, trying to dodge in midair, but he managed to stab me deep in my side.

I landed on my feet but staggered, my body screaming, the strength gushing from me along with the blood from where Cash had stabbed me.

Cash's laugh was demented as he twirled my sword in his hand. He began to stalk toward me.

"You're dead now, betrayer spawn bitch—"

A monster bellowed in the woods.

Cash paused, no longer laughing.

The basilisk tore out of the trees, roaring his head off. He was a wall of gray-green scales, yellow eyes ablaze, wraith guts splattered across his face.

Cash was frozen in place, his head tipped back to stare into those burning eyes. He dropped my sword. "Oh fu—"

Elijah unhinged his terrifying jaw and struck.

He snatched Cash up into his mouth and swallowed him whole.

Holy shit.

The world spun around me.

I lay down on the grass and blinked up at my basilisk. Glowing yellow eyes regarded me from above. He dipped his big serpent head to nuzzle gently at my fur.

Elijah came for me.

Of course he did.

Cool scales wrapped protectively around my beast body. I let out a big feline sigh and relaxed into him.

The last thing I saw before I surrendered to the darkness was Kellan, standing at the tree line, sword in hand, gaping at me like he'd seen a ghost.

35

AVERY

I awoke to kind, dark eyes and the face of an angel.

"Hey, there she is," Dr. Lee cooed.

An angry hiss sounded somewhere above me.

"Cut it out, Elijah." That was Heath's voice. "You know the doctor has to see how she's healing."

There was a snort, and the cool, firm body encircling me shifted irritably.

"How are you feeling, Avery?" Dr. Lee asked. He reached over the wall of scales and pressed soft fingers to my side, just below my ribs.

I tried to take stock of myself and my surroundings, which was a challenge because I was so groggy. I was back in my human body, somehow wearing a baggy T-shirt and underwear. I didn't feel any dirt or blood or wraith guts on my body, so someone had managed to get me cleaned up. I was on the floor, wrapped in a pile of blankets, lying on a pillow that felt like mine. Elijah's basilisk was curled around me. Sunlight streamed through the windows.

"Um, I feel okay," I said. "Tender where you're pressing. But mostly just... sleepy."

Dr. Lee hummed. "Good. That's good."

Heath's face appeared. He leaned over Elijah's body and stroked my hair lovingly.

I smiled at him. "Hi."

He looked so tired, but he returned my smile. "Hi, Killer."

"Are we in my cabin?"

"Yes. Elijah carried you five miles through the woods and all the way back here. Your doorframe didn't survive, unfortunately."

The warm tingly magic of Dr. Lee's healing ran up and down my entire right side. I sighed contentedly. "Did Elijah... make me a nest?"

"He sure did. He's, um, going to be a basilisk for a while longer."

The events of the night came tumbling back into my foggy brain, and I gasped. "Heath, Elijah ate—"

"I know, baby." Heath shut his eyes and took a deep breath, his jaw tensing. "Kellan told me."

"Oh." I sank into my blankets and reached above my head to stroke Elijah's scales. "I see."

"Elijah won't be able to shift back until he finishes... digesting."

I wrinkled my nose. "Ah."

"He should be good in another six to eight hours," Dr. Lee said lightly. He patted the basilisk on the neck, and Elijah let out a prissy snort. "Fascinating, isn't it?"

I nodded sagely. "So fascinating." I turned back to Heath, his face framed by the gentle rays of the morning sun. A golden summer prince, watching over me. "Kellan saw my beast," I murmured.

"He told me that as well. But it appears he is going to treat that information with the appropriate care. He actually finished off Trent before he called me and sent me after you and Elijah."

"I'm not hearing any of this," Dr. Lee said in a sing-song voice. "La la la."

"Mmm," I said, petting Elijah's cold, smooth nose as he nuzzled me. "Good."

Heath's face crumpled. "I am so sorry, Avery. We failed you again. We somehow managed to let you run through the woods, injured and alone, *again*, and you were attacked by people I should've killed a long fucking time ago."

"Hey." I grabbed his hand and squeezed it weakly. "Everything was fucked up last night. I had to leave Aiden with Wyatt, and you weren't with me because you were saving my brother's life, remember? How is he?"

Heath rolled his eyes. "Throwing a tantrum in the infirmary because Dr. Lee won't release him until tonight."

"He's healing nicely, Avery," Dr. Lee added. "But you know I like to keep an eye on my patients."

"What about Wyatt?" I asked. Horrifying memories flashed like gunshots in my brain. Wyatt laying naked in the creek, battered and trying to hold in his own guts. I began to tremble. "Heath, he was hurt really badly."

Heath caressed my cheek. "We got to him in time, baby. He's recovering, sedated and healing. Aiden's keeping an eye on him. You saved his life, and I know he doesn't intend to let you down by not pulling through this."

I nodded, sniffing as I blinked away tears. "Okay. I wish I could see him."

"Soon, Killer. You have your own recovering to do, okay?"

"Yeah." My eyelids fluttered. "I feel foggy and tired."

Heath nodded, looking pained. "Your tiger overextended herself to a dangerous degree, Avery. I can hardly feel her.

She has to recharge, and the best way to do that is for you to sleep."

Dr. Lee stood up and slung his medical bag over his shoulder. "Like your basilisk, another six to eight hours of rest should be enough to get you and your beast, the nature of whom I am now privy to and will never reveal to anyone, back on your feet. Being in such close proximity to your scaly mate here will be a big help."

He winked at me, and then he left, strolling out through the hole in the wall that used to be my door.

I shut my eyes and clutched Heath's hand. "There are other things I need to tell you," I whispered. "That Cash said."

The weight of Heath's wolf filled the nest, surrounding me as protectively as Elijah's body. *Mmm.* "You can tell me when you're better, baby. That's all I want right now. Just for you to get better."

"Okay," I murmured, and then I slipped under again.

SOMETIME LATER, I BLINKED AWAKE ONCE MORE. THE SUN WAS high and blazing outside, and a warm breeze wafted in through the screen windows. Elijah had tucked his big beast head next to me in our nest, and he was sound asleep, slow breaths puffing from his slitted nostrils.

I felt for my tiger. She was also sleeping, the low thrum of her magic a bit stronger than it had been when I'd awoken earlier and talked to Heath.

Heath....

Careful footsteps sounded as someone entered my cabin.

Elijah popped one yellow eye open to examine our visitor. He snorted and went back to sleep.

Aiden knelt next to us and peered into my nest. "Hey," he said softly. "You're awake."

I smiled at him. "Mmm. For a minute, maybe. I'm still so sleepy."

His jaguar caressed me, and I let the energy seep into my center. "Your tiger feels much stronger than when I checked on you a few hours ago." He laid a hand on my cheek and tried to smile, but pain filled his hazel eyes. "Wyatt's bear is the same. Dr. Lee thinks he'll be able to discharge him tomorrow, just in time for us to pack up and head home."

I sighed in relief. "Thank the Moon."

"And Ian is up and about and carrying on about whether this is a summer camp or a prison. I left George with him."

"Oh, good. He'll make sure Ian stays put."

Aiden grinned. "Exactly. And I think you just need a few more hours of rest. Heath and I will come back by before dinner."

"Mmm, okay," I murmured. "They always feed us well on patrol nights."

Aiden's face hardened. "We are not going on the last patrol tonight. I told Commander Moss we'd walk if he tried to make us."

My empty stomach soured. "Does he, um... know what happened? Aiden, I killed Alex and Jared. And I mostly killed Trent."

"Yes, he does, and yes, you did. Kellan took Ward, Commander Moss, and me out there at sunrise. We saw the aftermath. Ward and the commander are incensed, to put it mildly. They would've killed all four of them again themselves if they could've."

Aw. "Did you find my swords?"

"I did, sweetheart. I cleaned and sharpened them for you." He grinned, and this one was real and savage. "You gutted those moronic fucking wolves, didn't you? You didn't even have to shift."

My face heated at his jaguar's glowing pride. "I had to work fast. I couldn't let them win, Aiden. I had to get back to you."

His expression softened, and he ran his thumb lightly across my cheekbone. "I am in awe of you, Avery. You are the most incredible woman I've ever met." Pain clouded his face. He shut his eyes and dropped his head. "And yet, I did it *again*. I sent you away and allowed you to be viciously attacked. Again. I just...." He looked up at me, his eyes shining with tears. "How could I ever expect you to forgive me?"

"Hey," I whispered, rubbing the back of his hand where it rested on my cheek. "I do forgive you, Aiden. You would never purposefully endanger me, even back then. I know that now."

"No," he said fiercely. "Never. I'm contemplating never leaving your side again, actually."

I melted into my blankets, feeling floaty and content. "I wish you could lay in my nest with me. But Elijah didn't really leave much room."

He chuckled. "No. He's being very selfish with you, but he's probably earned it."

"It's a good thing he ate Cash," I whispered. "It forced him to be sluggish and lazy in here with me rather than out on a rampage."

Elijah snorted and burrowed his big head deeper into my side.

"That's very true." Aiden leaned down and kissed my forehead. "Rest now, sweetheart. We need you to get better."

As I drifted off, he whispered, so softly I almost couldn't hear it, "We won't survive without you."

THE NEXT TIME I AWOKE, THE SUN WAS BEGINNING TO SET, AND my tiger was purring up a storm in my chest.

My scaly cocoon had disappeared.

Instead, I found myself buried in my blankets and wrapped around a warm, naked man.

Elijah was sleeping soundly. I was lying on his chest, the steady beat of his heart under my cheek and the gentle rise and fall of his breathing threatening to lull me back to sleep. Strong arms held me tightly, and our bare legs intertwined.

I lifted my head to study his face. So peaceful, my monster.

Sleep had softened his sharp angles into something almost sweet. His unruly dark hair fanned out over my pillow, and his thick eyelashes brushed the tops of his cheekbones. I traced those cheekbones lightly with the pad of my finger, making my way across his rough stubble and over to his ear. I caressed the shell of his ear and touched each of the thin gold hoops in his lobes, marveling at how those and the one he wore through his septum survived his shifts when the rest of us could only manage that with studs.

I moved to the snake tattoo around his neck, tracing the intricate lines of the head where it was nestled right over his firm chest. He was warm—not as warm as one of the others would've been—but just right to keep me comfortable as I was pressed against him. Only the thin fabric of my panties separated my most intimate parts from the muscle at his hip.

My body was healing. I was still sore, especially where Cash had stabbed me with my own fucking sword, but I couldn't remember a time when I was able to get such a long or restorative rest, even after a patrol. My beast was back online, luxuriating in the kills we'd made and the touch of our mate, and it had all awoken a deep ache within me.

A need so intense, I could only cling closer to Elijah, as though touching more of his skin with mine would cure me.

He stirred in my arms. His eyelids fluttered before snapping open.

Rounded pupils in a sea of liquid gold took me in. They constricted into the vertical slits of his beast for a blink and then bounced back to round. He sucked in a shaky breath, licked his lips, and then let out a tortured groan.

I opened my mouth to say something—anything, I didn't know what—but before I could make a sound, Elijah rolled me onto my back and covered my body with his.

Smoldering eyes searched my face with desperate hunger. His warm skin was a delicious contrast to the chilly tingles of the basilisk now licking up and down my body. He was hard and heavy between my thighs, his cock resting on my lower belly and my dampening panties.

He didn't speak. The wild and desperate way he looked at me said everything.

Asked me everything.

I stared into those mesmerizing eyes and whispered my answer like a prayer.

"*Yes.*"

36

AVERY

For the briefest moment, Elijah stared down at me, a look of wonder on his face, and then he slammed his lips to mine. I dug my fingers into his hair and let him consume me. I wanted him. Needed him. Was never going to get enough of him.

He shifted our bodies just enough to slide his long fingers between my legs. He traced the seam of my panties before dipping beneath the fabric, and another tortured groan escaped him at the wetness he found there.

I moaned against his lips. "*Pl—*"

He tore my panties from my body and buried his cock inside me.

"Fuck," he hissed against my ear. "*Dove.*"

I whimpered as he began to thrust. He was long and thick and a perfect fit, as the Moon knew he would be.

"Yes, Elijah. *Yes.*"

He pressed his forehead to mine and fucked me harder. His pupils slit into those of the basilisk. "You are *mine,*" he hissed.

"*Yes.*" I dug my nails into the taut muscles of his back. "Yours."

He licked into my mouth, his long tongue caressing mine. His thrusts became even more frenzied.

Brutal.

Proprietary and *desperate*.

He didn't let up, fucking me and kissing me and driving me higher and higher. I lost track of where he ended and I began as I wrapped my legs around his waist and urged him on.

"Elijah," I croaked. "I'm.... I'm going to...."

He pinned my arms above my head and ground down into me, his thrusts gentling, replaced with the slow roll of his hips. The hard muscles of his pelvis worked against my clit while his dick filled me to bursting. The basilisk's gaze bored into mine. "We're together now, Dove. I'm not talking about bonding or anything with the others. This is about you and me. I love you, and I'm not leaving your side for as long as we live."

Tears pricked in my eyes even as I skated along the edge of the most intense pleasure I'd ever experienced. "Yes," I sobbed. "I love you, too, Elijah."

He shut his eyes and let out a pained noise, like I'd kicked him in the stomach. When his eyes snapped open, they were his human eyes, their glow soft and warm. He dipped to kiss me again. "*Mine,*" he purred.

And then he held me down and went back to fucking me ruthlessly, until white-hot ecstasy ripped through my body.

I screamed into our kiss, and he groaned, following me over the edge.

As I came back to earth, he pressed kisses to my forehead, my cheeks, my nose, and finally my lips. His cock softened inside me, but he didn't seem in a hurry to remove it, nor was I in a hurry to make him.

Being connected to him, having him as a part of me, if only for a little while longer, gave me more contentment than anything had in quite some time.

"I'll never stop trying to be worthy of your love," he whispered, "even if it takes me our entire lives to get there."

I shook my head. "You are worthy, Elijah. You've made caring for me the center of your whole existence. You've stayed with me and loved me, even when I was trying desperately to push you away."

"You were ambushed and almost killed," he hissed, and the air turned icy around us. "*Again*, Dove. If I hadn't arrived when I did...."

I cupped his face in my hands. "But you did. You gave Cash the end he deserved, and you even managed to get me out of the woods without anyone else seeing my beast."

His expression softened. "Dove...."

"The Moon gave you to me, and I've decided to keep you."

The sly smile I loved so much finally crept onto his striking face. "Then you'll have me. I hope you know what you're in for, my sweet dove. There's hardly been room in my thoughts for anything but you since the moment I laid eyes on you in our shared class."

I brushed a lock of his hair over his ear. "You were pretty memorable yourself."

"And now that I have you?" He dipped his head to run his tongue along the side of my neck. "Now that I can taste you, and hold you, and *fuck* you to my heart's content?" His tongue found the shell of my ear, and he rasped, "I'm only going to fall deeper, Dove. I'm only going to grow more obsessed."

A shiver racked my body. "Yes," I whispered.

He kissed along my jaw. "If anyone even *breathes* incorrectly in your direction, I will consume them and make them into nothing."

"Elijah," I gasped.

His chuckle was sinful. "I want to be where you are, always. I would crawl inside your skin and live there if I could."

Only Elijah could make that sound so intensely romantic. I grinned and wiggled my hips. "You are still inside me, it seems."

"Indeed." He thrust his hips playfully, and I bit my lip at the sensation he elicited in my oversensitive pussy. "And I apologize for not inquiring before I came inside you, my love, but I'm aware you have a contraceptive implant."

"I do," I said slowly, narrowing my eyes at him. "How do you know that?"

He grinned, showing me those sharp canines. "Heath scented it."

"Oh." And reported back to the group, apparently.

He began to kiss down my neck, stretching the collar of my oversized T-shirt so he could move down my chest. "How long do you think the others will leave us to luxuriate in each other before they come in here to fuss over you?"

"Until right now," Heath said gruffly.

Speak of the devil.

Elijah blew out a defeated breath and sagged in my arms, which made me laugh. When he finally rolled off me, the mess he'd left between my thighs leaked onto the blankets. He swirled his fingers at my entrance one last time, humming a pleased noise.

I bit off a moan and snuggled into his side.

Heath stood in the opening where my door had once

been, leaning against the wall with his arms crossed over his chest. He wore a tight white T-shirt and sweatpants that clung to his thick thighs, and he had the look of a man who was amused but trying very hard to appear stern instead.

Aiden was with him, dressed similarly and smelling like a rainstorm, his wavy chocolate hair damp. He caught me checking him out and raised his eyebrows, also trying for a stern look and succeeding more than his brother.

"As quintet leader, I am here to fuss over both of you," Heath announced, striding over. He knelt next to me and ran his hand over the side of my body still healing from being stabbed, beginning from where my T-shirt had ridden up to my breasts and all the way down to the exposed skin of my hip. The blanket tucked around me only just obscured my bare ass. His nostrils flared, and he groaned softly. "Did Elijah take good care of you, Killer? Your tiger feels very happy right now."

She sure was, though not entirely satisfied, apparently. She licked a claw and flicked her tail at Heath's wolf.

I smiled dreamily at our leader. "Elijah and I are together now."

His face split into a grin. "Are you?"

Elijah kissed the top of my head. "It's true. And yet, I suspect you two are here to cut our honeymoon short."

Aiden stood at our feet, arms crossed, surveying Elijah with a critical eye. "How are you feeling after... you know," he asked.

He shrugged. "Surprisingly good, though I'd prefer not to dwell on it all." He shuddered dramatically. "*Meat.*"

I patted his chest. My poor vegan monster.

Heath scooped me into his arms. I squeaked in surprise and threw my arms around his neck as he lifted me out of the nest. "Get dressed and report to the infirmary," he said to

Elijah, nudging him with his foot as Elijah grumbled in protest. "Dr. Lee wants to check you over to make sure there aren't any lingering... issues."

"And we'd appreciate it if you looked in on Wyatt," Aiden added.

I gasped. "Why? Is something wrong? Is he okay?"

Aiden ran a soothing hand down my arm. "Wyatt is just fine, sweetheart. We just ran into Ward, and he told us that Wyatt is healing well and that his bear is strong. He should be awake soon."

Elijah stretched his long limbs, blankets falling away and exposing his sinewy body and olive skin from head to toe. He rose from the nest, completely and unabashedly naked. He tossed me a heated glance before turning to Heath. "Fine. I'll go check on our bear and let Dr. Lee poke at me." He leaned in and planted a lingering kiss on my lips. "Be good for our boys, my love."

"I'd planned to take you to the shower and scrub you clean of anything left over from our night from hell," Heath said, and then he narrowed his eyes at Elijah. "And now I'll also have to wash all of your cum off her before we parade her through a cafeteria full of shifter males."

"Green looks good on our leader, doesn't it?" Elijah purred, winking at me. He pulled on some shorts and sauntered to the doorway, shirtless and barefoot. "I'll see you at dinner, Dove," he called over his shoulder before he ducked outside.

Aiden sighed and squinted at the doorway. "I'll follow him for a bit to see if he's actually headed in the direction of the infirmary." He stole a quick kiss and whispered against my lips, "I'll meet you at the showers and make sure you have some privacy, okay, sweetheart?"

"Okay," I whispered back, though I hated to see him go, even for just a few minutes.

Heath tightened his grip, still holding me bridal style. I was pretty sure I'd recovered enough from my injuries—and from Elijah fucking me until I was a gooey pile of bones—that I could walk on my own, but after the events of the past twenty-four hours, I'd decided to take some time off from being a stone-cold, certified badass. It was safe and comfortable here in Heath's arms, just as it had been safe and comfortable wrapped up in Elijah's arms and scales.

So, I'd stay for a little while.

Heath carried me out to the small concrete building behind my cabin that housed the bathrooms and showers I shared with the handful of female staff. At this hour, Aisha would be in the infirmary, and the rest were probably in the kitchen, preparing dinner.

My Alpha was all business. He took me straight to the largest shower stall in the corner and threw the curtain back. He set me gingerly down on the bench in the spacious changing area in front of the shower, and then he cranked on the water. As steam began to fill the stall, he tossed the curtain aside and marched back out.

He returned a few seconds later with a clean towel from the towel bin and the shower caddy I stored in my assigned cubby.

I didn't ask how he knew which one was mine.

I tipped my head back to rest against the wall and watched him, fondness welling within me. Heath was a true Alpha—noble, unwavering, and impressively powerful, all in the name of caring for his pack. It was obvious he'd hardly slept since the night his wolf had spent in my cabin. He'd been running around, putting out fires and keeping everyone in our family *alive*, including my brother.

My stomach sank as I remembered I had one more thing to add to my Alpha's burden.

After he'd set my caddy on the cement floor of the shower, he knelt at my feet, bringing him eye level with me. He ran his warm hand up my leg. "Ready, Killer? I'm physically incapable of leaving you right now, but I can turn around, if you'd prefer."

I cupped his stubbled cheek. "I want you to stay, and you don't have to turn around. But I need to talk to you first."

He sighed, frowning. "Is this about whatever Cash said to you before he became basilisk food?"

I nodded. "He raged at me for a bit, and of course he couldn't help crowing with victory at my imminent demise." Heath's expression turned thunderous, and I ran my fingers soothingly through his hair. This wasn't going to get any easier for him to hear. "He didn't name names, but... I'm pretty sure this involves your father."

37

HEATH

The carefully built composure I'd been wearing like kevlar since the moment I'd had to leave my quad and my mate in the middle of a war zone crumpled like fucking tissue paper.

I could only stare silently at Avery—the beautiful, savage queen who was the love of my fucking life—as she told me every word of bile Cash had decided to spew before he and his quad tried to kill her.

Before they'd attempted to rip my soul and my wolf's from my body.

That's what would've happened if Avery died. I'd be a husk, and so would my brother. Wyatt would probably be dead, and no one would ever see Elijah in his human body again.

"I just...," Avery whispered. "I don't think it's a coincidence the wards failed only a few weeks after your father ambushed me in the arena hallway. He may not know about my tiger, but he knows I'm a female Prime whose power rivals his own."

I managed a stunned nod. "And he's on the Council. He

has the ability to fuck with the school's wards. And he knows Cash's fathers, who sit on the Northeastern Council, which means he also knows Cash. He had an in—someone within the Guardians who had access to you and was sympathetic to their... cause."

"Right," she said softly.

This was so fucking devastating.

The thing I'd been worried about since the day she'd told us that he'd accosted her in the arena had *already happened.*

My wolf howled his fury, creating a crushing pressure in my chest. I wrapped my arms around Avery's legs and buried my face in her lap. "I am so sorry, baby. *Fuck.* I knew my dad had regressive views about female shifters, but I didn't think he was a murderer. What the fuck is wrong with him?"

She played with my hair, soothing me when I didn't fucking deserve to be soothed. "Maybe this is another clue, Heath. Another piece of the puzzle we're trying to solve."

I lifted my head to stare into her gorgeous eyes. "You think my dad's involved in the belladonna murder ring?"

She lifted a brow. "Do you?"

The dread that overcame me as I wrestled with that question made me sick to my fucking stomach.

I wouldn't lie to Avery. Never again.

Holden was absolutely capable of something that sinister, and there was no way Stephen wasn't complicit.

"*Fuck,*" I bellowed, the sound echoing off the walls of the shower. I let go of Avery's legs and fell onto my ass.

I didn't deserve to touch her or hold her or be comforted by her.

Phantom claws had wrapped around my lungs, every breath scraping against my rib cage. I scooted backwards until I hit the wall of the shower. I sat there like a fucking miserable asshole, elbows on my knees and my head in my hands while the spray of the water hit a few feet away from me, the mist dampening my clothes.

"My dads are fucking scum," I rasped. "And I let them hurt you. I've failed you, just like I've failed my sister."

"Hey," Avery said gently. She crawled into my lap, straddling me.

Even through the physical pain I was experiencing due to my failures as a mate and quad leader, I was hyper-aware that Avery had no panties on under her T-shirt. Blood rushed straight from my brain to my cock as she pressed her bare pussy right up against it through my thin pants.

"Avery," I groaned.

She cupped my face in her hands, and I could only gaze up at her in awe. "None of this is your fault, Heath. You haven't failed me or Clara, and you saved my brother's life last night. I owe you *everything*."

"I would do anything for you," I whispered. "But *fuck*, baby. Cash. My own *father*—"

"Your father has probably been at this evil villain thing for longer than you've been alive. We're onto him now, and I'm here with you. He doesn't stand a chance against us together."

Those were words I'd scarcely dared to dream of hearing from the girl I was so fucking madly in love with that it was a miracle I was able to function outside her presence.

My eyes felt hot and wet, and I couldn't blame the shower. I sucked in a deep breath and tucked my face into her chest, desperate to just breathe in her scent and feel her body wrapped around mine.

A quiet rustle of the curtain sounded.

"Aiden," Avery whispered. "He's okay. I just told him some things—"

"I heard," Aiden said, his voice pained. "I was standing guard out there to make sure you two had some privacy, and I heard everything."

"Oh," she said quietly, stroking my hair.

I could feel my brother's despair, his helplessness, the way his jaguar paced the cage of our circumstances. I'd felt it before, and I hated it for him.

"I would take all of this from him if I could," Aiden said to Avery. "It's hard, you know? I'm the older brother. I should be protecting him. Handling our fucking parents. But that wasn't the way it worked out."

Aiden was an extremely powerful shifter and the largest jaguar in a generation. He could've easily led his own quad, but we'd always been inseparable, a united front against our fathers since childhood. We'd never considered anything other than sharing a quad together.

It just happened that my beast was even higher on the power and dominance scale than his. Being the quad leader suited me and my wolf just fine.

My brother had never wished for it, until I'd decided to challenge my dad. Aiden would've taken that from me in a heartbeat.

I'd never let him.

"It wasn't," Avery agreed. "But only the Moon knows why we're made the way we are. And you do take care of him, Aiden. I've seen it. You're a good brother. A good man."

I finally lifted my head from Avery's chest and peered over her shoulder at my brother. "Listen to our mate. She knows what she's talking about."

He gave me a half-hearted smile. That smile turned hungry as his gaze traced the lines of Avery's leg where it wrapped around my waist. He watched as I slid my hands from her hips down to her bare ass, giving those perfect globes a squeeze.

Avery's lips brushed my ear. "Are you feeling better?"

"Your naked pussy pressed against my cock could cure me of anything, Killer."

Aiden floated further into the shower stall, and then he knelt behind Avery, the water soaking into the knees of his gray sweatpants. He pushed her wet shirt up to her neck and then began kissing a path down her spine.

I took advantage of her shirt being around her neck to fill my hands with her perky tits.

She dropped her head to my shoulder and let out a tiny little moan.

"What do you say to Aiden and me helping you shower off, Killer?" I rasped against her cheek. "Let us take care of you."

"That depends," she said, arching into Aiden's touch as he pressed his lips to the crook of her neck. "I don't just shower with any males. Will you both agree to be my... boyfriends?"

Aiden swatted her ass lightly, and she made a growly little kitten noise.

"I don't know if I like that," he said between the moments when he didn't have his mouth on her skin. "*Boyfriend* doesn't feel like enough, sweetheart. You're my mate."

I grasped her chin and brought us nose to nose. "He's right, baby. We're your Fated, and we hope that one day soon we'll be your bonded mates. But, I'm a benevolent leader. We're going to be whatever the fuck you want us to be, *for now*, as long as it involves us being yours."

She nodded, pressing her forehead to mine. "I don't

know if I'd have been able to do what I did to survive against Cash's quad if my beast and I hadn't needed so badly to get to you, Heath. If I hadn't needed to survive for Wyatt, and Aiden, and Elijah. We belong together. I'm sorry I fought it for so long."

"No," I growled. "We deserved that. We hurt you, baby. *I* hurt you. Even if you forgive me, I don't know if I'll ever truly forgive myself."

She took my lips in a ferocious kiss, which I returned with equal fervor. *I'll devour you first, Killer.*

After our tongues had battled for several long, glorious seconds, she pulled away to growl in my face. "Shut up. I told you to stop saying that shit about yourself."

My dick was so hard, I was in physical pain. My wolf loved playing dominance games with this girl.

"You heard our girlfriend," Aiden said. He pulled her shirt off over her head, leaving her gloriously naked in my lap. He swatted her ass again. "Up, sweetheart. Let's get you showered."

She let him pull her to her feet, and she stepped gracefully over me and moved under the showerhead.

"Fuck," I muttered, my gaze glued to the rivulets of water sluicing down her tight body as she wet her hair.

"Fuck," Aiden agreed.

She arched a brow at us. "If you're both going to wash me, I want your clothes off."

You'd never see two males strip so fast. I managed to peel myself off the floor as I kicked off the last leg of my sweatpants. I snagged Avery's shampoo from her caddy and squirted some in my hand before taking my place behind her.

"Oh," she moaned as I massaged the shampoo into her hair.

The steel pipe that was my dick was cradled against her back and the crevice of her ass. We were past the point of no return. I knew it. She knew it. Aiden also knew it.

We would not be leaving this shower before I bent her over and showed her what it meant to be mine.

Aiden had managed to get her little shower puff soapy, and he was now running it all over her body, paying special attention to her tits. After she was covered in suds, we rinsed her body and her hair, exchanging smug looks at her little mewls and happy sighs as we worked.

I grabbed her conditioner and began to work it through her long hair while Aiden gave up all pretense and shoved his tongue into her mouth. She moaned, and the heady scent of shifter lust saturated the steamy air.

When Aiden finally deigned to let her breathe and began making his way down her body, I grasped her chin and turned her head to face me over her shoulder. Hooded blue eyes gazed into mine, a soft smile on her face. She was perfect, and I rumbled my approval.

"I love you, Avery Baxter," I growled, my lips a mere inch from hers. "I've loved you since the first day I watched you swing your swords in the arena. I loved you even when I acted like I didn't, and I loved you even when you hated me. I'm going to take care of you for the rest of our lives, and I will *never* hurt you again, do you understand me?"

Her eyes misted, and she blinked the tears away. "I love you too," she whispered. "So much."

Euphoria. I took her lips in a rough, possessive kiss. "Good girl. Now get ready, because we have plans for you."

38

AVERY

I leaned into Heath's embrace, my back to his solid, wet chest, as Aiden wrapped his lips around my nipple. He flicked his tongue, teasing me, and then he switched to the other side and gave it the same treatment.

"I've never seen such a perfect pair of breasts," he mused between sucks and nibbles. "These taunted me during our tutoring sessions. I was dying to know how they'd feel in my hands."

Heath chuckled, his lips pressed just below my ear. "He was always crankier than usual those nights."

Aiden kissed a path down my stomach until he was on his knees in front of me. He lifted my leg to rest on his shoulder, and then he feathered a few kisses over my inner thigh, his eyes holding mine. Could he see how desperately I wanted him, even without his glasses? The turquoise glow that ringed his irises was as bright as I'd ever seen it, so his beast was at the surface, lending a hand.

"*Aiden,*" I whined, which just made him grin and nip my thigh again. "Please."

"This feels familiar," Heath mused. "Except Aiden stole my spot, didn't he, Killer?"

"Do you two—*ah.*" I gasped as Aiden licked a long stripe through my aching core. "Do you two share like this a lot?"

"No, baby," Heath said. "We always knew we would eventually, but he and I hadn't met a girl we were both that seriously into. Not until you."

"We should've known then that it was the Moon at work," Aiden said. He swirled his tongue around my clit. "What idiots we were. All four of us were somehow obsessed with the same girl, and we thought we could just ignore it."

"It was misery," Heath growled. I gasped as Aiden threaded a finger inside me, and then another. "How fucking consumed we were by the girl we thought we couldn't have. Do you know how many times I fucked my fist in the shower, thinking about the taste of your pussy?"

Aiden sucked my clit into his mouth and rumbled a pleased noise. "It's un-fucking-believable, isn't it?" he said between lashes of his tongue. "Poor Heath."

"I—*oh.*" I squirmed, digging my nails into Heath's arm where it was banded across my chest. "Aiden, I'm so close."

"Mmm," he hummed against my slick skin. He hammered his fingers harder into me and flicked his tongue, driving me right over the edge.

I cried out, but Heath was there to consume my screams. He slammed his lips onto mine and growled in satisfaction as my climax shot through my body, leaving me shaking and limp in his arms.

Aiden ran his tongue languidly through my folds, pressed one last kiss to my inner thigh, then climbed to his feet. I took in his gorgeous body, all lean, carved muscle and skin almost as tan as his brother's. His cock was long and thick, hanging heavy between his thighs.

He held my gaze as he wiped his mouth with the back of his hand, and then he hit me with that haughty grin I used to hate to love whenever he'd done something impressive during our tutoring sessions.

Heath kissed my cheek and nudged me toward Aiden. "Go to him. I'll wait."

Aiden grabbed my hand and yanked me into his embrace. As our hot, slick bodies collided, I threw my arms around his neck and kissed him hard.

He groaned against my lips, shuffling me backwards until my back hit the shower wall. "Avery," he breathed between kisses, "I love you, sweetheart. You're my whole world."

I pulled away from our kiss so that I could stare into his vibrant eyes and comb my fingers through his thick, wavy hair.

My brilliant jaguar.

He was breathtaking, and he was mine.

"I love you too," I said softly, and then I gave him a teasing grin. "Professor."

"Brat," he rumbled, and then he hoisted me up so that my legs were wrapped around his waist. With one skilled flick of his hand, he lined himself up and drove his cock into me, swallowing my moan with another kiss.

He took me hard against the wall, grinding into me, the taut muscles of his lower abs rubbing deliciously against my clit, his cock rubbing just as deliciously against every sensitive spot inside me. He was precise and relentless, and in minutes, I was falling apart in his arms.

"Fuck *yes*," he growled. "That's so good, sweetheart. Give it all to me."

As I shattered, I met Heath's gaze over Aiden's shoulder. He was standing under the shower, stroking his cock as the hot water streamed over his golden body and the starbursts of his wolf blazed in his eyes.

Aiden groaned into the side of my neck. His thrusts slowed, and then we enjoyed a few more unhurried kisses while he still had me pinned to the wall with his hips.

"All right," Heath rumbled. "Hand her over, man."

Aiden grinned against my lips and pulled us away from the wall. He carried me the few steps needed to get to Heath, and then he finally set me down, extricating his dick from inside me at the very last second.

Heath positioned me back under the shower, and I let the warm water run down my body and wash away the mess Aiden left dripping down my leg.

Aiden kissed my cheek. "I'll go grab us more towels and dry clothes. Be good for Heath, sweetheart."

"Not likely," I said, grinning.

He chuckled as he wrapped my towel around his waist, and then he ducked out of the shower stall.

Heath stepped in front of me and cupped my cheek in his big, calloused hand. "Got one more in you, Killer?"

"You think I can't handle you, Alpha?" I asked, baring my teeth at him.

I let my tiger off her leash.

He sucked in a breath and cracked his neck. His wolf met my tiger in the tight space between us, the force of his dominance never failing to keep me on my toes. He leaned in and gave me a savage grin. "Is that how it is, baby? Want me to come and take it?"

Boy, did I.

My tiger answered for me by dripping so much lust into

her display of dominance that she'd practically turned around and lifted her tail for this Alpha.

Heath's nostrils flared. "I see," he growled, and then he struck.

In a blink, he had me flipped around and pressed against the wall, his hard chest at my back and my wet hair wrapped around his fist. His heavy cock slotted against my ass, teasing me the way he had earlier when he'd washed my hair.

I jutted my ass back against him, and he let out a pained groan. My tiger was putting up a token resistance, pushing her will onto him as if to hold him in place, but Heath's wolf slipped right through my beast's defenses. His dominance was more consuming than I'd ever felt before.

"*Mine*," he growled, and then he sank his teeth into my neck. He didn't break the skin, but there was a sharp nip of pain in that proprietary bite.

I loved it.

"Yours," I gasped as he yanked my hair tighter and bit me again.

He thrust his cock inside me. He didn't ease in. He didn't begin gently or try to warm me up. He filled me to the hilt in one smooth, brutal stroke, and my scream shook the cement walls of the shower.

"*Fuck*," he groaned, long and low. He began to snap his hips, every thrust harder and deeper than the last. "Never keep this pussy from me again, Killer. I'll die without it."

I made a garbled noise of agreement. He was fucking me into the wall, demolishing all my senses. There was only the sound of his skin slapping against mine, his hot breath on my neck, and the torrid climax he was about to unleash on my body.

"*Heath*," I whined. I was strung so tight, already so sensitive after Aiden, clinging to the precipice amidst Heath's onslaught. "It's so much. I need—"

"I've got you, baby. I've always got you."

Rough fingertips found my clit, and he fucked me mercilessly until my muscles spasmed around him, forcing me to come yet again.

He groaned a string of obscenities and came with me, holding me tight. He gentled, kissing my shoulder, then the crook of my neck, and finally behind my ear.

I sighed happily.

He pulled out and flipped me back around, moving us under the streaming water one last time.

"This is the best day of my life," he said, cradling my face and staring down at me with such devotion that tears welled in my eyes once again. "Thank you for letting me in, Avery. For giving me a chance. For loving me. I don't deserve it—"

"Shut up," I said, sniffling.

"—but I'll spend the rest of my life making sure you don't regret it."

I kissed him. "I know you will. Now take me to dinner. I've used a shit ton of energy healing my body and my beast and letting my boyfriends bang me into next week. I'm starving."

He laughed. "You got it, Killer."

As I walked with Heath and Aiden down to the chow hall, I searched my memories for the last time I'd felt this good. The aches and pains I'd awoken with after healing from my injuries had been replaced by the delicious soreness of marathon sex with the men I finally allowed myself to admit I'd fallen for.

Heath held my hand, our fingers threaded together, while Aiden's hand was on the small of my back. It was easy and natural, and my tiger purred with satisfaction at their touch. I could now look forward to a lifetime of being between these two men in all kinds of ways, and the thought made me shiver with pleasure.

Heath exhaled roughly. "Baby, whatever you're thinking about is going to have to wait, unless you want to be bent over a table while I stake my claim on you for everyone to see."

"A gratifying thought," Aiden mused. "But then I'd have to kill everyone you let see her like that. The ones Elijah doesn't get to first, anyway."

I elbowed them both. "Quit it. No one is claiming me, in public or in private, for the rest of the day."

One shadow still lingered over this little bubble of bliss, but I planned to remedy that after dinner.

As we approached the chow hall, a few familiar faces came down the path from the infirmary.

It was Ian, hand-in-hand with Brody, and they were escorted by Elijah, who'd found a shirt somewhere, and George.

I dropped Heath's hand and bolted.

"Aves—*oof*," Ian said as I slammed into him and threw my arms around his neck. "For the love of the Moon—oh fuck, are you *crying*?"

"*No*," I sobbed into his shoulder.

He rubbed my back. "There, there. I'm okay. I've been okay, I swear. It turns out Dr. Lee is a hot jailer in addition to being a hot doctor. I would've broken out and come to see you, except Blackwell told me you were fine and babysitting your insane snake boyfriend."

Said boyfriend winked at me over Ian's shoulder.

I wiped my nose on Ian's T-shirt—"*Ew*, Aves, what the fuck?"—and turned to raise an eyebrow at my Alpha.

He had definitely not given my brother all the facts.

Heath shrugged. "You can fill him in when you're ready."

"Fill me in on what, exactly?" Ian asked, his tone deceptively light as he glared daggers at Heath.

"Later," I replied.

I released him and composed myself. Ian was here, walking, talking, and staring down the most powerful Alpha wolf in a generation. He was fine.

I kissed Brody's cheek, and he squeezed my hand, giving me a knowing look, which meant he had also been keeping things from Ian.

Good. Ian would've compromised his healing and probably pissed off Dr. Lee, camp leadership, and the basilisk if he'd been informed of everything that'd happened. He was a wrecking ball when he wanted to be.

I bent down to stroke George on his shiny head, and then I jumped into Elijah's arms.

He kissed me, slow and deep. "Hello, Dove. You taste like heaven. I think Heath and Aiden did a little bit more than just get you clean in the shower, didn't they?"

I grinned. "They got me dirtier first."

"Avery, for fuck's sake," Ian moaned behind me.

"We're so happy for you guys," Brody said brightly.

"Thank you," Heath replied. "We're pretty damn happy too."

With that, we finally went to dinner, where I sat sandwiched between Elijah and Aiden and inhaled a burger. Heath sat directly across from me, and for the duration of the meal, his gaze never strayed from my face.

My tiger, though. Even surrounded by her mates, she grew restless.

One last stop, I told her. *Then we'll be complete.*

39

———————

AVERY

After dinner, Elijah and Aiden promised to see Ian back to his cabin. Ian had protested, and I told him in no uncertain terms that seeing him run through by a wraith was going to haunt my nightmares for years and the least he could do was literally anything I needed him to do so that I could feel some peace.

He shut up after that.

After a goodnight kiss each from my jaguar and my basilisk, Heath escorted me to the infirmary. The two nurses manning the front desk didn't even glance up at our entrance. Heath had probably come and gone from here an awful lot over the past twenty-four hours, and it didn't surprise me in the least that he'd decided visitor protocol didn't apply to him.

We shoved through the metal doors that led to the patient treatment area. The fluorescent lights and stark white of the room never failed to be jarring, despite the number of times I'd been here over the summer. Tonight, it was busier than I'd ever seen it.

Almost every bay, each containing a bed separated from its neighbor by pale-blue curtains, had a patient in it.

Last night had really done a number on us all.

Aisha and several other medics I didn't recognize flitted around the room, tending to the patients. It was quiet, save the low, no-nonsense voices of the medics and the occasional beep of a machine.

Heath squeezed my hand. "This way."

He led me to a bed at the far end of the long room, then shoved the curtain aside to reveal Wyatt.

He was sound asleep, a mess of cords connecting him to an IV drip and several monitors.

I choked back a sob. My poor, brave bear.

"Hey," Heath said softly, rubbing my back. "Feel him. He's going to be just fine, baby. I promise."

I approached the side of the bed and then laid my hand on his forehead. He was warm, and his cheeks had good color. His breathing was deep and even, and his bear radiated quiet strength, flashing with extra vibrance at my touch.

"I'm still mad at you, Gale," I whispered. "But I'll forgive you if you wake up and show me that cocky, sexy smirk."

He stirred and mumbled something unintelligible.

Come on, Wyatt. Please.

Dr. Lee stepped around the curtain, tablet in hand. "Ah, hello, Avery. I'm so happy to see you up and about."

I managed a smile. "Yes, thank you again for treating me under... alternate circumstances."

He waved a hand. "Don't mention it. That's my job. And it was actually a great study in how our bodies and beasts are able to heal when we're in physical contact with our Moon-blessed mates. You are so rare, as you know."

"Right." I stroked Wyatt's silky auburn hair. "Would Wyatt heal faster if I stayed with him?"

"I suspect so, yes," he replied. "But he is very much out of the woods, Avery. I don't want you to worry. His wound is healing nicely, and the energy of his bear is healthy. I should be able to discharge him tomorrow."

I sniffed and rubbed at my eyes. "Okay."

Dr. Lee checked Wyatt's monitors, making notations on his tablet as he went. He slanted me a sympathetic look, and then he pulled the sheet down, exposing Wyatt's bare torso and the waistband of his shorts. Dr. Lee peeled away the large bandage covering Wyatt's stomach, revealing the angry red scar that bisected it.

The memories of Wyatt in the creek came crashing back. I batted them away. Those would be a mark on my soul forever, but I had to be strong for my bear.

"All is well," Dr. Lee said reassuringly, placing the bandage back on Wyatt's wound. "He's a hero for our community, and so are you, Avery. You and your mates and everyone in this camp. I'm just happy to be able to do my part."

"Thanks, Doc," I said softly.

He winked at me and ducked out of Wyatt's bay, clapping Heath on the shoulder as he passed.

I carefully maneuvered myself under the IV line connected to Wyatt's hand and then slipped into the bed, curling my body around his and laying my head gently on his chest.

Heath kissed my hair. "I'll be back in the morning, Killer. Sleep well."

"You too," I whispered. "I love you."

His smile was a bright, beautiful thing. "I love you too. So fucking much."

He left, and I settled in, content to listen to the steady, reassuring beat of Wyatt's heart. After a while, the staff dimmed the lights, and I drifted off to sleep.

SOMETIME LATER, I AWOKE TO THE SOUND OF A LOW, SEXY groan.

"Fuck," Wyatt rasped. "This is the best dream ever."

I clutched him tighter, suddenly fearful he would slip away. "It's not a dream," I whispered. "I'm here. I'm here with you."

He groaned again, shifting us in the bed so that I was lying in the crook of his arm and we were nearly nose to nose. His emerald eyes gleamed, and he thrummed with the sturdy aura of his bear. "Wildcat," he murmured. "You're really here?"

"Yes."

"Are you okay?"

"Am I.... *You're* the one in the hospital bed," I hissed.

He grinned lazily. "I'm healthy as a horse, thanks to you."

I tried to stare him down, but my lip trembled.

His smile fell away. "Baby, no, shhh." He kissed my forehead. "It's okay. I'm okay."

The tears came anyway. "I thought I was going to lose you, Wyatt. I've never been so scared." I sniffed, and he wiped the tears from my cheek with his thumb. "And then when Cash attacked me, and I thought I wouldn't get back to you—"

"When Cash *what*?" he growled.

Bear rage blanketed our corner of the infirmary. One of his monitors chirped irritably.

"Shit, I'm sorry," I whispered, stroking his hair. "We can talk about that later—"

"We will talk about it right the fuck now."

I heaved a sigh and gave him the highlights, ending with Elijah's extended nap in my cabin.

Wyatt buried his face in the crook of my neck and took several deep, shaky breaths. "I cannot believe.... After the promises Dad made.... He *swore* you'd be safe from that motherfucking sadist—"

"Wyatt, your dad couldn't have—"

"And then he almost *killed* you." His voice hitched, and he brought his face back to mine. The red sheen of an enraged bear rolled over his irises, but his expression held only anguish. "And I wasn't there for you because I was lying in a fucking ditch."

"Stop it," I pleaded. "You saved my life, Wyatt. And you almost got yourself killed in the process." I let my tiger peek out of my eyes. "Never do that again."

His hand slid from my cheek into my hair, and he grasped a handful in a tight fist, making me gasp. His irises had turned a brilliant ruby-red color I'd never seen before. "I thought I was going to die, yes," he growled. "I thought that Giant was going to finish me off. But it was only when I thought I was going to have to watch it kill you first that it broke me. Hear that? It. *Broke.* Me."

"*Wyatt*—"

"You want to threaten me with your beast? Good, I fucking love it, but this time I'm going to threaten you right back. Do something like that again, and I'll handcuff you to me and never let you out of my sight again. Got it, Wildcat?"

I glared at him. He glared back. We both knew we'd do exactly what we did, again and again.

"I'll always save you," I said after a minute.

"I'll always save you too."

A smile pulled at my lips. "Because I love you, Wyatt."

He stared at me, blinking, and the red vanished from his eyes, replaced by his gorgeous green. "Thank *fuck*," he breathed. "I'm so in love with you, it hurts, baby. I've been a goner since the second you wrapped your pretty hand around my throat."

The last piece clicked into place. The euphoria I should've felt the moment my tiger laid eyes on my Fated finally bloomed within me.

Wyatt must've felt it, too, because his eyes went wide, and he broke out in a big, beaming smile.

Then he kissed me. Slowly, carefully, worshipfully. I basked in his touch and his reverence and his love. For a few blissful moments, I forgot we were in a hospital bed with only a thin curtain separating us from the rest of the world.

Wyatt rumbled a pleased noise and bundled me closer, hiking his leg over mine. He let out a sharp hiss at the effort, and a quiet cry escaped me at the reminder of his pain.

"Shh, baby. It was just a little... sting."

"I don't care," I said. "You need to rest. It's—" I lifted my head and looked for a clock, finding one on the nearby monitor. "—three in the morning. Let's go back to sleep. I'm not going anywhere. Ever."

"Mmm, I like the sound of that." He snuggled me back into his chest. "Did the others take care of you, at least?"

I grinned into his firm pec. "I've had, like, four orgasms since I woke up from my healing sleep, which was right before dinner."

"*Fuck*," he groaned. "As soon as I'm back at fighting weight, baby—"

"I know. Trust me, I remember."

He chuckled. "That's right. We all know who was first."

I kissed his chest. "Sleep, please."

"Yes, ma'am," he said, already sounding drowsy. "Anything for you."

His breathing slowed as he fell asleep, and I followed him soon after, my beast purring contentedly in the arms of her bear.

40

AIDEN

"**W**yatt," Avery growled. "You're not supposed to lift heavy things."

Wyatt continued to wheel Avery's trunk off the stoop in front of her cabin and into the grass. "Babe, I'm not *lifting* anything," he said with a guileless smile. "I'm dragging your practically weightless trunk a very short distance."

She tossed her ponytail over her shoulder, crossed her arms over her chest, and hit him with her sternest glare.

His grin only widened. Avery had to know by now that behavior accomplished nothing except giving Wyatt an erection.

He set her trunk down gently next to the duffle bags I'd already collected from her cabin and lined up at the edge of the path. Heath and Elijah would be arriving soon with Heath's SUV so that we could cram her luggage in with ours.

It'd taken a lot of negotiating with Ian at breakfast, but he'd eventually agreed to "let" us drive Avery home before we would return to the Gale Estate. We'd agreed to "let" her have a full forty-eight hours of family time before we'd be dropping back by for a visit, and even that amount of time apart from our mate had nearly given Heath an aneurysm.

I'd bet my entire trust fund that he'd already found us a short-term rental in her neighborhood for these last few weeks before school would begin.

Avery had watched our back and forth with an amused smile on her face, eating her waffle with one hand and clutching Wyatt's thigh with the other as he demolished three plates of pancakes.

A night sleeping with our mate in his arms had done that bear good.

I itched for my turn.

My jaguar bristled. *Soon.*

"Oh, look who it is," Wyatt said dryly as George slithered out of the bushes. "I heard you were being a menace in the infirmary while I slept."

George hissed at Wyatt and then made himself at home on top of one of the duffles.

Avery cooed at him and tickled his chin. "Such a good boy. Thank you for keeping my brother in line."

I walked over and tucked her into my side. "He's going to try to stow away in your luggage," I said.

"I know. He's not as sneaky as he thinks he is."

Wyatt retrieved the last of Avery's items from the cabin, returning with her swords in their harness and her backpack. He set her backpack down on top of her trunk and then held up her blades. "Where do you want these, Wildcat?"

She gave him her back. "I'll wear them for now."

He shot me a sly grin and then slowly slipped the straps of her harness over her shoulders, which were bare beneath the flimsy little tank top she wore. After she'd shrugged them on, he slid his hands down her arms, over her rib cage, and then settled them on her hips. He dipped down and kissed her shoulder, and then he continued a path along her neck.

She bit her lip and arched for him, sighing happily as he worked.

I took a moment to bask in our new, incredible normal.

And then I struck while the iron was blazing hot.

I grabbed Avery's face and kissed her hard. She moaned into my mouth as Wyatt and I pressed her between us. She writhed in our hold, her little moans siphoning every ounce of blood from my brain and sending it straight to my cock. Coherent thoughts escaped me, other than that I couldn't wait to do this exact thing for the next hundred years of our long shifter lives.

She gasped as I lovingly cupped her tits in my hands. "We can't.... Anyone could walk by...."

A car horn blasted through the air.

I hugged Avery to my chest and turned to glare at the black SUV that'd just pulled up in front of the cabin.

Heath gave me a droll look from the driver's seat. "Really? Just out here where we can all see and smell what you're up to?"

Elijah leaned across the console and waggled his brows. "Dove, are you enjoying yourself?"

"I was, actually." She kissed my cheek, squeezed Wyatt's hand, then extricated herself from our clutches. Grinning, she slinked across the grass and over to Heath's window.

She propped herself on the frame and said something to him. He lost the stern Alpha face and went moon-eyed at our girlfriend. A few more words were exchanged, and then he growled and yanked her head into the car so that he could make out with her. Elijah cackled in the passenger seat.

"This is the life," Wyatt said, coming to stand next to me. "Imagine what it'll be like when we're actually bonded to her."

"I'm almost afraid to. I'm terrified I'll wake up and this will all have been a dream."

A dream I'd thought was just that. I'd hurt my mate. I'd looked her in her gorgeous eyes while she stood in front of me, looking more beautiful than I'd ever comprehended a female could, and called her *no one*. I'd dismissed her in a forest full of wraiths and nearly gotten her killed.

I didn't deserve this new life, but I'd cling to it until my fingers bled all the same.

When Heath finally released Avery, we got to work loading her luggage into the car. Well, three of us did. Avery forbade Wyatt from lifting anything. He just smiled and told her to try and stop him, and she did—by inviting him to pin her to the side of the car and shove his tongue down her throat.

Heath and I were arguing over the best way to stash all the bags around the car and still leave room for five tall shifters and a snake when a large white Suburban rolled slowly up to the cabin and parked a few feet behind Heath's car.

I squinted at it. "Who the hell—"

The doors opened. Kellan emerged from the driver's seat and the rest of his quad from the back.

An older man I didn't recognize climbed out of the passenger seat. His hair was long—not as long as my dad's or Kellan's, but shoulder-length—and white, streaked with a touch of the blond it must've been years ago. He was in good shape and looked to be in his sixties, but he was almost certainly shifter, which meant he was probably closer to eighty.

Like us, Kellan's quad wore the T-shirts and jeans of the civilians we were finally free to be, but the older man wore slacks, a perfectly pressed dress shirt, and shiny black shoes. Kellan and the others fell in behind him as he walked toward us, his amber eyes taking in Avery with covetous interest.

I went from confused to murderous in a blink.

That fucking bastard griffin.

The others clocked it, too, and we surrounded our mate. Avery watched the group approach with a placid look, but her tiger had been roused and was ready to kill at the slightest provocation.

Our beasts responded in kind. I didn't know what Kellan was trying to pull, but he was walking his quad and this elderly shifter into an active minefield.

"Hello, there," the older man said with a friendly smile. He held up his hands in surrender. "Now, now, there's no need for the violence I can feel brewing from the rather impressive beasts in this group. I completely understand the concern, but I assure you I mean no harm to any of you, nor do my grandson and his quad."

Ah. This was Jeremiah Crimson.

Kellan's grandfather. Ex-Council member. His tenure had ended a few years before my fathers' began. Like Kellan, he was a griffin—an aging one who'd retired from public life decades ago.

"And what exactly is the purpose of this visit?" Heath asked. His wolf had not turned down the temperature, so neither would the rest of us.

"Ah, well." Jeremiah set his sights on Avery again. "I am

actually here to speak to Miss Baxter. I must say, I am a bit disappointed to find you in the company of Holden Blackwell's sons and their quad, my dear."

"I can assure you that Holden Blackwell's sons are disappointed every day they wake up and are still related to him," Avery replied, her voice dry as the desert.

No truer words. As it turned out, my father was a horror that Heath and I hadn't yet even begun to comprehend.

Jeremiah arched a white brow. "Is that so? Well, perhaps they are more promising young men than I'd thought."

"Get to the point," Heath growled.

"Yes, quite right." Jeremiah beamed a worshipful smile at Avery. "My name is Jeremiah Crimson. I'm Kellan's grandfather, and you, my dear, are a true treasure of our kind, to put it mildly. The moment my grandson told me of your beast, I had to meet you."

Avery glared at Kellan over his grandfather's shoulder, and he at least had the modicum of decency to appear apologetic. It didn't matter, though, since he'd been staring at Avery all summer in the same way his grandfather was now, and knowledge of her tiger had only made it worse.

"I'm sorry," Kellan said to her. "I promise your secret is safe with my grandfather, Avery. He's on your side."

"No," she said, her voice that calm quiet that spelled danger. "I suspect your grandfather is on *your* side, Kellan."

He winced.

"We are all on the same side, I assure you," Jeremiah said smoothly. "Now, Avery, I wonder—how much do you know about the legend of the White Tiger?"

"I know the same bullshit that everyone else is taught," she replied.

Jeremiah grinned. "Do you? How do you know it's bullshit, then?"

"Because she didn't betray her people, she didn't die, and she wasn't barren," Avery spat. "At least, that's the story that's been passed down through my family. She lived on with her bonded mates and had children that I am, in all likelihood, descended from."

It took everything I had to not let the surprise show on my face. We'd spent all summer just trying to heal the rift between us and our mate, and now that we were finally together, we still had so much to learn about her.

Jeremiah gave her an indulgent smile. "Indeed. But there is so much more to it, my dear. And that's why I'm here. I am part of a group of... scholars, let's say, who have strived to uncover and safeguard the truth about our ancestors and the events surrounding the First Guardians. As you know, it is the stories of those events that have so strongly shaped our society today."

"What group of scholars?" I asked. I'd never heard of such a group, and the Moon knew I'd spent the month before camp began frantically researching this very thing.

He shrugged. "We don't really have a name, but more just a shared thirst for knowledge and"—he went back to staring intently at Avery—"a desire to right some wrongs done to the females of our kind."

"And what is it that you want with Avery?" I pressed.

"Simply to help her learn where she comes from and what role the Moon, in her infinite wisdom, may have for our glorious tiger," he replied. He sobered, the kindly grandfather giving way to a hardened shifter elder. "And to have a frank discussion about those forces lurking out there who would seek to harm her and those like her."

Every single one of us went on high alert.

This was knowledge we *all* needed—to protect our mate

and to help us uncover who had done unspeakable harm to her family and Elijah's.

But at what cost?

"You have my attention," Avery said. "What's the catch?"

He chuckled. "Well, I had hoped you wouldn't see it as a catch, but you're correct that I do have my own motives. I won't lie to you, my dear."

"Great," Avery said. She was still remarkably calm, but her tiger was pacing with increasing agitation, and it was driving my jaguar up the wall. We'd all been through a whole fucking lot in the past forty-eight hours, and this was a curveball we didn't need but couldn't ignore. "Let's hear it."

"I'd like to invite you to come with us today and spend a week at my lakeside manor," Jeremiah said. "I have in my library many of the apocryphal texts that those of us seeking truth have collected over the generations. I will share them with you and tell you everything I know about where you come from."

Apocryphal texts. That was *exactly* what I'd been searching for—esoteric writings whose existence I'd only theorized about with Elijah as I tore apart my dad's home library.

But there was no way this bastard was offering up this sacred and likely dangerous knowledge out of the good of his heart.

"That's very generous," Avery replied. She snaked an arm around my waist and snuggled into my side. "I'll bring Aiden here along with me. He's a professor of magic and history, so he'd be best to help me sort through that." She grabbed Elijah next and pulled him into her other side. "Or how about I bring my basilisk? Like me, he has a particular interest in learning more about nefarious groups who are harming female shifters."

A chill seeped into the air and surrounded us all. I didn't have to look at Elijah to know that he was putting all his energy into keeping his beast from committing additional murder.

Jeremiah's smile slipped. "Ah, well, that's the crux of the problem, my dear. My offer is only good if you come alone."

"Hell no," Heath growled. "Do you think we're stupid?"

"Let me guess," Avery said. "None of these men are allowed to accompany me, but Kellan and his quad will be present the entire week?"

Jeremiah shrugged helplessly. "I said I wouldn't lie to you. I want to give you a chance to get to know my grandson and the fine men of his quad outside of the Guardian program. As I'm sure they've mentioned, they do not hold the same prejudices against bonds with a beast soul as their peers." He narrowed his eyes at Heath. "And I am a bit suspicious regarding the intentions of this group of young men, my dear. Holden Blackwell is the last male on earth who would raise his sons with progressive views on females with a beast."

Heath bared his teeth. "You're not wrong about my father. But you're dead wrong about our intentions regarding Avery."

Avery gave me a reassuring squeeze, and then she took a step forward and lifted her chin. "Kellan," she said, addressing the scheming griffin over his grandfather's shoulder. "This needs to stop. I appreciate your open-mindedness regarding shifting females and bonds, but you need to know that Heath, Aiden, Elijah, and Wyatt are my Fated."

Jeremiah's eyes widened.

Kellan, however, did not look surprised. "I thought that

might be the case." He gave her a wry smile. "But I don't give up that easily, Avery."

"Are you insane?" she asked incredulously. "Their beasts are not rational when it comes to me, Kellan. You watched Elijah swallow a man whole with your own two eyes."

Jeremiah slanted Elijah an uneasy look, and Elijah gifted him with his most unhinged smile.

Kellan's face hardened. "Avery, they found out you were Fated before camp started, right? It would explain the seismic shift in their behavior. And yet, you were at odds with them for most of the summer. You're not bonded. If it were us—if we'd found *our* Fated, especially if she was *you*—there'd have been no fucking questions. We'd have been bonded by the first Full Moon. But you weren't. They didn't want you until they did, and they hurt you in the process. I want the chance to show you that we're a better choice."

"Do you wanna fucking *die,* Crimson?" Wyatt growled. "I have had a hard fucking couple of days, and you're trying to keep my mate from me. I will rip your throat out."

"Okay, okay," Jeremiah said, waving his hands. "I understand this is a... complication, but my offer stands. One week, Avery, and you'll have full access to my entire library, including everything I know about the insidious work of *legatum menidis.*"

I sucked in a breath.

Avery whirled. "Aiden?"

"*Legatum menidis* is Latin. *Legatum* is like a bequest, in the written and codified sense. It could be understood as a precursor to the notion of 'heritage,' which didn't come to be used in English to mean 'something passed down from the ancestors' until the 1600s. *Menidis* is a latinized form of a Greek word for Moon."

She blinked at me, and then realization dawned. "Lunar Heritage."

Elijah swore.

Avery pressed her lips together and shut her eyes for a moment. She took a single fortifying breath, and then she turned back to Jeremiah.

"One week," she said. "I'm not a prisoner. If I decide I want to leave, I leave."

"Of course," he said easily.

"I'm allowed contact with my family," she went on.

He nodded. "Certainly. But I'm afraid I have to insist that you do not have contact with the gentlemen behind you for the week you're with us."

Heath was vibrating with barely restrained violence. The rest of us were not any better, but we had to keep it together.

If there was even a chance of learning something that could help us shed light on who killed Avery's mother and Elijah's, on who wanted to hurt Avery....

We had to let her go.

"Fine," Avery said tersely. "But George is coming with me."

"Hell no," Kellan spat.

Jeremiah frowned. "Who?"

On cue, George emerged from behind Heath's car and slithered over to Avery. He hissed at Jeremiah, and then he wound himself around Avery's leg.

"My python," Avery said. "He comes with me, or no deal."

"Avery, come on," Kellan said. "You'll be perfectly safe. You don't need a rabid snake bodyguard."

"He. Comes. With. Me. Or. No. Deal," she bit out.

"Yes, yes, that's fine," Jeremiah said, waving a hand.

"Your week starts now, my dear. Let's get your luggage into the Suburban."

Fuck.

I can't do this.

"Hey," Avery said, gathering us in close. We all put our hands on her, desperately, wherever we could reach. "I have to do this. He knows *something* about Lunar Heritage. We can't afford to ignore that."

"I know, but fuck," Heath said. "We just…. We just came together, Killer. The thought of being away from you for even a week feels like someone is tearing my lungs from my chest."

"We can do it," she said. "It'll suck, but I'll bail as soon as I can. And you trust me, right? I don't want anything to do with Kellan's quad."

I stroked her cheek. "Of course we do. That was never a question."

"Elijah?" Avery asked tentatively.

His eyes glowed yellow, his pupils slitted. The beast was fighting him hard, poor guy. "Don't worry, Dove," he said, his voice a soft hiss. "I'll never be far from you."

"Okay." She blew out a breath. "Okay. I'm doing this. George will be with me, and I'll be okay. It'll be over before we know it. Please let Ian know everything. I love you all."

As Kellan and the assholes in his quad moved her bags from Heath's car to the Suburban, we kissed her goodbye, one by one.

And then we watched as she donned the uncompromising focus she always had before battle and climbed into the front seat, George draped over her shoulders like armor.

Doors slammed, and then they drove off, spiriting away the beating heart of our quad.

"We're not going to take this lying down," Heath said after they'd disappeared. "But we have to play it right."

"Yes," I said.

Wyatt and Elijah grunted their agreement.

"All right, huddle up," Heath said. "This is what we're going to do."

To Be Continued...

Avery and the boys' story concludes in *Rage of Beasts*. Want a sneak peek at a draft of the first chapter? Sign up for my newsletter at www.elizabethdearwrites.com.

ACKNOWLEDGMENTS

Oh, hey. You made it! That one wasn't so bad, right? *Right??*

As always, you can check out the (very) draft first chapter of the final installment of Avery and the boys' adventures, *Rage of Beasts*, when you sign up for my newsletter. I also like to send out little excerpts and teasers of the book I'm currently writing to my newsletter subscribers, so don't miss out on that.

Thank you first to you, readers, for making *Clash of Claws* my best release ever. I remain astounded by the response to that book, and I have probably peaked in my author career. I can only hope *Edge of Steel* gave you what you were looking for (mostly! nothing's perfect!), but no matter what, I appreciate you being here more than I can say.

I'm hard at work on *Rage of Beasts*, but I have set up a LOT OF THINGS to tackle, not to mention I owe you all a lot more spice, so strap in for what is probably going to be a long one (for me). I've set the pre-order date back as far as Amazon allows, and I'll move it in once I firm up the timeline.

Thank you also to:

Morgan, for everything, everywhere, all at once.

Blake, for the grovel coaching.

Kaitlin, for saving my sanity.

Jade, for the Latin lesson.

Anna, for signing on to be intimacy coordinator.

Cherie, for the fantastic cover.

McKinley and Jamee, for the most enjoyable editing experience of all time.

Everyone who posted so enthusiastically about CoC on social media, for making my morning, afternoon, or evening, every single time.

And my husband, for supporting my dreams. I don't think that 3D-printed dick given to you by one of my readers at your first book con will be your last.

ALSO BY ELIZABETH DEAR

Shifter Guardians Academy

Paranormal/Modern Fantasy Why Choose

Clash of Claws

Edge of Steel

Rage of Beasts

A Knight's Revenge

Dark Contemporary Academy Why Choose

Storm the Gates

Seize the Castle

Kill the King

Max & Frankie: A Knight's Revenge Novella *(M/M)*

A Knight's Revenge: The Complete Series

The Dylan St. James Omegaverse

Contemporary Why Choose A/B/O

Dylan St. James: Omega Concealed

Dylan St. James: Omega Revealed

Seraphina Bryce: Omega Unleashed

Daisy: TBA

Blackstone Academy

New Adult, Paranormal Romance

Mave Fortune: A Rejected Mates Story *(M/F)*

Ben Fortune: A Shifter Love Story *(M/M)*

Knox: An Alpha's Redemption Story *(M/F)*

Asher's Story: A Blackstone Academy Novella *(M/M)*

Standalone Shorts

Haunted Games: A Masked Man Romance Novella *(M/F)*

ABOUT THE AUTHOR

Elizabeth is a corporate girl who recently discovered she's also a dreamer and storyteller. She's a military spouse, a mom, and a lover of genre fiction, especially romance and urban fantasy. Academy romances were her first love. When not writing or spending time with her family, her favorite pastime is going on a journey with a powerful heroine, her sexy, obsessed love interest(s), and a cast of characters she'll still think about days later.

While always a romance writer, Elizabeth tends to jump around the subgenres and romantic pairings. Her specialty is strong and uber-competent female leads with a backbone and a smart mouth. Elizabeth also discovered that readers love that her heroines tend to have supportive, loving families—particularly strong sibling relationships—so she tries to incorporate that into each of her series. She loves to write action, suspense, banter and steam.

For info and links to all the things, including my newsletter sign up, please visit my website at elizabethdearwrites.com.